'Meticulou: this sweeping story will keep a tight hold on your heartstrings until the final page' *Iona Grey*

'A marvellous story: gripping, romantic and evocative of a turbulent and fascinating time' *Lulu Taylor*

'Just magical. At the last line, tears rolled down my cheeks. Highly recommended' *Louise Beech*

'A heart-warming affirmation of the tenacity of human love' *Liz Trenow*

'Gill Paul has clearly done her research in this absorbing story that cleverly blends imagination with historical fact. The closeted and ultimately doomed Romanov family have always fascinated, especially the four grand duchesses, and the older strand of this dual narrative story is told by one of the girls' secret loves. Tragic, touching and authentic-feeling' *Kate Riordan*

'This is an intriguing and involving book that explores a really fascinating period in time in a clever and highly enjoyable way. I was hooked into both timelines from the start' *Joanna Courtney*

'A beautiful and moving story, beautifully and movingly told. I read it in just two sittings . . . I enjoyed every page' *John Julius Norwich*

Praise for Gill Paul's other novels

'A marvellous moving adventure, full of vivid colour and atmospheric detail' *Lulu Taylor*

'A stunning epic' *Claudia Carroll*

'A terrific adventure story, full of romance and atmospheric detail – a great escapist read' *Liz Trenow*

'A gripping historical read . . . with an ending which is at once uplifting and heartbreaking. I couldn't put it down' *Julia Williams*

'A wonderful story of love, romance, bravery' *One More Page*

'A love story that will squeeze your heart tight – this is the perfect all-consuming summer read'
Random Things Through My Letterbox

'I thoroughly enjoyed reading this book . . . Brilliantly written, with great descriptions about places and events'
Boon's Bookshelf

'It is full of emotions and so many details, but the details are described in a wonderfully colourful, engaging way . . . Brutally honest, and I can only imagine how much thorough research went into writing this book' *I Heart Chick Lit*

'A wonderfully imagined peek into the fabulous excesses of the Burton-Taylor relationship, from booze-fuelled spats to their intoxicating chemistry' *Hello magazine*

'A stunning new voice – I was hooked from the first sentence of the prologue. With beautifully drawn characters and sensitive detail – *The Affair* draws you in and you won't want it to end. An accomplished, energetic, original new voice in fiction'
Kate Kerrigan

'Loved *Women and Children First*. Interestingly it deals with the aftermath/guilt/angst of surviving *Titanic* – gripping read'
Chrissy Iley

'A warm-hearted and engaging novel that breathes fresh life into the well-known tragedy of the *Titanic*'
Amanda Brookfield

'Paul keeps the narrative up, making a virtue of pace' *Guardian*

'A sexy, pacy, thoroughly modern novel' *Ham & High*

'Enough twists and turns to keep even the most devious plotmaster turning the pages as rapidly as possible'
Middlesborough Evening Gazette

The SECRET WIFE

Gill Paul is a Scottish-born, London-based writer of historical fiction and non-fiction. Her novels include *Women and Children First* (2012), which was shortlisted for an RNA award, *The Affair* (2013), and *No Place for a Lady* (2015), which was shortlisted for a Love Stories Award. Her non-fiction includes *A History of Medicine in 50 Objects* (2016), *World War I Love Stories* (2014) and *Royal Love Stories* (2015). Gill has written about relationships for a number of newspapers and magazines, and has an occasionally successful sideline in matchmaking. She swims year-round in an outdoor pond.

By the Same Author

Women and Children First
The Affair
No Place for a Lady

GILL PAUL

SECRET WIFE

avon

AVON

A division of HarperCollins*Publishers*
1 London Bridge Street
London
SE1 9GF

www.harpercollins.co.uk

A Paperback Original 2016

Image on page 397 courtesy of the Library of Congress

A catalogue record for this book is
available from the British Library

ISBN-13: 978-0-00-810214-2

Typeset in Minion by Palimpsest Book Production Ltd, Falkirk, Stirlingshire

Printed and bound in the United States of America by LSC Communications.

17 18 19 20 LSCC 10 9 8 7

Find out more about HarperCollins and the environment at
www.harpercollins.co.uk/green

For Richard, with love

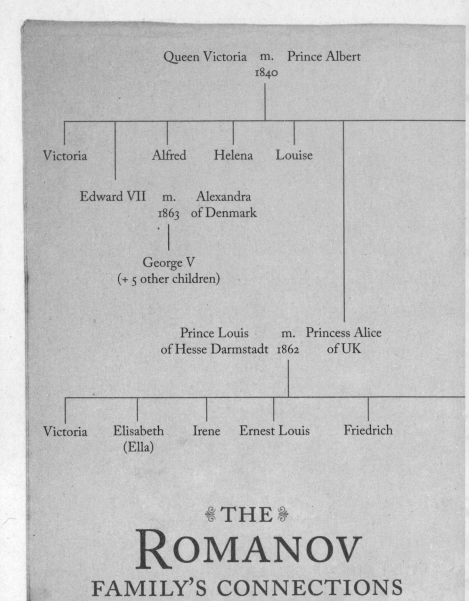

Queen Victoria m. Prince Albert
1840

Victoria   Alfred   Helena   Louise

Edward VII m.   Alexandra
1863   of Denmark

George V
(+ 5 other children)

Prince Louis   m. Princess Alice
of Hesse Darmstadt 1862   of UK

Victoria   Elisabeth   Irene   Ernest Louis   Friedrich
(Ella)

❧ THE ❧
ROMANOV
FAMILY'S CONNECTIONS

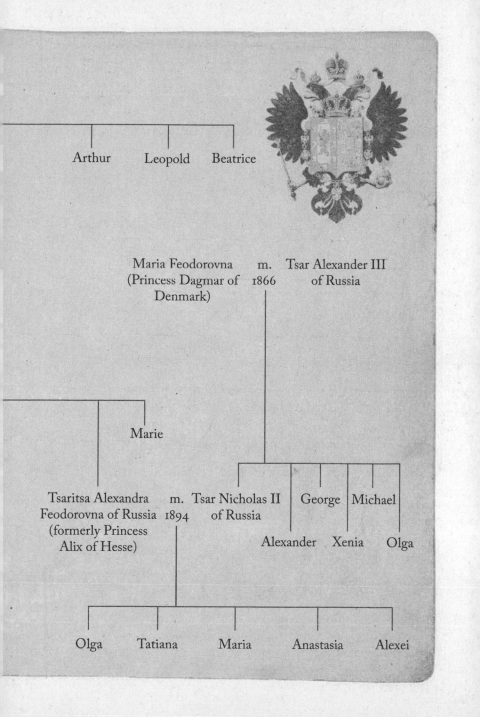

Arthur   Leopold   Beatrice

Maria Feodorovna   m.   Tsar Alexander III
(Princess Dagmar of   1866   of Russia
Denmark)

Marie

Tsaritsa Alexandra   m.   Tsar Nicholas II   George   Michael
Feodorovna of Russia   1894   of Russia
(formerly Princess   Alexander   Xenia   Olga
Alix of Hesse)

Olga   Tatiana   Maria   Anastasia   Alexei

Prologue

Lake Akanabee, New York State, 19th July 2016

It was twenty-nine hours since Kitty Fisher had left her husband and in that time she had travelled 3,713 miles. The in-flight magazine had said there were 3,461 miles between London and New York, and the hire car's Sat Nav told her she had driven 252 miles since leaving the airport. A whole ocean and half a state lay between her and Tom. She should have been upset but instead she felt numb.

Back in the UK it was four-thirty on a Sunday afternoon and she wondered what Tom was doing, then grimaced as she pictured him pottering around the house in his jogging bottoms and t-shirt. He would no doubt have called her closest friends, all innocence, asking if they knew where she was. How long would it take him to work out she had flown to America to look for the lakeside cabin she'd inherited from her great-grandfather?

She had been careful not to leave any paperwork behind so he didn't have the address. Let him stew for a while. It served him right for his infidelity. She shuddered at the word, an involuntary image of the messages on his phone flashing into her brain. She was still in shock. Nothing felt real. *Don't think about it; stop thinking.*

The woman on the Sat Nav was comfortingly sure of herself: 'In two hundred yards take a left onto Big Brook Road.' It felt nice to be told what to do; that's what she needed when the rest of her life was falling apart. But a few minutes later the voice-lady seemed to get it wrong. 'You have reached your destination' she said, but all Kitty could see was dense forest lining the road on either side. She drove further but the voice urged her to 'Turn around'.

Kitty got out of the car to explore on foot and, peering through the trees, discovered a track overgrown with waist-high grass and hanging branches. She consulted the map that had been sent with the cabin's ownership documents and decided this must be it. The car's paintwork would get scratched if she tried to drive down so she set off on foot, pushing her way through the thicket. There was a droning of insects and a strong smell of greenness, like lawn cuttings after rain. Before long she could see the steely glint of Lake Akanabee, with pinpricks of light dancing on the surface. When she reached the shore she looked around, squinting at her map. The cabin should have been right there.

And then she noticed a mound about twelve feet tall, camouflaged by creeping plants. It was thirty years since anyone had lived there and Kitty was prepared for the cabin to be reduced to a pile of rubble. Instead it was as if the forest had created a cocoon to protect it from the elements. Weeds wrapped themselves around the foundations, pushed in through broken windows and formed a carpet over the roof. The entrance was barely visible through a mass of twisted greenery. But the cabin's location, nestled on a gentle slope just yards from the pebbly shore, was stunning.

She walked over to look more closely. A jetty sticking out into the lake had long since collapsed, leaving a few forlorn struts. A sapling had grown up through the four or five steps to the cabin's porch, causing them to buckle and snap, and its roots tangled through the fractured wood like a nest of snakes. But the corrugated steel roof appeared to have stayed watertight, protecting the walls beneath. 'Concrete foundations,' she noted.

Treading with care, Kitty climbed onto the porch, where rusty chains hanging from the ceiling and some fractured planks on the floor indicated there had once been a swing seat. She imagined her great-grandfather sitting there, looking out at the view, perhaps with a beer in his hand. Pushing aside the foliage, she reached the cabin door and found it wasn't locked. Inside it was dim and musty, with a smell of damp mushrooms and old wood. Dust motes danced in shafts of light pouring through gaps in the creepers. When her eyes adjusted, Kitty saw there was one large room with a rusty stove, an old iron bed topped by a mouldy mattress, a wooden desk, and heaps of rubbish everywhere: yellowed news-papers, ancient cans of food and a pair of perished rubber galoshes.

She stepped carefully across the room. Through a doorway there was a bathroom with a stained tub, basin and toilet; a cobweb-covered shaving brush nestled on a shelf. To her astonishment, the toilet flushed when she pulled the handle, and after a low creaking sound dark water came out of the tap. She guessed they must be hooked up to a water source on the hill behind and that there was a below-ground septic tank, but it must be at least thirty years since that tank was last emptied.

She turned back into the bed-cum-sitting room and walked around, checking the condition of the walls and ceiling. Thankfully the floor held firm underfoot. She reckoned she could even stay the night once she'd cleared the rubble and torn back the jungle to let in some air.

Out on the porch she took in the view. A couple of silver birch trees stood between her and the beach, which was lapped by tiny waves. No signs of human habitation were visible, and no traffic sound intruded; the opposite shore about a mile away was thick with forest. It was just her and the trees and the lake, and it was glorious.

Kitty walked back to the car to retrieve her bags and drag them down the track, flattening the grass in her wake. She ate a salt beef and gherkin sandwich from the selection she had bought at the airport, drank a can of Seven-Up, then donned some sturdy gloves to start tearing at the creepers that smothered her cabin. Already it felt like hers, she noted. Already she was falling in love with it.

One of the plants was what she and her school friends called 'sticky willy'. They used to try and stick it on each other's backs without being noticed. Another type of creeper filled the air with spores that tickled the back of her throat. She was careful not to let any leaves touch her skin because she knew they had poison ivy in America but she wasn't sure what it looked like. A swarm of tiny black flies rose into the air and floated away in the breeze. She worked with grim determination, hoping that by totally exhausting her muscles she could quell the panicky thoughts that clamoured in her brain. *Don't think about Tom. Stop thinking.* She had brought her mobile phone and laptop through force of twenty-first-century habit, but both were switched off. She couldn't bear to listen to his excuses and self-justifications, simply didn't want to deal with any of it.

When she had yanked back most of the overgrowth, she saw that the weathered wooden slats made the cabin look like an organic part of the wooded landscape. Despite having just one room it was big, perhaps twenty feet long, with windows all around, and the sloping roof had a little chimney sticking out. She went inside again and loaded debris into some heavy-duty bin bags she'd brought along, stopping to read a few yellowed news headlines: the accident at the Chernobyl power plant in Russia; the explosion of the *Challenger* space shuttle. The springs on the bed had long gone, so she hauled it outside to dispose of later then unrolled the sleeping bag she had brought and spread it in one corner.

By the time she finished, the sun was lowering over the lake and birds were squawking loudly, expending their final burst of energy for the day. She went to sit on the porch to listen. A whip-poor-will called, and it sounded for all the world like a wolf whistle. Shadowy bats zipped by, and frogs croaked in the distance.

4

Suddenly she saw something glint under the fractured wood of the steps, nestled amongst the tree roots. She lay down full length stretching her arm to grasp it and was immediately surprised by the weight of the object. She pulled it out and saw it was a golden oval, less than an inch long, studded with tiny coloured jewels – blue, pink and amber – set within swirls of gold tendrils, like flowers on a vine. It looked expensive. On the back she could make out some scratched engraving but it had been rubbed away over the years. There was a hole in the top and she assumed it had been threaded on a chain. Someone must have been upset to lose such a stunning pendant. She'd never seen anything quite like it.

Kitty slipped it deep into the pocket of her jeans and opened another airport sandwich, turkey and salad this time. She ate it for supper, washed down with a miniature bottle of Chenin Blanc she'd brought from the plane, as she sat with her legs dangling off the edge of the porch. In front of her, the trees swayed in a slight breeze and the smooth surface of the lake reflected the dramatic colours of the sky, changing from pale pink to mauve to gold and then bronze, as vivid and surreal as the painted opening title shots of a Hollywood movie.

Chapter One

Tsarskoe Selo, Russia, September 1914

Dmitri Malama drifted to consciousness from a deep slumber, vaguely aware of murmuring voices and the whisper of a cool breeze on his face. He had a filthy headache, a nagging, gnawing pain behind the temples, which was aggravated by the brightness of the light. Suddenly he remembered he was in a hospital ward. He'd been brought there the previous evening and the last thing he recalled was a nurse giving him laudanum swirled in water.

And then he remembered his leg: had they amputated it in the night? Ever since he'd been injured at the front he'd lived in fear that infection would set in and he would lose it. He opened his eyes and raised himself onto his elbows to look: there were two shapes. He flicked back the sheet and was hugely relieved to see his left leg encased in bandages but still very much present. He wiggled his toes to check then sank onto the pillow again, trying to ignore the different kinds of pain from his leg, his head and his gut.

At least he had two legs. Without them he could no longer have served his country. He'd have been sent home to live with his mother and father, fit for nothing, a pitiful creature hobbling along on a wooden stump.

'You're awake. Would you like something to eat?' A dumpy nurse with the shadow of a moustache sat by his bed and, without waiting for an answer, offered a spoonful of gruel. His stomach heaved and he turned his head away. 'Very well, I'll come back later,' she said, touching his forehead briefly with cool fingers.

He closed his eyes and drifted into a half dream state. He could hear sounds in the ward around him but his head was heavy as lead, his thoughts a jumble of images: of the war, of his friend Malevich shot and bleeding on the grass, of his sisters, of home.

In the background he heard the tinkle of girlish laughter. It didn't sound like the plain nurse who had tended him earlier. He opened his eyes slightly and saw the tall, slender shapes of two young nurses in glowing white headdresses and long shapeless gowns. If he'd just awoken for the first time in that place, he might have feared he had died and was seeing angels.

'I know you,' one of the angels said, gliding over to his bedside. 'You were in the imperial guard at the Peterhof Palace. Weren't you the one who dived into the sea to rescue a dog?'

Her voice was low and pretty. As she came closer, he realised with a start that she was Grand Duchess Tatiana, the second daughter of Tsar Nicholas. While Olga, the eldest, looked like her father, Tatiana had her mother's faintly oriental bone structure. She was gazing at him with intense grey-violet eyes, waiting for an answer.

'Yes, I'm afraid that was me. My uniform was ruined, my captain was furious, and the dog was a stray who shook himself down and ran off without so much as a thank-you.' He smiled. 'I'm surprised you heard about it, Your Imperial Highness.'

She returned his smile. 'I heard some guards discussing it and asked them to point you out. You must be a dog lover.'

'Very much so. I have two at home, a Borzoi and a Laika. They're scamps but I miss them terribly.'

'My father is fond of Borzois. He had one he said was more intelligent than most human beings, and he was grief-stricken when it died.' She wrinkled her nose prettily. 'But the ones we keep in the kennels bark constantly. I'd love to have a dog of my own in the palace but it would have to be quieter. Perhaps you could advise?'

He felt honoured that a grand duchess was conversing with him in this natural, everyday fashion. 'Of course, Your Imperial Highness. Do you prefer small or large dogs?'

'I think small. And there's no need to call me "Your Imperial Highness". I am a nurse here, not a royal. Mama, my sister Olga and I are all training as nurses to help the war effort. These days I am known as "Nurse Romanova Three", while they are One and Two.'

He chuckled at the impersonal moniker. 'Do you like Terriers, Nurse Romanova Three? The Black Russian Terrier is a clever dog and not too boisterous. Spaniels are also popular with ladies for their silky coats. And then there are small breeds of Bulldog. I rather like French Bulldogs.'

She clapped her hands. "Oh yes! I love those serious wrinkled faces, as if they have the cares of the world on their shoulders."

Her sister Olga, the other angel in white, called to say she was going through to the next ward. Dmitri expected Tatiana to follow but instead she lingered.

'I see you have a leg wound,' she said. 'Is it terribly painful? Can I get you anything?'

He shook his head. 'Thank you, I'm fine. I'm just annoyed that I was careless enough to get myself wounded in the first week of war.'

'Is it a bullet wound?'

He thought back to the moment when he ran out to collect Malevich from the field, dragging him by his collar. In retrospect he'd felt a blow on his thigh but thought nothing of it as he concentrated on saving his friend. 'Yes. I didn't realise I'd been hit until we got back to base. It was odd because the pain and bleeding didn't start until then.' All of a sudden the blood had begun to gush and he'd collapsed on the grass. It was a mystery why it hadn't bled earlier, out on the field – as if one of the saints was looking

9

after him. After his collapse he remembered feeling very hot and starting to shiver, his teeth clenched, and they'd ripped off his trousers to see a ragged hole going all the way through his left thigh and grazing the right. Fortunately the bullet had not lodged inside. Perhaps that's what had enabled surgeons to save the leg. Over the last weeks he'd been transported back from the front at Gumbinnen, East Prussia, via various medical stations, to the Catherine Palace in St Petersburg, where the grand staterooms had been converted into wards.

Tatiana asked his regiment and exclaimed when she heard he was in the 8th Voznesensk Uhlans: 'You are one of my own men! I must take especially good care of you.' Both Olga and Tatiana had been given honorary command of their own regiments on their fourteenth birthdays.

'It's a great honour to be nursed by my colonel.' He grinned. 'But I suppose I will have to behave myself with you around.'

They chatted for a while about the war, triggered only a few weeks earlier by the German Kaiser's rampant militarism. It was still a shock to Dmitri, and Tatiana told him it was even more shocking to them as they had so many German relatives, their mother having been born there. She called the Kaiser a swine. Olga glanced in to look for her sister and made a brief, impatient gesture with outspread hands.

'I must get to work,' Tatiana said. 'I am supposed to accompany a more experienced nurse and she will be waiting. But tell me, is there anything I can do to make your stay more comfortable?'

'I don't suppose you could lend me a book? Any book at all. I love to read.' He hoped he wasn't being presumptuous. 'I would return it, of course.'

She seemed delighted. 'I too love reading. Who are your favourite authors?'

He hesitated. So many good writers these days were anti-tsarist: Alexander Kuprin, Maxim Gorky, Ivan Bunin . . . he must choose from an earlier era: 'Tolstoy, of course. And Chekhov.'

'I agree with you,' she said. 'I much prefer the classics to the modern writers. My absolute favourite is Turgenev. Have you read *Fathers and Sons*?'

Dmitri was surprised, as the novel dealt with the younger generation rejecting the values of the old aristocratic order. 'Not since I was a boy. I love the poetry of Turgenev's language. He conjures images that stir the soul.'

She was amused: 'You sound like a writer yourself.'

He made a face. 'I used to keep a journal as a youth but not for a long while now. It was rather whining and self-indulgent.'

'Really? I keep a journal. I try to describe events of the day truthfully. I like the challenge of finding exactly the right words and often they come to me when I am doing something completely different: working here in the hospital, or doing my embroidery, or . . .' She stopped, colouring slightly.

He liked the way she spoke, slowly, considering her words, and the intelligence he could see in her eyes. 'In that case you have the instincts of a writer.'

She laughed. 'Oh, I could hardly pretend . . . no one reads my journal but me.'

'Without an audience, you can express your truest feelings. I used to find writing very useful for understanding myself. You know how sometimes you react instinctively in ways that puzzle you? You think: why am I angry? Why does that make me sad? It's fascinating to unravel the tiny spark that provoked the reaction, perhaps just an unintended nuance, something that struck a chord and triggered the emotion of a much earlier experience . . . human nature is the most compelling study of all.' He stopped, feeling he was talking too much and perhaps boring her, but she seemed to be listening intently.

'I know exactly what you mean,' she said, biting her lip as if some example were flitting unseen through her mind.

Dmitri watched, thinking what an open, natural girl she appeared to be. He had expected the tsar's daughters to be haughty and sophisticated, like the grandest ladies of the St Petersburg aristocracy, but Tatiana did not seem to have any airs. She spoke to him as if to an equal.

'Nurse Romanova Three,' a woman called from the doorway.

'I'm coming, Sister Chebotareva.' She gave Dmitri a quick, warm smile, said, 'Till tomorrow,' then hurried from the ward.

Dmitri watched her go with a smile on his lips, having completely forgotten his pain. He wondered what age Tatiana must be, then worked out that she was seventeen, six years younger than him. In her manner she seemed younger still. And she was much more beautiful than he had ever imagined when he'd seen her from a distance. Her skin was creamy perfection, her eyes like deep pools, her lips stained as if by wild berries . . . If she had not been a Romanov, Dmitri would have flirted with her. Over his years in the imperial guard he had made a number of conquests amongst the young titled ladies of St Petersburg, although none had captured his interest for long. But here, he thought, here was a girl he could easily fall in love with.

Chapter Two

Next morning, Dmitri opened his eyes and gazed up at the ceiling, where cupids, griffins, and other mythological creatures danced in cornflower-blue semicircles. A vast chandelier of multiple tiers glinted in the sunlight. The walls were of white silk with delicately painted blue flowers. He was in the Blue Drawing Room of the Catherine Palace, a place he had sometimes glanced into when serving in the imperial guard. His neighbour in the next bed, a man named Stepanov, told him that the staterooms of the Winter Palace had also been converted into makeshift wards for wounded officers. Surfaces had been cleared of ornament and the priceless furniture replaced by hospital beds, but the andirons and fireguard were gilded bronze, and the elaborate clock on the mantel showed the Greek gods Bacchus and Momus in marble and bronze. The wealth of the Romanovs was unfathomable.

The royal family no longer lived in the Catherine Palace, preferring the relative intimacy of the nearby Alexander Palace in winter, the Peterhof in summer, and the extravagant luxury of the royal yacht, *Standart*, or their Crimean palace at Livadia for holidays. Most of the stately palaces lining the Baltic shores in St Petersburg, where Dmitri had worked, were kept for ceremonial purposes: to entertain visiting dignitaries, and as the setting for state occasions.

What must it be like to grow up with such limitless wealth, Dmitri wondered? To have an elephant house and Chinese theatre in your garden, to be driven around in shiny new automobiles by uniformed chauffeurs, to be able to buy whatever your heart desired? Tatiana seemed an unspoiled girl, but the sheer grandeur of her upbringing must set her apart. He knew her clothes were made by French couturiers and her hats shipped from a fashionable store in London; that her perfume came from Brocard & Co and her shoes from Henry Weiss. He had often noticed deliveries arriving by special messenger. Although he was the son of an army general, a member of a well-connected upper-class family, surely he couldn't ever hope to become close to Tatiana? It was impossible, wasn't it?

He watched the clock, wondering what time she would arrive. The previous day it had been mid morning when she stopped by his bed. He managed to eat some breakfast and had his dressing changed by the moustached nurse. She brought him a bowl of water and a razor and he shaved then combed his hair, keen to look presentable for Tatiana's visit.

She bounced in at ten, her cheeks flushed from hurrying, three books tucked under her arm.

'I hope I didn't keep you waiting. I had lessons to attend, then I had to go to the Znamenie Church to pray for our soldiers. Here – would any of these interest you?' She placed the books on the bedcover then pulled up a chair and sat by his bed.

'How kind of you, Nurse Romanova Three.' Dmitri smiled. He picked up the first book: Turgenev's *Fathers and Sons*. 'I will enjoy re-visiting this to see if it lives up to memory.' She watched eagerly as he examined the others. 'I've never read Tolstoy's *Kreutzer Sonata* so I look forward to that. And Gorky's short stories are perfect: I remember one about the cutting of a tunnel through a mountain – have you read it?'

'Ah, that was so haunting. Do you think it can be true that mountains have a spirit that can harm those who damage them?'

Her eyes looked grey today, with flecks of violet round the edge of the irises. A tendril of auburn hair had slipped from the side of her white headdress.

'I remember seeing such a tunnel being dug and thinking that it looked like an offence against nature. Gorky has captured that sense of a wound being inflicted. Thank you for the books. I will stop being such a disruptive, demanding patient now I am so well occupied.' He stroked the expensive Morocco leather binding.

She glanced around, unsure whether to believe him, then realised he was pulling her leg. 'Perhaps we might discuss them when you finish. I love to talk about books. I often write critiques of them in my journal.'

'I can't imagine when you find time to write your journal. It sounds as though your days are fully occupied: nurse, grand duchess, colonel . . .' He was fishing, eager to know more about her life.

'I write every evening before bedtime. In fact, I wrote about you last night.' She coloured. 'Mama tells me you are a hero, that you rescued a wounded officer while under enemy fire. She is going to award you the Golden Arms sword.'

Dmitri was surprised: 'It's an insurance policy all soldiers follow. If you see a chance, you slip out to bring back the wounded, hoping that one day someone will do the same for you.' He didn't tell her the officer was a friend, and that he still had no word about whether Malevich had survived his wounds. He knew he would choke up if he spoke of it.

'Nevertheless, I'm sure they don't give bravery awards to just anyone. I suspect you are being modest. You have a heroic air.' Her eyes were sparkling.

Now he laughed. 'I'm not sure what a heroic air is! My father was a genuine hero. He was a cavalry general in Tsar Alexander's army, who served in many campaigns, and in 1904 became Viceroy of Georgia. He has so many decorations pinned on his jacket it is heavy as a suit of armour. I'm just a simple cavalryman following orders.'

15

'Does your father fight in the present war?'

'No, he has retired to my home town of Lozovatka, in Evkaterinskaya Province.'

'I have never been there. Is it beautiful?'

Dmitri wrinkled his nose. 'It's a very small town, set on a pretty river not far from the Sea of Azov, but Your Imperial Highness would have no reason to go there. They have no society to speak of. In my childhood it was rural, but they have started mining for minerals and great slashes are being torn through the landscape, just like Gorky's tunnel.'

'Do you come from a large family?' She was regarding him intently. 'What kind of childhood did you have?'

'Not as large as Your Imperial Highness's. I have two elder sisters, Vera and Valerina, but no brothers. The girls were always trying to rope me in to their games, dressing me in costumes and making me perform in their plays. You have no idea how character-forming it is for a young boy to be forced to wear a wig and gown and have his cheeks rouged! I escaped around the age of nine after I befriended one of the groundsmen on our family's estate. He taught me how to hunt and fish, since my father was often away from home. All in all, it was a fairly average childhood.' He did not tell her about the fierce rows when his irascible father came back, and the vicious beatings he had endured, sometimes with a horsewhip.

'Tell me, are your sisters married now?'

'Vera is married to Prince Alexander Eristavi-Ksani of Georgia, but Valerina still lives at home with our parents. She is twenty-six years old and I hope she will yet find a husband, but she is the quieter of the two, a little shy perhaps. I'm very close to her.'

'I would love to meet them!' Tatiana exclaimed. 'I know hardly any women outside our family. Mama had just begun to allow Olga and me to attend the occasional ball or soirée when war broke out. We used to hear music floating up to the windows, and see fine ladies ice-skating on the Baltic, but no matter how hard we pleaded we were scarcely ever allowed to join them. Aunt Olga

– Papa's sister – would occasionally invite us, but I think the ladies felt awkward about introducing themselves to us. I should probably never have met you, Cornet Malama, had it not been for this war, and your injury.'

'I am very glad we met, Nurse Romanova Three. Our conversation is helping to relieve my frustration at being stuck in bed, my ears assailed by the grunting and snoring of my fellow officers.' Her hand rested on the covers not far from his, and he longed to touch it, or even raise it to his lips. He might have done so with another woman, but dared not attempt it with a Romanov grand duchess.

Her sister Olga came into the room and approached them. She was shorter than Tatiana and not nearly as pretty, with coarser features and plain blue eyes. 'Who is this patient who occupies all your time?' she asked, her eyes merry. 'Could it be Cornet Malama, the officer about whom you regaled us all last evening?' Tatiana blushed scarlet, and Dmitri bowed his head, saying 'A votre service.'

'I beg pardon for interrupting,' Olga continued, 'but Sister Chebotareva has asked if we will go to the annex and change dressings.'

Tatiana rose.

'Thank you again for the books,' Dmitri said. 'I will begin the Turgenev immediately.'

'I'll stop by later to check how much you have read,' Tatiana promised.

The girls scurried out of the room and Dmitri lay in a daze. She seemed to like him. At least she enjoyed chatting with him, and she had mentioned him to her mother and sister. Did that mean there might be a chance of a match between them? His family owned a large estate but their wealth was nothing compared to the immense riches of the Romanovs. Would he be considered too lowly? Were they hoping to find foreign princes for all four Romanov girls, or might a Russian general's son suffice?

Stepanov called over: 'Congratulations! I heard her say you are to be awarded the Golden Arms!'

Dmitri frowned, wondering how much of the conversation Stepanov had heard. He did not feel like talking. He wanted to close his eyes and remember the sweet jasmine scent of Tatiana's skin, the directness of her gaze, the soft tone of her voice, the way her emotions flickered across her face for any who cared to read them. He opened the cover of the Turgenev novel and saw that she had written her name on the frontispiece, in both Russian and English, her lettering neat and evenly spaced. He ran his finger over it lightly, then lifted the book and breathed in the smell of the pages. Should he try to stop himself falling in love with her? Already he suspected it might be too late.

Chapter Three

'Did you hear the news of Tannenburg?' Stepanov called, interrupting Dmitri's reverie. 'It's catastrophic: 78,000 killed or wounded, 92,000 captured, and General Samsonov dead by his own hand.' He was reading the figures from a newspaper.

Dmitri already knew that the Russian Second Army had been encircled by the Germans but hadn't heard the casualty figures till now. He felt sick to his stomach at the enormity of the slaughter. 'How could it have happened? Why is German intelligence so much better than our own? It seems they intercept all our messages, yet we are in the dark about their plans.'

Stepanov grimaced. 'They are better equipped too. Their guns have longer ranges, more explosive power. Our superior numbers count for nothing when we are sent into battle with nineteenth-century weapons.'

Dmitri thought of the friends he had left behind at the front: were any still alive, or had they been struck down by the indiscriminate big guns? The Russian army was the largest in the world, but the German foe was nimbler, more flexible. 'This war will be lost within months if we don't get modern equipment and become faster in the field. Our chain of command is too slow and dithery. Changes in orders take so long to be implemented, the enemy has moved on.'

Stepanov was gloomy. 'According to this newspaper's editor, we can't compete with the rail network supporting the German army. We're still riding around on horseback but the days of using cavalry in battle are numbered. A horse presents a large target, and the big guns terrify them.'

Dmitri agreed, but it meant everything he had learned at the prestigious imperial Corps de Page and then in the Uhlan Lancer Guard Regiment was out of date. He was a skilled horseman but knew nothing about the positioning, loading and firing of the big artillery shells now in use. He had achieved distinction in his examinations in science, military history and mathematics but had virtually no experience of the devastating new military technology.

At ten o'clock the following morning, Tatiana bounded into the ward full of excitement: 'Malama, why did you not tell me you won the Stoverstny?'

Dmitri had led the field from the start of the previous year's prestigious horserace on Ortipo, his cognac mare. 'That was many moons ago,' he said. 'I'm flattered that you have been researching me.'

'Well, of course I have,' she said, sitting on the edge of his bed since there was no chair in sight. In any other girl he would have thought it a flirtatious gesture, but Tatiana did it naturally, without guile. 'I am trying to discover what makes you tick.'

'I fear I will prove a very dull study.' He smiled. 'I am an army officer and keen to return to my regiment as soon as I can, to fight for my country. I'm so predictable, I make myself yawn.'

'I shan't allow you to leave,' Tatiana said playfully. 'As your colonel, I order you to stay.'

He looked further down the ward to where Olga was sitting on the bed of an officer called Karangozov before replying: 'I cannot disobey a direct order. Perhaps you think the army will fare better without me?'

She giggled: 'Rushing out and getting yourself shot is a drain on manpower. You must stay here to keep me entertained.'

'But you are the one doing the entertaining, while I lie here like a useless lump. Life on the ward would be insufferably tedious without your visits to look forward to.'

'Perhaps you will soon be able to walk in the grounds with me? The temperature is mild and the leaves are turning to brilliant reds and yellows.'

He glanced out of the tall windows at the clouds scudding past. Every time Tatiana said something personal, his heart leapt. Did she speak to other patients so kindly? Certainly, on their ward, she stopped by his bed far longer than at the others.

'I'd like that, my colonel,' he replied, a little hoarse.

Her mother, Tsarina Alexandra, swept into the room, and Olga and Tatiana leapt off the officers' beds. 'Why don't you change Cornet Malama's dressing?' the Tsarina instructed Tatiana, giving Dmitri a quick nod of acknowledgement. 'Olga, come with me to the annex.'

Tatiana went to fetch water, scissors and lint, and Dmitri cringed at the thought of her seeing the ugliness of his wound. He knew he was not a bad-looking man, with his dark-blond hair and chestnut eyes, but his left leg was scored by deep gashes on either side that were healing with hideous colours: jagged plum-purple lines surrounded by grey and orange swelling, the skin bald where the hairs had been shaved. At least the wounds no longer bled or oozed pus, but they were imperfections he would rather have hidden.

He couldn't watch as her cool fingers cleaned around the wounds. Her touch was causing his manhood to stiffen and he wriggled to rumple the bedcovers over the spot so she would not notice. It was agonising and wonderful at the same time. They didn't talk, didn't look at each other, and he wondered if perhaps she was embarrassed too.

'You're not bad,' he told her as she tied the last knot on the dressing and began to collect her instruments. 'There could be a career in nursing for you, if you get bored of being a grand duchess.'

21

'Why thank you, sir.' She bowed with mock politeness. 'I aim to please. I shall be back later to check you are not being disruptive.'

She gazed straight into his eyes as she spoke and he felt a jolt, for all the world as if he had been shot by Cupid's arrow. The words of poets through the generations, words he had previously thought trite and clichéd, suddenly made sense to him. He felt deliriously happy and wildly anxious at the same time. Did Tatiana have romantic feelings for him or did she simply enjoy his company? How could he let her know he had fallen in love without causing embarrassment or spoiling the intimacy that was developing between them?

During the interminable hours of bed rest, Dmitri pondered ways of ascertaining her feelings, then decided that he should give her a gift: something personal, something she would treasure. A book? He had no way of knowing what she had or had not read, and it felt rather a staid present. Jewellery? The family had more ostentatious gold and precious stones than he could ever afford. And then he thought back to the subject of their first-ever conversation and the answer came to him: he would get her a puppy.

He knew a St Petersburg breeder who had some gorgeous French Bulldogs. One of them would be perfect, but how would he get it to Tatiana? He wanted to watch her reaction on receiving the gift so he couldn't simply have it delivered to the Alexander Palace.

That evening, the Tsarina's lady-in-waiting Anna Vyrubova came by to straighten his pillows. She was a plump-faced kindly type, a friend with whom his mother often stayed when she came to St Petersburg for the social season, and she enquired after his family. Dmitri decided to ask her advice. Did she think it would be acceptable for him to buy a gift of a puppy for Grand Duchess Tatiana? He explained that he wished to surprise her.

Anna's face lit up with pleasure. 'How adorable!' she exclaimed. 'I'm sure she would love it. What can I do to help?'

Dmitri told her the whereabouts of the breeder and detailed the type of animal he wanted: not the runt of the litter, but a pup that was confident around people and did not scare easily. 'Choose the one that comes over to sniff an outstretched hand and squints at you sideways. Avoid any that stand back and bark or bare their teeth. I want a pup who is playful but does not use his teeth. We can't risk him biting the grand duchess.'

Anna agreed she would help with the choice, following Dmitri's advice. She seemed thrilled to be part of the secret.

Two days later, she stopped by his bed to whisper that the breeder had a perfect pup and she had placed the order but that it would be another week before it would be ready to be taken from its mother. Dmitri was frustrated by the delay. He saw Tatiana every day and as well as their morning visits, she and Olga now came back in the evenings. They had a lesson with Dr Vera Gedroits at six o'clock, after which they sterilised the instruments for the following day. If there was time after that, Olga would play piano and they would sing along to some well-known songs, like the Latvian favourite 'Kaut Kur'. Tatiana sang quietly, but Dmitri could hear she had a pure, tuneful voice.

On the day the puppy was ready to be handed over, Dmitri gave Anna Vyrubova his final instructions about purchasing a basket in which to transport it, a collar, some food, a water bowl and a litter tray, and he gave her the money to pay for it. When she returned an hour later with the precious cargo in a box, Dmitri glanced in and grinned: it was perfect. Anna went to find Tatiana, who was in the annex.

Soon she arrived in the ward, looking flustered. 'Anna Vyrubova said you needed to see me.' She noticed the box. 'What is this?'

He held it out: 'A gift, to thank you for your patience with me.' Snuffly panting sounds were coming from within.

Tatiana took the box and opened it warily. A tiny black face leaned out to lick her hand and she squealed in delight. The dog fitted easily into her cupped palms and she examined the pointy ears, the frown line between the eyes, the wrinkled snout, then bent and kissed the top of its velvety head.

'Malama . . .' she began, looking up at him, but could say no more. She was overwhelmed, virtually speechless, but it didn't matter because Dmitri could see it written in her eyes that she loved him. And now she must know that he loved her too. His heart swelled with such profound happiness he could scarcely breathe.

Chapter Four

October brought chill winds from the Arctic, along with showers of blustery rain. One day, when the rain had eased off, Tatiana found a wheelchair and pushed Dmitri into the beautifully manicured formal gardens of the Catherine Palace so they could start training the little Bulldog she had named Ortipo, after Dmitri's cavalry horse. Dmitri showed Ortipo a titbit of chicken then held out his palm, loudly instructing the dog to 'sit', while Tatiana pushed on her backside to demonstrate. But as soon as she removed her hand Ortipo leapt at the wheelchair, trying to grab the chicken. Tatiana tried again, only for the pup to jump up and leave muddy paw prints on her white nurse's uniform.

'I think we have an untrainable one here,' she laughed, brushing at the marks.

'No dog is untrainable,' he replied. 'But this one seems more of a challenge than most. I suspect you are spoiling her when I am not around.'

At least Ortipo had mastered the art of waiting till she got outdoors before relieving herself, which proved a level of obedience – but not much. Despite their efforts she jumped up at every passerby, barked furiously at the gardeners, and refused to come when called unless food was offered. They laughed till their sides ached as she cavorted around the lawn trying to catch leaves blowing in the wind, or chased huge seagulls, who took off into the air when she was just a few feet away.

'What do you think she would do if she caught one?' Tatiana asked.

'She'd get the fright of her life. These giant gulls can be fierce.' He felt as though they were proud parents and was delighted the dog gave them a pretext to spend time together without anyone questioning it. They didn't even have a chaperone.

Tatiana had pushed his wheelchair as far as the limestone grotto at the edge of the Great Pond when a few spots of rain fell so they hurried into the grotto to shelter. The exterior walls were decorated with seashells, and the watery theme continued inside with masks of Neptune on the windows, and dolphins and tritons carved on the pillars that supported the domed ceiling. Ortipo scooted around sniffing corners while Dmitri and Tatiana waited by the door for the rainclouds to pass.

'Aunt Ella was asking about you yesterday evening,' she said, glancing at him shyly. 'She joked that we seem to be having a romance. She teased me about it.'

He hesitated. 'Do you think she disapproved?'

'No, not at all,' Tatiana said quickly. 'She said she knows your mother and that you come from a good family. Olga is sweet on an officer called Mitya – do you know him?' Dmitri nodded and bit back a retort; he found Mitya rather crass. 'She talks about him all the time. Even little Alexei teases her, but I suspect she enjoys being teased.'

'And you do not?'

Tatiana hesitated. 'I am a private person and prefer to keep my feelings for my journal instead of being the subject of gossip.'

'How I would love to read that journal,' Dmitri twinkled. 'Could you bring it to the ward later?'

'Never!' she exclaimed vehemently, making him laugh. 'Do you think this rain will pass soon or should we dash back and risk a soaking?'

'Let's linger a while. I might try walking a few steps, if you will lend me your arm.'

He pushed down on the arms of the wheelchair to raise himself then swung the injured leg to the ground, wincing slightly as it took his weight. Tatiana steadied him, and for a moment they were so close he could feel the warmth of her body and hear her breathing. He longed to put his arms around her. If only he dared!

She stayed close as he hobbled a few steps to the opposite window then paused to recover.

'I don't want you to get better so quickly,' she cried mournfully. 'They will send you back to the front and then you will forget you ever knew me.'

He spoke with passion: 'Tatiana, I will *never* forget you. *Never*. If I should be mortally wounded on some foreign battlefield, I swear your name will be the last word on my lips and your face the last image in my head.'

Tears sprang to her eyes and she blinked them away, turning her head to the side. 'But might the story have a happy ending?' she asked quietly.

'I will do all I can to make sure it does,' he breathed. Her face was so close that he could have kissed her by leaning forward just a few inches, but it would be presuming too much. He was sure she could hear how hard his heart was hammering in his chest, because he was certain he could hear hers too.

By mid November, Dmitri could walk across the ward unaided and he wasn't surprised when he received a letter informing him that he had been passed fit for duty and must report to his regiment by the 12th of December. He kept the news from Tatiana for a while, not wanting to distress her. The thought of causing her pain made his chest tighten and a lump form in his throat, but at the same time he hated to keep such an important communication from her. When there were just two weeks to go, he took her for a walk through the park, past the pyramid where tiny gravestones marked the burial places of Catherine II's three dogs. Ortipo nosed the frozen earth as if she could detect something, most likely the scent of a fox.

'I knew this day must be close,' she said bravely and turned her head away, but he could hear that she was choking back tears. 'I have some gifts for you. You will be surprised how busy I have been.'

'Really? What kind of gifts?' He glowed at the thought.

'I have knitted you a muffler, gloves and several pairs of thick socks. I don't want to think of you freezing in some bleak, wind-swept tent.'

He was so touched he could barely speak. Was this the moment to kiss her? He hesitated too long and she had turned to call Ortipo, who was chasing a squirrel.

'We must take some photographs,' she said. 'I'll bring my Box Brownie to the ward this evening.'

'You have hundreds of photographs of me already–' he smiled '–and I look ugly in all of them.' She and Olga were keen photographers.

'Will you write to me?' she asked, her tone a little plaintive.

'Of course! You shall have a letter every week, which is at least ten times more than my mother gets.'

'I shall write to you every day,' she declared, her eyes glassy.

Impulsively he took her slender hand and pressed it to his lips, lingering to savour the sensation and inhale her precious scent. She did not pull it away.

Dmitri dressed in his navy and yellow uniform and set off early on the morning of the 12th of December, along with two other officers and a dozen soldiers all heading for Poland, where the remnants of the Russian First Army were attempting to hold the German Ninth at bay. Dawn had only just broken but Tatiana appeared in the palace driveway, looking pale in the wintry sunshine, and stood by the gate to wave. As their truck passed Dmitri saw her eyes were red with crying and his heart felt as though it were breaking in two.

Chapter Five

London, April 2016

At first Kitty thought the letter was junk mail and was about to toss it in the bin. It was written on expensive-looking watermarked paper from a company called Inheritance Trackers Inc., and as she skimmed the first paragraph her eye was caught by the name Yakovlevich. She was pretty sure that had been her Grandma Marta's maiden name, so she went back to read it properly. It said that she was the great-granddaughter and only living descendant of Dmitri Yakovlevich, who had died in America in 1986, and that his estate had not been claimed. Should she wish Inheritance Trackers to reunite her with this fortune, they would handle all the legal work and would take a fee of only fifteen per cent. There was a thirty-year deadline for claiming lost estates and if she did not act soon, the property would be forfeited to the government.

Kitty was instantly suspicious: this was an era of scams, when you were offered millions of pounds if you would only advance a couple of thousand to help get someone through customs in an African country; when boiler rooms located in the Bahamas claimed they could quadruple any investment within a year. Besides, Grandma Marta had been alive in 1986, so why had she not inherited Dmitri Yakovlevich's money? Why had Kitty never even heard of him?

Marta had been a fun grandmother, who kept delicious sweets in her pottery rabbit candy jar, and was always happy to get down on the floor and play Hungry Hippos or Mouse Trap. Kitty couldn't recall her mentioning her father, but then Marta had died when Kitty was eight. She would probably find pictures of him in the old suitcase of family photos she had stowed in the bedroom closet after her parents passed away. She must take a look some time.

She rang the number on the company's letterhead and was put through to someone called Mark, who told her that the inheritance concerned was worth over fifty thousand dollars in cash. There was also a cabin on Lake Akanabee in the Adirondack Mountains of northern New York state, which had been uninhabited since her great-grandfather's death, and royalties for some books he had written. *He was an author! How intriguing.*

'So what do I have to do to claim it?' she asked carefully, picking up a pen.

'We'll send you some forms to fill out,' explained Mark, 'and you return them to us, along with a copy of your birth certificate – and a marriage certificate if you're married – and we'll do the rest.'

'Do I have to pay anything upfront?' she asked suspiciously. 'Legal fees or anything?'

'No, we take our cut when the money and the ownership papers for the cabin come through,' Mark told her. 'Do you want me to send you the information?'

'Why not?' she agreed.

She forgot to tell Tom that evening, but when the paperwork arrived confirming the totals, she showed it to him. He didn't seem particularly impressed.

'Fifty K minus fifteen per cent is forty-two and a half thousand dollars and at today's exchange rate that's about twenty-seven thousand quid. Better than a poke in the eye. Do you want me to give you the number of a financial advisor who can give you some ideas on investing it?'

She looked at him across the table and wondered about this stranger she had married. The Tom she had known back in college would have suggested blowing the windfall on a round-the-world trip for two, or perhaps buying a yacht and learning to sail. They were only in their mid-thirties, they had paid off the mortgage thanks to the inheritance when her parents died, neither of them wanted to have children, and now all Tom could think of was saving for the future? She felt she was seeing him through different eyes than she had a decade ago; or maybe she was the same person and he was the one who had changed. It was hard to tell.

Back then he'd wanted to be a composer and had spent most days writing songs on his keyboard and sending demos to record companies. After they failed to leap at the chance of buying his creations, he chucked it all in, took an accountancy course and was now working as an auditor for the City Council. He had become serious and precise, leaving home at the same time every morning in a neat predictable suit, the kind of outfit no one would ever notice. If he committed a crime and witnesses were asked to describe him they'd struggle to come up with anything because he was so nondescript: short brown hair, hazel eyes, medium height, grey-blue suit, no unusual features.

Kitty made fun of him for his plain ties that were always in the same shade as his plain socks, for his trousers that were hung in a trouser press overnight so the crease fell in exactly the right place. It made her want to raid his drawer and leave only mismatching socks; or to get him drunk and drag him to a tattoo parlour to have a gothic emblem etched on his forearm. She found it irritating that he drank sensible decaf coffee and brushed his teeth for exactly two minutes; she was bored with the weekend sex routine of an orgasm for her, one for him, invariably achieved the same way.

He was a good provider – they were lucky not to have money worries – but at some point they had stopped having fun and she couldn't think when that had happened. The holiday in Costa Rica the previous autumn had been glorious; Christmas with his extended family had been nice. But since then life had felt monotonous, with nothing interesting on the horizon.

It didn't help that her own career had stalled. She'd studied journalism at college and always imagined herself flying first-class to LA to interview celebrities for *Vanity Fair*, or breaking the story that David Cameron had a secret lover in a *Guardian* exclusive, but instead she reviewed theatre for the local paper in their part of north London. She earned a pittance and had to sit through dire shows at least three evenings a week then churn out five hundred words of lively copy that didn't betray how deeply disenchanted she was with theatre as an art form.

Her mother's oft-repeated view that writing was a hobby, not a reliable way to earn a living, kept echoing in her head. She'd wanted Kitty to study law, but memorising all those endless judgements sounded unbearably tedious. Should she have listened? Or should she push herself harder to succeed as a writer? There seemed no urgency when Tom earned enough for them both. She kept planning to write a book but changed her mind about the subject before managing more than a few thousand words. If she couldn't maintain an interest, how could she expect to hold her readers' attention?

'You've always had a lazy streak,' her mum used to say. 'You get it from your dad's side.' Perhaps it was true.

She wondered what kind of books Dmitri Yakovlevich had written. She vaguely remembered that Grandma Marta had Russian roots; the surname certainly sounded Russian: perhaps his work was all in his native language. She'd find out when the royalty statements came through.

There was nothing that seemed suspicious in the Inheritance Tracker forms so she signed on the dotted line and sent them back with the required certificates. She and Tom vaguely discussed what to do with the cabin in upstate New York, and he was in favour of selling it.

'After it's lain empty for thirty-odd years, the level of repairs needed to make it habitable would cost more than the thing is worth,' he said with his business head.

'It might be a good investment,' Kitty maintained. 'We could renovate then rent it out through a local agency.' She had a flair for DIY. Her father had taught her carpentry skills and she had already done up three properties in London: two she sold on at a profit and one in which they still lived.

'We'd only be able to rent it three months of the year,' Tom said. 'No one wants to holiday in the Adirondacks in winter, and it wouldn't cover its annual costs on the summer rental alone.'

Kitty yawned. He didn't seem to see the romance of owning a cabin in the American wilderness. Why had Dmitri bought it? She imagined it must be very beautiful. And then it slipped to the back of her mind over the next few weeks as she wrote her theatre reviews, had lunch or an early-evening drink with friends, took her yoga classes and ran the household she shared with her sensible, risk-averse husband.

Chapter Six

London, 18th July 2016

Kitty could not put her finger on what made her pick up Tom's mobile phone when he went for a run one Saturday morning, leaving it on the hall table. She'd never done that in all the years they'd been together, even though she knew his password and he knew hers. It wasn't a conscious decision to check his texts but the phone was lying there, she was standing looking at it, and somehow she found herself flicking through his messages. Almost immediately she found a photo of a naked woman with huge breasts and a message that read 'Want more of this, baby? How about my place, 11 on Saturday morning.' It finished with a heart emoji.

Kitty's throat seemed to close up and she could feel the blood pumping in her temples. The sender of the text was called 'Karren', with two 'r's, and when she scrolled down she found several more texts, telling Tom he was the hottest lover she'd ever had, and making arrangements for other trysts. It appeared they'd been having an affair for at least two months; he hadn't even bothered to delete the evidence.

She glanced at the clock: ten to eleven. He would be at Karren's any moment now. What should she do?

Her closest friend, Amber, lived two streets away so Kitty jumped in the car, revving the engine as she raced round there. Amber was breastfeeding her youngest, only six weeks old, while her husband played with their two toddlers in the garden. Kitty didn't bother with any preamble, simply handing her the phone with Karren's nude photo on the screen.

'Can you believe it? Look what Tom's been up to behind my back! The utter bastard!'

She expected Amber to be shocked or perhaps try to think of innocent reasons why he might have such a picture on his phone. Instead she hesitated a fraction too long, not meeting Kitty's eye, and the penny dropped.

'You *knew* about this?'

Amber looked up miserably, and handed back the phone. 'I'm so sorry. I thought I had persuaded him to knock it on the head without you finding out. I didn't want you to be hurt.'

'You *knew*!' Kitty repeated. She couldn't believe it. This was the woman with whom she shared her innermost secrets. They discussed everything from their most embarrassing sexual experiences to their fake-tan disasters, from their career dissatisfactions to their secret celebrity crushes. She was the one who had said the right things after Kitty's parents' deaths, the only person she could bear to discuss them with. Amber's face was a study in guilt.

'Kitty, I . . .' she began, but Kitty shook her head, mouth open in astonishment and held up a hand to stop her. There was nothing to say. Amber had known and hadn't told her. She turned and rushed from the house, knowing that Amber would never catch up with a baby in her arms.

She got back in the car and drove home, ignoring the persistent ringing of her phone on the passenger seat. Tom would be back soon, with a false smile and another woman's scent clinging to him. The thought made her stomach heave. She didn't want to be there, couldn't face confronting him and all that would entail. The life she thought she was leading had fallen apart in an instant.

Every plan she had made for the future, every dream assumed that Tom would love her forever and now it was clear he didn't and wouldn't. It felt like a double betrayal that Amber had known and not told her. She had to get out of the marital home, but where could she go that he wouldn't find her?

And then it came to her: the documents making her the owner of the cabin on Lake Akanabee had come through just a few days earlier and the cheque had cleared in her current account. Why not fly out to see it? It felt like a suitably dramatic gesture in response to such a huge betrayal.

She grabbed a suitcase and threw in whatever came to hand: outdoor clothing, a sleeping bag, some toiletries, a few basic tools, all the paperwork relating to the cabin. Tom would never remember the name of the lake. Now she thought about it, he'd been distracted these last few months. Perhaps he was in love with Karren. Tears pricked her eyes and she shook herself, before picking up her laptop and mobile phone, leaving Tom's phone in the middle of the kitchen table. She debated leaving a note but decided against it. Let him work it out for himself.

She drove to Heathrow, parked the car in a long-stay car park then went to the British Airways desk and booked a ticket on a six o'clock flight, which would land in New York at nine o'clock the same evening, due to the five-hour time difference.

'You need a return ticket within ninety days if you don't have a visa,' the carefully made-up saleswoman explained, beige shellac nails tapping on a keyboard.

Kitty ran her finger along the desk calendar and picked a date just before the ninety days would be up. She was paying full price so she could always change the flight if she decided to come back sooner.

In the departure lounge she used her laptop to book an airport hotel room in which to rest on arrival, then organised a hire car for the next ninety days, which cost an eye-watering sum. By focusing on practicalities, she tried to stop herself thinking that

Tom would already be home. He'd probably be wondering why she wasn't there to prepare lunch – unless Amber had called to warn him that Kitty knew his secret. What would he do next? Which friends would he phone? Would he notice that her passport was missing?

On the flight she drank four miniature bottles of white wine, ate a re-heated dinner and dozed off in front of the new Ridley Scott movie. The time passed quickly, although she felt nauseous with sleep deprivation when she queued to get through customs in John F Kennedy airport. She conked out in the anonymous hotel room and slept for a few hours, waking as dawn broke outside the hermetically sealed windows.

She went to collect her car from the rental agency, typed the zip code of the cabin into the Sat Nav and let the woman's confident voice guide her off Long Island and due north towards the Adirondacks. It was 254 miles, she was told, and would take over four hours. Kitty was a confident driver, and she hoped to get there around lunchtime to give her time to decide in daylight whether the cabin was habitable.

The traffic thinned after she left the interstate and for a while the road skimmed the shores of Great Sacandaga Lake before heading up into the mountains. It was warm and sunny and the views were glorious: hills covered in forests like plush green velvet, a flash of blue denoting a lake between the trees, a few white clouds against a bright sky. Her heart wouldn't stop pounding though. She tried to find a music station on the radio but the reception was too crackly. She hadn't eaten breakfast and her stomach growled, but she was pretty sure she would throw up if she ate anything. *You bastard, Tom,* she thought from time to time, but mostly she tried to keep her mind blank and focus on the driving.

Chapter Seven

Postal deliveries to the front line were erratic but Tatiana wrote so frequently that Dmitri seldom had long to wait between her letters. He thrilled at the sight of her handwriting on the envelope, at the way she always called him 'Malama sweetheart', at the faint hint of her scent that he imagined he could detect on the pages, and at her sentiments, which became more affectionate with each exchange. She wrote that Ortipo's snoring kept Olga awake at night, and that she had been playing a game called ruble with her sisters; she told him of her patients on the wards, of books she had read, and always she told him that she missed him.

Dmitri found it easier to overcome his natural reserve and express his feelings in letters than he had done in person, and Tatiana reciprocated his endearments. They became bolder and he felt he learned more of her character with each letter. He imagined she must seem very private and reserved to those who didn't know her, but to him she wrote with a straightforward honesty that was unprecedented amongst the women of his acquaintance. There were no games, or sulks or flounces.

Was there a chance he might one day be her husband? Or did her parents have other suitors in mind for their eldest daughters?

He plucked up the courage to ask and was overwhelmed by her reply:

Malama sweetheart,

You asked about the marriages my parents have considered for Olga and me and now I think I will make you laugh because we have endured so much speculation on the subject based on virtually no substance.

First of all, I am told that David, the eldest son of the British King George V, is believed to have taken a liking to me when we visited there in August 1909. Of course, I was only twelve and far too young to be aware of it, although I remember dancing with him at a ball on the *Standart*, while fireworks lit up the sky. He was rather a good dancer, and I recall he was wearing a uniform because he was at naval college, but I can't remember making conversation. Mama said to me afterwards that she was only twelve when she first met Papa, and that it is possible to know your own mind at that age. I think she was keen that either Olga or I should one day be Queen of England but nothing came of it. We haven't seen David since then and I imagine he must be terribly busy with the war.

Then in 1912, I think, the newspapers started reporting that Olga was to be married to Grand Duke Dmitri Pavlovevich – which was news to Olga, who had always found him rather coarse. The rumour persisted for years with absolutely no foundation, much to Olga's annoyance.

You must have heard about the marriages with Balkan princes that our parents have been rumoured (erroneously, I believe) to be arranging for some time. For a while I corresponded with my cousin George of Battenberg, but never with any intention of marrying him, let me assure you! Olga was asked to consider Prince Carol of Romania, who came to visit us in Livadia last summer, but she does not want to leave Russia when she marries, so we came up with a cunning plan: we both suntanned our faces before they arrived, knowing that in royal circles it is considered *paysan*. We were polite to Carol but I think he took the hint because no further meetings have been arranged.

Olga and I are agreed on two things: that we only want to marry Russian men, and that we want to marry for love, as our parents did. I can imagine nothing worse than being forced to marry someone I do not like for political reasons, but am assured by Mama that will never be the case and that we may choose our own husbands. Now I am embarrassed to have told you so much, but you asked and so here is my answer.

I hope you are keeping warm, *mon amoureux*, and not straying into the way of any more bullets. Do you ever think of me or is your life too full of plans for defeating the Kaiser's army? Are you comfortable in your bunker at night? Are you getting enough to eat? Is there snow where you are? The snow here is five foot deep and I worry that you may catch cold. Every night as I lie in my cosy bed, I worry about where you are lying and wish you could hear my thoughts through the frosty night.

Did you receive my letter in which I told you of Anna Vyrubova, Mama's lady-in-waiting, being in a train crash? She is most seriously injured and we are all terribly concerned but at least she is conscious and able to eat a little. Mama is nursing her personally. She is so very dear to us.

As you are very dear to me.

Que Dieu vous garde.

Tatiana

It was minus five degrees outside but Dmitri was flushed as he sat in his bunker reading and re-reading this letter by candlelight. The earthen walls glittered with ice and his breath misted the air. *We only want to marry Russian men and we want to marry for love.* Surely it was a hint, perhaps even an invitation? He could imagine her blushes as she wrote and wished he could kiss those pink cheeks over and over.

All of a sudden he yearned for her with a passion that was tantamount to madness. He couldn't bear their separation one moment longer; it was tearing him apart. What was it about her that moved him so? His feelings could not be reduced to logic; quite simply, he adored the very essence of her.

Dmitri felt so sick with longing that it could only be assuaged by writing back to Tatiana straight away and spilling his feelings on paper. Recklessness took hold and he wrote with the question that was foremost on his mind:

Mon Ange,

Your letter has filled me with hope and drives me to write that I wish with all my heart and soul I might one day be the Russian man you choose to marry. I don't have royal blood or a fortune anything like the size of your family's, but I promise I would alternately worship and tease you in exactly the right proportions for the rest of our lives. The possibility that I might have a chance of gaining your parents' approval fires me with renewed determination to survive this grotesque war. My love for you gives me an invisible cloak that bullets and shells cannot penetrate.

Please do not tell anyone of this proposal lest your father think it disrespectful that I have not asked his permission first . . . but a private understanding between us would make me the happiest man in the world.

When the letter was finished Dmitri lay back on the wooden pallet that served as his bunk and daydreamed about marrying Tatiana. Maybe the wedding could take place in the Romanovs' private chapel, the Grand Church at the Winter Palace, with its ostentatious gold stucco and its dome with lunettes picturing the Apostles. He imagined his parents and sisters sitting alongside the Tsar and Tsarina. His father was a stern, critical man who believed Dmitri was not rising through the army ranks as rapidly as he should, but surely he would be proud of a son who married a Romanov? His sisters would love to become acquainted with the grand duchesses, and undoubtedly the relationship would enhance Valerina's marriage prospects. Dare he send the letter?

Dmitri thought about it overnight and when his feelings were the same the following morning, he rushed to give it to the postal clerk before he could change his mind. As was his habit, he addressed the envelope to Tatiana's maid, Trina, so that the officer who censored their mail would not discover the true object of his affections. He could not risk gossip leaking out.

All that day he did not tell anyone, not even his friend Malevich who had at last returned to the front fully recovered from his wounds. That evening as they sat around the fire slurping bowls of watery venison stew, his fellow officers teased him for being silent and withdrawn and Malevich led the ribbing.

'I think Cornet Malama has a sweetheart,' he joked. 'Have you noticed how eagerly he awaits postal deliveries, and how he rushes to his bunk to read any letters in privacy? Pray tell us, Malama, who is the lucky lady?'

Dmitri shook his head, grinning. 'As if I would tell a bunch of delinquents like you lot!'

'See how he blushes,' another mocked. 'He definitely has a secret.'

'It's the heat of the fire,' Dmitri maintained.

He wished he could talk about Tatiana – he wanted to tell the world of their love – but any wrong move at this stage could spoil his chances, especially if it spilled into the newspapers. His heart was so full he scarcely felt the biting cold of the Prussian plain where they were dug in. Huddled in his bedding roll that night, he imagined Tatiana's arms around him, her face against his, as he sank into dream-filled sleep.

Chapter Eight

The war continued to go badly for the Russians. The Germans introduced the new long-barrelled howitzers, which they hauled around on wheeled carriages, and now they could wreak destruction wherever they chose. Massive shells hurtled down without warning. The ground shook, stones rained from the sky and more bodies had to be buried after each ear-shattering explosion. It took hours of hacking at the frozen earth with a pickaxe to dig a grave, and many bodies were piled in together, without the dignity of solitude in their final resting place. Dmitri spent his days trying to direct their own shelling towards the howitzers but felt they were making no progress.

When he came off duty each evening, he rushed to the postal clerk. A few letters arrived that Tatiana had sent before receiving his; they were charming, but he was going mad waiting for her response to his proposal. When it came, he knew instinctively this was the one. The envelope was of the same type as the others, it was sealed in the same way, but his heart pounded and he felt sick with nerves as he tore it open.

Malama sweetheart,

I received your letter of the 28th of January this very
morning and have rushed to my room to write as soon as I
could. The answer to your proposal is yes, yes, yes; with all
my soul I wish to be your wife. You should see how I blush to
say these words. I know Mama and Papa will agree, since you
are so courageous and noble and true. Mama has already
told me she admires you, and I know Papa will too. I can't
wait for the day when I can call you my husband. If only the
war could be over next week and you could rush home to
claim your bride! I fear the waiting will be unbearable.

Dmitri read and re-read the paragraph, unable to believe his
eyes. Was he misunderstanding it? The underlined 'yes, yes, yes'
seemed unequivocal. Was it really true that he might become
Tatiana's husband? He read on, giddy with excitement:

I understand that until then we must keep our engagement
secret but I hope you will not mind that I have confided in
Uncle Grigory. Do you know him? The Siberian spiritual
leader they call Rasputin, who is a great friend of our
family. He saw me sitting pensive by a window and guessed
that I was pining for a loved one so I found myself telling
him about you. He asked to see a letter from you, because
he says that men can judge other men's intentions far better
than women. After some hesitation I produced your
proposal letter from the folds of my gown, where I had
tucked it to keep it close. He read it, and when he finished
he handed it back, saying 'He truly loves you, and he is
obviously a good man.'
I was overjoyed, as you can imagine, and told him how
much I want to marry you. I explained that my mother and
sisters do not yet know we are in love, although they have met

and admired you, and I made him promise to keep our secret. Uncle Grigory closed his eyes and held my hand for several seconds, one finger on my wrist as if he was feeling for the truth. He has mystical powers and his predictions always come true. 'Yes, you will marry him,' he said. 'Yet there are dark days ahead.' I suppose he means because of the war.

I hope you do not mind me telling him, Malama. Since your letter arrived I have been bursting with the news that we are to wed. I find it hard not to tell anyone else, but I agree that is how it must be since you must apply to my father for permission and I can't see how he might give it till the war is over. Until then it will be our precious secret, something I can hug to my breast to ease the agony of missing you.

I must go to the hospital now but will write later. When I am writing I feel close to you and wish there were more hours in the day so I could write more.

Mon amour est pour vous, à jamais.

Tatiana

Dmitri stared at the letter, with a tumult of emotions. There was the exhilaration of Tatiana accepting his proposal but also irritation and alarm that she should have told Rasputin about it. Dmitri had not been introduced to the bearded wild man, but had heard only ill of him. The thought of him touching Tatiana's wrist and reading the intensely private letter made Dmitri wild with jealousy. What if Rasputin told the Tsarina, to whom he was said to be very close? It could utterly spoil his chances of one day being accepted into the family. What had Tatiana been thinking?

'What do you make of Grigory Rasputin?' he asked the men that evening as they ate their meagre bowls of stew, accompanied by hunks of rough, gritty bread.

'Who is he?' a young officer asked.

Malevich replied: 'He's a self-seeking charlatan who presents himself as a man of God while spending his time carousing in brothels and bars. He has inveigled his way into the Romanovs' inner circle and their relationship with such a reprobate does them no favours. I hear the Tsar would banish him to Siberia but the Tsarina has fallen under his spell and will not hear of it.' He shook his head in disbelief.

'What do you think he seeks from them?' Dmitri asked sarcastically. 'Surely not riches, power and influence?'

Malevich snorted. 'Of course. It's a very lucrative connection for him.'

Another joined in. 'It's a shame the assassination attempt in May was unsuccessful. I hear he is trying to convert the Tsarina and her daughters to the Khlysty sect, who believe that you must sin as much as possible and then ask for forgiveness later. They claim repentance is only genuine for the greatest sinners: a very cynical philosophy and one that suits Rasputin right down to the ground.'

'That would certainly account for his many transgressions,' Malevich agreed. 'Nude swimming; wandering round the palace in his nightshirt; even entering the bedroom of the grand duchesses while they lie sleeping. It is not a healthy association. I heard he makes love to every lady he meets – including his own daughter.'

'Oh, that's vile ...'

Dmitri was disturbed. How could the Tsarina not see through such a man, with his crazy eyes, dishevelled clothing and disrespectful manner? Back at his tent, in a burst of ill humour, he scribbled off a hasty note to Tatiana:

My very own angel, I wish you had not been so trustful of Rasputin. No doubt he is all smiles and weasel words inside the palace walls but believe me when I tell you that in the outside world he is known as a scoundrel. I am afraid that if he spreads our secret it could ruin any chance of us one day being wed. Of course, I understand your desire to tell someone of our love – I feel the same way myself – but could you not have whispered it to Ortipo instead? She would have made a better choice of confidante than the wild Siberian, and I expect her response would have been more intelligent. I cannot stop to write more now but will try to find a moment soon.

Your very own, Malama.

He sealed the note and hurried to the postal clerk's tent to send it, still feeling discomfited. How could Tatiana not see through such a ruffian? Was she so lacking in judgement?

He pondered the question as he lay in bed that night, unable to sleep, and it came to him that her very limited exposure to the outside world must mean she did not have well-tuned instincts about human nature. She was a good creature who saw only good in everyone she met. It would be his role gently to teach her more of the world.

As soon as he realised this, he regretted the pompous tone of his note and hoped it would not upset her or even change her opinion of him. He lay awake long into the night worrying and as soon as the camp awoke the following morning he rushed to the postal tent to retrieve his letter, only to find it had already been dispatched.

Chapter Nine

All day Dmitri agonised over his note. Would Tatiana be hurt that he sounded critical? Might she even fall out of love with him? His turmoil continued till nightfall, when he was distracted by devastating news: the Russian XX Corps had been surrounded in Augustow Forest by four German corps without any Russian commander getting wind of it. For five days they had held out under intense gunfire, in a snowstorm, until all hope was lost. It sounded as though most of the 70,000 men had been killed outright and the remainder taken prisoner. Yet again it had been possible because of lack of information about German troop movements.

There were urgent meetings of Russia's commanders and a counter-attack against the right flank of the German front was called for the next day. *Too little, too late*, Dmitri thought gloomily as he prepared his horse, oiled his pistol and sharpened his sabre in a biting wind beneath dark grey, snow-heavy clouds. He couldn't bear the thought that he might die the following day and the last correspondence Tatiana would receive from him would be that curt rebuke, so he sat down to compose another letter, hoping it might overtake the first.

Mon Ange,

Forgive your jealous lover for his temper of last evening. I could not bear to hear of your intimacy with another man, one who is renowned for his promiscuity, no less. It was agony for me to think of him close to you, reading my most personal letter. Like an impetuous fool I responded in haste but now repent and beg you not to love me any less for my outburst.

Affairs go badly in our part of the front. It seems we will not be able to defeat the German army with any speed, although I hope we will now restrain them at the border so they cannot sink their boots into Russian mud. If only this war would soon be over so that I can rush home to your arms. I yearn to hear your pretty voice and look into the depths of your eyes. Forgive me, angel.

Your Malama

He kissed the envelope tenderly before taking it to the postal clerk, although he knew it would pass through many hands before hers. Oh, if only he could deliver it in person!

Over the next few weeks, Dmitri's regiment was forced to retreat rapidly as the German and Austro-Hungarian armies combined to push through Poland. It would have been suicide for the Russians to stand and fight because they did not have the artillery and ammunition to rival their opponents. At times the Germans were so close Dmitri could hear them calling to each other, could smell the smoke of their campfires, could see their sentries shivering in the deep snow. He hoped the conditions would be harder for them, as Russians are used to snow. Sometimes he crept out under cover of the forest to set eyes on the enemy but he never asked his men to fire at the German lines for fear of those big guns. Until they had such weapons themselves it would be foolhardy to give away their location.

All this time, he heard nothing from Tatiana. Postal deliveries were scarce while the army was on the move, and the severe weather meant supplies did not reach them regularly. They shot deer and picked berries for food, and melted snow for drinking water because the rivers and lakes were covered in impenetrable ice. Dmitri knew his comrades had received no letters from their families and sweethearts, but still he feared the silence must mean Tatiana had changed her opinion of him. Perhaps she had found a new beau at the hospital, with whom she now passed her time. Would she be so fickle as to abandon him after a few months' absence? He couldn't believe it of her . . . but still, she might be cross about his rebuke over Rasputin. It was entirely his own fault.

Winter blew itself out with one last icy storm and watery sunshine began to thaw the snow. Icicles broke off and hurtled from the treetops like daggers thrown by invisible hands. The ground became boggy with snowmelt and occasional rabbits, fresh from hibernation, began to grace the camp's cookpots. Meanwhile, the Germans took Warsaw and Krakow, and pushed on towards Lithuania and Belarus; seemingly nothing could stop them. Privately, Dmitri grew contemptuous of the commanders who could think of nothing to stop this assault, and was not remotely reassured when he heard that Tsar Nicholas intended to take personal command of the army. There was much muttering round the campfire that Nicholas knew nothing of military strategy and might as well put his young son Alexei in charge for all the good he would do.

At last, when over two agonising months had gone by without word from Tatiana, Dmitri received a bundle of letters one evening, all of them from her bar one from his mother. He hurried to his tent and began by sorting them into date order before he opened

51

the first one, which was dated February 12th, just after she must have received his rebuke.

My dearest Malama,

I have read your note and your explanation sent the following day and of course I can understand why you resent me showing your letter to Rasputin. If our situations were reversed and you had shown one of my letters to a comrade I would have been hurt and surprised. However, I assure you that Rasputin has never been anything but respectful to my family and to me personally.

I believe Mama and Papa first met him in 1905, and were immediately impressed by his inspiring interpretations of the scriptures. When Prime Minister Stolypin's daughter was injured in that dreadful bombing, he cured her against all the odds simply by laying his hands on her wounds. He now treats Mama for her headaches and sciatica, and helps my little brother Alexei when he suffers from painful joints. There is no doubt in my mind that he has healing powers.

One day, when you are back in Tsarskoe Selo, I will introduce you and you will see for yourself that he is a force for nothing but good. I hate to disagree with you by letter when we have no immediate prospect of being together. If only we could look into each other's eyes and know that all is well. Believe me when I tell you that my feelings for you have not changed one little bit because of this difference of opinion. I am glad we can speak our minds with each other and am sure this is a healthy sign for our married life.

The letter finished with many endearments and Dmitri buried his face in his hands, overcome with emotion that she was still his Tatiana, his beloved. He kissed the paper and clasped his hands in prayer, thanking God for ending his weeks of mental torture.

He opened the next letter, then the one after, and read through all in sequence. She wrote of her sadness after the death of a young patient at the hospital. She drew a picture of the special tag, encrusted with tiny jewels set in filigree vines, she had commissioned Fabergé to make for Ortipo's collar then wrote that the little floozy did not deserve it, having got pregnant by another of the palace dogs, provoking quite a *scandale*. She wrote of the books recommended by her English tutor, Pierre Gilliard, and of all she was learning from Doctor Vera Gedroit, who flattered her by saying she had a talent for nursing. And as the letters progressed she became increasingly anxious about Dmitri's welfare, saying she had received no word from him throughout the spring months when it seemed all news from the front was worse than the last.

Mon chéri,

I beg you to send two lines telling me you are safe. I'm full
of such fear that I find it hard to concentrate on my work.
My sisters talk to me and I realise after several minutes that
I have not been listening because all my thoughts are with
you in Poland. I will not rest easy until I hear you are safe.

The most recent letter told him that in October she and Olga would be joining their father at Stavka, the army headquarters in Mogilev, where Alexei was visiting the troops. It was her fondest hope that Dmitri might be close enough to ride over for even an hour: 'To see your face and hear your voice would be bliss, even if we cannot be alone together. I will only be assured that you are well when I can see it in your eyes.'

Dmitri cursed. Mogilev was several hundred miles south of his current position. He went to ask his commander if there might be some mission that could take him down that way, perhaps delivering a message to the Tsar, but was told that he could not be spared.

It was unbearable to think of Tatiana coming comparatively close yet not be able to see her. Mogilev was not on the front line but if the Germans made a sudden push forwards it was not unthinkable that their shells might penetrate so far. What was Tsar Nicholas thinking? It proved he had no concept of how strong this German opponent was or he would not have considered bringing his family to the area. Dmitri tortured himself with images of Tatiana being torn apart by a howitzer shell and knew he would not sleep easy till she was in St Petersburg once more.

Chapter Ten

Lake Akanabee, New York State, 20th July 2016

The morning after her arrival at Lake Akanabee, Kitty drove into the nearby town of Indian Lake to buy tools and provisions. A row of purply-red clapboard houses and shops with white eaves and sloping roofs were set along a dusty main street, with skeins of overhead wiring looping from lamppost to lamppost. There were no traffic lights and she hardly saw another car as she crawled along looking for a hardware store.

The road was lined with fast-food outlets, camping equipment stores and adventure sports shops with racks of canoes outside. She drove straight past 'Lakeside Country Stores' first time and it was only on the way back that she noticed their sign advertised hardware, plumbing and decorating materials as well as camping gear. She pulled into the yard and dug out the list she'd scribbled. She needed a battery-powered chainsaw, a drill, woodworking tools, a spade, and a brush and shovel; she also needed a gas cooking stove, an oil lamp, and some cups, plates and cutlery. The man behind the counter piled up her purchases, obviously delighted to make such a substantial sale.

'Do you have a sliding bevel?' she asked, checking against her list.

'You sure you need one?' he asked, an eyebrow raised in a manner that indicated he didn't think women knew about such things.

'Yes. I have some steps to rebuild and need to get the angles right.'

He shrugged and began searching the shelves. 'Just arrived?'

'Yesterday.'

'Your husband with you?'

Kitty bristled. Why did men in DIY stores always assume there must be a man behind the scenes? 'Nope,' she said shortly.

He produced a bevel and she unfastened then retightened the wing nut before adding it to her pile.

'You've come at the right time,' the storekeeper said. 'We're nearing the end of bug season. A couple of weeks ago you would have had to fight your way through swarms of them.'

'I did get a couple of bites last night,' she admitted, scratching her neck. 'Is there anything you recommend?'

'Yup,' he said, and added a large bottle of insect repellent to the pile. 'Round here we wear this twenty-four seven, April to October.'

The chip and pin machine wasn't working so she had to sign for her purchases.

'Is there a supermarket nearby?' she asked.

He directed her to one further down the main street. 'You can't miss it.'

'How about a jeweller's?' She fingered the pendant she'd found, which she'd slipped inside her purse. It would be interesting to get it valued.

'Lake George is the nearest jewellery store, but my brother-in-law used to work in the trade and he still keeps a stock of gift items. You'll find him down Bennett Road.' He wrote the name and address for her on the back of his business card. 'Say Chad sent you.'

Kitty went to the supermarket first and stocked up on the type of tinned foods that could be heated over a camping stove, as well as crackers, cheese, apples, coffee and a few bottles of wine. The car was full to bursting as she drove down to Bennett Road, which was easy to find as there were hardly any other cross streets off

the main road. When she rang the bell, two Great Danes came bounding across the yard, followed by a bearded man in a disconcertingly bright cerise shirt.

'Hello,' she began. 'Chad said you used to work in the jewellery trade. I was hoping to get a valuation on a pendant.' She took it from her purse and handed it to him.

He had a quick look. 'Sure. Come inside.'

She took a seat at his kitchen table, which was covered in a floral waxed tablecloth. The man fetched a jeweller's loupe from another room and held the pendant up to the light of the window before giving a low whistle. Kitty waited. He examined the setting of the stones then turned it over and squinted at the back. There was silence while he concentrated, then finally he turned to Kitty.

'This is Fabergé! It's one of the most beautiful pieces I've come across.'

'You're kidding!' Kitty was not a jewellery expert but Fabergé was probably the world's best-known luxury brand. Her grandfather must have been wealthy; or perhaps it was a family heirloom.

'If I'm not mistaken, it's rose gold set with a sapphire, a ruby and imperial topaz. The engraving on the back is a maker's mark. It's a little worn but it looks as though the workmaster's initials were H.W.'

'Can I see?' Kitty peered through the loupe but couldn't make out anything that looked like either 'Fabergé' or 'H.W.'

'It's the Cyrillic alphabet,' the man told her. He produced an iPad from a drawer and typed in a password then looked something up. 'As I thought . . . it's Henrik Wigström, who was their head workmaster from 1903 through to 1918.'

'Was he Russian?' Kitty asked, wondering if Dmitri had brought the object over from Russia with him.

'Wigström was from Finland but he worked at the company headquarters in St Petersburg, under the great Michael Perchin, the most famous Fabergé workmaster.' He glanced up to see if she recognised the name, but she looked blank. 'The company was so popular in the late nineteenth and early twentieth centuries that they used independent artisans to make up orders based on sketches supplied to them by Fabergé's designers. You'll have heard of the famous Fabergé eggs . . .'

'Erm . . . I think so.'

He seemed disappointed by Kitty's ignorance. 'They were extraordinary jewelled creations that the royal family gave each other for Easter, with hidden surprises inside. Only sixty-five of them were ever made and recent prices at auction have reached close to ten million dollars each.'

'Oh my God!' Kitty was stunned. 'For an Easter egg?'

The jeweller laughed. 'Yeah, well, the one Tsar Nicholas gave to his mother in 1913 was made of platinum and gold, studded with' – he read from his iPad – '1,660 diamonds on the outside and 1,378 in the little basket inside. Not your average Easter gift, I agree, but they were by far the richest family in the world. It was an absolute monarchy for three hundred years and the Russian people were serfs, so all the country's wealth flowed into the family coffers.'

Her eyes widened. 'Does that mean my pendant is valuable?'

'It's only small but I reckon it would fetch several thousand dollars at auction. Do you want to sell?' He weighed the object in the palm of his hand. 'I still have contacts in the business.'

'Sorry, no. It's a family piece. I just wondered . . .' He looked disappointed so she continued: 'Perhaps you could sell me a gold chain to wear it on?'

He padded off and came back with a small tray of neck chains. She chose one with fine links that complemented the filigree setting of the stones and paid cash for it.

'If you change your mind about selling, you know where I am,' he called after her.

As she drove back towards Lake Akanabee, with the pendant resting on her breastbone, Kitty was overcome with curiosity about her great-grandfather. If he could afford a Fabergé jewelled pendant, he must have been rather a good writer. Why had she never heard of him?

A mile or so before the track to her cabin, she passed a vacation park with a coffee shop and reversed to have a look. On the sign it read 'Free Wi-Fi', so she parked and went inside with her laptop tucked under her arm.

'Hi, can I be cheeky and ask for your wi-fi code and some electricity?' she began, explaining that her cabin, a few miles up the road, had no electric hook-up.

'Be my guest,' the lad serving the coffee said, pointing to a socket where she could charge her laptop. His name was Jeff, he told her, pouring her a latte, and he worked there for the summer then went back to college in the fall. She explained about her inheritance and Jeff was amazed when he heard which cabin she was renovating. 'I thought that was a goner. You must know what you're doing.'

'I've never taken on a challenge quite like this,' she told him, 'but I'll work it out as I go along.'

When her laptop had charged sufficiently, she opened her browser and googled the name Dmitri Yakovlevich. First of all she found biographies for a Russian Arctic explorer, a Jewish composer and a Constructivist artist, but none of their dates seemed to fit. She added 'writer' after her search term and up came a short Wikipedia page about a man who had been born in 1891 in Russia and had written five novels: *Interminable Love* (1924), *Exile* (1927), *The Boot That Kicked* (1933), *In the Pale Light of Dawn* (1944) and *Toward the Sunset* (1947). There was nothing else about him, not even a date of death.

Next she went to the site of a second-hand book dealer and entered Dmitri's name in the search facility. The only book of his in stock was *Interminable Love*. Kitty ordered a copy, paying for it with her credit card, and Jeff said she could have it delivered to their office, since the local mailman was unlikely to trek down to her cabin.

Next she hovered over the icon for opening her email account. It was tempting to click on it and see what mails came in. She had texted her editor at the newspaper to say she'd been called away on family business, so she wasn't expecting any work emails. There would almost certainly be some mails from Tom – either pathetic attempts at self-justification or perhaps he would be asking for a divorce. The thought made her shudder. She was sure Amber would have been in touch as well, but if she contacted Amber she would have to discuss Tom's infidelity and that would mean thinking about it and she simply did not feel ready. Out there in the wilderness, on a separate continent, she had already begun to feel like the independent, capable person she used to be before she got married. To get back in touch with Amber and Tom – with anyone from her old life – would make her feel sad and anxious and needy.

So many questions would have to be considered. If Tom wanted a divorce, what would happen about money? She couldn't live on the pittance she earned writing theatre reviews and the money she'd made doing up properties had been swallowed up by the house they lived in now, but her pride wouldn't let her take a penny from Tom. They'd have to sell the house and she'd need to get a proper job doing God knows what. But if he wanted to save the marriage, would she ever be able to trust him again? Would she be able to make love without thinking about 'Karren' with the double 'r'? Memories of the naked woman on Tom's phone made Kitty's gut clench and tears welled up in her eyes. She took her last sip of coffee.

Let him wait. Maybe it would give him time to get Karren out of his system. Meanwhile she would fix up her cabin. When she had woken that morning, she'd gone for an early swim in the shimmering crystal water, listening to the noisy chatter of birds disputing their territory. There was dense green forest, sparkly blue water and hazy blue sky for as far as the eye could see. The sense of being part of this awe-inspiring landscape brought a kind of clarity in the midst of her emotional turmoil. After one night there, she was already falling in love with Lake Akanabee.

Chapter Eleven

Eastern Front, Lithuania, 5th March 1916

Time weighed heavy for Dmitri during the winter of 1915 to 1916 and made him yearn for Tatiana more than ever. Both the Russian and German armies had dug into the earth, trying to find shelter from the brutal blizzards that obscured their vision two feet ahead and made it impossible to venture out of the trench for fear of accidentally wandering into no man's land. Dmitri still rode out on reconnaissance missions but it was clear that cavalry would play little part in the next stage of the war so he also took lessons on how to position the big guns that were just beginning to arrive from Russian armaments factories, guessing that this would be the only way to drive the Germans back from the territories they had captured in Poland, Lithuania and Belarus.

He got through the days by dreaming of the life he and Tatiana would lead together once the war was over. Would they stay in St Petersburg in a wing of one of the palaces? He would prefer to be in the country; he was more at home in wide open spaces. Still it didn't feel real; he couldn't allow himself to believe they would be married until her parents had given consent. In truth they had not known each other long. They'd had less than three months together before he came back to the front, and he could sense

61

Tatiana had changed while he was away. Before she had been light-hearted and almost carefree; now she had grown up. She said as much in her letters:

Malama sweetheart,

Can you believe it is fifteen months since that December day when I waved farewell to you outside the Catherine Palace? I was a mere child in those innocent weeks at the start of the war, with no idea of what I would have to confront. Now I often assist as surgeons amputate men's limbs; I dress stinking gangrenous wounds; I give injections and distribute medicines; I comfort those who are dying; and yesterday I was even able to calm a man who had some kind of fit of terror. He was staring straight ahead, rocking backwards and forwards and uttering a moaning sound that disturbed the other patients. At first I just talked in a low voice but he didn't seem to hear or see me. Finally I began to sing, upon which he stopped moaning to listen, and at last he fell asleep for the first time since he arrived on our ward. I think my singing must be particularly soporific!

The patients give me a little insight into the life you are leading at the front and I am terrified on your behalf. I know that you are holding the line somewhere in Lithuania and are not currently in battle, but that shells pound the earth and snipers watch for any careless movement. Malama, I beg you to be extra-cautious and avoid any heroics. *Souvenez vous que vous tenez mon coeur entre vos mains.*

Tatiana's endearments still amazed Dmitri after all this time. He was loved by his mother and sisters – perhaps his father even loved him in his own strict, old-fashioned way – but they were family and were supposed to love him; Tatiana had *chosen* to love him and he couldn't understand why. What was special about him? He could list a thousand reasons why he loved her but they only made him feel even more unworthy: her gentle nature, her quiet dignity . . . he loved the way her eyes sometimes seemed to be gazing from a place deep inside her and focusing somewhere far in the distance, hinting at the intelligence of her inner world.

He glowed with pride when she sent him a newspaper clipping describing Olga and her as 'The White Sisters of the War'. As well as nursing, Tatiana told him she headed a committee that helped to provide aid for the refugees who had poured into Russia from German-occupied territories, and she travelled the country inspecting facilities. Dmitri knew she was being modest in her letters when she wrote that she felt shy at committee meetings and wanted to dive under the table. He heard from other soldiers that Tatiana's was by far the most popular of the picture postcards of the grand duchesses being sold to help fund the war, and surely that spoke volumes about her achievements as well as her beauty.

Her mother, on the other hand, was increasingly criticised in the press. 'Rumours Spread that Rasputin urges Alexandra to Broker Peace with Germany', ran one headline that reached them at the front, followed by: 'A Third Government Minister Sacked by the Tsarina for Daring to Criticise her "Close Friend"'; 'Tsarina will not Believe Stories of Rasputin's Corruption'. Perhaps it was inevitable that the populace would be suspicious of Alexandra, as she had been born in Germany and still had family there; certainly it had been short-sighted of Nicholas to leave her in charge when he went to take command of the troops, allowing the disreputable Siberian to stay by her side.

One day Dmitri overheard a group of soldiers speculating that Alexandra was having an affair with Rasputin. This was treacherous talk and he could have disciplined them for it but he knew such sentiments were widespread and decided to pretend he hadn't heard. He couldn't discipline every soldier who thought that way, although he didn't believe the rumour for one second. Alexandra was too proper, too insistent on recognition of her exalted position to entertain such a scruffy fellow in her bed. She seemed to him rather a cold mother, although Tatiana always sang her praises.

He wondered if Alexandra ever read the newspapers? Certainly Tatiana could not, because she seemed oblivious to the criticisms of Rasputin's relationship with her mother. Since their argument she was cautious when she mentioned him in letters and there was no more 'Uncle Grigory'. Still she maintained that Rasputin increased her understanding of God and Dmitri felt sure that her rather eccentric views on spirits almost certainly came from him. One day she wrote of a woman who came to the hospital to read soldiers' palms:

She was a hearty type, like any farmer's wife, but there was a mysterious look in her eyes when she communed with the spirits. Every soldier she spoke with seemed convinced of her powers, so I asked her to read my palm. She wondered if I had a question to which I sought the answer, so I asked if she could see when I would marry. She held my right hand and pored over it for some time, tracing the lines with the tip of her finger, then she said that my love line is strong and I will marry someone I love truly. She hesitated before adding that the line of fate is interrupted, making a sharp turn off to the right, and that this means I will pull off something extraordinary in the future. She would tell me no more, but I am greatly cheered that we will marry, Dmitri, because it must mean you will survive this war.

Dmitri rolled his eyes. So did it mean he could walk unguarded onto the plain separating them from the German front line without being shot? He found it amusing that someone as clever as Tatiana should be taken in by this spiritualist nonsense. He would tease her about it when next they met.

'Oh God, I can't wait,' he breathed.

On the 7th of March 1916, new orders arrived for Dmitri. He ripped open the envelope and couldn't believe his eyes: Tsar Nicholas ordered him back to St Petersburg to serve as an equerry at Tsarskoe Selo. Dmitri was stunned. It was completely unexpected, and he wasn't immediately sure how he felt. Of course it would be wonderful to be reunited with Tatiana but he would feel as though he were abandoning his comrades. Instead of firing shells at the Germans, he would be supervising the care of the Tsar's horses. It was a great honour, certainly, but it felt like a soft option.

His orders were to leave the day after next, so he just had time to write a quick note to Tatiana and tell her the news. As he scribbled, he wondered how she would feel about his return. She had been a girl when he left and now she was a woman. Despite her affectionate letters, perhaps their romance had been a childish whim for her. Perhaps, when they met again, she would wonder what she had seen in him. His own feelings had not wavered for a second, but she might look at him critically with her newly mature eyes.

He caught a train to St Petersburg and continued the journey to Tsarskoe Selo in a military truck he had spotted pulling out of the station. It was early evening and he wondered if Tatiana would be in the hospital with her patients, or at home with her family, or possibly off touring medical facilities in another city. His truck pulled up at the gates of the Alexander Palace and he presented his credentials to the guards and swung his knapsack over his shoulder to head towards the stables.

Suddenly a slender figure appeared from a palace doorway, all in white like a ghost. She seemed to fly across the distance between them and straight into his arms. Dmitri encircled her and squeezed tight, breathing in her scent before he looked down. Her face was thinner and her cheekbones more pronounced but otherwise she was the same Tatiana.

'How did you know when I would arrive?' No one knew. He himself hadn't been sure whether he would get a lift that evening or would have to wait till the following morning.

'I've been watching from the window all day.' She seemed short of breath and he wasn't sure whether it was from the run or because her emotions overwhelmed her. 'Oh, Malama, promise you won't ever leave me again.'

Chapter Twelve

Far from the long separation lessening Tatiana's feelings for Dmitri, if anything it seemed the reverse was true. When they were together it felt as if a bewitching aura surrounded them. Colours were more intense, the sun shone brighter, the grey days of winter's final weeks seemed to flash past. Once again Dmitri's head swirled with the words of the great love poets as he gazed into Tatiana's eyes and listened to the soft tones of her voice – but now he knew more of her personality from the hundreds of letters she had written, their love felt stronger and more unshakeable.

He hadn't been back a week before she came running into the stables on her way to the hospital and announced, 'Mama would like to invite you for luncheon tomorrow at noon. Do say you'll come.'

He was astonished. 'Your Mama has invited *me*? Whatever for?'

'Because I asked her to!' Tatiana grinned impishly. 'Don't worry. She likes you. And you'll get to meet my siblings as well.'

Dmitri had been in the company of members of the imperial family on numerous occasions but only as a member of the guard, never as a guest, and he was nervous about the protocols. He wished he could consult his mother, who was an expert in such matters, but his parents had not yet had a telephone installed at their home. Instead he had a chat with Anna Vyrubova, the Tsarina's lady-in-waiting, who assured him that luncheon in these days of wartime was very informal and that he should just be his amiable self.

The following afternoon Dmitri presented himself at the Alexander Palace, his boots and buckles shiny, his chin clean-shaven and his hair carefully oiled and combed flat. A butler showed him to the Formal Reception Room and as the double doors opened, the brightness from the ceiling-high windows reflecting off the mirrors and the lavish gilt décor momentarily blinded him. He blinked and saw Alexandra sitting at a writing desk and her five children on sofas round the fire. Tatiana leapt to her feet to welcome him then led him around, making the introductions. It seemed they spoke English to each other and Dmitri had to concentrate to keep up because he did not often use the language.

'You've met Mama, of course, when she awarded your St George medal.' He bowed to Alexandra, who gave him a cordial nod then returned to the letter she was writing, but not before Dmitri noticed a strong smell of garlic about her. He wondered what she could have eaten for breakfast.

Next Tatiana led him to her brother, who lay with his feet up on a sofa. 'This is Alexei, who is recently returned from the front line.' It was some years since Dmitri had seen the boy. He was now thirteen years old but looked much younger, and Dmitri was shocked to note the deep purple shadows under his eyes and his general air of frailty.

'Did Your Imperial Highness see any action?' Dmitri asked

The boy replied with a dejected tone: 'Sadly, I was not allowed anywhere within range of the German guns.'

His sisters laughed, and Tatiana remarked, 'I should hope not.'

Next he greeted her older sister, Olga, and Tatiana introduced him to Maria, a slightly plump sixteen-year-old with merry eyes, and fourteen-year-old Anastasia, whose waist-length hair still hung loose in the childish fashion rather than being arranged on top of her head.

'Don't ever play a board game with Anastasia,' Maria warned him, gesturing at a chequerboard and some scattered ivory pieces. It looked as though they had been playing halma. 'She is an appalling cheat.'

'There speaks a poor loser,' Anastasia replied, sticking her tongue out at her sister.

Tatiana quickly interrupted to tell Dmitri that the younger girls had begun visiting the hospitals to entertain the soldiers, and that they were already very popular.

'I am sure they are.' He smiled as Tatiana beckoned him to sit in an armchair close to her. 'Their spirit and beauty would cheer any man.'

Maria asked him about the retired imperial horses who now lived in stables behind the Alexander Palace, where they were able to enjoy their old age. Alexei wanted to know which of the imperial racehorses Dmitri considered would be the fastest when the Stoverstnöm resumed after the war. They all seemed very keen on horses and Dmitri gave his opinions, conscious that while the girls were competent horsewomen, Alexei had never been allowed on horseback because of his frail joints.

A butler announced luncheon and they seated themselves around a table near the window. There was a bunch of peach-coloured roses in the centre, and Dmitri assumed they must have been cultivated in the palace greenhouse; how else could they have roses in April? The cutlery was heavy silver, although Alexandra apologised that they were not using the best plate and that the meal was very plain. Dmitri thought it not at all plain, with a cream soup, followed by fish fillets in a light-as-air sauce, mutton in gravy, and then a dainty dish of apple compôte. The girls led the conversation, alternately teasing each other, asking Dmitri whether he had seen any wild bison or bears at the front (he had, but only from a distance), and discussing patients in the hospital. Tatiana seemed reserved in their company, often stepping in to broker peace between her two younger sisters, and Alexandra seemed distracted, scarcely talking at all.

After the meal, Dmitri was surprised when Alexandra asked if he would join her for tea in the adjoining Portrait Hall. He immediately rose to his feet and followed her, with just a glance of farewell to Tatiana. What did she want to talk about? How much did she know about his relationship with her second-oldest daughter? Might she be about to ask him his intentions towards her, and if so what would he reply?

The Portrait Hall was vast and airy, with burnished gold pillars, a slippery parquet floor and the most exquisite chandelier Dmitri had ever seen, with cascades of what looked like millions of tiny crystals. Alexandra sat on a settee under a huge portrait of Catherine the Great and he took a chair nearby as a waiter poured steaming cups of tea from a heavy silver *samovar* and set a little bowl of chocolates between them. Dmitri was tempted to take a sweet, because they looked scrumptious, but Alexandra didn't so he felt it might not be correct etiquette. On a side table, there was a display of the elaborate Fabergé eggs the family gave one another for Easter, each worth thousands of roubles.

Tatiana had told him the family had stopped buying new clothes with the outbreak of war and were having to patch and mend old garments, but the Tsarina looked very grand in a chocolate-brown gown with embroidery of bronze foliage. She wore four strings of pearls around her neck, a diamond-encrusted Star of the Order of St Alexander Nevsky on her breast and a huge aquamarine ring on her finger.

'Tell me, when you left the front line, had any of the mobile field guns arrived?' Alexandra began. Her manner was austere but not unfriendly.

'Yes, they had, but the men have not had much practice in firing them,' he replied.

'Is it difficult to fire them?'

'The machines are heavy. One man in my company was seriously injured by the backwards thrust of a . . .' He hesitated, struggling to think of the English word for a shell casing. Alexandra nodded to indicate she understood.

'Do you think they will make a difference?' she asked. 'You may speak freely. I know there are some successes in Galicia but we seem to have reached a stalemate to the north of the line. What do you think it will take to push the invader back behind their own borders again?'

Dmitri noted the term she used: 'the invader'. These were her own people by birth. What an awkward situation she found herself in. He told her his opinion, that there was no point in pushing forwards at one point in the line only. As they had discovered early in the war, the German troops were quick to cut off and encircle advance parties, with catastrophic consequence. 'I believe we should not mount another attack until the whole line from north to south has the new weapons and the men are ready to use them in one concerted push.'

She nodded, as if he had confirmed her own views. 'Tell me, are supplies reaching the men? Were they adequately fed in your part of the line?'

Dmitri hesitated. 'There were supply problems during our retreat but now that we are static, the situation has improved.' He could still smell the garlic scent, which seemed to emanate from her pores rather than her breath.

After ten minutes of war talk she announced abruptly that she must retire to rest before her afternoon's duties and Dmitri leapt to his feet and bowed as she walked out. At the doorway she turned and regarded him with a friendly smile: 'Please take those chocolates with you, Cornet Malama. They are too sweet for my tooth.'

'Thank you, Your Imperial Highness.' His face was scarlet as he bowed again. Had she noticed him eyeing them? All the same he decided to accept her offer, so he scooped up the contents of the bowl before the butler showed him to the door.

Walking back to the stables, rich chocolate melting on his tongue, he mused over what had passed. Had he been invited solely so that Alexandra could pick his brains about the war? What had she thought of him? Should he have been less frank, more obsequious?

He got his answer that evening when Tatiana rushed into the stables in her uniform, fresh from her evening lesson with Vera Gedroits. 'My darling, you have charmed the entire family. I *knew* you would. Mama wrote to Papa this afternoon telling him she thought you would make an admirable son-in-law. Can you believe it? I've been so excited, I couldn't wait to tell you.' She was bouncing up and down like a gleeful child.

Dmitri blanched. 'She wrote that? Does it mean . . .? Do you think she might let us marry soon?'

'Oh, *mon chéri*.' She cocked her head. 'Not during wartime. We wouldn't be able to make suitable arrangements, and our wedding must be a state occasion. Besides, my sister Olga should be allowed to marry first. I will urge her to hurry and choose her husband. She has too many favourites and must try to narrow it down to one!'

'Can we at least announce our engagement?' Dmitri asked. 'Many have guessed we are close and I would not like to compromise your reputation.'

'I will ask Mama, but I get the impression she wants it to be an unofficial engagement for now. It's good for us to have this time in which our love is secret, so we can get to know each other better without the eyes of the world watching . . .' She glanced at the door. 'I can't stay now as I must get back to sterilisation duties. I simply couldn't wait to tell you the news.'

They embraced quickly and Dmitri inhaled the scent of her hair. It made him remember something from earlier: 'What is that strange perfume your mother wears? I didn't recognise it.'

Tatiana glanced round to check no one was listening, then wrinkled her nose. 'She smells peculiar, doesn't she? I give her daily arsenic injections for exhaustion and it appears to cause that odour. Olga has it too – didn't you notice? I'll see you tomorrow, dearest. By the side gate at two-thirty.'

They slipped into the habit of spending an hour together each afternoon. In fair weather, they took Ortipo for a walk round the park, trying in vain to teach her to fetch a ball, or rode out on horseback; on rainy days, they played card games, read poetry to each other or simply sat conversing. They never ran out of conversation, and Dmitri saved things to tell her: snippets of conversation he'd overheard, or amusing anecdotes about the horses, sometimes a joke. Usually there would be a ladies' maid somewhere in the background, acting as chaperone, but she tactfully kept her distance and it was easy to feel as though they were alone.

One morning Dmitri turned a corner in the park and overheard some guards gossiping about the elder Romanov girls. He should have stopped them straight away but instead he paused to listen.

'They've both got favourites amongst the men, I hear. Olga is completely smitten with that Mitya and Tatiana's in love with Volodya.'

The pain in Dmitri's heart was like a stab wound. Who was Volodya and what was he to Tatiana? He rushed to the guardroom and made enquiries, learning that he was a second lieutenant in the 3rd Guards Rifles Regiment, who had spent several weeks in hospital the previous autumn. He was a friend of Olga's sweetheart Mitya and had a reputation as a ladykiller. It seemed the four of them had sometimes played croquet together, before Volodya had been cured and sent back to the front the previous Christmas.

Just as well for him, Dmitri thought grimly. He was consumed with such raging jealousy that had the man still been in town, he would have been tempted to seek him out and beat him to within an inch of his life.

73

Chapter Thirteen

At the beginning of May 1916, just over a month after Dmitri's return, the Romanovs, including Tsar Nicholas, went on holiday to Crimea. It was their first trip since 1913 and Dmitri knew how much Tatiana loved it there, but watching their Delaunay-Belleville automobile disappear down the road towards the station made him feel ill. His limbs were heavy, his brow fevered and his head aching. How would he last three weeks without her? She had promised to write, but letters were no longer enough to satisfy him. He only felt truly alive when in her presence. 'I am so terribly glad to see the sea,' Tatiana wrote.

Olga and I have been lying in the sun so I hope you will not mind your fiancée's face being brown as a nut. The warmth appears to be helping Mama's health, and little Alexei is quite animated, badgering the sailors to tell him stories about German U-boats. We sailed from Odessa to Sevastopol but do not have time to travel to Livadia as Father and Alexei must soon return to the front.

Dmitri read her letter with a sour feeling in his stomach. How could she enjoy herself when he was bereft without her? And then he rebuked himself: what kind of lover would resent his loved one's happiness? Was love always so selfish? He should be pleased for her, and he tried, but he was out of sorts and moody with the staff in the stables and didn't regain his cheerful spirits until her return.

Tatiana's nineteenth birthday fell on the 29th of May, and Dmitri bought her a pair of amethyst drop earrings, which he thought would bring out the violet in her eyes. They were well beyond his means on army pay, and would involve repaying his debt to the jeweller monthly for over a year, but it was worth it to see Tatiana's delight with the gift. She hugged him and kissed his cheek before threading them through her earlobes and seeking a mirror to check her reflection.

'I have far less jewellery than you might suppose.' She turned her head one way and another, admiring the effect. 'Mama used to give us each a single pearl on our birthdays so that by our sixteenth we would have enough for a pearl necklace, but I have few pairs of earrings and certainly no amethysts. I do believe this is my favourite stone.'

'Will you celebrate with your family later?' Dmitri asked, smiling at her girlish excitement and delighted by the apparent success of his gift.

'Just my sisters. Papa and Alexei are at Stavka.' She hesitated. 'I believe Mama has asked Rasputin to stop by.'

Dmitri glowered. 'On your birthday? Is he so close to the family?'

Tatiana pursed her lips. 'Yes, he is. I must introduce you so you can see he is nothing like the image you have. He's a very sweet, gentle man.'

Dmitri snorted. 'Even if he is a good man and all the stories I have heard are wrong, the fact remains that the Russian people mistrust him. They blame his influence for all that is wrong with the country: for the food shortages, for the lack of progress in defeating Germany, for the railway strikes . . . He boasts of his power over your mother, saying he can make her do anything.'

'I didn't know there were food shortages and railway strikes.' Tatiana frowned. 'But how could these be Rasputin's fault? He is a holy man, a healer.'

'Of course they are not his fault *directly*, but people think they are, and that's what matters. Your mother would do well to ban him from the palace while she is running the country's affairs. Perhaps he should go back to Siberia, at least till after the war.' He worried about speaking so frankly to Tatiana, who looked upset and bewildered, but it felt as though he had a duty to do so when he might one day be a member of the family.

'There's something I must explain,' she said quietly. 'Come, sit down.' They were in the grounds of the Catherine Palace and she led him to a bench with a view over the chain of waterfalls that gushed into the Great Pond. He waited as she chose her words.

'It is a family secret but, as you are to be one of us, I think it is time you were told . . . You know that Alexei has frail health?'

Dmitri frowned. Everyone knew that.

Tatiana bit her lip. 'I am worried that you might change your mind about marrying me if I tell you the rest.'

Dmitri grabbed her hand and squeezed it tightly. 'Whatever the secret, I promise I will not change my mind.'

She nodded, as if she had known this would be the case, then continued. 'Alexei suffers from the bleeding disorder known as haemophilia that also afflicts some of my cousins in Prussia.' Dmitri gave a sharp intake of breath and Tatiana continued: 'When he bumps his leg even mildly, it can mean bleeding into his joints and he has almost died several times in his short life. Back in 1912 after he injured himself jumping onto a boat, he was so poorly that he was given the last sacrament. But every time, Uncle Grigory manages to heal him where the doctors have failed. He has brought Alexei back from the edge of the grave many times. This is why the family cannot be without him. But of course we can never explain this to the Russian people because Alexei is the male heir who must carry on the Romanov line . . .'

Dmitri could see the problem; they could not admit to such fragility in the succession. 'I'm so sorry, angel. It must be a terrible worry for you all.' Suddenly Alexandra's reliance on the wild man and Nicholas's forbearance of him made sense.

'It is something you must consider,' Tatiana told him. 'Were we to have a son, there is a chance of him inheriting this vile disease because it is passed through the female line. That's why it is only fair to warn you now in case you wish to reconsider your proposal.'

Dmitri was aghast: did she know him so little? He fell to his knees on the path in front of her, his voice shaking with emotion. 'There is *nothing* that would make me reconsider – *nothing*. Now I know the truth about your brother, I love you more than ever.'

'You are so pure and unselfish,' she marvelled, placing her hand on his shoulder.

He felt unworthy, remembering his recent burst of selfishness when she went on holiday. Sometimes his love felt like a kind of uncontrollable madness. But he was proud beyond measure that she had shared with him the very sensitive family secret.

The trust between them had grown daily that spring. She had often confided in him when her sisters annoyed her, or when her mother's illnesses were hard to bear, but to share this particular confidence meant she considered him one of the family, and he was deeply honoured.

After Tatiana went back to work, Dmitri pondered what she had said. If Alexei proved too frail to produce an heir, how would it affect the succession to the throne? Would Nicholas be succeeded by Olga and her husband, followed by their children? And what if Olga failed to marry, like his sister Valerina? Would the succession pass to Tatiana and himself? He did not want to be tsar. The desire to rule was not in his nature. His deepest wish was that one day he and Tatiana would have a home in the countryside where they could keep horses and dogs, and have children of their own, God willing. If one of their sons inherited the bleeding disorder, they would deal with it in due course.

He felt as though it was tempting fate to think so far ahead. What if the war continued to go badly for Russia? How many years might it be until they could marry? What if she fell for someone else before then? Was there a possibility that Tatiana could be forced into an arranged marriage as part of a peace treaty? He tortured himself with these imagined scenarios, and only relaxed during his afternoons with Tatiana when he felt the sureness of her love calming him.

The weather in St Petersburg that June was magnificent: warm and cloudless, with just an occasional overnight shower to freshen the flower displays that bloomed profusely across the royal estates in both formal and informal gardens. At last the news from the front was encouraging: General Brusilov's offensive had forced the Austro-Hungarian army to retreat and by the end of the month they had advanced sixty miles and taken 350,000 prisoners. It proved what the mighty Russian army could do when they had a decent leader at the helm, and gave them all succour.

However, the picture changed in July when German troops were diverted from the Western Front to fight back and Russian casualties once more began to mount. On the 27th of August, Romania decided to declare war on Austro-Hungary, and as a result Brusilov had hundreds more miles of front line to defend, right down into the Balkans. Suddenly, there were whispers in the guardroom that all able-bodied men were to be called back to the front and Dmitri prayed fervently he would not be among them.

One evening in early September he heard that a new influx of wounded officers had arrived at the Catherine Palace and among them was the man named Volodya, with whom Tatiana was rumoured to have formed an attachment in his absence. He had suffered a spinal injury, Dmitri heard, and could be there for some time. Jealousy gnawed his insides like a hungry rodent.

He had never asked Tatiana about Volodya, partly because he was too proud but also because he feared that some tiny passing expression would give away the truth that she'd had feelings for him, and he couldn't bear that. He considered visiting the hospital to catch sight of his rival but couldn't face the anguish if he walked in and found Tatiana chatting to him, smiling at him.

Then, as cruel fate would have it, the morning after Volodya's arrival a letter came with fresh orders for Dmitri: he was to report to a post in Moldova by the 20th of September. He slumped to the ground, his heart beating rapidly. How could he leave Tsarskoe Selo when his rival was there and Tatiana would see him every day? Dmitri sat breathing hard, all kinds of crazy plans flashing through his mind. He would sneak into the ward by night and hold a pillow over Volodya's face. He would ask Tatiana to elope with him and they would run off together to a country that was not involved in this bloody war.

And then came an idea that was not quite so far-fetched. There was only one way he could return to the front with any kind of equanimity. It had to be worth a try.

Chapter Fourteen

Dmitri told Tatiana of his orders while they sat in the wildflower meadow just beyond the Llama House in the grounds of the Alexander Palace. She had woven a garland of camomile flowers and placed it around his neck, where it hung over his uniform, the white petals already drooping.

Immediately she burst into tears. 'Oh, Malama, I can't bear it. How shall I live without you?' She clutched his arm, distraught. 'You have no idea how scared I was when you were at the front line before. I woke every morning with a lump in my throat, as if a stone were lodged there. And now we are so much closer, it will be unbearable . . .' Her shoulders shook with sobbing.

'Hush, angel.' He put an arm around her, close to tears himself. Tatiana brought out a softness in him that he was not familiar with.

She continued: 'At least with Papa and Alexei, I know they will be kept out of danger. But you – you are the type who rushes out in the face of enemy fire. I can't lose you, Dmitri, I simply can't.'

He kissed her hair, his insides melting at her anguish, then he leaned over so his forehead rested against hers. 'Can you read my thoughts?' he asked.

She shook her head and a silky strand of hair tickled his cheek.

'I have faced death many times during this war,' he told her quietly, seriously, 'but never when I had so much to lose. The strength of our love has grown so vast these past months that I find myself unable to risk losing you.'

'You will never lose me,' she replied huskily.

He breathed hard, his forehead still resting on hers, and continued: 'I'm going mad, Tatiana. I feel like banging my head against a wall with frustration that I must wait till this infernal war is over to marry you – and that I might die without ever knowing that sweet joy. The only thing that would make this parting bearable would be if you would marry me before I go.'

She drew a quick surprised breath and he spoke hurriedly.

'I know we can't have an official state wedding but why not a secret ceremony, just for us? I am not asking that we lie together, much as the idea thrills me. I only want us to be united in God's eyes so that if my time is up I will go to Heaven knowing that you truly loved me and that you will one day join me for all eternity."

Tears pooled in her eyes. 'I couldn't bear for you to die. Please don't talk that way.'

'Being married to you, I would have everything to live for. I would know for sure you'd be waiting for me on my return and that I could trust your love to be as strong as ever. I promise you, Tatiana, that if you do this for me, I will ensure I survive."

She leaned her head back to look him in the eyes. 'But who would perform such a ceremony?'

'A friend of mine, Father Oblonsky. He is a priest from my hometown. I have already asked if he would be willing to conduct a secret ceremony between me and the girl I love, and he has agreed. His chapel is a few miles down the Kuzminka River. We could go there by night to avoid being seen. No one need know.' He waited for her to drink this in, grateful that at least she hadn't ruled it out straight away.

'But if we then married formally after the war, would it not be bigamous?'

'Father Oblonsky says not.' He had only half-listened to the old priest's explanation about how it could work, overjoyed to hear that he was prepared to conduct a ceremony. He watched as love and duty wrestled in Tatiana's mind.

'My parents must never find out. And you must promise with all your heart that you will not make me a widow.' Her eyes were sad, but she had a determined air. It was only then Dmitri realised with a start that she must love him almost as much as he loved her; otherwise she would not take such a risk.

'I promise.'

He touched her eyelashes with the tip of a finger to brush away a tear caught there.

Three nights later they met at a side entrance of the Alexander Palace at midnight. Dmitri led two horses, and they jumped on horseback and rode to the riverbank, where he had moored a rowing boat. He lit a candle for Tatiana to hold as he rowed downstream, and her eyes were wide in the flickering light. Neither spoke, each lost in their own thoughts, with the lapping of the water against the edge of the boat and the hoot of an owl the only sounds.

'Are you sure about this, angel?' Dmitri asked as he helped her ashore at a little mooring.

'I'm sure.'

The door of the chapel was open and Father Oblonsky was waiting in his vestments of rich red and gold pattern, with a gold mitre on his head and a heavy gold cross around his neck. He ushered them in, quickly blessed the rings Dmitri handed over, then began the age-old rituals to bind them for life. They were each given a candle to hold. Tatiana's hand was trembling and she looked dazed but incredibly beautiful in her chaste white gown with throat-hugging neckline. The sweet fog of incense rising from the censors, the priest's deep lilting voice, the glittering gold icons of the chapel interior made it seem like a dream.

'Eternal God that joinest together in love them that were separate, who hast ordained the union of holy wedlock that cannot be set asunder . . .'

They followed instructions as the priest asked Dmitri to put his larger ring on Tatiana's finger, then her smaller one on his own little finger, and signed them with the cross.

'O Lord, our God, who hast poured down the blessings of Thy Truth according to Thy Holy Covenant upon Thy chosen servants, our fathers, from generation to generation, bless Thy servants Dmitri and Tatiana, and make their troth fast in faith, and union of hearts, and truth, and love . . .'

This was the moment at which they officially became man and wife, and they caught eyes shyly: Tatiana smiled but Dmitri was too overawed to react. His ears were buzzing, his legs like jelly, his brain on fire: it was the most precious moment of his life and yet he felt he was barely conscious. He wanted time to slow down so he could savour each second, analyse each word of the service, live this moment to the full. They both took sips from the proffered cup of rich altar wine then the priest wrapped his stole round their joined hands, to unite them till kingdom come.

All too soon it was over and they embraced, letting their lips graze the other's, the most delicious sensation Dmitri had ever experienced.

'May God bless you and keep you safe for the rest of your lives,' Father Oblonsky said in farewell. 'I wish you all the happiness in the world.'

They did not have time to linger as it was already three in the morning. Back on the river, Dmitri had to strain to row against the current. Black trees waved their branches against the moonlit sky. Tatiana was silent and he wondered what she was thinking. Even at this moment when they should be closer than any two people in the world, he was frustrated by the ultimate unknowability of another person. Was she regretting their actions? Did she feel he had forced her into it?

'Are you all right?' he asked tentatively.

She sighed, sounding blissfully happy. 'I am going over the priest's prayers in my head. I never want to forget a single detail of this night. No grand state wedding could ever compare to the beautiful simplicity of the promises we have made.'

A sob escaped from Dmitri's throat and he lifted an oar from the water so he could wipe his eye with his sleeve. His father used to chide him for crying, saying he was like a silly chit of a girl who needed to learn to control his emotions. A few moments later a bend in the river brought his face into the moonlight and he knew Tatiana would see that his cheeks were glistening with tears, but he also knew it didn't matter because she would understand.

Chapter Fifteen

Lake Akanabee, New York State, end of July 2016

Kitty threw herself into work on the cabin with a passion. First she used her chainsaw to hack down the branches overhanging the track so she could drive along it. That was vital so she could transport planks of wood and panes of glass for her repairs, as well as take away all the rubbish and the old bed to a dump. She climbed onto the cabin roof and mended a rusted patch then pushed her broom down the chimney to clear the abandoned birds' nests inside. She cut down the sapling that had grown up through the porch steps, chopping it into lengths for firewood. She painstakingly rebuilt the steps, planing, sanding and weather-proofing the wood then adding curved banisters on either side. In her head was her father's quiet voice: 'Slow and easy, now; don't cut corners or that's where the rot will set in.'

She scrubbed the interior of the cabin, clearing out age-old spiders' webs, the skeletons of small rodents and clusters of fungi. She patched a couple of gaps in the walls forced open by creeper roots and hired a local firm to empty the septic tank. They confirmed her water came from a well and advised her it couldn't be drunk because of rust in the supply pipes but was perfectly good for washing.

Every morning she set herself tasks for the day: replacing the window glass, scrubbing the ancient grime on the bathroom fittings, digging a fire pit for barbecues, reconstructing the swing seat . . . there was always more to do. She bought a camp bed, a little folding chair and a coolbox to keep insects out of her food supplies, but otherwise left the cabin unfurnished, apart from Dmitri's old desk and the stove that looked nice but was too rusty to use for cooking. Her bags were piled in one corner of the spacious main room, and the only decoration was a bunch of wildflowers thrust in a plastic tumbler on the desk. She rather liked the minimalist look.

At the end of each day, when she had achieved her goals, she had a long swim round the tip of her bay and into the next, to cool down and cleanse the dirt and sweat from her pores. Afterwards she sat on the edge of the porch with a glass of wine, letting the breeze dry her hair, looking out over the lake and planning what she would tackle tomorrow. Thoughts of Tom hovered in the periphery but she kept them there. As an only child she was good at managing without company, but it wasn't easy to forget a marriage; at some point she would have to decide what to do. Later. For now she was focused on making her cabin perfect. The surroundings were so stunning that she wanted to do them justice; she decided this would be her finest building project ever.

Jeff at the vacation park proved very helpful, letting her drop in to recharge her power tools and advising on local suppliers. One day when she stopped by he handed her a parcel: the copy of Dmitri Yakovlevich's novel *Interminable Love* had arrived. Its old-fashioned cover with a pattern of bottle-green, taupe and black swirls gave no clue as to the contents, and there was no description on the inside flaps of either the story or its author. She took it back to the cabin and sat in her little canvas chair by the water's edge, naked because the heat of the day was stifling. She kept a big t-shirt nearby in case any ramblers appeared but clothes seemed superfluous so far out in the wilderness.

The story began with a young country boy called Mikhail who sees a local girl, Valerina, falling off her bicycle and rushes to help. The grazes on her hands and knees are bleeding and obviously painful but she bites her lip and blinks away the tears and at that moment he finds himself starting to fall in love with her.

The translation of the text was uneven with some awkward phrasing but Kitty was soon hooked as young Mikhail explored the sensations of love: he wished he could get inside Valerina's skin and experience her every thought and feeling so that he would never say or do the wrong thing; he was tortured with jealousy when he saw her in conversation with anyone else; he felt as though he was losing his mind to some overpowering affliction that brought more pain than it did reward. Soon his devotion paid off and she fell in love with him too but he found it hard to believe. His emotions swung from exhilaration one moment to anxiety the next and, without meaning to, Kitty found her thoughts wandering back to her early days with Tom.

She had first spotted him playing his songs to a small group at the students' union, and she liked his absorption in the music, his unruly hair, the striped Pierrot t-shirt and braces he was wearing, and his grin when everyone applauded at the end. For a few weeks she stalked him, looking for a way to introduce herself, but in the end he made the first move, appearing by her side when she was placing an order at the bar and saying, cheekily, 'Mine's half a bitter.'

'Can you add half a bitter?' Kitty asked the barman, and Tom was shamefaced.

'I was joking. You don't have to buy me a drink. Let me give you the money.'

She insisted on paying and he followed her over to join the group she was with, introducing himself around the table. He was affable and everyone seemed to like him, but Kitty was so attracted to him at close range that she could barely focus on the conversation. She longed to place her hand on his thigh, nestle into his shoulder, press herself against him. She'd never felt such lust for anyone and wondered how he could be oblivious to the sheer force of it. But it seemed he wasn't: at the end of the evening, as the others rose to leave, he took her hand and whispered, 'Can I come back with you please?'

Kitty was staying in student accommodation, where they weren't supposed to have overnight guests, but she sneaked him in. As soon as the door closed behind them they ripped off their clothes and spent the night in a frenzy of steamy, compulsive sex that left her head feeling as though it was stuffed with cotton wool. When she got up to make tea in the morning, Tom said, 'This is a little awkward, but I'm sorry, I didn't catch your name.' And they both collapsed in giggles; it still made her giggle now. And then she remembered Karren with the double 'r' and stopped abruptly.

She got up and laid the book to one side while she waded into the cool waters of the lake. It was shallow close to shore but she always swam out until the cabin was barely distinguishable amongst the dense woods that surrounded it. From that distance she could see how isolated it was, with no other man-made structure for at least a mile on either side.

It was three weeks since she arrived at Lake Akanabee and she hadn't been in touch with anyone back in England. She knew this might be construed as eccentric behaviour but the solitude was feeding something within her. She could feel herself getting stronger with each day of self-sufficiency and she supposed before long she would be tough enough to go home and deal with her marital problems. Perhaps she could also deal with her discontent about the whole fabric of her life. She was thirty-five years old and it was time to decide how she wanted to spend the next few decades. If she wasn't going to be with Tom, she should look for someone else before the wrinkles and grey hairs set in. She shook her head to dispel this image. The thought of being with another man filled her with dismay: all that adjustment as you learned someone else's tastes, their sleeping habits, their moods . . .

She dived down through the clear, cool water. She could see the bottom but it was further than it looked and she had to turn and come up for air before she reached it.

The heat was too intense for hard physical work so Kitty decided to take a day off and immerse herself in her great-grandfather's novel. It was strange to get a glimpse of his personality through the story while living in his cabin and walking in his footsteps. She felt a kinship with him as she lay in the shade of the trees he must have looked up at, and read *Interminable Love*, his first novel.

Civil war separated Mikhail and Valerina when their families were sent to opposite sides of the country and he was forced to fight, but their love remained strong as ever. Neither would marry; neither could contemplate being with anyone else, so they lived half-lives shadowed by the memory of their first and only love.

As the sun set, Kitty lit a fire, cooked herself a burger on a rack set over the flames, opened some wine, and continued to read in the orange flickering glow. In the final chapter, Mikhail tracked down the remote Siberian village where Valerina now worked on a collective farm. He asked around to be told she was out in the fields operating one of the new-fangled tractors that had just been delivered. Modernity was often portrayed as evil in the novel, with machines taking the place of people in a metaphor that suggested the unquestioning obedience to the regime of its cowed citizens. Mikhail spotted Valerina from afar and began to run towards her. She saw him approaching, realised who it was, and tried to turn off the tractor's engine – but something went wrong and it started to accelerate. It was heading straight for Mikhail so she pulled down hard on the steering wheel and as the vehicle turned it toppled onto its side, crushing her underneath. Mikhail struggled to lift the tractor but it was far too heavy. He called for help but there was no one in earshot. Valerina's injuries were too severe for her to survive so he lay on the earth beside her, kissing her face as she slipped off into the blackness of death.

It was something of a clichéd ending but tears were streaming down Kitty's cheeks. She wiped them on the hem of her t-shirt but couldn't stop crying and soon she was sobbing out loud, with huge painful spasms that hurt her chest. She hugged herself and buried her face in the crook of her elbow, crying with the abandon of a child. She hadn't even cried like this when her parents died. Was it because she was tipsy? What was this about? And as soon as she asked the question, she knew: it was because she missed Tom. There was so much she wanted to tell him. She wished he could see the work she had done on the cabin. She wanted to tell him about this Russian great-grandfather who had been an author. Perhaps he could help her to decide how to make her life more fulfilling … But he was not 'her Tom' any more. She couldn't talk to him because the huge matter of his infidelity lay between them and until she could decide how to deal with that it was easier not to be in touch at all.

As she lay in bed that night, wrung out from crying, Kitty's thoughts turned again to Dmitri Yakovlevich: he must have been a romantic soul to write so movingly about love. Why had he been living in such a remote spot? Was he alone there? Did he ever come to London to meet his great-granddaughter or was he too elderly and frail to travel by the time she was born? His bed had been in the spot where she now lay, in a corner beneath the window, so he must have looked out at the silver birch tree branches swaying in the moonlight just as she was doing now. She didn't believe in ghosts but at that moment she felt as if she could almost sense his presence, standing a few feet away, calmly watching over her.

Next morning, she drove to the coffee shop with her laptop and tried to find out more about Dmitri. She went to an ancestry website she had used for journalistic research at college. It had a US immigration section, but she couldn't find anyone with Dmitri's name. She tried her grandmother Marta's maiden name and the search engine whirred and finally came up with a child of eight years old, who had entered the United States in 1934. That sounded about right. Travelling with her, in a second-class cabin, were her mother, Rosa Liebermann – a name Kitty had never come across – and her brother Nicholas, aged nine. She'd heard there had once been a great-uncle Nicholas, so this must be them. She looked further up the page and there it was: Dmitri Yakovlevich Malama, aged forty-three years and four months. Was his real surname Malama? Why had he used Yakovlevich on his novels? The party's place of departure was given as Berlin. It took Kitty only a few seconds to speculate that the reason for their departure from Germany in 1934 might lie in Rosa's Jewish-sounding surname. But how had Russian-born Dmitri come to be in Berlin in the first place?

She tried several other searches but with no more success. She couldn't find where Dmitri and Rosa had lived on arrival in the US, what schools the children had attended, or where he had worked.

She closed the computer and drove to Indian Lake for some pots of varnish. She wanted to cover the entire cabin with a weather-proof coating while the weather was dry. The man in Lakeside Country Stores recommended the type he said was most effective against the cold, snowy winters in these parts. He was respectful now, as if he'd accepted she knew what she was talking about.

While she worked on the front wall that afternoon, she heard an outboard motor on the lake and turned to see a mahogany-skinned, silver-haired fisherman close to the shore. She waved and walked down to the broken jetty to greet him.

'Y'all bought the cabin, have you?' he called, squinting up at it.

'I inherited it,' she explained. 'My great-grandfather used to live here.'

'Well, I'll be!' he exclaimed. 'You're Dmitri's kin? I thought that cabin was a write-off but he would be happy to see you doing it up all nice.'

Kitty blinked. This man had known Dmitri. Rather than spend an hour on the internet, why had she not thought to ask around locally? 'Can I offer you a beer? Or a coffee?' she asked.

'A beer'd be nice.' He tied his boat to one of the broken struts of jetty and leapt to shore. 'Name's Bob. I live over the far side.' He gestured.

Kitty fetched two Buds and a bottle opener and they sat on the grass facing the water. He offered her a Marlboro and lit up himself when she refused.

'It's funny you should come along because I've been trying to find out about Dmitri,' she began. 'Were you two friends?'

Bob shook his head. 'We said hi when we bumped into each other at the store, but he never invited me here and I never invited him to mine. We lived our own lives.'

'Did his wife stay here with him?'

Bob frowned. 'I never saw a woman. Just him padding around on his own, with his dog at his heel. He was a writer so I guess the solitude suited him.'

'I read one of his books yesterday. Until recently I had no idea we had a writer in the family.'

'Yeah, I've got all his books. He gave them to Sue and me as a wedding present. My wife likes reading but I've no time for it.'

'That's amazing!' Kitty was delighted. 'Have you still got them? Do you think Sue would mind lending them to me?'

'I'm sure she wouldn't mind.' He glanced over towards his home and chuckled. 'See that glint in the trees over yonder? It's probably her looking out for me with the binoculars. She'll be wondering what I'm doing drinking beer with a pirtty lady.'

Kitty saw a dancing point of light in the direction he indicated. She hadn't considered anyone might be watching through binoculars and flushed to think they could have seen her wandering around naked.

'You not lonely here?' Bob asked. 'Is your boyfriend coming over?'

'My husband's back in England,' she said. 'I'm keeping myself busy, as you can see.' She waved an arm at the half-finished coat of varnish.

'Let me give you my cell,' Bob said. He scribbled the number on the back of the foil in his cigarette pack with a pen from his shirt pocket. 'You call if you need anything. It's a remote spot for a young girl like you.'

She was touched by his concern. She felt completely safe in the cabin but it was good to have a neighbour's number in case of an emergency. When he left, he promised to return in a day or so with Dmitri's books.

She went back to her varnishing, annoyed to see that the stretch she had already coated was now covered in dead and dying flies, like the bloody aftermath of some miniature battle.

Chapter Sixteen

Moldavia, December 1916

By the time Dmitri arrived in Moldavia, a hilly country squeezed between the Russian Empire to the East and the Austrian Empire to the West, winter was closing in. There could be no fighting while mountain passes were closed due to thick snow and the ground was too hard to dig trenches, so all sides hunkered down. Dmitri was furious to find he had travelled hundreds of miles south simply to spend the next few months living on meagre rations in an army bunker when he could have been in Tsarskoe Selo, close to his beloved wife. It was characteristic of the complete lack of foresight amongst the Russian high command.

Looking back, his wedding seemed like a dream. He still could not believe that he was married to the most beautiful, most talented of the Romanov grand duchesses. Tatiana's letters came regularly, and there was a new air of intimacy about them. She confided in him about family matters that she would have considered disloyal to discuss before their marriage:

Olga finds it too hard to continue working in the hospital: she does not have the stomach for watching operations or cleaning wounds. Her nerves are suffering from the prolonged absence of our father and brother, and she has transferred all her attention to Mitya (yes, he's here again). I swear she talks of nothing but him and I am fed up hearing of his every word and breath! Meanwhile, she never asks about you, sweet Malama. I think she is *jalouse* of our closeness and prefers not to hear of it.

She wrote that Anastasia and Maria fought more than ever, sometimes wrestling on the floor pulling each other's hair and having to be separated by force. She wrote that her mother was taking increasing doses of Veronal for her many ailments, which made her so sleepy that Tatiana invariably had to attend the tedious refugee committee meetings on her own. And always she wrote with concern for Dmitri's safety, begging him to keep warm and stay out of harm's way.

While she was anxious about him, he was becoming increasingly alarmed about the safety of the Romanovs. Now he was back amongst soldiers, he realised many were saying openly that the royal family had to be overthrown. Nicholas no longer had the support of a large number of his men, who were fed up being sent on suicide missions against a better-equipped, better-managed opponent. The territorial gains made by General Brusilov's advance had already been reversed by the Austro-German Ninth Army and there seemed little hope of victory on that front. Meanwhile the letters the men received from their families back home told of dire food shortages and dread of the starvation winter would bring. Even the army survived on what they could hunt in lieu of regular rations. And now that Nicholas was at the front and Alexandra was in charge in St Petersburg, there were louder rumblings that she was too much influenced in her decisions by Rasputin.

'I reckon they are German spies who send Russian military secrets to the enemy; that explains why the Germans are always one step ahead,' Dmitri heard a soldier telling his friends. He wished Alexandra had a wider circle of advisors, but she had always remained aloof from the St Petersburg aristocracy and trusted no one except her husband and Rasputin, laying them open to all sorts of allegations.

On the 18th of December, Malevich came to Dmitri's tent with alarming news from the city: Rasputin had disappeared and foul play was suspected. Instantly Dmitri was worried for Tatiana's sake, knowing how distressed she would be, and quickly sent off a letter expressing his sympathies. He had never met the man: an opportunity had not arisen for Tatiana to introduce them. Despite his instinctive mistrust, he understood how strongly the family felt they needed him and knew the loss would hit them hard.

The following day a letter came by messenger from Tatiana telling him the horrific news:

Uncle Grigory has been murdered, hideously murdered, and it seems it happened at the home of Prince Felix Yusupov, who is married to my cousin. I can hardly bear to write the words, but perhaps you know already because it is all over the newspapers the men were reading in the hospital this morning. One of them even showed a gruesome photograph of his corpse with an eye gouged out. His poor eye! Dmitri, they say he was poisoned, stabbed, shot and still he did not die until they drowned him in the Malaya Nevka River, where his body was discovered beneath the ice. What has happened to our country? Why would anyone do this to a holy man? I simply don't understand . . .

Dmitri guessed Yusupov might have done it in an attempt to protect the family from the insidious rumours about the holy man. If only it would stop the rot, it would be worthwhile, but he couldn't say this to Tatiana so he sent back a note repeating how sorry he was and how much he wished he could be there to comfort her in person.

The following day another letter came, only slightly calmer than the last:

I am comforting myself by looking through a notebook I have kept over the years in which I wrote down his wisest teachings. One day I will show it to you, Dmitri, so you understand his true goodness. Mama is inconsolable at the loss. She says Uncle Grigory is a martyr who deserves to be sanctified, and begged that he should have a state funeral. Papa, who has returned from the front, disagreed and this morning he arranged a simple service at which we all paid our respects. Mama laid an icon on Uncle Grigory's chest before the coffin was sealed and we dropped white flowers in his grave as we said our desolate farewells . . . I just don't understand a world in which such a thing can happen. I wish you could explain why . . .

Dmitri hoped word of this funeral did not become public. Tatiana had no idea about the mood of the populace, which turned uglier by the day. The common soldier was jubilant about Rasputin's murder, while in the streets of St Petersburg he heard they lit candles in celebration and chanted 'A dog's death for a dog'.

Dmitri dreaded what this might portend for the royal family. If men dared to murder someone their sovereigns held dear, it meant that the last vestiges of respect for the monarchy were ebbing away. But if it was overthrown, what would take its place? A republic, as in France? What would that mean for the Russian people? Who would uphold the traditions of their great nation? And, more urgently, what would happen to the Romanovs?

If only Dmitri were close enough to protect his new wife! He felt impotent to be stuck hundreds of miles south. It was unbearable to think of her coming face to face with a stone-throwing mob, such as were said to be attacking public buildings in St Petersburg.

The Alexander Palace had no regiment to defend it – merely a few under-qualified guards.

Unable to contain his anxiety, he wrote an impassioned letter to Tsar Nicholas, saying that in such inflamed times there should be plenty of loyal retainers stationed in Tsarskoe Selo to watch over the Tsarina and the grand duchesses. The old imperial guardsmen with whom he had trained would have laid down their lives to protect the family, but they had all been sent to war and the current royal escort was composed of raw recruits with less dedication and training. He begged Nicholas to recall him to the palace to do what he could to keep them safe.

Dmitri did not expect his letter to have any effect – he had little faith in his Tsar's perspicacity – but perhaps the man had more of an inkling of the state of the nation than he revealed, because he replied by return that Dmitri should travel to Tsarskoe Selo post-haste to take a place in the royal escort. He added: 'I know that you are a good and true friend to my family, and trust you will report to me directly any concerns you might have.'

Dmitri packed his kit and caught the first train for St Petersburg, arriving on the 7th of January, the Russian Orthodox Christmas. He travelled on to the Alexander Palace at Tsarskoe Selo and before even going to his quarters he asked the butler to deliver a note requesting that Tatiana come down to the side entrance.

He had been waiting just ten minutes, shivering in the brutal cold, when Tatiana appeared in a thin gown. She gave a little cry when she saw him and hurled herself into his arms. 'For the rest of my life, no Christmas gift will ever mean as much as this.'

Dmitri opened his coat and wrapped it tightly around them both so their bodies were pressed together for warmth. He vowed, silently, that as long as he had breath in his lungs he would not let anyone harm a hair on her head. If necessary, he would lay down his life to protect her.

Chapter Seventeen

Tsarskoe Selo, Russia, February 1917

Tsar Nicholas stayed in the Alexander Palace at Tsarskoe Selo for two months after the murder of Rasputin, making plans for a spring offensive against the Germans. The billiard room was covered in maps marked with a profusion of arrows, crosses and scribbles, which he pored over night and day. Dmitri thought he was deluded to imagine he was capable of planning such a campaign. Did he have any idea that levels of desertion from the Russian army were rising daily and that there was a growing threat of all-out mutiny? Like them, he had no faith in his Tsar's abilities as a commander and wished he would hand over the reins to one of his experienced generals. Nicholas sometimes acknowledged him with a quick nod when they passed in a corridor, but never spoke to him, and Dmitri wasn't sure that he knew who he was.

For six blissful weeks he was able to see Tatiana every day. She was hard at work in the hospital while he had many duties as a member of the royal escort but they sought each other during breaks, when they would talk and play with Ortipo, just as in the old days. He teased her that her training of her pet had been so lax that when they went for walks, Ortipo chose the route; that when she threw a ball for her, she invariably ended up fetching it herself. Ortipo was the boss.

In the evenings he sometimes joined her in the wards to listen to a group of Romanian musicians who had been hired to play chamber music to the patients, and they sat close, not quite touching. Dmitri felt the air between them charged with the delicious secret that they were man and wife. He heard Volodya had been transferred elsewhere to convalesce and was relieved not to come face to face with his erstwhile rival.

Tatiana had no inkling of life outside the palace and Dmitri decided not to enlighten her. It would cause her distress to no purpose because she could not solve the country's economic problems. For ordinary Russians bread was scarce, meat unheard of, and prices in the few shops that still stocked food were sky-high. Her father had outlawed the production and sale of vodka at the outbreak of war and men were brewing home-made versions that made them wild drunk and uncontrollable. Ugly mobs burnt pictures of her parents in the streets and cartoons in the press showed the Tsar and Tsarina eating meals of caviar and lobster or lighting cigarettes with hundred-rouble notes while their people starved. Tatiana would have been baffled and greatly upset had she seen them.

The mood of the public was the foremost worry preying on Dmitri's mind until in mid February, Tatiana came to tell him that both Olga and Alexei had succumbed to fever and hacking coughs and the doctor had diagnosed measles.

'Poor little Alexei,' she sighed. 'He so wanted to return to Mogilev with Papa. I think the men there are very kind to him.'

'You will stay away from the sick room, won't you?' Dmitri urged. 'I don't want you to catch it.'

'Mama is nursing them as she has already had measles and I don't think you can catch it twice. I have moved into Maria and Anastasia's room.'

That evening, Dmitri thought Tatiana looked a little flushed as she went about her duties in the hospital. 'Do wrap up warmly for your journey back to the palace,' he cautioned, but it was too late: the following morning his fears were confirmed when her ladies' maid, Trina, came to tell him Tatiana too had fallen ill. She sent a quick note but her handwriting was scrawled and quite unlike its normal copperplate: 'I pray I have not passed the sickness to you, my darling. This really is the most horrid affliction. Forgive me that I do not feel sufficiently well to write more.'

Dmitri sent her a note with an early snowdrop pressed between the pages, saying that he was sure she would still look dazzling, even when covered in spots. There was no reply and within days Trina brought news that the illness had worsened. Tatiana developed abscesses in her ears that made her deaf and the doctor was concerned her hearing might be permanently affected. It was agony for Dmitri to think of her suffering. If only it were possible, he would have taken the measles upon himself to spare her; he had already had a dose as a child and did not suffer too badly. Trina told him that Tatiana's beautiful auburn hair had been cut short to quell the fever, and he begged for a lock. When she brought one he slipped it under his pillow and every night he stroked the soft hair across his cheek and in his head he whispered words of love to his secret wife. He pined for her.

Dmitri's thoughts were focused on the invalids, but he heard rumblings from the town that thousands of women had taken to the streets to protest about the food shortages and that their numbers were being swollen by the hour. On the afternoon of the 25th of February he heard the sound of gunfire outside the palace gates and gathered a handful of guards before running out to seek the cause of the commotion. Several hundred townspeople were protesting, many waving placards and some of them armed.

'Pray calm, I beg you,' he shouted over the noise. 'The royal children are critically ill.'

'Let them rot in hell!' a woman yelled. 'At least they are fed, unlike my children.'

Dmitri sent two guards to fetch bread from the palace kitchen and a telegram was dispatched to Nicholas in Mogilev to ask what he would have them do. While they waited for a reply Dmitri urged the kitchen staff to bake as much bread as they could for distribution to the crowd. What they would do if supplies ran out, he could not imagine. Perhaps by then some solution could be reached.

The following day, Nicholas telephoned from the front and ordered the captain of the guards to suppress the demonstrations by force. He was incandescent with rage that the mob were scaring his sick children and said the men should not hesitate to open fire. Dmitri felt sick to his stomach. Had the Tsar learned nothing from the revolution in 1905, when he had been forced to hand many of his powers to a newly created government body known as the Duma? His only option was to negotiate because most of his army was at the front and, besides, he could no longer rely on the troops' loyalty.

After the telephone call, the captain convened a meeting of the guard to pass on this order and Dmitri knew from his colleagues' grim expressions that it was useless.

'I've had enough,' one man said, laying down his weapon. 'The army opened fire in St Petersburg and hundreds are lying dead in the streets. Me, I won't shoot my own people.'

A chorus of voices joined him, all in agreement. Dmitri and the captain remonstrated, but half-heartedly. They knew there was not enough manpower to hold back a determined mob, and any more casualties would only inflame tensions. The Tsar's orders would not be carried out.

Every day brought news of further regiments that had mutinied. This revolution had been building for a long time but now it had begun no one knew what would happen next or which direction it might take. It largely depended on Nicholas. If he was determined to try and shoot his way out of trouble, Dmitri feared the consequences – for him and for the country as a whole.

He and his royal escort comrades patrolled the palace grounds with rifles and bayonets shouldered, ignoring the shouts of the crowd and the intermittent sounds of gunfire in the city. The snow was deep and the temperature bitterly cold but he marched with determination: no one would break into the palace where Tatiana lay while he was on hand to protect her.

On the evening of the 28th of February Alexandra came out into the courtyard to talk to the guard, swathed from head to toe in furs. 'For God's sake, I ask all of you not to let any blood be shed on our account,' she pleaded. Dmitri was shocked to see how much she had aged in a few days, her complexion pale as parchment.

'How are the grand duchesses, Your Imperial Highness?' he ventured to ask.

She shook her head. 'Not yet recovered. The Chairman of the Duma has advised that we evacuate the palace but the girls simply cannot be moved.'

'You can count on us to remain at our posts,' Dmitri promised. 'No matter what.'

She pursed her lips and nodded her thanks, anxiety etched on her brow.

Dmitri couldn't believe it when rumours began to spread on the 2nd of March that the Tsar had abdicated. It didn't ring true. Nicholas was too arrogant, too wedded to the idea of his divine right. At first it was said that he had stepped down in favour of Alexei, which seemed ridiculous given the boy's frailty and lack of experience. Next came word that Nicholas wanted his brother Michael to take the throne, but Michael had refused. Gradually Dmitri realised the gossips must be right. Who would lead the nation now?

Orders came that the Guards Equipage were to vacate the palace, leaving officers of the royal escort as the only force guarding the perimeter. They rearranged their rotas and cut down on sleep so there would always appear to be enough guards on view to deter the mob from breaking in. It was a game of brinksmanship. As Dmitri marched by the railings, someone with a harmonica began to play the 'Marseillaise', the anthem written after the French Revolution of 1789. Dmitri's fingers tightened on his rifle: he felt like shooting that man on the spot. Everyone was jumpy, but none could have as much at stake as him, with his wife desperately ill inside the besieged palace.

Still there was no word from Nicholas. He had promised to return to Tsarskoe Selo on the 1st of March but the days dragged by without any sign. On the 5th of March the telephone and electricity lines to the palace were cut and food supplies were beginning to dwindle. When Dmitri rushed to the kitchen after an overnight shift to thaw his fingers and toes in front of the great ovens, the only food he could find was a tough loaf and some chicken bones from the day before.

As he walked through the courtyard, charred scraps floated from the chimneys and drifted on the breeze like oversized black snowflakes. A colleague told him Alexandra was burning her correspondence and diaries. Why would she do that if she had nothing to hide? Dmitri could not help wondering what injudicious disclosures might have graced the pages of her letters to Rasputin. Better if they did not reach the hands of the new rulers, whoever they might prove to be. One scrap still had some legible words on the edges and he ground it to dust beneath his heel.

During the morning of the 8th of March a delegation arrived from the provisional government. Dmitri recognised the politician Alexander Kerensky among them and was faintly reassured; he had seemed a moderate influence in the Duma. They marched briskly into the palace and were occupied inside for several hours. Dmitri watched the entrance, scarcely daring to breathe. Was Kerensky telling the family what their fate was to be? Was Tatiana well enough to attend the meeting? He glanced up at her bedroom but the curtains were drawn.

At noon their captain called them for orders. 'We must leave the palace this afternoon,' he said, eyes downcast and the words sticking in his throat. There was a chorus of disbelief as he continued: 'The 1st Rifles will replace us. They are in town this very moment and due here imminently.'

Dmitri felt sick to the pit of his stomach. The 1st Rifles had vowed allegiance to the revolutionary government.

'The Tsarina asks that we go peacefully and refrain from any action that might delay the Tsar's arrival and affect the fate of her children.'

He passed round some small jewelled icons of the Holy Mother that Alexandra had given him for all the men of the escort who had served so faithfully.

Dmitri fingered his icon, fluttery panic in his chest. What should he do? He couldn't bear to leave the palace. It was insufferable to be so powerless. He considered hiding somewhere in the building so as to remain close to Tatiana, but knew he would be arrested if he were discovered. Instead he sought Trina, the ladies' maid, to ask for news of Tatiana's health. He hoped it might be possible to see her, to explain that he must leave but would remain nearby.

'She still cannot receive visitors,' Trina told him. 'But I have been given a pass to get in and out of the palace. If you like I can meet you and convey letters between you.'

Dmitri arranged that he would meet her at a side entrance every morning then, with feet dragging, he went to his quarters, took off his imperial guard's uniform and changed into civilian clothes, packed his knapsack and wandered out into the grounds.

He gazed up at Tatiana's window, willing her to look out. He yearned to see her, both to reassure her and to reassure himself. Who knew how long before they would be reunited, or under what circumstances? Walking out the palace gates and away from her felt wrong, as if he was wrenching off a limb.

Chapter Eighteen

Tsarskoe Selo, Russia, March 1917

The vitriol directed against the Romanovs in Tsarskoe Selo was staggering. Everywhere Dmitri went, townsfolk gossiped about Alexandra's supposed promiscuity, speculated that Alexei was not the Tsar's son, and even cast aspersions that the grand duchesses took lovers amongst the palace staff. It was hard not to lose his temper and lash out, but he restrained himself and occupied his time writing to old friends from the imperial guard, men such as Malevich, whom he knew would be loyal to the Romanovs. Surely together they could find a way to help them? In public, he was careful not to identify himself as a scion of the family, because the mood was so ugly he could have been attacked by a mob. He saw one aristocrat fleeing on foot after his carriage was overturned.

Every day, Dmitri scanned the newspapers, trying to work out, like other Russians, who would be their new leader. Prince George Lvov seemed the current face of the provisional government but a council in St Petersburg, the Petrograd Soviet of Workers' and Soldiers' Deputies, was increasingly influential, and more soviets were springing up around the nation. The stridency of their pronouncements alarmed Dmitri: what Russia needed more than anything was a wise leader who could get food to the people and quell the urge to blame all the country's ills on one absurdly wealthy family.

Tatiana was slowly recovering from her illness and, judging by her letters, seemed to have no idea of the danger the family faced.

My dearest love, I wish we could meet but at the same time I am far too vain to allow you to see me like this. You will be shocked to learn that my remaining hair has been falling out in clumps and I must wear a headscarf to cover the bald patches. I know how you loved my hair and promise I will grow it again as soon as I can! I am also much thinner but can eat solid food once more and aim to gain weight very soon . . . We are all in reasonable spirits. I think we are going to sail to England for a holiday with our relatives, George V and his family, until the revolution is suppressed. We are waiting to be told when a ship will arrive to collect us. I miss my work in the hospital but am occupying my time with reading and trying to stop the younger ones from arguing (a mammoth task). I miss you and wish I could be with you even for just one moment to lean my forehead against yours and see if I can read your thoughts.

Dmitri was glad she could not read his thoughts, because he couldn't imagine how the British would simply send a ship through the Baltic, which was patrolled by German warships. Would Germany guarantee them safe passage? That would not go down well in revolutionary Russia. But in his reply he did not mention his doubts:

Now that your vanity has returned, I am reassured you will soon be yourself again . . . Once you sail for England, I will follow hot on your heels. Perhaps your parents will allow us to be officially wed there if the revolution is prolonged. We could buy a manor house in the countryside and keep horses and dogs. I will have to polish my English, which is nowhere near as fluent as yours, and adopt an accent that sounds like a man being strangled, such as their aristocrats use, but all in all I think it a good plan.

Every day he strolled up to the Alexander Palace to deliver a letter to Trina and receive the one Tatiana had written for him. Afterwards he walked along the road outside hoping in vain for a glimpse of her. He often saw Tsar Nicholas cycling around on an old bicycle, wearing a workman's jacket and cap like a country peasant. Sometimes he was chopping wood or breaking ice, but always his head was down and he did not notice Dmitri pass by. From the newspapers he knew that Nicholas and Alexandra were under house arrest to prevent them trying to retake the throne, but to Dmitri's eyes it did not look as if they had any such intention.

The gates were patrolled by revolutionary guards, identifiable by their badges showing a factory worker carrying a red flag. Dmitri could tell they were inexperienced from the awkward way they held their fixed bayonets, and their jumpiness at any sudden noise: these were eager new recruits jumping on a bandwagon. Townspeople stopped to gawp through the fence and one whispered to him that the guards would take you inside the grounds for a glimpse of the family for a fee of twenty roubles. Tatiana had not mentioned this in her letters and the disrespect horrified him. It was as if they were exotic creatures in a zoo rather than monarchs from a centuries-old dynasty.

Spring came, the snow and ice began to melt and trees burst into leaf almost overnight. Every day he missed Tatiana more and his fears for her increased. Why had nothing happened? Still there was no word of when the ship might arrive to take her family to England and, unable to bear the suspense, Dmitri made an appointment to visit the British ambassador, Sir George Buchanan, in St Petersburg. He used his status as a member of the royal escort to gain admittance, which was risky, because identifying yourself as a Romanov acolyte was inadvisable in the current climate. It was better to be a worker. If anyone asked, Dmitri claimed to be a common soldier of lowly birth.

Recently his mother had written that his father had been questioned by revolutionary guards and told he might have to stand trial on charges that were not yet specified. How could a general who had earned so many medals for service to his country be under suspicion? Anyone wealthy or well connected seemed to be a target. Many of the Romanovs' friends had been arrested: Anna Vyrubova, Alexandra's lady-in-waiting, was being held in the Peter and Paul Fortress, and several members of the extended family were under house arrest in case they tried to help Nicholas regain his throne.

'I'm afraid that the British Foreign Secretary has recommended that the Russian government make some other plan for the future residence of their imperial majesties,' Ambassador Buchanan told him, peering through half-spectacles. 'The difficulties of transporting them to London in wartime proved insurmountable. Besides, the new government are not keen for the Tsar and Tsarina to leave, since they are privy to so many of the country's war secrets. You understand, there is nothing more I can do . . .'

Dmitri was horrified. 'You must help! What will become of them without the aid of their British cousins? There are calls in the press for them to stand trial as traitors to their country. Who knows what might happen?'

The man shifted in his seat. 'We will, of course, continue to apply pressure and ask that they are treated with humanity, but as a rule the British government tries not to interfere in the affairs of another sovereign nation.'

Dmitri felt a clenching of his gut, and a sense of dread that made his heart heavy as he left. If the British would not save them, then it was up to pro-monarchist Russians. He had located around twenty colleagues who promised to help but that was nowhere near enough to launch an armed rescue attempt and spirit the Romanovs out of the country. The railway workers were a militant bunch who would never allow them onto a train, and they had no hope of stealing a ship from the heavily guarded harbour. Besides, he remembered what had happened to Louis XVI of France and his wife Marie Antoinette after they tried to slip out of France in 1791 following the revolution there: they'd been intercepted, tried as traitors and beheaded. He shivered. If the Tsar and Tsarina were being accused of betraying their country, then it was important not to give the prosecutors any ammunition.

He did not tell Tatiana of his discovery, but he could sense from her letters that her mood was darkening.

The doctor tells us that Olga's heart has been weakened by the measles, and Maria still cannot walk. I do my best to cheer the invalids by reading aloud to them, and in fair weather we take them out in wheelchairs to the formal gardens. We are allowed to wander deep into the wood, where it is quite wild. I avoid coming round the front of the house where people stare at us through the fence, but I would do so if I thought I would one day see your dear face there.

We have occasional visitors, but I do not wish you to become known to our revolutionary captors or else you might end up in prison, like poor dear Anna Vyrubova. How could they do that to a cripple? What treason could she possibly have committed?

Oh, Dmitri, I yearn for you with my entire soul. If we could but have five minutes alone . . . The thought of your passionate nature and fine mind, your sparkling eyes and strong arms, make me feel I can cope with anything so long as I am assured we will be together again some day soon.

Dmitri was encouraged to hear they were allowed to wander into the wood and it occurred to him that perhaps there was a chance he could meet her there. He borrowed a horse and rode around the edges of the palace grounds, looking for less well-defended points. He was able to make his way into Alexander Park through the graveyard for imperial horses and rode on past the farm to the woods, searching for a place where he might meet Tatiana. There was a gothic White Tower just five minutes from the front entrance of the palace, a place where servants used to sleep. It did not appear to be in use any more so he slipped inside and climbed the winding staircase to the sixth floor then walked out onto the turreted battlements. He could see across the park all the way to town. Would the guards let Tatiana walk that far? It was a short distance from the formal gardens. Perhaps she could try.

Rather than put his message into a letter, which might be intercepted, Dmitri asked Trina to tell Tatiana he would wait in the White Tower at ten o'clock each morning. If she was able to join him for a few minutes that would be wonderful, but he emphasised that she should not dream of putting herself in danger.

The next morning he got there at nine-thirty, hiding just inside the entrance to the tower in a spot where he could look along the path Tatiana would have to take. He did not have long to wait before he saw her strolling past the lake, stopping to pick wild-flowers and placing them in a basket she carried over her arm. She was very thin, in a grey gown with a grey scarf tied over her head. Dmitri admired her elegant walk: she looked like a grand duchess even in peasant-style clothing. She bent by the water's edge to pluck a white iris, checked the coast was clear, then scur-ried across to the tower's entrance.

In an instant Dmitri pulled her into his arms and covered her face, her dear mouth, with kisses. 'Oh my love,' he breathed, but was unable to say any more. She still looked ill, her complexion pale and her cheeks hollow but there were no scars from the measles rash. He stroked her cheek with his finger and looked deep into her grey eyes, overwhelmed by the strength of his emotions.

'I cannot stay long in case they miss me,' she whispered, 'but it is wonderful to see you.'

'How are things in the palace?' Dmitri asked. 'Tell me the truth.'

111

She hesitated. 'It's full of drunken soldiers, smashing our precious belongings and carousing till all hours. There does not appear to be any discipline. Papa seems resigned to it and wanders round on his own without talking to any of us. Mama has taken to her bedchamber, where she works on her embroidery. I am the one who must raise everyone's spirits and sometimes I confess it takes more energy than I can summon. But being here, with you, has revived me.'

'I will be here every day at ten. And I am doing my best to secure your release.'

'If only the British would hurry . . .' she sighed.

Dmitri looked away. He couldn't bear to be the one to tell her the British were no longer planning to rescue them. Instead he asked how she passed her days.

'Papa and I are planting carrots and summer vegetables in a plot near the palace. I enjoy working with the soil, although my nails are suffering.' She held out her hands to show him, and he kissed each palm in turn. 'And you? What are you doing?'

'I have lodgings in town where I await news from the various quarters I am talking to about your rescue. But I often wonder if I should tell the new government of our marriage so I can be detained with you and stay by your side.'

'No!' she cried. 'You mustn't! We need you outside. If you joined us, you would be unable to help.' She kissed his lips. 'I love that you would be willing to give up your own freedom and of course it would be wonderful to see you every day, but for now it must be this way.'

'Perhaps we can see each other more often. I will come to the Tower every morning and you should join me whenever it seems safe. Don't take any risks, though.'

They had one last, lingering kiss before she turned to walk back into captivity with only a quick final glance. As she disappeared round the corner of the palace, it flashed into Dmitri's head that this might be the last time he ever saw her, and the pain was like a stab wound. He couldn't bear her to be in danger. He yearned to snatch her and ride off into the countryside, just keep riding till they reached safety. But she would never leave her family. That wasn't an option.

A few days later Tatiana came to the tower again, and every few days after that, as spring turned to full-blown summer. The meetings sustained them: she was able to unburden herself and Dmitri could revel in the sheer exhilaration of being with her. Afterwards he relived every embrace, every tender word, and felt warmed by the certain knowledge of her love.

On the 12th of July, he was waiting in the White Tower when he saw her approach just as two revolutionary guards appeared from the other direction, their routes set to intersect. Dmitri could sense Tatiana's confusion as she tried to decide what to do and he willed her to turn back, but it was too late.

'Oy, who are you?' one of them called out. Dmitri couldn't hear her response but it seemed she told the truth because the soldier replied, 'Your lot aren't allowed over here. You shouldn't be outside the palace courtyard. Get back right now, whore.'

Rage filled Dmitri with a red-hot fire. He had a knife in his belt and he was pretty sure he could kill the two of them before they were able to raise the alarm. Tatiana glanced quickly in his direction, shook her head almost imperceptibly, then turned and hurried back along the path to the palace. Dmitri was still shaking with rage that they should speak to her so insultingly. He watched closely as the men passed, memorising their faces, vowing that when the revolution was overthrown he would have them jailed.

When he rode round to the side gate to meet Trina, she had a hurried letter from Tatiana:

I was so sad not to be able to hold you earlier today, but in my daydreams I am pretending those soldiers did not stop me and we were together. I try to fill my head with joyful images and I wish you would do the same . . . I am sorry to say that we may not have another opportunity to meet at the tower because we were told this morning that we are leaving Tsarskoe Selo on the 31st of July. They have not said where we will be taken, only that we are heading south, so we hope the destination is Livadia. How wonderful that would be! We will take as much as we can, because who knows when we will return? Anyhow, my dearest one, I will write as soon as I know our destination in the fervent hope that I will see you there before too long. I love you with all my heart, now and always.

Dmitri made sure to position himself near the gates of the Alexander Palace from dawn on the 31st. It seemed word of the family's move had leaked out because there were hundreds of people there, some of them jeering and calling names, others just come to gawp. The disrespect made him very cross, although he understood the desperation of the thousands upon thousands of starving families whose male breadwinner had been killed in the war. He saw an official emerge with a message for the guards and wormed his way close enough to hear that the royal party was being taken out of the west gate of the park on their way to the railway station.

He leapt on his horse and rode at speed to intercept them, arriving at the station just as they were disembarking from a convoy of shiny automobiles. His eyes sought Tatiana amidst the throng and found her at the exact same moment as she spotted him. He touched his fingers to his lips and blew her a discreet kiss and she did the same then folded her hands as if in prayer. Seconds later she had stepped up into a carriage and disappeared. He felt an enveloping sense of emptiness in his core and a fore-boding deep within his bones.

Chapter Nineteen

Lake Akanabee, New York State, 12th August 2016

A violent storm swept across the lake one night and the rain woke Kitty at four in the morning, sounding like stones hurled from the heavens as it pelted on the tin roof. She lit her oil lamp and went to the door to watch. Trees were bending sideways in the wind, lightning forked across the lake and her fire pit had already filled with water. At least there didn't appear to be any leaks in the walls she had patched.

The howling of the storm and the clattering on the roof were so loud she couldn't get back to sleep, so she opened her great-grandfather's second novel, *Exile*. Bob had brought all the novels round a few days earlier, neatly inscribed to him and his wife, Sue. *Exile* had originally been published in 1927 but this was an American reprint dated 1950. The writing was beautifully lyrical but the story was bleak. It told of a man who had been forced to leave his homeland, for reasons that are never explained. He arrived in a bright city full of corruption, where everyone was trying to sell something: drugs, useless modern gadgets, or themselves. She wondered if this was how Dmitri saw New York then remembered he had not arrived there till 1934. Maybe he was writing about Berlin. The man in the story is haunted by some wrong he has committed in the past. He falls in love with a beautiful woman but is unable to commit to their affair because of the damage to his soul, and in the end she leaves him.

One thing was for sure, Kitty thought, rubbing her eyes: this man understood depression. She'd never read a book that took you so deeply inside the head of a depressive and it was a disturbing experience, which was somehow mirrored by the cataclysmic weather. Dawn was breaking outside with a faint pink glow but still the rain hammered down, bouncing off the sun-parched ground, and the opposite shore of the lake was obscured by low-hanging cloud. Even at eight o'clock it was still so dark that Kitty needed to use her lamp for reading. She decided to drive to the vacation park coffeehouse for a latte and some human company. The novel had put her in a gloomy, introspective mood.

Jeff wasn't there, but the coffeehouse was full of campers sheltering from the elements. Kitty found a corner and plugged in her laptop to charge, listening to the complaints of the holidaymakers who had hoped to go hiking, canoeing or rafting and instead found themselves with long hours to fill and squabbling children to entertain. The windows misted up with their breath and the loud babble made Kitty feel desperately lonely and, for the first time, homesick. No one paid her any attention as she opened her laptop. First she went to the *Guardian* website and read about the news back home and the issues that were concerning *Guardian* readers: government cuts, immigration; the usual stuff.

Her cursor hovered over her email icon and, steeling herself, she clicked to open it. One thousand eight hundred and seventy-five emails were waiting, she was told, and she sipped her latte as they began to flash into her inbox. Tom's name was prominent among them – the name 'Tom Fisher, Tom Fisher, Tom Fisher' flashed past her eyes like strobe lighting – and her chest felt tight. Whatever he had to say, she wasn't ready to hear it, but she couldn't help noticing the email headings: 'I'm so sorry', 'Please get in touch', 'Urgent – I need to speak to you', 'I will always love you', 'Please can we talk?' She let her eye skim down the list but didn't open any of them. There was a pain in her chest, beneath the ribs on her left side: a hard rock that nagged like a tumour. She tried taking a deep breath and letting it out slowly but the pain persisted. She put her hand over her heart and felt it beating more rapidly than usual and that made her panic. She couldn't breathe.

Kitty yanked the plug from the wall and closed the laptop, tucking it beneath her arm as she squeezed past the huddle of campers, stepping over backpacks and small children to reach the exit. There was a yell of communal protest when she opened the door, letting in a gust of rain, so she stepped out into the squawl and closed it quickly behind her. She got behind the wheel of the car and pulled out of the car park but her heart was hammering too fast and her breathing was too jagged for her to drive. After a few hundred yards she pulled in to the roadside and bent forward, resting her head on the steering wheel.

What did it mean? Was Tom saying 'I will always love you but I love Karren as well'? 'I will always love you but I want a divorce'? What kind of love was he talking about exactly? A month had gone by since that morning when she checked the messages on his mobile phone but she wasn't ready to hear from Tom yet; that much was obvious. She had been foolish to open the email account. It would take more time before she was able to deal with that situation and all its repercussions. It merely underlined her sense that her marriage had failed, that she had failed.

In her head she heard her mother's voice berating her: 'Why are you such a quitter? You take piano lessons then get bored; you start tennis coaching then don't want to go back. You never stick at anything.' Was it true that she was a quitter? She had stopped piano and tennis and drama and all those other extra-curricular activities because her mum had such high expectations; she had to be a prodigy at everything. When she rang home with the news she'd got a 2:1 in her journalism degree, her mum had commented, 'What a shame. If only you'd done a bit more work . . .' She could just imagine the deep sighs if her mum could see her now, hunched over a steering wheel, her heart overbeating with anxiety.

She forced herself to breathe regularly, counting to five between breaths and trying to make her mind go blank of everything but the in breath and the out breath, as they taught at her yoga class. A truck sped past with a whoosh, covering her windscreen with a wave of surface water.

She knew she needed to keep herself occupied, and reading Dmitri's next novel was not going to hack it. Then she remembered the overgrown patch of weeds behind the cabin that she'd been waiting for the right moment to deal with. It should be easier to uproot them now the earth was softened by rain. She'd get soaked to the skin but it would give her a real sense of achievement to clear that patch. It was flat and treeless so maybe she could do some planting there. Keeping busy was the best way to cope with a broken heart.

Chapter Twenty

The rain continued all week but at least it was still hot. Kitty spent her time clearing the earth around the cabin and it was like working under a power shower as the torrents beat down on her back and steam rose from the freshly dug earth. It was tough work that left her streaked in mud, with muscles that ached in new places every day. She used her camping stove to heat noodles and make tea indoors, and spent the evenings sitting in her swing seat on the covered porch, drinking wine and reading Dmitri Yakovlevich's remaining novels.

They were rich and in some ways surprisingly modern stories, with an overriding theme of love and loss. His male characters were more in touch with their emotions than any man she knew, endlessly analysing their reactions to events, but his women were all slightly idealised, a little too perfect, maybe. Could any male writer create convincing female characters? she wondered. The last two novels, the ones written in America, could easily have been published in the present day. The writing was clean and spare, but evoked glorious images that filled her head until she felt she knew the people in his stories as well as if they were her companions in the cabin. They were complex and flawed but never dull. Was that what Dmitri was like?

Kitty remembered that she held the copyright to these novels, as part of the inheritance. She should try to get them reissued. Perhaps she would contact his last publisher, Random House, and ask if they might be interested. She could imagine them selling well with modern covers and intelligent broadsheet reviews. She could write a feature about her great-grandfather and explain how she came upon his story . . . but she would have to find out more about him first. He was still a shadowy figure with a biography that consisted of a few dates and places and huge gaps in between.

One afternoon, when the rain was coming down in sheets, she heard a car pulling down the track towards her cabin and she dropped her spade to watch. It was a police car with two officers inside. One of them opened his window and called out: 'You Kitty Fisher?'

She was astonished, and before she answered 'yes', her mind had invented a dozen different reasons why they might be there. Had she breached her car-rental agreement? Was there a problem with the ownership of the cabin? Did she owe local taxes for something?

'Your husband reported you as a missing person back in England,' the closest officer explained. 'They tracked you down from your credit card use and the vacation park told us you were here. Is everything OK, ma'am?'

It had never occurred to her that Tom would call the police. What an idiot! 'I'm so sorry you've had to come out all this way,' she gasped. 'Please – come in for coffee and I'll explain.'

They followed her to the cabin door, carefully wiping their feet before entering. Kitty lit the gas stove.

'I'm sorry I only have one chair,' she told them. 'You're my first guests. I've been here a month doing up the cabin. I recently inherited it.'

'You didn't tell your husband you were coming?' One of the policemen did the talking while the other wandered round examining the work she'd done patching the walls.

She turned away to spoon instant coffee into cups. 'I decided I needed a break. He'd been cheating on me.'

'So you're teaching him a lesson?'

'No.' Kitty shook her head. 'I couldn't decide what to do, and I wanted to see if I could rescue this cabin, so it fell into place.'

'Looks like you've done a good job here – but you should let your husband know you're safe. He thought you might have done something stupid . . .'

Kitty frowned. 'You mean suicide? Tom knows me better than that . . .' Her voice trailed off. Did he? Could he really have believed she might have killed herself over Karren with the double 'r'? That implied a level of arrogance she hadn't thought him capable of.

'He's gone to a lot of trouble to find you, so he must be pretty torn up.'

Kitty considered this. Tom was torn up? Well, good! But still she couldn't face talking to him and listening to all the pathetic excuses he was bound to come up with. 'I don't suppose you could pass on a message that I'm safe, and that I'm staying here for the rest of the summer? But please don't give him the address. I don't want him turning up.'

'Why? Is he violent?'

'No,' she said quickly. 'It's not that.'

They looked at each other, and the talkative one pursed his lips before replying. 'You're awfully isolated out here. You sure you don't want him to visit?'

She tried to picture Tom at the cabin, but it felt wrong. The cabin was hers, not his. And, as her panic attack the other day showed, she wasn't ready to talk to him, not yet. She was acting instinctively, protecting herself from further pain, and when she felt strong enough she would get in touch. 'I'll call him, but not yet. I apologise for taking up your time. I'm sure you've got far more important things to do.'

'No, ma'am. It's pretty quiet out here. The odd car accident, a few DUIs . . . we're not a crime hotspot. If you're sure that's what you want, we'll email the police back in England and tell them you're fine. Thanks for the coffee.'

They looked around for somewhere to put their cups. Kitty smiled and took them. The officers paused for a moment peering out the cabin door, waiting for a lull in which to dash to the car without getting soaked, but no let-up appeared to be on the way.

'Keep safe, ma'am,' they called as they ran out into the downpour. She waved from the porch then came indoors and sat on the bedding roll, hugging her knees to her chest and rocking back and forth. How stupid Tom was! He'd be lucky not to get charged with wasting police time. He must have guessed where she'd gone before they tracked her credit card use . . . he just hated the fact that he couldn't control this situation.

In a flash of insight, Kitty realised they had slipped into a pattern in which Tom always made the decisions in the marriage. Perhaps it was because he was the one with the regular salary. He decided which holidays they could afford or when they needed new cars. He had wanted to move to Crouch End, a smart middle-class area, even though it meant all the profit she had made on property developing, as well as her inheritance from her parents, was swallowed up. She would have been quite happy staying in the multi-cultural whirl of Turnpike Lane, but Tom thought the crime rate was going up and the final straw came when his car window was smashed in an attempted theft.

It hadn't been like that in the early days when money was scarce. Holidays had been spur-of-the-moment, and they never booked package tours – simply got a cheap flight to Bangkok or Mumbai and travelled around by local transport, finding basic accommodation in beach huts or rooms in villages where tourists were a rarity. Suddenly she remembered the delicious smell of the fresh tea growing in the mountains of southern India, where they had stayed in a tiny hostel. They'd hiked in the hills by day and sat outside in the dusk eating mango and chatting with local people who passed on their way home from the fields. She remembered the day Tom saved her life by throwing a well-placed stone when a black snake appeared on the grass beside where she was sitting. She remembered the scent of the garland of white jasmine he bought from a street seller for a few pennies and placed around her neck. She remembered how they used to talk and talk and never run out of conversation, endlessly fascinated to hear each other's point of view. What had happened to that?

Something in Dmitri Yakovlevich's last novel came into her head: a male character ponders why his relationship is so different twenty years down the line; the dynamic has changed, the power base has shifted. And he realises that as his own position in life has changed, it has skewed the way he views his partner. Kitty mused on this. Tom was not a dictator. She had let him drift into becoming the one who took responsibility for mortgages, cars and holidays. He hadn't taken the power – she had given it up. She didn't like making decisions of that sort because she found them stressful – it was easier not to take the risk of what her mother deemed 'failure' – and by default had slipped into a role that was almost like that of a child. It was an interesting theory, and the more she thought about it the more true she realised it was. She had been coasting along, not being a full partner in the marriage. Perhaps Tom would have liked her to pull her weight more.

Of course, none of this excused the fact that he had been unfaithful to her. She was still furious when she thought about that. Was she punishing him with her silence? Probably. But the main obstacle was that when she thought about calling or even emailing him, she began to feel panicky. It brought up such a host of anxieties – about money, security, family, what she was doing with her life – that she had to shut the lid on the box quickly and busy herself with something else.

Chapter Twenty-One

Tobolsk, Siberia, 6th August 1917

Malama sweetheart,

We have arrived in Tobolsk, after a long journey by train and then steamer. How remote and strange this countryside is: flat and marshy, with swarms of insects and wide open skies. I'm told it is only possible to reach here in the summer months because as soon as winter sets in the river freezes and no traffic can get in or out. Perhaps this is why they chose to send us here: shut away and forgotten, where Papa can cause no political problems for the new government.

We are staying on the steamer for now because the Governor's House, where we are to be accommodated, was recently used as a barracks and is in desperate need of cleaning and refitting. We are able to walk around the town and I have found the people curious but friendly. Everyone asks why we girls have short hair, thinking it is some new fashion in St Petersburg, and they don't know what to say when I tell them the real reason, that we have been ill.

I will mail this letter quickly in the hope that you will come to join us in this little hamlet. I wish I could say more to recommend it, but as you know we will make the most of it. I require little to make me happy: merely to know that my family – and that includes you – are safe and well.

Tenderest love from Your T

The letter reached Dmitri in Tsarskoe Selo two weeks later and he went straight to Malevich's lodgings. Rather than reveal the truth he told him he had heard from some contacts about the Romanovs' latest location.

'Why Siberia?' Dmitri worried. 'It's the landlocked dead centre of the country. They obviously don't plan to send the family overseas any time soon.'

'I suspect they don't know what to do now the British have refused to take them. But why couldn't they could go to Denmark, where Nicholas's mother hails from?'

'If the government won't do it, then we must try to get them there. I will travel to Tobolsk, look at the lie of the land, and see what can be done.'

Malevich agreed. 'And I'll stay in St Petersburg and find comrades prepared to help. We can communicate by telegram. But be careful what you say, because there is no doubt it will be read by the new power-crazed authorities. Let's pretend to be businessmen and refer to the family as cargo.' Dmitri flinched. 'Yes, I know it's insensitive, but needs must . . .'

The thought of a Siberian winter filled Dmitri with gloom but he packed a bag with snowshoes and his wolfskin coat and hat and set off for the long journey to Tobolsk by train and then river steamer. His only consolation was that each mile brought him a mile closer to his beloved wife.

As he walked up from the docks on the Irtysh River the skies were leaden, although the temperature was sweltering. He asked directions to the Governor's House, assuming the family would be installed there now, and was directed to a square, white building of two storeys, in the classical style, with a courtyard around it bordered by a ten-foot fence. A couple of guards stood by the gate. There was no sign of the family, but he caught a glimpse of movement by a first-floor window that made his heart lurch. Was that Tatiana? If only she would glance out. He ached to see her.

Dmitri hung around until the guards were beginning to eye him with suspicion, whereupon he wandered round a corner and was overjoyed to encounter Trina, the ladies' maid, coming up the hill with a basket.

'Thank goodness you're here!' he cried. 'I've just arrived. Are the family well?'

'As well as can be expected,' she told him. 'The Tsar is frustrated by the lack of space for outdoor activity; you can walk round that yard in three minutes or less and there's nowhere he can plant his vegetables. The Tsarina has made a chapel in the old ballroom and prays there daily, but otherwise keeps to her bedchamber. And the girls and Alexei are bored. They're only allowed into the yard between eleven and twelve, and then from two until dusk.'

'Are you able to pass letters to Tatiana? The guards don't search you?'

She nodded. 'Of course. I'm staying in a house down the hill so walk up here every morning at seven-thirty, and I often come up and down on errands.'

'I'll bring you a letter each day at seven-thirty. Bless you for your loyalty.' He clasped his hands together. What would he do without Trina as a conduit? She must have guessed they were lovers but had been utterly discreet.

'If you like, I'll ask Grand Duchess Tatiana to come out onto the balcony and wave to you,' she offered.

'Is that safe? Won't the guards notice?'

'The girls often sit on the balcony and watch people go by. Come at a quarter to two.'

At twenty to two Dmitri walked up the hill, trying to appear as if he was strolling casually. From afar he could see the silhou-

126

ette of Tatiana on the balcony: she was taller, more slender than her sisters, and she held her head high, almost like a ballet dancer. As if she felt his gaze, she turned and saw him and they stood for a few moments watching each other from afar. It was intensely moving for Dmitri. To know she was safe, to see it with his own eyes, was overwhelming and he realised that throughout the journey to Tobolsk he had been afraid of arriving to find her dead. The example of the king and queen guillotined after the French Revolution was stuck in his head. On the one hand he was sure no loyal Russians would kill their imperial family, but this spirit of revolution that had been unleashed was volatile and unpredictable.

The guards did not appear to be watching, so Dmitri sauntered along the road bordering the garden, glancing up whenever he thought it safe. Tatiana touched her fingers to her lips then clasped her hands to her heart.

He wanted to walk past again, but a guard turned to watch him so he crossed the road as if he had just remembered some errand. If he were careful, he would be able to catch a glimpse of Tatiana every day; that was something to look forward to. Goodness knows what these guards would do if their marriage was revealed; he would probably be arrested on the spot.

The letter Trina gave him the next morning detailed a little of life inside the house and no matter how hard Tatiana tried to be positive, Dmitri could tell she was miserable.

Malama sweetheart,

I thank you from the bottom of my heart for following us to this remote place. We have done our best to make a comfortable home, with all the photographs and nick-nacks we brought from Tsarskoe Selo, but the lack of freedom weighs heavily. Most of all I miss being able to walk in the woods and meet you inside the tower. It seems no such thing will be possible here. Did you know Dostoevsky was briefly imprisoned in this town, in 1850? I often wonder what he made of it.

Our days are spent reading, playing bézique or dominoes, exercising in the yard, praying, or eating meals, and the time drags interminably. I look at the clock, thinking an hour must have gone by and realise it is only minutes. We have one light on the horizon: we have been given permission to attend Blagoveschensky Church this Sunday, the first church service we have attended in six months, so all are very excited. Perhaps you could be there too? I would love that.

I know you will never abandon me but all the same do not think I am unappreciative of the sacrifice you have made in following me here, and the possible danger it could mean for you. I love you for it. I love everything about you. My sole happiness lies in daydreaming about a future in which we are together.

Dmitri made sure he was in the church well before the service, on a side from which he could survey the rest of the worshippers. To his surprise, the royal party were led in through a side door, which meant they had to pass directly in front of him. Tsar Nicholas was lost in thought but the Tsarina gave a slight nod of acknowledgement. Tatiana gave a quick smile, while Olga looked astonished as she glanced from him to Tatiana. Her sister obviously hadn't mentioned that he was in town.

He watched Tatiana as she crossed herself then lit a candle. She was wearing a cornflower-blue dress with a high neck and her short hair was arranged in fetching waves, almost reaching her shoulders. She looked solemn as she stood alongside her mother and sisters, but as soon as the singing began she joined in, and she turned to catch eyes with Dmitri several times.

Orthodox services were always long but this priest seemed determined to impress his royal visitors with his stamina as one hour stretched to two. Dmitri would have liked him to preach all day just so he could stand and watch his beloved. It was wonderful to be under the same roof as her after the weeks of separation, and to see for himself that she was healthy.

At the end, the family walked in front of him once more and Tatiana let her hand brush his arm as she passed.

Dmitri had rented lodgings in town and that evening he sat and wrote to Malevich, telling him of the situation in which he had found the Romanovs ('the cargo'). He described the layout of the town and the position of the guards around the house, but really he knew rescue from this place was impossible. Already, in early September, the temperature was dropping rapidly and in just a few weeks they would be unable to leave Tobolsk for the eight months of winter. Perhaps the following spring, the revolutionary government would relent and allow the youngest family members to go free. No one could possibly think them guilty of any crime, no matter what the sins of their parents.

Dmitri felt furious with both of them for their blinkered, outdated approach to monarchy. The Romanovs had made their vast fortune from the resources of the nation, yet Nicholas had not seen fit to open the coffers when his people were starving. Alexandra had been remarkably short-sighted in using Rasputin as an advisor when she was seen by ordinary Russians as allied to the enemy. Between them they had turned the once-revered imperial family into a hated institution. But the children were so young – Alexei only thirteen, Tatiana only twenty – surely they could not be blamed?

Yet again he thought of poor Marie Antoinette, the French queen, whose only 'crime' was to have been born Austrian in an era when Austria was France's bitter enemy. Her eldest daughter, Marie-Thérèse, had been held prisoner for six years before being released into exile. Would Alexandra's German roots and Nicholas's imperious style yet count against them all? Could an accident of birth mean years under house arrest for the younger Romanovs?

Chapter Twenty-Two

Tobolsk, Siberia, winter 1917

On the 28th of October Dmitri bought his usual newspaper from a street seller and recoiled as he read the headlines: there had been yet another coup in St Petersburg. Three days earlier Bolshevik leader Vladimir Lenin and his comrade Leon Trotsky had led a successful coup against the provisional government in St Petersburg. It had begun at 9.45 p.m. with the battleship *Aurora* firing shots at the Winter Palace and ended at 2 a.m. with the taking of the Palace by rebels. The provisional government had been imprisoned in the Peter and Paul Fortress.

Dmitri was stunned. Both Lenin and Trotsky were lunatic extremists, who had been forced into exile after the 1905 Revolution. When Lenin arrived back in Russia in April 1917, everyone expected him to join the provisional government but instead he published his own radical agenda in *Pravda*. He believed peasants should seize land from rich landlords, that factory workers should take over the factories, and that manual workers should receive higher wages than office workers. Everyone Dmitri knew dismissed Lenin as mad. No one thought he could possibly succeed – yet somehow he had. The change had come over the summer, when Lenin announced his intention of withdrawing

Russia from the war with Germany without delay. While the provisional government tarried, pressing for better terms, Lenin promised battle-weary soldiers that they could come home immediately, and finally they had switched allegiance. It was a short-term measure that would cost the country dear, almost certainly losing them control of the Baltic states.

Dmitri wondered what would become of his parents, back home in the comfortable estate that had been in his father's family for centuries? What would happen to the Romanovs in the new 'workers' paradise'? Dmitri realised straight away that these events would split Russia down the middle and change the country he loved forever.

Shortly after the coup, a letter came from his mother telling him his father had been arrested. It seemed the Bolsheviks were taking a hard line with what they called the 'bourgeoisie'. Dmitri worried that his proud father would not submit easily to captivity and prayed he would not be foolish enough to resist his captors. He wrote to his mother and instructed her to engage a good lawyer. In other circumstances he would have ridden home to protect his mother and sisters and to agitate for his father's release from prison, but for the time being his first loyalty must be with his wife.

He wondered if news of the Bolshevik coup had reached Tsar Nicholas, and asked Tatiana in his daily letter, but it seemed from her reply that she did not appreciate the implications of the change of government:

I am glad the war is over if it means no more Russians will be killed, but Papa is worried that the Baltic lands currently occupied by the Germans may be lost in the peace negotiations. He has requested that he might be included in the discussions . . .

After that she changed the subject:

Did I tell you we are now keeping five pigs in an old stable in the yard? They are very sweet and come when called, like dogs. Ortipo barks at them but is too much of a coward to venture close. I must not let myself become over fond of them, as I suspect they are intended for our table this winter . . . We also have chickens, turkeys and ducks, and Father has dug a duck pond for them. I have begun to reread the works of Tolstoy, since it seems we are stuck here for the next few months. I'd forgotten what a great story-teller he is! Do you like *Anna Karenina*? We are also rehearsing a production of Chekhov's *Three Sisters* to enter-tain our parents. I am the director and play the role of Masha. I only wish you could come to watch . . .

Dmitri was astonished by Tatiana's everyday tone. Did she realise that the nation was rift in two? He supposed that in captivity her horizons had narrowed; either that or she was putting a remark-ably brave face on events. He thought he had grown to know her rather well but found it impossible to guess what she was thinking deep down. Was she simply being cheerful for his sake?

Dmitri wrote to several aristocrat friends asking what they planned to do about this so-called workers' revolution. Surely they wouldn't give up their property without a struggle? It was agony to be stuck in Tobolsk, powerless to help resist the coup, but he couldn't leave Tatiana when every day he felt the danger increasing, like a dark shadow sweeping across the land, set to envelop them completely.

20th December 1917

Malama sweetheart,

The temperature today is minus nineteen and the windows are draughty, so I am huddled in my warmest coat and shawl, and have tempted Ortipo to sit on my lap, where she acts like a hot water bottle. Still my freezing fingers make it hard to hold the pen so forgive me if my writing is shaky. We are occupied with making Christmas presents since we cannot buy them. I am painting bookmarks to give to all our guards here, and embroidering or knitting gifts for the family. What can I make for you, my dearest? Would you like a scarf or some socks? Be sure you are in church for the Christmas Day service so we can see each other. I do love Christmas. As I write, my nostrils are full of the citrusy scent of a balsamic fir Christmas tree that stands just outside my bedroom door.

Dmitri was in his usual place in Blagoveschensky Church for the Christmas Day service. These brief occasions when he could be in close proximity to his beloved were like a balm to his anxious soul. The Romanov family arrived, huddled in their coats and mufflers, and Tatiana had a smile in her eyes as she passed him and pushed a tightly wrapped parcel into his hands. No one noticed in the bustle of worshippers and he quickly secreted it inside his coat. He had earlier given Trina his Christmas gift for Tatiana – an amethyst brooch he had purchased from his landlord's wife – and as she unfastened her coat he could see that she wore it on her collar. She turned and caught his eye.

The Christmas service was interminable. It was conducted by a new priest and when he called out the names of those taking communion, he used the old, forbidden title 'Tsar Nicholas II, Emperor and Autocrat of all Russias'. A gasp went around the church and the guards standing by the doors glanced at each other. This priest obviously did not know that monarchy had been abolished and the former tsar was now referred to as Citizen Romanov. Again, when it came to the Tsarina, he called her 'Empress Consort of all Russias'. There was a stirring movement in the crowd and more soldiers filed in. Dmitri fingered the knife he always kept tucked in his belt. If the soldiers became violent, he planned to grab Tatiana and bustle her from the church and out of harm's way.

All through the service, Dmitri kept an eye on the guards, but it appeared they had no orders to intervene. At the end, they surrounded the Romanov family and herded them up the street to the Governor's House as fast as they could. Dmitri caught sight of the Tsarina's face and she seemed bewildered.

The following morning Trina brought a letter from Tatiana, and this time there was no pretence of cheerfulness.

The Bolshevik authorities are so incensed by the use of Papa and Mama's titles in church that we have been banned from attending any more services. I am desolate because it was the only chance we got to step beyond the confines of the yard and my only opportunity to see you, my precious one, up close. Without that, I don't know how I will remain optimistic.

He fingered the knitted waistcoat that had been in the parcel she slipped to him. The wool was of a rich auburn hue similar to the shade of her hair. It fitted snugly and kept him warm, almost like having her arms around him. It was lovely but at the same time it reminded him that he had no idea when – or if – he would ever feel her embrace again.

The temperature dropped still further in January, to a bitter minus twenty-nine degrees, and the skies were clear blue in the brief hours of daylight. The Romanovs built a snow mountain in the yard and enjoyed tobogganing down it when they were allowed outside. Dmitri offered to walk the smelly mongrel kept by a neighbour of his landlady's, as it gave him an excuse to loiter outside the Governor's House listening to their shrieks. When Tatiana stood on top of the mountain she could see over the fence and wave to him, sometimes even calling a word or two. Olga called greetings as well, and the younger children waved. There were moments when the situation almost felt normal, until the reality struck when a guard yelled at him to move along.

As he made friends in the town of Tobolsk, Dmitri realised there were many monarchists there. Hushed conversations in the town's teahouses frequently concerned plots to rescue the Romanovs and spirit them overseas. He listened hard, then walked out to inspect waterways or cattle roads that had been mentioned as possible escape routes. Some of them seemed as though they might be useful once the thaw came. The guards around the house were careless and there were windows of opportunity when the family could have been rescued with minimal manpower.

That all changed on the 14th of February when the guards at the Governor's House were replaced and a new, stricter regime put in place. Tatiana wrote that the old guards were accused of being too friendly with the family and the new ones were much sterner. They wasted no time in destroying the snow mountain and reducing the income the Romanovs were allowed.

'Only 600 roubles a month,' Tatiana complained in a letter. 'How can anyone live on that? We shall have to let ten servants go and cut back severely on our food consumption.'

Dmitri wondered if she knew that unskilled workers in Russia earned an average of 200 roubles a year on which to feed their families? Probably not. She had likely spent as much on Ortipo's Fabergé dog tag without a second thought. It wasn't her fault: it was the way she had been raised. He had also grown up with servants but being in the army had made him self-sufficient, so he was able to do his own laundry and prepare an edible meal. Tatiana would not know where to start. She was a skilled nurse, though. Her talents were currently directed to looking after little Alexei, who was bedridden after a fall on the snow mountain.

I have to massage his limbs several times a day to stop him getting cramp, but unless I am very gentle it can aggravate

135

his swollen joints and he cries out with a sound that is unbearable. He is a stoic boy but has known more pain in his short life than most know in a lifetime.

The cold seemed to linger even as the days grew longer. Dmitri filled his time by trying to plan the rescue, reading borrowed books, walking the dog, meeting friends and writing his daily letter to Tatiana.

Under the new regime she was no longer allowed to step onto the balcony or wave from the windows, so they had no way of seeing each other in the flesh but fortunately Trina was still able to transport their letters, secreting them carefully at the bottom of her basket.

Dmitri's world shrank, just as the Romanovs' had shrunk, just as the world of all the people of Tobolsk shrank during the winter months. And then came a communication from the outside world: a telegram from his sister Valerina. He ripped it open and felt the floor dissolve under his feet as he read: FATHER DIED OF HEART ATTACK IN PRISON STOP MOTHER AND I STAYING IN GAMEKEEPER'S COTTAGE AS HOUSE TAKEN OVER BY BOLSHEVIKS STOP.

He felt as though he had been punched in the gut. He sank to his heels and buried his face in his hands. It seemed impossible that his indomitable father could be dead, no longer breathing, eyes closed, his flesh stiff and cold. While their relationship had always been more formal than loving, Dmitri was proud of his father. He had hoped that his wedding to a grand duchess would augur a new closeness between them, when his father would learn to respect him in return – but it wasn't to be.

Suddenly a suspicion entered his head: the general was a tough man, and very fit at just sixty years of age. Had he really suffered a heart attack or was this regime executing its high-ranking opponents? There was no way of knowing but the idea his father could have been murdered made him sick with rage.

That night in bed, the tears came and he wept with frustration that he could not travel from Tobolsk to attend the funeral and comfort his mother and sisters, that he could not pay his final respects. Through his tears he remembered his father chastising him for being too emotional. 'Emotion is a weakness,' he'd often said. Perhaps that was true. But Dmitri felt unbearably sad that he and his father hadn't ever got to know each other – and now they never would.

Chapter Twenty-Three

Tobolsk, Siberia, spring 1918

In April, the ice covering the Tobol and Irtysh rivers began to thaw, great chunks breaking off with a cracking that sounded like gunfire and floating downstream before melting to slush. The first boats arrived, bringing fruits, vegetables, fuel, newspapers, and among the passengers was a new commissar tasked with the care of the Romanov family – a man of around thirty-five years of age named Vasily Yakovlev. Dmitri was slightly acquainted with him from the winter of 1916–17 when they were both at the front in Moldavia, and he knew him to be a cultured, well-connected man, despite his newfound Bolshevik credentials. He gave it a couple of days then went to the local soviet building, where the workers' councils met, to greet him.

Yakovlev rose from behind his desk to shake Dmitri's hand but was suspicious in his greeting. 'What on earth brings you to this part of the world, Malama?'

Dmitri sat down. He had a story prepared. 'I am planning to make excursions into the surrounding countryside and test for minerals. And you?'

Yakovlev smiled, clearly not believing him for a second, and answered: 'I am in command of the Tobolsk Red Guard.'

'How odd. Why do they need someone of your seniority in such a small town?' Dmitri asked, all innocence. 'Is it because the Romanovs are imprisoned here?'

'I expect that's the case,' Yakovlev replied, and they exchanged a look.

There was a moment's silence before Dmitri asked, 'What do you think will become of them?'

Yakovlev narrowed his eyes. 'I have heard Citizen Romanov will stand trial on charges of treason, and his wife will join him if her correspondence with Rasputin proves incriminating. Investigators are combing through letters found in his lodgings and collecting evidence that they colluded with the Germans.'

Dmitri nodded, as if in approval. 'And the children?'

'I don't think it has been decided . . .' He gave Dmitri a sharp look. 'I suppose you must know them from your time in the imperial guard.'

'Hardly at all.' Dmitri shook his head quickly. 'They wouldn't talk to the likes of me.'

Yakovlev nodded, slowly. 'And yet you are here.'

'By coincidence. Still, I am glad that a man of your sensibilities is in charge and that their fate is not left to the mob.'

'Indeed.' They looked at each other and Dmitri thought the beginnings of an understanding flashed between them.

He rose. 'I must let you do your work, Yakovlev, but I hope we can talk again soon. If there is anything I can do to help you in your work, you need only ask.'

He left the building feeling slightly reassured. A man who read books, who enjoyed theatre – surely such a man had a compassionate soul? And even if the Tsar and Tsarina were tried for treason, even if they were found guilty, there could be no such charges against their children, against Tatiana. She and Olga were the White Sisters of the War; Tatiana's had been the most popular picture postcard. The public wouldn't stand for any harm coming to them.

*

Two days later, Yakovlev sought Dmitri at his lodgings and asked if he would like to take a stroll along the Tobol River. Dmitri grabbed his coat and hat and came straight away. The ground was marshy underfoot, the trees black and leafless, the river high and fast-flowing with snow melt from the mountains. The roar of the water forced them to raise their voices as at first they talked of their families. Dmitri felt choked when Yakovlev expressed his sympathies on the death of his father.

Once they had passed the edge of town and there was no one in sight they began to talk of the Revolution, and Yakovlev told him that aristocrats across the country had lost their lands and possessions. There had been fierce resistance in Moscow, and both Ukraine and Estonia had declared themselves independent republics, but elsewhere local soviets were exerting their influence and crushing opposition.

'Why do you work for them?' Dmitri asked.

'I am an army officer; this is my life. Besides, I hope to be able to exert some influence to moderate the extremists.'

'I hope that may be the case but what I hear makes me gloomy.'

They were silent for a while, each with their own thoughts, when Yakovlev mentioned, almost casually, 'There is a reason why I was sent here at this time. The Romanovs are to be moved soon to a secret destination and I am to supervise their transfer.'

Dmitri's chest tightened. 'Will they be safe in this destination, wherever it is?'

'I am not convinced they would be safe in the place that has been suggested,' Yakovlev continued carefully, 'so I am considering taking them to Omsk instead. Do you know Omsk? A very pleasant town.' He walked with his eyes downcast, not meeting Dmitri's surprised glance. He knew that Omsk was not under Bolshevik control and wondered at Yakovlev's motives in telling him this.

'When must they leave?' he asked.

'Ah, that is a secret,' Yakovlev continued, 'but it will be soon. Later this month, probably. That should give time for plans to be put in place.' His tone was strange. He would not state his intentions outright but it was clear he hoped Dmitri would pick up on his subtext.

'I should think plans could be made in that time,' he agreed, and Yakovlev nodded and murmured, 'Good. I hope so. Perhaps it would be doing our new leaders a favour if circumstances prevented them from showing their worst face to the watching world.'

It couldn't be clearer, Dmitri thought. He was asking him to arrange a rescue from Omsk.

'How is your mineral hunting, my friend?' Yakovlev continued in a brighter tone.

'Very fruitful,' Dmitri agreed. 'I am certainly glad I came.'

They chatted about old acquaintances from wartime, about the peace treaty that had surrendered the Baltic states to Germany, and about the slow rise in temperature as spring arrived in Siberia. They acted for all the world as if this were an innocent meeting between two old army comrades but Dmitri knew there was an underlying agenda in which each would play a role.

As soon as they parted, he hurried to send a telegram to Malevich saying that the cargo they had discussed would be arriving in Omsk before the end of the month and asking if he could deal with its onward dispatch. Suddenly, rescuing the Romanovs seemed a real possibility. From Omsk, they could be spirited by automobile to Crimea and taken by boat to Constantinople without having to pass through Bolshevik-held territory. It was a perfect location.

His heart sang and he longed to tell Tatiana, but it was too dangerous to risk putting it in a letter. The less she knew, the safer she would be.

Chapter Twenty-Four

Tobolsk, Siberia, April 1918

Dearest Malama,

We had a visit yesterday evening from the very charming Commander Yakovlev. Papa trusts him and I hope he is right to do so. He tells us that we are to be moved but yet again he will not say where, although he hinted we would go north and west. The trouble is that Alexei is not well enough for the journey. He has a haemorrhage in his groin, which has been causing excruciating pain. Papa explained this and Yakovlev tried to overrule him but after seeing Alexei with his own eyes he reluctantly agreed that some of us may stay behind to nurse him. Mama was torn: should she go with her husband or stay with her sick son? Eventually she decided that Papa needs her most, so Olga, Anastasia and I will remain behind with Alexei, until he is sufficiently recovered.

Dmitri gasped with horror – 'No!' She should have told him Alexei was ill. Why had she not? He supposed she was trying to spare him from worry, just as he had spared her by not telling her of his father's death, but it ruined his plans. He snatched up his pen to reply:

My love, I beg you to reconsider. It is essential that your family stick together at a time like this. Believe me when I tell you I have reasons that I cannot share in a letter. Please do not be alarmed but consider whether it might be possible to make Alexei comfortable enough to travel with cushions spread all around him. Any comforts that would help, you can rely on me to find. Please do this for me, Tatiana. Please keep the family together.

She replied that she was alarmed by the tone of his note but maintained that it would be impossible to move her brother. Dmitri clutched his head in despair. If only he could see her face to face for just one minute, he could explain this was their only hope of rescue. But it was impossible.

He quickly sent a telegram to Malevich, who had already arrived in Omsk, telling him that the cargo they had discussed was being sent in two batches. Would there be any way to keep the first batch safe until the second arrived in a month or two? Malevich replied that it would be difficult but he would endeavour to do as he was asked.

Dmitri had planned to travel close behind the Romanovs and to help with the operation to smuggle them out of Omsk and overseas. Once they were on board ship, he hoped to have time to visit his mother and sisters and to arrange their escape as well. But now all his plans would have to be changed. A car came to pick up the Tsar and Tsarina along with their middle daughter, Maria, leaving the remaining children inside the Governor's House with their guards.

'I am reading to Alexei from *Tales of Shakespeare*,' Tatiana wrote immediately after the departure.

143

He is especially fond of *Julius Caesar*, in particular the murder scene. Why do boys relish violence?

I have a feeling from your letter that you know more than you are telling me about our parents' destination and I wish you would share it with me. I wonder if they are headed for Sweden or Norway, since Yakovlev hinted they were to go north and west? But he also said the journey would take five days, so perhaps that is too far. I hope it is not to Moscow. This new government does not seem well-disposed towards us. Do tell me what you know, Malama, or else I will be fearful.

Dmitri was more than fearful: he was terrified that when the Bolshevik government realised Yakovlev had taken the royal couple to Omsk, outside the territory they controlled, they would take revenge on the remaining children. He replied to Tatiana's letter, trying to calm her fears, but at the same time he bought several rifles and distributed them amongst monarchist sympathisers in the town in case it became necessary to storm the compound. He watched the house night and day for any change in routine that could signal trouble and he wrote to Tatiana suggesting that she stow her valuables securely in case a journey became necessary sooner than expected. If they could have spoken directly, he would have trusted her with all, but he could not risk writing anything that would give the game away should the guards decide to search Trina.

The poor communications between Tobolsk and the outside world were infuriating, especially when Dmitri received a telegram from Malevich saying that the expected cargo had not arrived in Omsk. What had gone wrong? Where were Tsar Nicholas and his wife?

Dmitri's nerves were in tatters. If only Yakovlev would send him a telegram; but he supposed he would not dare, since all telegrams were routinely read by the local soviets.

A week after the royal couple's departure from Tobolsk, Dmitri was walking along the street when he heard a news vendor crying out the day's headline: 'Tsar and Tsarina moved to Ekaterinburg.'

Ekaterinburg! There could be nowhere worse. It was a town in the country's industrial heartland, home to the most militant workers, who were fiercely hostile to the monarchy. His heart sinking, he grabbed a paper to read the story: it said the royal party had arrived in the city two days earlier and had been jeered by crowds at the railway station. They were being accommodated in the merchant Ipatiev's house, to be known henceforth as the 'House of Special Purpose'. Everything about it sounded ominous.

Dmitri wondered what had happened to Yakovlev's plan? It had obviously failed, because rather than taking the Romanovs to a city where they would be among supporters, they were now surrounded by fervent supporters of the Revolution. Dmitri punched a wall in frustration; the chance of rescue from there seemed remote.

Back at his lodgings he fingered one of the rifles he had bought. With a lover's selfishness, he wondered whether it would be possible to rescue Tatiana on her own: to sneak in by night, rouse her from her bed on some pretext and spirit her away. But he knew she would never forgive him. She would be furious at being tricked and desperate to return to her family.

Was she safe inside the Governor's House without her father's protection? Would the guards treat her with respect? He wrote telling her where her parents and Maria were staying and asking if all went well for them. 'If you have any concerns, I will immediately make my status known and offer my protection,' he wrote pointedly.

Tatiana wrote back in the strongest of terms:

Do not even think of it, not for one second. I need you exactly where you are. Knowing you are there is the one thing that gives me strength. If ever we are threatened,

Trina will let you know. For now we are treated well enough, although the food is poor and Alexei does not have all the medicines he needs. The warmer weather gives me hope that there are better times ahead. I miss you with a constant ache. I sometimes think it must be even harder to be you than it is to be me, because you are alone while I have my siblings. But this is how it must be for us. Only think how much sweeter it will be, having experienced this hardship, when we are finally together once more.

Dmitri hurled his boot across the room. It was unbearable for a man of action, a soldier, to be unable to help the women he loved most in the world. He was failing his mother and sisters because he dare not leave Tatiana, and he was failing Tatiana because he had not managed to rescue her family and get them out of Russia after more than a year of house arrest. Reluctantly he had to accept that this was how it had to be for now, but it made him feel like a failure as a husband, a son and a brother.

Chapter Twenty-Five

Lake Akanabee, New York State, late August 2016

Dmitri Yakovlevich was never far from Kitty's thoughts as she worked on the cabin or sat by the lakeshore, gazing out across the dazzling beauty of the wilderness. What had brought him to live here? Why was he alone? Had he found contentment in the tranquillity? She wondered yet again why her mother had never mentioned there was a writer in the family, even when Kitty had told her of her own ambitions to write. Surely she must have realised she would be interested? But then her mother had never encouraged her to write: it wasn't a prestigious enough career for her only daughter.

She thought back to the suitcase full of family photos in her bedroom closet in London. Were there any of Dmitri? She had dipped into it when looking for pictures to reproduce on the order of service at her parents' joint funeral but had never explored further. She knew there were albums stretching back through the twentieth century from both her mother's and her father's sides of the family and wished she had them there, to study. If only there were someone she trusted who would send that suitcase out to her without any questions asked. Someone who had a key to the house. Someone who wouldn't tell Tom.

All of a sudden the answer came to her: their cleaner, Marion, was a dependable type. She would do it. The more she thought about it, the more compelling the idea became. Kitty leapt into her car and drove to the vacation park. While her mobile phone charged up, she opened her email account and sent a mail to the enquiries address at Random House publishers in New York, asking if there were any remaining members of staff who had known her great-grandfather. She explained that he had been published by them between the 1930s and 1970s. An automatic reply bounced back saying her enquiry would be dealt with shortly.

She switched on her mobile phone, ignoring all the bleeps indicating texts and voicemail messages, and dialled Marion's number. It was early evening back in London and when she answered, Kitty could hear her children squabbling in the background. She had no idea how Tom had explained her absence to Marion and decided not to offer any more information than she had to.

'I'm out in the States and need a case sent over by courier. Do you think you could do that? And would you mind not telling Tom? It's a surprise.' She held her breath.

'Of course,' Marion replied. She was a single mother whose husband had abandoned her and she did not have a high opinion of men in general. 'Let me find a pen.' There was a pause and a shuffling sound before her voice came back on the line. 'Fire away!'

Kitty described the whereabouts of the suitcase. It was an old brown leather one but appeared sturdy enough and just had to be labelled with the address. There was a Fedex office locally and Kitty would call them to pay with her credit card. Marion would have to fill out the export forms and get a receipt.

Marion wrote down the address of the vacation park, then asked: 'Is it urgent? I wasn't due at the house till Friday but could stop by tomorrow if you want.'

'Oh please ... that would be amazing.' Suddenly Kitty wondered whether Karren had taken advantage of her absence to move in with Tom. Did she ever spend the night there, in her bed? Would Marion tell her if that was the case? Did she want to know?

'Are you OK?' Marion asked.

Kitty paused, then decided to leave it. 'I'm fine,' she said.

The suitcase arrived at the vacation park two days later and Kitty couldn't wait to get back to the cabin and examine the contents. Marion had wrapped so much tape around it that she needed to cut it open with a Stanley knife. Inside there was a mixture of photograph albums, framed portraits and loose snaps, all muddled together. No care had been taken as to the order, everything shoved in higgledy-piggledy with the decades mixed up, so Kitty began by sorting them into piles according to age and which side of the family they came from.

Once she had them in rough order, she focused on the oldest, sepia-coloured prints from her mother's birth family. Someone had helpfully scribbled names in pencil on the backs of some: 'Rosa, Nicholas and Marta, Coney Island, 1937' – that was three years after they arrived in America. There was an amusement park in the background and they looked like any family on a fun day out. She imagined the photo must have been taken by Dmitri. Another showed the children peering out from the observation deck of the Empire State Building, looking slightly older. Kitty tried to remember her grandmother's date of birth and reckoned it must have been around 1925 or 1926. Marta looked maybe thirteen or fourteen in the picture, with skinny legs, straight brown hair held in place by an Alice band, and teeth too big for her face. Nicholas was taller, his hair cut short, wearing long trousers and an open-necked shirt.

Marta seemed more popular than Nicholas; in these childhood pictures she was usually surrounded by groups of friends, and as she got older there were boyfriends – dozens of them, it seemed. Her grandmother hadn't been a great beauty but she was always smiling or laughing in her pictures, and she dressed with great style. Even as an old lady, Kitty remembered her wearing tailored trouser suits that made her look years younger than her age, often accompanied by a man's trilby hat.

Many pictures showed dark-haired Rosa with friends, smiling in the garden of a weatherboard house or sitting on the sofa with a dog by her side. Kitty had to search long and hard before she found one of Rosa with a man who looked as though he might be her husband, an arm around her waist. He was very handsome, with slicked-back hair and a white-toothed smile, like a matinee idol. Was this Dmitri? He was tall and well dressed, his posture erect. She found one more shot of the same man, this time standing in his garden, leaning on a hoe, with the same straight, almost military posture, although his hair was unruly from the effort of toil. She felt sure this was her great-grandfather and strained to make out details of his face: a high forehead, brows like a shelf beneath which dark eyes stared out, sharp cheekbones, full lips. A face that looked as though it had been carved from hardwood. Did he have a melancholy air or was she projecting? She thought she could see a family resemblance with her and her mother, perhaps in the shape of the face, the chin.

Why were there not more photographs of him? The answer came to her that in those days men were the ones wielding the camera. Even two generations later, her father had been the family photographer, quipping that her mother always cut off the tops of heads.

Amongst the photos there were postcards from holidays in Switzerland, Cornwall, Santa Barbara and Vancouver Island, with a variety of signatures, the ink old and faded. There were letters from people who appeared to be family friends, telling news of children and grandchildren, illnesses suffered and house moves. Kitty didn't recognise any of the names.

At the bottom of the suitcase she found a battered, ancient-looking notebook with black leather covers. Inside, every page was covered top to bottom in handwriting in what she assumed were Russian characters. Straight away she guessed it must be Dmitri's. Perhaps they were notes for his novels. The writing was small and incredibly neat but she could not make head nor tail of it. Why keep this notebook but not more of the many notes and manuscripts he must have produced during his writing career? He must have had a reason, and Kitty decided she was going to find out. If only she had known her great-grandfather; somehow she felt they would have had a lot in common. Maybe this note-book would help her get closer to understanding him.

Kitty drove to the vacation park coffeehouse for the second time that day and opened her laptop to search for Russian to English translators. There was one called Vera Quigley in the town of Gloversville, about seventy miles away. She called and made an appointment to drop by the following afternoon.

Chapter Twenty-Six

Gloversville, New York State, 1st September 2016

Vera Quigley lived in a tiny two-storey house with a door that opened directly from the street. Inside it was like a dolls' house, with bookshelves lining the walls from floor to ceiling and furniture crammed in so tightly there was barely space to squeeze between. She appeared to be in her sixties and she was short – under five feet, Kitty reckoned – with a cap of very soft, fine baby hair that looked as though it might recently have regrown following chemotherapy. Vera waved Kitty to an armchair and as she sat, she could feel the springs through the fabric.

'Are you Russian-born?' Kitty asked, glancing round at a set of matryoshka dolls laid out on a shelf in height order.

'No, my parents came here in 1917, but I was brought up bilingual. I used to work in the Slavonic Languages Department at Yale but moved here when I retired and now I do a bit of translation on the side . . . Can I offer you some lemonade?'

A jug stood ready on a side table and Kitty was happy to accept because it was a hot day and her mouth was dry.

'This is the notebook I told you about.' She passed it over. 'I think it may have belonged to my great-grandfather, who was a novelist.'

Vera took the notebook, put on a pair of reading glasses and opened the first page. 'This is a diary,' she said straight away. 'These short lines' – she held it out to show Kitty – 'are dates. Do you see? That one reads March fifteenth, Wednesday.'

'Which year?'

Vera looked at the front cover of the notebook. 'I can't see a year. Would you like me to translate a little so we can discover what it is about?'

'Oh, yes, please!'

Vera opened it to the first page and spoke slowly: 'February eighteenth, Sunday. We had *obednitza* at 11.30.' She glanced up to see if Kitty had understood – 'That's a liturgy in the Russian Orthodox Church' – before continuing. 'Then we worked outside in the garden, digging over the soil. A letter from the outside world made me laugh with M's description of his landlady's cabbage soup tasting as if she had boiled up some dirty stockings from her laundry bag. He writes that he is teaching tricks to a foul-smelling mongrel with traces of so many breeds that it is impossible to guess its parentage. The dog is a fast learner who will wait in a corner for several minutes until given a signal, upon which it will retrieve a ball and drop it in his lap in return for a crust of bread. It would put to shame certain other dogs of our acquaintance!'

Vera stopped and looked up to see if this made sense to Kitty.

'I wonder why he talks about a "letter from the outside world". Where was he?'

Vera shrugged. 'I don't know. Shall I carry on?'

'Why not try a later passage?'

Vera flicked to the middle of the book and chose a page: '30th April, Monday. Olga and I are learning to make bread, under the watchful eye of Trina.'

'Who is Olga? And who is Trina?' Kitty wondered out loud.

Vera shrugged and continued: 'It seems you must knead the dough for at least twenty minutes to get air into it, then let it rest for half an hour before moulding it into shape. Any activity that distracts us from missing Mama, Papa and Maria is welcome, and I expect that in my next life the skill of breadmaking will prove useful.'

'In my next life?" Kitty wondered, then answered her own question. 'Perhaps this was written at a time when Dmitri was planning to emigrate. He lived in Berlin between the wars.'

Vera flicked a few pages further: '4th June, Monday. We are all furious with Maria, who has been fraternising with the youngest guard, Anton, the one with the crooked nose. She thinks it is a joke, but it encourages them to toy with the rest of us. I had to push Anton hard tonight as he grabbed my breast on the way to the latrine, and he made a crude sound with his tongue, taunting me.' Vera looked up at Kitty. 'It appears this was written by a woman.'

Kitty was surprised. 'Who can it be? And why was there a guard? Where were they?'

Vera read on: 'I feel a growing sense of dread that we will die in this godforsaken house with whitewashed windows, denied even one ray of sunlight, and that I will never see my dearest love again . . .'

'It sounds as though they are in captivity. I wonder why.'

Vera gasped as she read the next bit. 'Tomorrow is Anastasia's seventeenth birthday.' She looked at Kitty. 'Do these names mean anything to you? Olga, Maria and Anastasia?'

'No. Should they?'

Vera skimmed down the page and translated another bit: 'Alexei is being very brave but he has not been well enough for us to wheel him into the garden since we arrived here.' She looked at Kitty. 'I suppose it could be a forgery.'

'A forgery of what? Who do you think they are?'

Vera frowned. 'These are the names of the Romanov imperial family, who were imprisoned after the Revolution in February 1917.'

'Surely it can't be!' Kitty racked her brains, trying to remember her history lessons. 'Why would Dmitri have a journal belonging to one of them?'

Vera placed the notebook on a side table as though it were a precious relic and stood up. 'I think I should wear gloves when handling this. It could be a document of historic importance.' She walked across the room and retrieved a pair of white cotton gloves from a drawer.

'Really? Do you think there's a chance it is genuine?'

'We know both the elder girls and their parents kept diaries. They are held in the State Archives of the Russian Federation but parts have been released in translation and this is remarkably similar in tone and content. That description of whitewashed windows sounds like the Ipatiev House in Ekaterinburg. It's well documented that Maria flirted with a guard there and the others were furious with her.'

Kitty was stunned and could barely take it in. 'What happened to them?'

'They were murdered in the early hours of July the seventeenth, 1918.' Vera sat down again and opened the diary to its last page. 'This diary finishes on the fourteenth, a Sunday.' She reached for an iPad that Kitty hadn't noticed before. Somehow it seemed incongruous in the dusty, bookish surroundings. She tapped on it for a few minutes then said, 'Yes, the fourteenth of July 1918 was a Sunday. Of course, there will have to be many tests if this is to be verified as genuine.'

Kitty was amazed. 'Whose diary do you think it is?'

'It must be Tatiana's. All the others have been mentioned.' She tapped on the iPad again then handed it to Kitty. There was a picture on the screen of a very elegant girl with short wavy hair worn in a side parting, dressed in an ankle-length ivory gown covered in embroidery, and wearing several necklaces and bracelets. She looked haughty, regal and suspicious, as if she was not someone who found it easy to trust.

'She's beautiful,' Kitty said. 'How tragic that she was killed!'

Vera took back the iPad and did another search. 'Look at that!' she exclaimed. 'That's Tatiana's handwriting. It's very sharp and graphic, with up and down strokes that are unusual for the period. It's identical to the writing in your diary, don't you think?'

Kitty looked from one to the other. The figures were written in the same way; they were indistinguishable. 'But why would my great-grandfather have had Tatiana's diary?'

'There are a number of possibilities,' Vera mused. 'A week after the murders, the Ipatiev House was opened to the public and sightseers wandered in and helped themselves to souvenirs. Dmitri could have been one of them, or it could have been passed on to him by someone else. I suppose he could even have been one of the guards at the house.'

'You mean one of the murderers?' Instinctively Kitty felt that couldn't be true. Any man who had written love stories as moving as the ones she had read could never have been a killer.

'No, historians are pretty sure they know who all the murderers were. Yakov Yurovsky, the head of the guards, and eight of his men.' She tapped on the iPad and read out the names when she found them: 'Ermakov, Kudrin, Medvedev, Nikulin, Kabanov, Netrebin, Vaganov and Jan Tsel'ms. He picked the most cold-blooded men he could muster. I believe several other guards refused to be part of it.'

Kitty shuddered and hoped Dmitri had not been involved. But if not, how did he come to have the diary? Suddenly she remembered the pendant and took it off to show Vera. 'I found this under my great-grandfather's cabin and a jeweller told me it is Fabergé.'

Vera peered at it. 'Michael Wigström, the Romanovs' favourite workmaster. It's lovely.' She handed it back. 'Why don't I lend you a couple of books so you can read about the family?' She rose and her eyes roamed along a shelf until she found what she was looking for. She picked out one book, then another.

'That's very kind. And would you consider translating the diary?'

Vera hesitated. 'My services don't come cheap. Why not donate it to a library or university and they will pay for the translation?'

'I don't want to give it to anyone else. It's one of the few things I have left of my great-grandfather, a memento of the Russian heritage I have only recently discovered. If I pay for the translation, what sort of cost are we talking about?'

Vera sat down to estimate the number of pages then sucked her lip and finally quoted two thousand dollars. She thought it would take her two to three weeks.

Kitty didn't have to think for long. Her great-grandfather had kept this diary for a reason and she was sure he would want her to read it. She could use some of the money she had inherited from him, which was sitting in her current account. 'I'd like to go ahead, if you're sure you want to . . .'

'Are you kidding?' Vera grinned, suddenly looking much younger. 'I can think of nothing I'd like more. What a fascinating project!'

Kitty held out her hand and they shook. 'It's a deal.'

As she drove back to Lake Akanabee, her mind whizzed through all the possible reasons why her great-grandfather might have had the diary of a Russian grand duchess in his possession. Had he known the family? Had he found it after their murder? Why had he kept it rather than donating it to a library? Or was it a clever forgery that he planned to use in a novel?

She wished Tom were there. He had a logical mind and often surprised her by suggesting answers she hadn't thought of. She liked the fact that their brains worked so differently.

And then she remembered the photo-message on his phone and grimaced. *You bastard, Tom. Why did you have to ruin everything?*

Chapter Twenty-Seven

Ekaterinburg, Russia, May 1918

Three weeks after the departure of the Tsar and Tsarina, Trina came to Dmitri's lodgings to tell him that Alexei had been judged fit for the journey and the remaining Romanovs were being taken to join their parents in Ekaterinburg. Dmitri packed his belongings and paid his landlady an extra week's rent to apologise for the lack of notice then hurried up to the Governor's House. Some old-fashioned *tarantass* carriages were standing by, presumably to take them on the first leg of the journey. Dmitri rushed to a horse dealer and bought himself a mount on which he could follow.

He watched as the royal party, twenty-seven of them including servants and tutors, were escorted into the carriages, along with the three dogs: Ortipo, Alexei's Spaniel, Joy, and the family's Pekingese, Jimmy. Alexei was carried out by a manservant with Tatiana close by, soothing him. She didn't look up, too concerned for her brother.

Dmitri rode behind the carriages, keeping out of sight amongst the trees and sleeping rough whenever the party stopped at an inn for the night. It was a bone-rattling journey on rough roads and Dmitri feared for poor Alexei, for whom every jolt would mean excruciating pain. His glimpses of Tatiana showed her looking harassed and anxious and he yearned to rush out and throw his arms around her. She was supporting everyone else and there was no one to support her.

Five days later they arrived at the railway junction of Tyumen, and Dmitri could see the girls looked bewildered as they were ushered onto a train, which had none of the comforts they were used to. The royal train had been like a palace, with sumptuous beds and sofas, chandeliers, dining tables and individual reading lamps. This train, by contrast, had hard seats in unadorned carriages leading off a bare corridor, and members of the public were also permitted to travel on it. He made sure Tatiana spotted him and caught the look of relief on her face when she realised he was travelling with them, although he couldn't get closer than two carriages away from the royal party.

The train departed with a screech and the air filled with the smell of smoke, while black soot smeared the windows. Dmitri tried to walk along the corridor to look in on Tatiana but was prevented by guards. When night fell he lay awake picturing her lying on exactly the same type of bench as him and wondered if she would get any sleep. Were their meals better than the tasteless soup and rough bread he had managed to procure? He hoped so.

On arrival in Ekaterinburg, he alighted from the train and watched as a contingent arrived from the local soviet. Crowds of townspeople jostled, eager for a glimpse of the royal visitors, and Dmitri mingled with them, trying not to attract attention. Several hours passed, during which officials came and went, before at last the royal children emerged with just three servants. It seemed the rest of the party were being left behind. They were instructed to carry their own bags, and Dmitri seethed with helpless rage as Olga, Tatiana and Anastasia struggled to lift them. The sole manservant couldn't help because he was carrying Alexei. As they staggered out towards the road, the crowd began to jeer. Dmitri yearned to remonstrate, to rush forward and carry their burdens for them, but had to stand by powerless as Tatiana rallied the others and they walked up the hill, heads held high, surrounded by Red Guards.

The first sight of the Ipatiev House was a shock. It was much smaller than the Governor's House and was surrounded by a tall fence just a few feet from the walls, so there would be hardly any space for them to walk outdoors. From what Dmitri could gather, it was built in the modern style but the windows were painted white to prevent anyone seeing in or out, and there were guards with machineguns sitting in sentry posts at every corner. This really was a prison and the gaolers were taking no chances. Tatiana turned and gave him one last haunting look before disappearing inside.

Dmitri walked around the house, noting where the guard posts were located, and listening for any sounds from within. It was unseasonably cold for May, with flurries of snow falling, and he supposed that might stop the family from stepping out of doors to stretch their legs. There was a knothole in the wood at one point and he bent to put his eye to it but was unable to see anything except the walls of the house with those spookily blank windows, as though the inhabitants had been erased.

He had to find lodgings but this time he judged it best to choose somewhere remote, in case he was able to rescue the family. He walked until he found an alehouse, where he asked if anyone knew of a farmer with a cottage to rent and a horse for sale; he had left his last horse in Tyumen when they got on the train. Word was passed around and finally it seemed someone had a friend who had a cousin who might be able to help. The friend's cousin was sent for and he arrived leading a horse, then took Dmitri to the outskirts of town where a little cottage nestled on the edge of a pine forest. A price was agreed, the horse was tethered, and Dmitri went inside to sit alone in the gathering gloom.

He felt sick with fear that Tatiana should be held in such a place amongst such people. Trina was one of the staff left behind on the train so he had no way of getting letters in or out. His wife was trapped behind that tall barricade by heavily armed guards in a town where there was only hostility towards her family. The end was drawing near. He could feel it in his bones. There wasn't much time left for him to find a way of saving her.

Next morning, Dmitri rode around Ekaterinburg getting his bearings. The town sat on the eastern side of the Ural Mountains and he could see scars on the towering rockfaces caused by mining. He knew they dug for precious stones here: the kind of stones the Romanovs had once used for their jewellery and Fabergé eggs without giving a thought to the source. There were some beautiful buildings – churches, cathedrals, theatres and private houses, built in the classical style – but there were also many factories spewing out smoke, noisy paper mills and foul-smelling tanneries where the working population earned their crust. Voznesensky Prospekt, on which the Ipatiev House stood, was the main thoroughfare. Dmitri rode past the house but even on horseback he was unable to see over the barricade and he could hear no signs of life from within.

Four houses down the hill, a brass plaque mounted on a wall indicated the British consulate and he pulled up his horse. Might it be worth enquiring within?

Dmitri was ushered into a hallway where he sat in a leather armchair for around twenty minutes until he was called to meet the consul, Sir Thomas Preston. He was a tall, distinguished-looking man, probably only in his thirties, with narrow eyes that scrutinised Dmitri as he entered the room. Dmitri introduced himself as a former member of the royal escort, one who was much concerned with the Romanov family's welfare, and asked if there was anything the consul could do to help them.

Sir Thomas tapped a pen on the desk, regarding him with regret. 'I make daily enquiries regarding the condition of the Tsar and Tsarina and will now include the grand duke and duchesses, but I probably have no more information than you. This morning I received a delegation from the staff members who still remain on board the train with nowhere to go and I am endeavouring to secure accommodation for them – although it appears some have been imprisoned. Information is sketchy.'

Dmitri was impatient. 'Can't the British government do something to help? These are relatives of King George V. I am outraged by their indifference.'

Sir Thomas pursed his lips before replying. 'Do you hear the news from the Western Front? Do you know how many are dying in the trenches? I'm afraid they are preoccupied with other matters back in London.'

Dmitri felt like shouting in frustration, but instead he buried his face in his hands and took a deep breath.

'I completely understand your alarm,' Sir Thomas continued, speaking quietly now. 'I myself am deeply worried by recent developments and if it were possible for me to assist any attempt to liberate the family without being directly accountable, then you can be assured I would do so.'

Dmitri looked up in surprise. At last an official seemed willing to help. 'My colleagues and I have formulated many plans but without success. The problem lies in freeing so many at once, including a boy who can no longer walk. And I have counted ten guard posts outside their new accommodation. It would take dozens of heavily armed men simply to get the family out of this town, never mind into safe territory.'

'Indeed,' Sir Thomas agreed. 'Let me be clear: the British government will not help in any official capacity. However, I have spoken to some British merchants who regularly trade within this region and take goods back to London, and we have discussed routes that might be used in the event of a rescue. They know ways of getting through the German naval blockade. Perhaps I should put you in touch.'

'You would do that?' Dmitri was astonished. Sir Thomas's sympathy was in complete contrast to the cold lack of interest he had encountered at the British embassy in St Petersburg. 'Why would you trust me?'

Sir Thomas smiled. 'I consider myself a reasonable judge of character after many years in this job. You took a risk in identifying yourself to me as a member of the royal escort. I could have called the local soviet and had you arrested. You'll find they are very militant in this town, so be sure to keep your counsel.'

An aide brought in a tray of tea and Sir Thomas offered Dmitri a cup. He hadn't eaten or drunk anything since the previous evening and it warmed his throat, slightly easing the tension in his ribcage.

'You are so close to the house . . . I wonder if you know of anyone who goes in and out who might be prepared to deliver messages for me?'

Sir Thomas shook his head slowly. 'I'm afraid not. Some nuns bring the family eggs and cream once a week, but their deliveries are searched with a fine-tooth comb. And a group of women go in to clean from time to time but they are recruited through the local soviet and I doubt you would find a Romanov sympathiser amongst them. It's unlikely Father Storozhev, the priest who visits to conduct Orthodox services, would risk falling out with the Bolsheviks. And otherwise, their only visitors are Red Guards. I tried to deliver a note of welcome to the Tsar and Tsarina on their arrival but was rebuffed. I'm sorry.'

Dmitri was crestfallen. How would he ever arrange a rescue if he could not communicate with Tatiana? How would he cope without their daily correspondence? Already he missed her letters, missed knowing the tiny details of her life. Were they rehearsing another play? How were her bread-making attempts progressing? These were the slender straws at which he had clutched to keep him sane, and without them he felt he was drowning in a vast sea of despair.

Chapter Twenty-Eight

Ekaterinburg, Russia, June 1918

Dmitri found excuses to walk past the Ipatiev House several times a day and gradually he worked out the family's routine. They were allowed to exercise in the garden for half an hour at eleven in the morning and then again between three and four in the afternoon. One morning when the guards did not appear to be watching, Dmitri pressed his eye to the knothole in the wooden fence and was able to catch a glimpse of the girls playing a game of tennis without a net. Tatiana was wearing a pale grey gown with a crimson-fringed shawl around her shoulders. He longed to call out but did not dare. Despite the fact that the weather had grown warmer, her mother and brother weren't there. Tsar Nicholas marched briskly up and down the bare yard, lost in thought, but Tatiana rallied her sisters to focus on the game and he could tell she was trying to keep their spirits up.

Suddenly, some instinct made her turn and look directly at the knothole. She stared hard for a moment and he blinked. Could she see his eye? Might she realise it was him? Dmitri quickly retrieved a scrap of paper from his pocket, scribbled '*Je t'adore. D.M.*', screwed it into a ball and wedged it in the hole. He walked off, swinging his arms, and ducked down a side street. Half an hour later when he walked back that way he was excited to notice that the paper had gone. Pray God Tatiana had retrieved it rather than a guard.

He returned that afternoon at four-thirty, after the Romanovs had been ushered indoors following their afternoon exercise, and saw there was a ball of paper in the knothole again. After checking that no one was watching he grabbed it and stuffed it in his pocket. He did not dare open it until he was several streets away. Fingers shaking, he uncrumpled the paper and read, in Tatiana's distinctive sloping handwriting, the words: 'All are coping as best they can but I yearn for you with all my heart. A thousand blessings upon you for following us and for giving me strength with your closeness. I adore you now and forever.'

A sob burst from Dmitri's chest and he struggled to suppress it. His beautiful, ethereal wife knew he was here and she loved him still. It was like a chink of light in a long, dark tunnel. They must be careful not to overuse the knothole as a method of communication because if they were caught, the guards might punish her and that avenue would be closed to them. He wrote explaining that in the note he left the following morning, and when there was no reply, he guessed she understood.

Dmitri felt immensely cheered by being able to write to Tatiana. He dropped by to see Sir Thomas Preston again later in the week and mentioned he had a line of communication with the Romanovs.

'Good,' Sir Thomas nodded. 'That will be useful. I also have a piece of news that may or may not be of interest. One of my staff knows a farmer, a man named Tolmachev, whose daughter is one of the cleaners at the Ipatiev House. He tells me that Tolmachev is no lover of the Bolsheviks, who have imposed all kinds of nonsensical legislation on farmers. I thought it worth noting.'

Dmitri was immediately interested. 'Will you give me directions to his farm?'

Sir Thomas took a sip of his tea. 'I think it would be best if my man introduces you. Next week some time. We'll arrange it.'

165

They spoke of the massive changes being imposed on Russian society by the new leadership – the plans for collectivisation of industry, the enhanced workers' rights – but agreed the immediate effect was that food prices were rising and the poor were struggling more than ever. Sir Thomas asked how Dmitri's own family were faring and Dmitri felt ashamed as he replied. 'My father was arrested soon after the Revolution and died in jail last winter. My mother and sisters long for me to visit but I have not . . . it seemed wrong to leave the Romanovs. My loyalties have been torn.' He blushed. 'I could not at any rate have attended my father's funeral because we were stuck in Tobolsk until the thaw. And now, it feels as though I am more needed here than at home in Lozovotka . . . If only it were closer. I feel horribly guilty every time I write yet again delaying my visit.'

Sir Thomas eyed him thoughtfully, then asked: 'Which one of the grand duchesses are you in love with?'

Dmitri was so startled, he sloshed tea into his saucer and it dripped onto his trouser leg.

Sir Thomas laughed. 'I knew I was right! Go on, which girl?'

'Tatiana,' Dmitri whispered, after a moment's hesitation. 'And she loves me too.'

'So she should, considering the sacrifices you are making for her. Well, I will do all I can to help.'

Dmitri rode out to Piotr Tolmachev's farm with a man from the consulate by the name of Henderson. The farmer was working in a wheat field. When he saw them waving he pushed through the tall stalks towards the fence.

'Have you heard the latest orders from Moscow?' he asked, continuing a conversation he appeared to have been having with Henderson at their previous meeting. 'I have to hand over all my excess wheat, beyond immediate needs, to a commissariat who will distribute it according to desert. Those doing hard manual labour will get the most, while those who do work that is not physical will scarcely get any. That means the likes of you will go hungry,' he told Henderson, glancing sideways at Dmitri.

'It sounds completely unworkable,' Henderson sympathised. He introduced Dmitri and they talked for some time about the new economic system the Bolsheviks planned to impose countrywide, with strict quotas for every commodity.

Dmitri had not heard all the details of the new plans and was horrified at how quickly the social structure of the country he loved was being ripped to shreds. Part of him accepted that the aristocracy, of which he had been a part, had no place in the twentieth century. For a privileged family to own the land and all its products by a chance of birth, and for those not so lucky in their parentage to have to work long hours on said land and pay taxes to boot, was a recipe for rebellion. But the alternative the Bolsheviks proposed seemed childishly simplistic. If land were owned communally, how would they make everyone do the same amount of work? Who would make the investment necessary to rebuild and renovate facilities, as his father had done on their estate?

The farmer's face was reddened by the elements but his eyes were a clear blue and his hair a short silver grey thatch. 'If I could afford it, I would move south to Crimea, which the Bolsheviks have been unable to take,' he said. 'My wife's family comes from there and it's good farming land. The extra hours of sunlight mean they get two harvests a year rather than our one. In Ekaterinburg we farmers are lucky to break even. I don't know how I am supposed to find "excess" to give the state.'

Dmitri bided his time until there was a lull in the conversation, then ventured: 'I hear your daughter works in the Ipatiev House. Does she tell you anything about the mood of the imperial family? I imagine they must be very fearful.'

The farmer shook his head. 'Shocking, isn't it? If the Bolsheviks have evidence the Tsar and Tsarina were traitors, let them produce it and try them in a court. If not, why can't they be released to

167

live in exile? Yelena, my daughter, says they are a charming family who are grateful for every little service. She feels sorry for them.'

'Is Yelena here today?' Dmitri asked, looking around.

'She's over tending to the pigs.' He waved an arm in the direction of a shed some hundred yards away.

They continued talking, but Dmitri kept an eye on the barn until a girl walked out carrying a bucket. He was too far off to tell much about her appearance but she looked tall and slender. She walked in their direction and as she got closer, Dmitri saw that she had shoulder-length brown hair. Suddenly a plan began to take shape in his head. Was it crazy? Could it possibly work? While Henderson and the farmer continued their discussion, he tried to think it through.

'How much money would you need to relocate to Crimea?' he asked the farmer abruptly, interrupting their conversation.

Tolmachev was puzzled. 'Why do you ask?'

'Name a figure,' Dmitri insisted, and the farmer thought for a moment then came up with the sum of two thousand roubles.

Dmitri continued: 'If I give you two thousand roubles, would you consider asking your daughter to help us communicate with the Romanovs? We are trying to get them overseas, and we need someone who has access to the house.'

The farmer was instantly suspicious. 'Who are you? How do I know you are not a Bolshevik spy?'

'I can vouch for him,' Henderson said quietly, and Dmitri gave him a quick nod of thanks.

'Well, I suppose I would consider it. What do you want her to do? Carry letters back and forth?'

'Not exactly,' Dmitri replied. 'First of all, I need you to find out the days on which she will be working over the coming weeks. Can you do that for me?'

'Two thousand, you say. In cash?'

'In cash.'

'It sounds as though we could work together, my friend.'

The farmer shook Dmitri's hand, and Dmitri could see the gleam of hope in his eyes, hope of a way out of an increasingly difficult life. This might work. It *must* work.

Dmitri rode back into town to see Thomas Preston. 'I need to talk to one of your merchants about the safest route out of Russia. Are any based in Ekaterinburg?'

Preston's eyes widened. 'You have a plan?'

'I'm working on it.'

'The best man would be Henry Armistead. Let me give him a call.' He lifted a telephone receiver and instructed the secretary on the other end to get Armistead on the line, then hung up and continued: 'Between ourselves, he was part of a plan to rescue the family from Tobolsk. They were going to travel down the River Enisei to the north coast then sail round to Murmansk on a Norwegian Arctic shipping line. The scheme had to be cancelled when they were moved to Ekaterinburg but perhaps he could arrange something similar here if you can get them out of the house.'

Dmitri spoke urgently. 'Please ask him to come as soon as he can.'

The phone rang, the connection having been made, and Sir Thomas spoke to the man on the other end, saying he had an important delivery for the Murmansk route they had spoken of before. There was a pause. 'Can you make it any sooner?' he asked. 'The opportunity could be lost by then . . . Oh, very well. And you will make the arrangements? Thirteenth of July it is.'

Dmitri's spirits fell. That was three weeks away. On the other hand, it gave him time to get the details in place. He had a lot to arrange. When he left the consulate he went to the town's telegraph office and sent a cable to his mother. APOLOGIES BUT URGENT BUSINESS KEEPS ME AWAY STOP CAN YOU WIRE TWO THOUSAND ROUBLES TO HELP CONCLUDE DEAL STOP HOPE ALL WELL STOP WILL VISIT SOON STOP YOUR SON.

Next he sent a cable to Malevich: CARGO WILL BE READY IN EKATERINBURG ON 13 JULY STOP COME A WEEK BEFORE WITH TWENTY *YELKA* STOP.

Spruce trees – *yelka* – were the largest and hardiest in the forests where they had fought during the war, and they had sometimes likened the toughest soldiers to them; he was sure Malevich would get the reference.

His stomach churning with nerves, he rode back to the cottage to think through every last detail. At last he was taking action. It felt as though he had delayed too long already and this would be his last chance.

Chapter Twenty-Nine

Lake Akanabee, New York State, September 2016

As September began, the weather at the lake was hot and sunny but with a fresh breeze. Kitty acquired a deep tan while her brown hair was streaked with blonde. She turned her attention to reconstructing the jetty, buying fresh planks of wood and tearing up the original in order to rebuild from scratch. She had always loved carpentry: the feel of the wood surrendering cleanly to her saw, the pleasure of joints that fitted snugly, the smoothness after sanding. Once the jetty was finished she took a canvas chair out there in the early evenings with a bottle of wine and sat reading the books Vera Quigley had lent her, staying until the light was low and the daytime bird calls were giving way to night prowlers.

Kitty was soon absorbed in the story of the Romanovs' life in the early years of the twentieth century, when they were the wealthiest family on the planet. She read of Alexei's haemophilia and his mother's growing dependence on Rasputin, the Siberian healer and mystic; then the suspicion that grew around them during the First World War, and the anger at their lavish lifestyles while there was famine across the country, leading to the 1917 Revolution. The book told of the family's fate in captivity, first at their home in the Alexander Palace in St Petersburg, then at the Governor's

House in Tobolsk, Siberia, and finally at the Ipatiev House in Ekaterinburg, to the east of the Ural Mountains. There was a map on which Kitty could see the mountains running north to south down the centre of Russia like a knobbly spine. She read that conditions gradually worsened for the family as Lenin and Trotsky took control of the western part of the country: their rations were reduced, many of their personal possessions stolen, and the guards treated them with increasing disrespect, forcing them to ring a bell when they wanted to use the lavatory and limiting their time outside in the yard. It was a far cry from the extravagant luxury they had been used to.

Vera Quigley had promised to send a first batch of her translation within a week, so Kitty went to the vacation park coffeehouse to check her emails. She dismissed the ones from Tom – 'Kitty, please, I LOVE YOU', 'We must talk!', 'Are you ever coming back?' Soon she would be ready to reply to him; just not quite yet. To concerned friends she sent a quick message saying that she was away for the summer in a place with no wi-fi but would be in touch on her return. As she had hoped, there was an email from Vera with a file attached and she downloaded and opened it. It seemed Vera had translated almost half the diary already, and she wrote that she was so absorbed in the task she kept forgetting to stop and eat. She was now convinced it was a genuine diary written by Grand Duchess Tatiana. Although the Romanovs had always spoken English in private, the Bolshevik guards insisted they spoke only Russian and she guessed that's why their diaries were in Russian too. She wrote that she felt immensely privileged Kitty had chosen her to translate it.

The diary began in February 1918 and ran through to July that same year. Kitty glanced at the earliest entries, in which Tatiana wrote about a play called *The Bear* she and her siblings had been rehearsing, and which they performed for their parents on the evening of the 23rd of February. She sounded like a teenager in places: 'I couldn't stop giggling when Olga began reciting Maria's lines rather than her own. It ruined the dramatic atmosphere somewhat.' Kitty googled and learned that Tatiana had turned twenty-one while in captivity, so she wasn't a child. Next she looked up Tatiana on Google images and was startled to find that there were hundreds of pictures of her: wearing a sailor suit on the royal yacht *Standart*; in formal court dress in 1913; in her nurse's uniform in 1915. The Romanovs obviously loved photography because there were pictures of them in all kinds of locations, and there were also some rather blurred home movies available online. Kitty watched one that showed the five children parading round a garden in order of height, like the Von Trapps in *The Sound of Music*, the girls wearing white dresses and wide-brimmed straw hats tied with ribbons.

Tatiana rarely smiled, Kitty noticed. She seemed more reserved than the others, more regal somehow, and she was easily the most beautiful, with her heart-shaped face, her penetrating gaze and soft cascades of brown hair. It seemed incredible that the diary found at the bottom of her suitcase of family photographs had belonged to this woman. It made Kitty feel there was a connection between them. *Who are you?* she wondered, gazing at the black and white image of a woman who had died a hundred years earlier.

Back at the cabin she read Vera's translation on her laptop. Some entries referred to people she didn't know:

March 22nd, Friday.

I wrote to Aunt Ella in Perm. We have such happy memories of the parties she took us to, but looking back we were
raw and uncouth, like country cousins. We huddled
together not knowing how to talk to anyone, and the other
guests avoided us, unsure how to introduce themselves. I
pray Ella is safe and sound, and Grandmamma, and
everyone else. I miss them all terribly. We have been

173

captives for over a year now, our fate in God's hands. I remain hopeful, although it seems our future will not be in Russia. I think I can be happy anywhere so long as M is with me.

Who was M? Kitty wondered. Her sister Maria? And which side of the family was Aunt Ella from? The entry finished:

At 8 o'clock in the morning we went to *obednitza*, and after dinner had *vechernaya* then Confessions in the hall. I read more of *Anna Karenina* before bedtime and keep wanting to give her a good shake! Vronsky was not worthy of her.

Kitty laughed. She had often felt the same way about the gullible heroine of Tolstoy's classic. As she read on, she got a sense of someone with a girlishness about her, yet at the same time a sense of responsibility for those around her. And although she didn't say as much, Kitty could tell she was anxious.

A week later another batch arrived from Vera, covering the months of April and May 1918.

8th April, Sunday.

Papa is upset because a new directive from the Red Guards forbids him and Alexei from wearing their epaulettes. It is ridiculous because no one can see us now that we are banned from leaving the grounds. I tried to commiserate but Papa never discusses our predicament. Perhaps he talks to Mama, but certainly not to me. Olga is sunk into depression and Maria and Anastasia seem not to comprehend our situation as they fight and play and fight again regardless of whether the guards are watching. Mama and Alexei are obsessed by their symptoms, and I can understand that with no distractions it is easy to think of nothing else, but I wish they would try. Forgive me my tetchiness this evening, dear diary. I hope it will evaporate overnight and I will wake in the morning with a soul of pure compassion.

In the early days of May, Tatiana described the tortuous journey they were forced to make from Tobolsk to Ekaterinburg. It seemed to have taken a week, which surprised Kitty because according to Vera's book the distance was only about three hundred miles.

Each jolt of the carriage makes Alexei gasp with pain. I know the driver can hear and is doing his best to avoid the biggest holes, but the road is in poor condition at this time of year straight after the thaw. I hope it was easier for Mama, Papa and Maria, when the ground was still hard with ice. If only we had been able to travel with them.

She wrote of their joy in joining their family in Ekaterinburg and described the accommodation:

OTMA [a note from Vera explained that this was the acronym the girls used to refer to all four of them] shares a room with floral wallpaper and an oriental-style rug. We do not have beds yet but are sleeping on the floor on our piled-up coats . . . In the afternoon we sat for half an hour in the garden, where there are beautiful lilac and honeysuckle bushes. It was a shame to come indoors where the air is stuffy and the heat intense. Some nuns sent eggs and cream to build up Alexei's strength, and it is encouraging to know there are good people in this town who are thinking of us.

On the 19th of May there was a strange entry about an eye in the fence. Vera wrote that she had translated it literally but wondered if it might perhaps be an obscure metaphor, possibly religious, with which she was not familiar:

I don't know what made me notice it, because we were several feet away, but there was a flicker that drew my attention. At first I thought I must be imagining it, then I supposed it must be a child because it is at the level of my chest, but there was something about the way it seemed to follow me that was familiar. And then I made the joyful discovery!

The entry finished right there and Kitty found herself as mystified as Vera had been. What was the discovery? It was frustrating reading a ninety-eight-year-old diary. At one moment she would begin to feel she was getting to know Tatiana and then some oblique reference made her realise that she knew next to nothing.

14 June, Thursday.

Papa has run out of tobacco and is irascible as a result. I went to speak with Anton, one of the guards, to ask if some might be found, and he made the most obscene request I have ever heard. If M were to hear of it, he would kill him on the spot.

The mysterious M again, and he seemed to be a man. She had no idea of his identity and supposed Tatiana disguised his name in case the guards demanded to read her diary.

Kitty knew from one of Vera's books that the girls had sewn their jewels into the seams and linings of their clothes, to protect them from the guards' pilfering, but there was no mention of this in her diary. She imagined it would have been uncomfortable to sit down while wearing a garment with jewels in its seams.

They must have been scared witless during those months of waiting to learn their fate but within the diary there was a focus on the daily routine of meals, prayers, exercise and reading. It was a quiet life.

When the final batch of translation came through, Kitty skipped ghoulishly to the last entry. It was dated Sunday 14th July and the tone was sombre.

> Father Storozhev came to conduct a service today with his deacon Buimirov. We were pleased to see him because it has been a long time since we took communion. He sang 'At Rest with the Saints' [Vera inserted a note that this was the Russian Orthodox prayer for the departed] and feeling the relevance of the words 'Give rest, o Christ, to the souls of your servants where there is no sickness nor sorrow nor sighing, but life everlasting' we all fell to our knees – apart from Alexei, of course, who cannot get out of his chair. None of us joined in the responses to the liturgy but at the end we came forward to kiss the cross and Mama and Papa took the sacrament. As Storozhev left, I whispered thank you to him. I can't say why but I have a feeling we will not see him again.

After that Tatiana had copied out some words that Vera said were those of a Russian holy man, Ioann of Kronstadt: 'Your grief is indescribable, the Saviour's grief in the Gardens of Gethsemane for the world's sins is immeasurable, join your grief to his, in it you will find consolation.'

According to the history books none of them had any idea they had just two days to live, but something about the tone of this entry made Kitty wonder if Tatiana perhaps had an inkling.

Chapter Thirty

Dmitri worked non-stop over the next three weeks while setting his plans in motion. He booked rooms to accommodate the twenty men he hoped Malevich would bring with him. Housing them all in one place would have raised suspicion so he chose lodgings spread around town and reserved two or three rooms in each. Henry Armistead would stay with Sir Thomas Preston, as he had on previous occasions.

When the two thousand roubles arrived from Dmitri's mother, he took the cash and went to visit the farmer, Piotr Tolmachev. They sat at his kitchen table, where a sheepdog nuzzled up to Dmitri's thigh, trying to ingratiate itself, as he placed the bag of money on the table and opened the top.

'What I want,' he said, 'is for your daughter to provide me with a plan of the inside of the house: where the family live, and where the guards are stationed. We need to know everything about the security arrangements.'

The farmer's eyes were transfixed by the glimpse of banknotes, and he nodded in agreement. 'No problem, my friend.'

'And then I want her to switch places with Tatiana, the second-eldest Romanov girl, for just one night.'

'You want *what*?'

Dmitri continued calmly: 'We need to talk to one of the family so that they understand the plans, and Tatiana has the most practical nature. Besides, your daughter resembles her in height, build and colouring.'

The farmer's face reddened: 'If she was discovered, she would be executed.'

Dmitri shook his head. 'She will not be discovered. The imperial family will be forewarned and will surround her so she looks inconspicuous. She will switch clothes with Tatiana and then switch back again the following morning. It is only one night. And in return I am offering your family the chance of a new life.' He gestured towards the bag.

'But they might not want the house cleaned two days running,' the farmer protested.

'I have noticed the women always work two mornings in a row and we will alter our plans to suit their schedule. I guarantee your daughter will only spend one night there. You have my word.'

The farmer lent his elbow on the table, hand over his mouth, as he thought. 'I cannot give you an answer now,' he said at last. 'I must discuss it with my wife and daughter.'

'Be wary, my friend. The more people who know, the more likely the secret is to be revealed, and if we cannot carry out the plan I will not be able to give you the money.' He closed the top of the bag and stood. 'I will return the day after tomorrow, when I am sure you will have further questions for me.'

As he rode back to his cottage, Dmitri was stricken with guilt. He knew what he planned was wrong; he knew he would be damned forever if it didn't work out, but he could not risk Tatiana being inside the house when Malevich's men stormed it. He would spring her free before the raid. With any luck, all would be released unharmed: the Romanovs would be spirited safely out of Russia, the farm girl Yelena would return home unsuspected, and Tolmachev could take his cash and relocate to Crimea. But he was taking the precaution of getting Tatiana out of the way in case the guards opened fire during the rescue. May God forgive him.

When Dmitri returned to the farm two days later, Tolmachev's wife and daughter joined them at the kitchen table.

'I will tell you what I know about the house,' Yelena agreed, 'but I do not see how I could pass for Grand Duchess Tatiana. I am nothing like her.'

It was true she was a rather plain, pudgy-faced girl, but her height and hair colour were right. 'You would be surprised to learn how little we look at another's face once we know them,' Dmitri told her. 'We form an impression and after that we glance into a room, see the right number of figures and think no more of it. So long as you do not engage directly in conversation with the guards, they will believe you are Tatiana because it will not occur to them to think otherwise.'

'But the other cleaners will notice. They all know me.'

'Can you trust them?' Dmitri asked. 'Or could Tatiana walk out separately at the end of the morning?'

'Perhaps my friend Svetlana will help,' she said thoughtfully. 'We've both become fond of the Romanov girls.'

'You will be the death of my daughter,' the wife hissed. She was a stocky woman and Dmitri could tell Yelena would look exactly like her in another twenty years. 'I want you to know I am against this.'

'Hush,' the farmer told her. 'This man is vouched for by the British consulate. I trust him.'

Dmitri felt shamed by his trust, and moved on quickly. 'Perhaps we could talk about the house?'

Yelena explained that the family all lived on the first floor, and she drew a plan of the rooms. She showed him where the guards took their meals, where the chapel was, and she drew a map of each of the entrances. 'There's a door leading down to the basement just here,' she pointed. 'Some of the guards sleep there.'

Dmitri looked at her sketch and asked questions until he felt he could picture every corridor and doorway. 'How far in advance do you know the days you will clean?' he asked.

'Only a couple of days,' she said. 'It is roughly once a week, although the actual dates vary. The next days will be Monday the eighth and Tuesday the ninth of July.'

Dmitri nodded. 'So after that it could be the fifteenth and sixteenth?'

'I don't know yet.'

'We'll speak again. Thank you with all my heart for this information.'

Malevich and his 'spruce trees' arrived on the 10th of July and they met at Dmitri's cottage. After they greeted each other and Dmitri handed round shots of illegal vodka he'd purchased from his landlord, they sat down to study the layout of the Ipatiev House and hear from him about the number of men in the guard posts and the hours at which the guard was changed. There were fewer guards on duty from one till five in the morning so they agreed the raid must be between those hours. The plan was to kill the external guards instantly before they could signal to waken their comrades indoors. It was made trickier because a curfew had been imposed on the town and all citizens were supposed to stay indoors after eight in the evening, but as yet it was not being strictly enforced.

'We shoot for the heads,' Malevich suggested. 'You say the sentry posts are around twenty feet tall and we will be on the opposite side of the main road? That's close enough range.'

Everyone knew it was risky. There were many ways the plan could fail but they talked it over endlessly, exploring every possibility, until it seemed as foolproof as such things ever can be. Dmitri trusted Malevich with his life, and the men he'd brought were former imperial guards, trained to a far more exacting level than any common soldier. He felt a thrill at the impending action.

At last he would be doing something after seventeen fruitless months of watching from the sidelines. At last Tatiana would be free.

No one except Tolmachev, his wife and daughter knew about the plan to free Tatiana from the house. Dmitri was too ashamed to share it with Malevich or Sir Thomas. It had no strategic advantage; it was purely his own selfish scheme to keep her out of harm's way.

Dmitri visited the British consulate every few days and Sir Thomas confirmed that Henry Armistead was still planning to arrive on the 13th, and that he had agreed to help. As the day grew closer, Yelena confirmed that she would be working on the 15th and 16th and Dmitri asked Sir Thomas to tell Armistead the cargo would be ready for dispatch in the early hours of the 16th.

He then wrote a note for Tatiana to warn her of what would happen. 'We need your help to plan a rescue. On Monday, a cleaner will switch clothes with you while they are working in the house and you should leave with the other cleaners and let her take your place. Don't be scared. I will be waiting outside.' It was only as he wrote this that it dawned on him what a huge risk he was asking her to take. What would happen if she were discovered trying to walk out? What if a guard intercepted this note? But still, he convinced himself, it was safer than being inside the Ipatiev House during the rescue operation.

He walked past the house on Friday the 12th, while the girls were in the yard, and looked through the knothole. Once he was sure Tatiana had spotted him, he stuck the note into the hole, so it protruded only slightly on the other side, then walked off. He turned back as he reached the street corner and could see the paper had already gone. There was no changing his mind now.

Chapter Thirty-One

Ekaterinburg, Russia, 13th–15th July 1918

On Saturday the 13th of July, Dmitri rode to the consulate in the afternoon hoping to meet Henry Armistead, only to be told he still had not arrived.

'Don't worry,' Sir Thomas assured him. 'I telephoned and was told that he left yesterday, so he should be here by nightfall. Come again tomorrow.'

The following day there was still no sign of him and no word either. Armistead must have been delayed on the journey. Dmitri felt he would explode with tension. He ran his fingers through his hair and hardly noticed when he yanked out a strand. Pain was a welcome distraction.

He met Malevich early on Sunday evening to discuss the options.

'I think we should go ahead. The arrangements are made, all the men are here,' Dmitri argued. 'The longer we wait, the more chance there is of something happening to them.'

Malevich was adamantly against it. 'There is no point freeing the Romanovs without a strategy to whisk them out of the country. They can't get on a train without the railway workers reporting it. It's too far to reach safety by road. We need Armistead's help.'

Dmitri had to accept he was right, but felt panicky at the thought of waiting. Anything could happen in a week.

After their meeting, Dmitri tried calling on Sir Thomas again but there was no sign of the merchant and Sir Thomas was at a loss to explain his absence. He tried to calm the increasingly distraught Dmitri. 'He has never let me down before. I'm sure he'll be here tomorrow.'

Dmitri didn't explain to him why he was quite so agitated. Sir Thomas didn't know that the following day Yelena would be going into the Ipatiev House to change places with Tatiana. Should Dmitri stop her? Or should he trust that Mr Armistead would appear and the plan could proceed?

Back at his cottage, Dmitri sat up late mulling over the options until his brain was frazzled, absent-mindedly stroking the waist-coat Tatiana had knitted for him. There was still time to ride to Tolmachev's farm and tell Yelena that the plan was delayed till the following week – but he was reluctant because he yearned so badly to see Tatiana. He had been counting the hours until he could hold her in his arms and a week seemed an impossibly long delay.

Eventually he decided that Yelena should go ahead and make the switch. If Armistead did not arrive, it could be a trial run for the following week, giving Dmitri a chance to brief Tatiana about their plans, so the family could take cover when the rescue began. He convinced himself it made sense.

Next morning, Dmitri watched as the party of cleaning ladies made their way into the Ipatiev House at 8 a.m., Yelena among them. He rode round the town, in an attempt to contain his extreme agitation. This was the moment when it could all go wrong. At eleven he enquired at the consulate, to be told that Mr Armistead had still not appeared, and he glanced into the exercise yard to see Tatiana strolling with her sisters. Was she going to do as he asked? She must be petrified. At twelve noon, he positioned himself on a street corner just a few houses further down Vozhnesensky

Prospekt and consulted his pocket watch, wearing an old jacket and cap like a factory worker.

The gates opened and a group of women walked out in a huddle. Dmitri strained his eyes to pick out individual figures but he couldn't see either Tatiana or Yelena. His heart was thudding against his ribcage.

The women wandered down the road, then the gate opened again and two more emerged, arm in arm. Straight away Dmitri recognised her: how could the guards not see? She walked differently from the other women. Even when wearing the plain bonnet and gown of a farmer's daughter she was transparently a grand duchess. He felt as if he might faint, such was the mixture of excitement and terror that swirled in his blood.

Neither of the guards at the gate gave her a second glance and she walked down the road with her arm through that of another cleaner, presumably Yelena's friend Svetlana. Only when she looked up and saw him could he tell she was terrified. It was an extraordinarily courageous thing to do, but Dmitri had never doubted she would manage. As she drew near, he took her arm and thanked Svetlana, who whispered, 'Good luck! See you tomorrow.' Tatiana's whole body was trembling as Dmitri led her round a corner and down the street to where his horse was tethered.

'I'm afraid I don't have a side saddle,' he apologised, his voice hoarse with emotion.

'That's all right,' she said quietly, and mounted, adjusting her skirts. Dmitri mounted behind her, glanced back at the house, then they rode off without any further words.

Tatiana was free! Dmitri's heart sang as he sat with his arms looped around her to hold the reins. She was here, with him, no longer a prisoner! He could feel the warmth of her flesh, and her hair blowing in the wind stroked his face. Behind them the road was clear apart from some peasants on horseback; there were none of the cars or trucks driven by Red Guardsmen. They'd got away with it!

Inside the cottage, she was still trembling when at last he enclosed her in his arms and held her tight. He unfastened her bonnet and caressed her as she clung to him.

'Oh Dmitri,' she cried. 'Why have you done this? What will happen to the family if my absence is discovered?'

Dmitri explained that he was waiting for a merchant to arrive that day, and they hoped to spring her family from captivity that very night. If not, she would return to the house the following morning and the plan would be carried out at a later date.

She listened carefully, her eyes widening. 'But how will you rescue them? Who will carry Alexei? Where will we go?'

He told her that these details had been worked out by his men, who were loyal retainers from the St Petersburg imperial guard.

'And I am to stay here tonight? With you?' She looked around.

'Yes. I must go out this afternoon to meet the merchant and if the rescue is proceeding tonight I will join the men, but I will return to you immediately with news. You will be safe here. It is very isolated.'

She needed time to take it in and sank down on a chair, laying her hands flat on the table to stop them shaking. 'It is as well you are doing this now. I did not like to warn you in a note but we all sense the end is near. The lack of respect with which the new guards treat us, the impertinence . . . We are an unwanted problem for the Red Guards. They resent the food we eat, the men it takes to hold us captive.'

'You think they plan to move you again?'

She shook her head. 'Perhaps. I don't know . . .'

'You are safe, Tatiana.' He knelt at her feet and leaned his elbows on her lap. 'Trust me. I won't let anything happen to you now – or to your family.'

She stroked his hair. 'My husband,' she said, her voice husky with love. 'I am so blessed.'

He had a little food in the kitchen but she said she was too anxious to take more than a cup of tea. They moved to the sofa

186

and cradled each other, talking about all that had happened during the months of separation, about the lowest moments of despair, about her exhilaration mixed with fear when she read his note and realised he had a plan to free them.

'There have been other plans too,' he told her, and explained about Yakovlev's scheme to get them to Omsk and Henry Armistead's plan to get them to Murmansk. 'The British consul is helping,' he said, and that seemed to reassure her a little.

They exchanged long, passionate kisses that afternoon. There was a bedroom just through a doorway but Dmitri did not dream of trying to make love to her. There would be plenty of time for that in their new life. For now it was sheer luxury to hear her voice, taste her lips, feel the softness of her cheek against his, and wrap her in his arms, safe at last. They leaned their foreheads together and this time both were able to read each other's thoughts because they were thinking exactly the same thing.

Time seemed to stretch, like a dream, but then Dmitri consulted his pocket watch and realised it was almost five.

'I must go to the consulate now to see if Armistead has arrived. Whatever happens I will be back within the hour,' he promised. 'Bolt the door behind me and don't open it again until you hear my voice.'

'Please be quick,' she pleaded, and he agreed, hand over heart.

'Rest now, my precious,' he told her with one last, lingering kiss. 'We may not get much sleep tonight.'

When he arrived at the consulate, Dmitri was met by a very apologetic Sir Thomas. Malevich was already there, looking downcast.

'I've just heard from Armistead,' Sir Thomas told him. 'He did his best to get through to Ekaterinburg but there are soldiers blocking all the access roads. You have no doubt heard about the advance of the Czech Legions through Siberia. Latest news is that they are less than a hundred miles away.'

Dmitri was appalled. 'Armistead can't let us down, not now. When will he come?'

'Don't you see? He may not need to come if the Czechs free Ekaterinburg. They are defeating the Bolsheviks wherever they go and have formed a provisional government in Omsk. At long last an effective White Army is fighting back against the Reds.'

This did nothing to lessen Dmitri's panic. 'But the Bolsheviks will move the Romanovs before they get here. They will never let the White Army claim such a prize.'

Sir Thomas had to agree this was likely, but had a suggestion. 'When they are a little closer, your men can make contact and arrange to hand over the family to their safekeeping . . . I can see it will be fraught but it's the only way to proceed.'

Dmitri paced up and down. 'Can't we go ahead with the rescue tonight? The Red Guard will become desperate as the Whites draw near. Anything could happen!'

Malevich intervened. 'But where would the family go? There's nowhere to keep them safe in this town and there are roadblocks all around. Wait a week, two at most. If there is any attempt to move them, we can intervene . . . It might prove easier to spring them loose while on the road than inside a heavily guarded house.'

Dmitri bit his lip. He wanted the rescue to proceed that night, but only because he couldn't bear to let Tatiana return to the house now he had her safe. 'Their lives are at risk. I can't just sit and wait.'

Malevich patted him on the shoulder. 'We will keep watch and move if we have to. Do not fear, Malama. Stay strong.'

Dmitri was close to tears as he rode back to the cottage in the dusk. He knew there was nothing he could say that would persuade Tatiana to abandon her family. She would have to be taken first thing the following morning to enter the house with the other cleaners. He couldn't bear the thought of saying goodbye to her again, not knowing when he would next hold her in his arms. Oh, if only she would choose to stay . . .

As he rode into the lane that led to the cottage he could see from afar that the front door was open. What was Tatiana doing? He had told her not to open it to anyone. As he got nearer he saw it had been smashed and hung from its frame in splintered pieces. Fear gripping his heart, Dmitri leapt from his horse and rushed inside.

'Tatiana!' He screamed her name and ran from room to room in blind panic. A chair lay overturned in the sitting room but she wasn't there. He checked again, looking inside cupboards, behind drapes. The bag stuffed with money was still beneath the bed so that ruled out robbery. Next he searched the outhouse and the nearby woods, with a pressure in his chest so painful that he staggered.

'Ta-ti-ana!' he screamed at the top of his voice and began the search all over again in case he had missed anything. *Where was she? How could she simply disappear?* Towards one copse there were hoof prints in the soil and possible signs of a scuffle. He leapt on his horse and set off in that direction but when he came to a fork in the road, he could see no tracks to indicate which way the riders might have gone. He was howling with grief, like a man possessed, as he picked one path and rode down it into the gathering night.

Chapter Thirty-Two

Ekaterinburg, Russia, 15th–16th July 1918

When Dmitri could control himself enough to think clearly, he realised one or more men on horseback must have followed them to his cottage. He had been looking out for Red Guards in a car or truck – their normal mode of transport – and had been so ecstatic to hold Tatiana in his arms once more that his professional caution had slipped at the most crucial moment. The pursuers must have waited till he left the cottage then snatched her. Did that mean she was back at the Ipatiev House already? He would not be able to tell until eleven the following morning when they came out to exercise in the yard.

What had made the guards suspicious? Maybe one of the other cleaning ladies told them of the imposter in their midst. Perhaps Yelena had panicked and told them herself. What would happen to her now? Might she be back at the farm, having secured her freedom with a betrayal?

He decided not to disturb the farmer and his wife with the news but rode to the Ipatiev House, keeping out of sight on side roads and alleyways. It was after eight so the curfew was in operation and the only signs of life were the night guards standing in their turrets. Next he went to the lodgings where Malevich was staying, got the landlady to fetch him, and explained in a shaking voice what he had done.

'We must storm the house straight away,' he insisted.

He could tell Malevich was horrified at his actions, although he hid his emotions beneath a professional soldier's veneer. 'If she is back inside the house, you can be sure they will have doubled the guard in preparation for an attack tonight. And the fact remains that there is nowhere to take the family. Let us sleep on the problem and consult Sir Thomas tomorrow. Perhaps he can make enquiries through official channels.'

'You don't understand, Malevich!' Dmitri was almost in tears. 'They might kill her tonight.'

'I think I'm beginning to understand,' he said gently, putting an arm round his friend's shoulder. 'You should have told me before. I did not realise you were in love with her.'

'More than love . . . much more than love . . .' Dmitri whispered, his eyes swimming.

'Come then. I will ride out with you around the town and its outskirts. I'll bring rifles.'

They trotted up and down the backstreets, one by one, stopping to watch and listen whenever they passed official buildings, ducking out of sight when they saw soldiers. It remained light until almost midnight but when the darkness fell it was hopeless to search further.

'What if it wasn't Red Guards who took her? Who else knew of your plan?' Malevich asked.

'Only the farmer, Tolmachev, and his wife and daughter, and the daughter's friend Svetlana.'

Dmitri's mind kept running through the possibilities. Could Tolmachev's wife have turned them in to protect her daughter? But then they wouldn't get the money, and her daughter might be imprisoned anyway, so that didn't make sense. He couldn't believe Svetlana had betrayed them, after the way she carefully guided Tatiana out of the house – but perhaps she had.

'Let's go to your cottage and try to retrace their steps,' Malevich suggested, and Dmitri was grateful for a plan. His own brain was overwhelmed.

As they approached, he prayed for a miracle: that they would go in and find Tatiana sitting on the sofa with a plausible explanation for her absence. He held his breath as they dismounted and ran indoors, but there was just echoing silence, the absence of the woman who filled all his waking thoughts, who had been there in the flesh just a few hours before.

'Isn't it strange,' Malevich mused, 'that if it was the Red Guards who took her, they didn't arrest you both?'

'Perhaps there were only a few and they feared I might overpower them.'

'But in that case, you'd think they would return with reinforcements.' He sat down. 'Perhaps it was not the Red Guards after all. Perhaps word reached the White Army and they sent an advance party to fetch her.'

Dmitri felt a ray of hope. 'Do you think that's possible? But how could they have heard she was here?'

'I don't know – maybe the farmer told someone. I will ride out and make contact with them tomorrow. They are led by Admiral Kolchak. Do you remember him from the war?'

Dmitri shook his head.

'He's a good man. I will ask if they have the Grand Duchess, and liaise with them over the rescue and handover of the remaining Romanovs. You stay here, keep an eye on the Ipatiev House, and see if Sir Thomas can exert pressure on the Red Guards . . . But now, I think, we should try to get some sleep, Malama. I will take the sofa.'

It took much persuasion but at last Dmitri went into the bedroom and threw himself fully dressed on the bed. As he lay there, eyes wide open, he noticed something sticking out from beneath a cupboard as if kicked there. He got up to retrieve it and found it was a notebook filled with Tatiana's impeccable handwriting. It was her diary. She must have brought it with her, concealed in her clothing. Did she want to keep it safe from the guards? Was she planning to give it to him?

She had written the last entry on Sunday, just over twenty-four hours earlier. He couldn't bear to read her words but he held the book to his face sniffing its pages. His fear for her was so acute it was like a hole gouged through his insides.

Malevich rode off at first light to locate the White Army head-quarters, which he had heard were in Kamensk, some hundred miles distant. Like Dmitri he was a skilled horseman and should make it in a day, whereupon he promised to send a telegram to the consulate with news.

Dmitri went out to examine the hoof prints he had spotted the previous evening. It looked as though there had only been two or, at most, three men, but still he couldn't find any trail beyond the crossroads. At eight, he rode into town and watched from a distance as the cleaning ladies entered the Ipatiev House, their number one fewer than yesterday. Next he went to call upon Sir Thomas and made his shameful confession: that he had rescued Tatiana then lost her again.

Sir Thomas looked stern. 'So you think the farm girl is still in the house?'

'I'll be able to tell when they come outside to exercise at eleven.'

'What will she do? My goodness, this is a muddle. I will send an immediate request for a guarantee of the Romanovs' safety and will make enquiries amongst my local contacts. If the farm girl does not emerge with the other cleaners, you must go and tell her parents. That will not be a pleasant task, I'm afraid. And then we will wait for news.'

Dmitri remained in the consulate all morning, watching the house from an upstairs window. He refused all offers of food and drink; even a sip of tea made him feel as though he was choking. He could see no signs of life at the blanked out windows, but at eleven o'clock five figures appeared in the yard and he sprinted down the stairs and up the road. He rushed round the side of the Ipatiev House and bent to peer through the knothole, every nerve on edge. He could tell the tall slim figure in Tatiana's gown was the farm girl long before she turned her head. The family all looked tense and scared, wandering around the yard without talking, and Nicholas paced up and down, as usual. Only the dogs displayed their normal exuberance.

Dmitri wished he could get a message to Yelena, telling her that she would be rescued soon. If only he had spoken to Svetlana that morning. If only he hadn't done such a despicable thing in the first place.

He was waiting on the corner when the cleaning ladies left the house at twelve and Svetlana rushed straight over, her face white with worry. 'Where is Tatiana? Yelena doesn't know what to do. How can she leave if they do not change places again?'

'I know, I'm sorry. We're doing what we can. Say nothing to anyone and your friend will be freed soon.' His promise sounded hollow even to his own ears and he could tell Svetlana was not reassured.

After that he rode out to Tolmachev's farm and told the farmer and his wife what had happened.

'*Svolach!*' The wife slapped him hard across the face. 'You promised us she would be safe.' She began to wail. 'I will never forgive you if . . .'

Dmitri quickly explained their plan to free the Romanovs and shepherd them into the hands of the White Army. 'It will be any day now,' he promised. 'I will keep you informed. The good thing is that none of the guards suspect the substitution has been made and the family are keeping up the pretence. Yelena is perfectly safe for now.'

'She must be so scared,' the farmer breathed. 'You guarantee it will be over soon?'

'I give you my word,' he told them. One way or another it would.

Before he left he placed the bag containing two thousand roubles on their kitchen floor. The farmer's wife kicked it. 'What use is your money without our daughter? Did you think of that? Or was she not a person to you, just a body you could buy? You disgust me.'

Dmitri hung his head in misery. He disgusted himself too.

Dmitri went back to the consulate that afternoon and Sir Thomas let him sit by the window to keep an eye on the Ipatiev House. At least he felt as though he was doing something, however futile. The family came out to exercise at three but Yelena wasn't with them, which sent Dmitri into fresh spiral of panic. Where was she? Had her identity been revealed? He noticed cars coming and going but wasn't sure if there were more than normal, and could not make out any of the occupants. His blood was pounding and he paced up and down, unable to keep still.

'Go home before the curfew,' Sir Thomas told him at seven. 'Your being here serves no purpose. We will have more information in the morning.'

Reluctantly, Dmitri rode back to the cottage, once again hoping that through some miracle Tatiana might have found her way back there. But she hadn't. He cried as he touched the space on the sofa where she had sat and listened to the silence all around. After two nights of very little sleep, he managed to doze for a few hours but woke with fear gripping his heart. What had he done? Had he ruined everything with his thoughtlessness? If so, he could never live with himself.

He rode to the consulate as soon as the curfew was lifted in the morning, and was met by Sir Thomas, who looked grey and worried.

'Sit down, Malama,' he instructed. 'I have some news which I think is credible.'

Dmitri felt his legs give way; he collapsed into a chair. 'Bad news?'

'I'm afraid so. It's being said that Tsar Nicholas was shot and killed by the Red Guards last night.'

Chapter Thirty-Three

Ekaterinburg, Russia, 17th July 1918

Dmitri couldn't breathe. His Tsar, his Commander-in-Chief, had been executed. His first thought was that it must be his fault for smuggling Tatiana out of the house. How would he ever live with himself? Tatiana was sure to hold him responsible.

'What of the others?' he croaked.

'Word is that the rest of the family have been moved elsewhere for safekeeping.' Sir Thomas looked grave.

'Moved where?'

'I was told by one source that they have gone to Verkhoturye, but there's no confirmation. I stress I don't know any of this for sure, but local people heard a disturbance around three in the morning and there are reports of a number of vehicles leaving the house.'

Dmitri leapt up. 'I will ride to Verkhoturye today. I must do something.'

'It's almost two hundred miles north.'

'I will telephone when I arrive.'

'Ah, yes. And your friend Malevich sent a telegram this morning. He has met Kolchak, the White Army commander, but says none of their men know anything of Tatiana's whereabouts.'

This was a blow. It meant Tatiana was almost certainly being held by the Red Guards. He must get to Verkhoturye as soon as humanly possible.

Dmitri knew Tatiana would take it very hard to lose her father. If only he could hold her in his arms and comfort her. He'd barely had time to mourn his own father but if he could just find her, he would try to help her recover from this shocking loss.

Dmitri rode day and night without rest, arriving in Verkhoturye at noon on the 18th of July. It was a tiny town on the Tura River, with historic buildings and a pretty cathedral. There were no more than a hundred private dwellings set along one main road and half a dozen cross streets. He should be able to find the family quite easily in such a place. But after riding up and down each street, he could see no house with guards posted outside. Wherever they were, there were bound to be guards. He knocked on the door of a female monastery and asked the elderly nun who answered if there had been any new arrivals in town over the past day, but she replied, 'Only yourself, sir.'

He spent the afternoon touring the countryside around the town, wondering if they might be in a remote building somewhere, his thoughts in turmoil. Could it really be true that Nicholas was murdered without a trial, with no chance to defend himself? What kind of people were these new rulers?

As evening fell he took a room in the area's only hotel and asked if he might use their telephone but when he spoke to Sir Thomas, the only further news was that the family appeared to have been transported from the Ipatiev House in trucks rather than carriages – yet another sign of the lack of respect now shown towards them. Sir Thomas's informant was a local woman, who had seen the trucks pull out between three and four in the morning. Perhaps they were slow-moving and the party had not yet arrived in Verkhoturye. Dmitri couldn't remember seeing any trucks on the road, but maybe he had overtaken them when they stopped for the night.

'I will continue my search tomorrow,' Dmitri said. It was the only thing he could think of. He had to keep himself occupied or he would go completely insane.

A week later, an inconsolable Dmitri returned to Ekaterinburg, having scoured every part of the countryside between there and Verkhoturye without finding a trace of the Romanovs. He discovered there had been dramatic changes in town since he left: the White Army had arrived, chasing out the Bolsheviks, and celebration was in the air. Flags hung from buildings, and flowers lay trampled on the streets where townspeople had tossed them at the liberating army.

'It is like emerging from a huge cave into the daylight,' Sir Thomas told Dmitri. 'We need no longer kowtow to those insufferable Red Guards.'

'But is there further news of the Imperial Family?'

'Nothing as yet. International pressure is mounting on the Bolsheviks to hand them over. King Alfonso of Spain and King Christian of Denmark are making diplomatic representations. I imagine we will learn their whereabouts very soon.'

Dmitri turned away. Every moment was sheer torture as he speculated what might have become of Tatiana. He prayed she had not been punished for attempting to escape. Surely they wouldn't do that? She was so young, so luminous . . .

'The Ipatiev House is abandoned,' Sir Thomas told him. 'No one guards the gates and curious townspeople have been wandering in.'

Dmitri glanced out the window. 'Perhaps there will be a clue to where they have gone. I'll go and take a look.'

He hurried across the road and joined a group going through the main gate. He knew the layout from the map Yelena had drawn, and headed up to the first floor then along to the bedroom the four girls had shared. Muted sunlight shone through the whitewashed windows and the air was stale and sour. Their four camp beds remained, the covers rumpled. On the floor lay odd items: a toothbrush, a prayer book, a needle and thread. He picked up the prayer book and saw Maria's name written inside. She must have forgotten it. A middle-aged peasant woman pulled a picture of the Holy Mother from the wall and clutched it like a prize. Dmitri searched through the other items lying around but did not find anything to indicate where the family might have gone. All that was clear was that they had left in a hurry. It felt strange and wrong to be in the girls' bedroom.

Next door was the Tsar and Tsarina's bedroom, with Alexei's bed at the foot of theirs, and the same scattering of personal items: bibles, images of saints, some porcelain dominoes. On the floor was the book *Tales of Shakespeare*, which Tatiana had mentioned she was reading to Alexei. He walked through the rooms occupied by Alexei's doctor and Alexandra's maid, the dining room in which the family ate their meals round a small carved oak table, the bathroom and water closet that all were forced to share. It was so cramped and uncomfortable he couldn't bear to think of Tatiana living there. The guard posts were connected by wires with bells on them, bells that Tatiana had told him the family had been forced to ring when they wanted to visit the water closet. It was intolerable that a royal family's bodily functions had been so closely observed.

The house had a horrible atmosphere that made the hairs on the back of his neck stand up. He hurried down the stairs to look around the ground floor where the guards had spent their time. No papers or telegrams gave any indication of the family's fate; drawers were empty, the walls cleared of notices. He walked out into the courtyard and round to look for the door to the basement but it was bolted shut. He rattled it but it wouldn't budge.

It was good to be in the fresh air again. Dmitri felt as though he were choking. Where were the Romanovs? Where was Tatiana? This 'house of special purpose' was offering no clues.

*

A few days later, Malevich arrived at the cottage and greeted Dmitri with a bear hug. 'You look terrible, my friend. Have you not been sleeping? Phew . . .' He wrinkled his nose. 'I can tell you have not been bathing.'

True enough, Dmitri couldn't remember when he last washed.

'I don't know what to do with myself,' he shook his head. 'I've searched everywhere. How can they have vanished into thin air?'

'We will find them,' Malevich promised. 'I heard they might be on the other side of the Urals, perhaps in Perm. There is talk of a sealed train that left Ekaterinburg in the early hours of the seventeeth and I'm willing to bet they were on it. The White Army is headed in that direction. Why not join us?'

Dmitri blinked hard. 'But what if Tatiana comes looking for me here? I can't risk missing her.'

'We will leave word of our plans with Sir Thomas. He will let you know if Tatiana returns to Ekaterinburg.' Malevich squeezed his shoulders. 'You are a great soldier, a brave man. The best thing you can do for the Romanovs is to free their country from the Bolshevik scourge and turn it back into the motherland we know and love.' He paused then added: 'You know it's what Tatiana would urge you to do.'

'What if the family are found while I am stuck fighting somewhere?'

'When they are found, I expect you will grab the nearest horse and ride off in a cloud of dust, not stopping until you have reached them.'

Dmitri nodded, his throat so tight it was impossible to speak. He would go with Malevich; it was better than doing nothing. Only by keeping busy could he hold at bay the terrible sense of doom that threatened to engulf him completely.

Chapter Thirty-Four

Lake Akanabee, New York State, late September 2016

It was a blazing hot day but Kitty shivered as she lay on the shore by her cabin reading about the murder of the Romanovs on the night of the 16th–17th of July, 1918. The account was based on a statement given by Yurovsky, the chief executioner, so was as close to the truth as would ever emerge.

It was around one-thirty when Eugene Botkin, the family doctor, was wakened by Yurovsky. He said that the situation was unstable as the Czech Army drew closer and that the Romanovs should be wakened and told to come down to the basement for their own safety until they could be moved elsewhere.

The family took forty minutes to pull on their clothes: Nicholas and Alexei in soldiers' tunics and Alexandra and the girls in white blouses and skirts. They were carrying small bags and seemed calm. Nicholas turned to the servants and remarked 'Well, it seems at last we are getting out of this place.' When Alexandra asked about their possessions, Yurovsky assured her everything would be packed up and sent on.

Kitty knew there had been a false alarm when they had thought they were being moved a couple of days earlier so perhaps they weren't sure if this was another one.

At 2.15 a.m., Yurovsky led the party of ten down the darkened staircase to the ground floor then out into the courtyard. Nicholas carried Alexei in his arms. Another door led down twenty-three steps to a basement and they were ushered into a bare room with an unshaded light bulb hanging from the ceiling.

Alexandra immediately asked for chairs: she could not stand for long because of her sciatica, and Alexei was too weak to stand at all. Two chairs were brought, and Yurovsky asked the girls and the servants to stand behind the Tsar and Tsarina, almost as if he were posing them for a photograph. He said a truck was coming to take them to safety, then left them alone while he went to check on the arrangements.

They must have been sleepy, Kitty thought, after being roused from their beds. None of them seemed unduly alarmed. Did they whisper amongst themselves? Perhaps they speculated on where their next destination might be.

Next door the guards sat drinking vodka and nervously checking their weapons. The Fiat truck Yurovsky had ordered pulled into the courtyard and, after checking it, at 2.45 a.m. he led his eight co-conspirators into the room where the Romanovs waited. They were alarmed to see faces they did not recognise, but hearing the truck outside, must have imagined their departure was imminent. Nicholas asked, 'What are you going to do now?'

Yurovsky produced a sheet of paper and began to read: 'In view of the fact that your relatives in Europe continue their assault on Soviet Russia, the presidium of the Regional Soviet, fulfilling the will of the Revolution, has decreed that the former Tsar Nicholas Romanov, guilty of countless bloody crimes against the people, should be shot . . .

Kitty tried to imagine the terror and confusion in the room. No one could have expected that, even after all the months of captivity. What kind of nation would execute their monarch without a trial?

Nicholas turned to look at his family. According to one report he cried, 'What? What?' before Yurovsky drew a pistol and shot him at point-blank range in the chest. He fell straight away, killed outright. The women crossed themselves as the guards began shooting, each at their designated target. A shot to Alexandra's head blew off part of her skull. Alexei remained rigid with shock in his chair, soaked in his father's blood, unable to try and save himself. His sisters fell to the floor, where they lay stunned and moaning in pain. The jewels they had sewn into their gowns deflected the bullets so they were badly injured but not killed. Some tried to crawl away but there was nowhere to hide in that bare room.

The air filled with smoke, making it difficult to see, and the guards panicked. They began stabbing viciously with bayonets to finish off their victims, turning the scene into a bloodbath. Some of the girls were murmuring prayers, others screaming. Bullet after bullet was pumped into little Alexei. Tatiana was shot in the back of the head as she and Olga huddled in a corner, her brain tissue spattering Olga's face. Anastasia survived longer than the others and pleaded for her life but was finished off by frenzied bayonet thrusts.

It was an unrelentingly horrific way to die. Kitty thought of the last entry in Tatiana's diary: although it was pessimistic, she could never have predicted such barbarity, the terror they must have experienced, the agony of the slash wounds.

Kitty's hand shook and she put down the book. She felt sticky and could almost smell the choking fog of blood and gunpowder. Suddenly she rose and ran into the lake, wading out deep and diving beneath the surface. The water was refreshing and she felt it easing a knot of headache in her temple. She turned to float on her back under the white pulsating sun.

Could Dmitri possibly have been there when the Romanovs were killed? If so, was there nothing he could do to stop them? She thought back through his novels, searching for clues to the nature of her great-grandfather. He was obviously articulate, very romantic, and prone to melancholy. She realised there was a theme running through the novels of a terrible wrong committed in the past which overshadows his characters' lives. Could Dmitri have been haunted by a sin he committed? She desperately wanted her great-grandfather to have been a hero, but what if he was complicit in murder? It would be horrible to learn that her ancestor had been involved in this evil assassination of innocents.

When she emerged from the water, Kitty twisted her hair into a ponytail and squeezed the water from it then sat down and read about Yurovsky's bungled attempts to dispose of the bodies:

Out in the remote countryside, when the guards stripped the family of their clothes, they found myriad priceless jewels stitched into their seams and linings. The Tsarina had rows of fine pearls in a belt around her waist . . . The corpses lay, blood-soaked, limbs askew, on the boggy ground. Yurovsky ordered his men to throw them down an old mineshaft where he hoped they would be concealed, but it was soon apparent that it was too shallow. His men doused the bodies with vats of sulphuric acid, and the air filled with the smell of burning flesh, but Yurovsky had failed to realise that acid would not dissolve teeth and bones. In desperation he threw a couple of hand grenades into the mine, hoping the shaft would collapse and cover the bodies, but they did not detonate properly in such an enclosed space. At last he realised he would have to remove the family and bury them elsewhere before suspicious local people came across the hideous scene . . .

Kitty read that when the graves were eventually discovered in 1979, there was a jumble of bones and teeth all mixed up together and it took researchers a long time to identify them. By then there had been more than six decades of controversy about whether all the Romanovs had perished, a debate fuelled by the fact that the evidence was contaminated by scientists who handled it over the years, and that Anastasia and Alexei were in separate graves some distance away. It was only in 2008 that DNA testing proved conclusively all five Romanov children, both their parents, and three household retainers had been massacred. Scientists took a DNA sample from Britain's Prince Philip, husband of the Queen, who was a close living relative of the Romanov family, for comparison.

Kitty closed the book and stood up. She needed to drive into town before the stores closed as she'd run out of wine. The quantity she was drinking had sneaked up during her stay until she was polishing off a bottle of a rather pleasant Californian Chardonnay every evening. Chilled in the water beneath the jetty, it slipped down like lemonade after a long day in the sun. She never had a hangover so reckoned her body could cope with that amount. Everyone knew those government guidelines were ridiculously cautious.

In the supermarket, she decided to buy a case of wine – twelve bottles in all – to save her having to come back so often.

'You having a party tonight?' the checkout girl asked, and Kitty smiled and said, 'Yes, something like that.'

*

In the early hours of the morning Kitty woke abruptly from a nightmare. All she could remember of it was the presence of something dark and evil in a house where she was trapped, possibly as a prisoner, although she never saw her gaolers.

She lay, heart beating hard, trying to adjust her eyes to the darkness, when suddenly she became aware of a faint movement in the far corner of the cabin. Terror gripped her. She pulled herself to a sitting position and groped for a box of matches. She couldn't hear any sounds now except the ones she was making, but it still felt as though something was in the room with her. The thought crossed her mind that it could be Dmitri's ghost, then she shook herself. *Stupid girl. No such thing as ghosts.* She struck a match but her hand was shaking so badly she couldn't get the wick of the oil lamp to take the flame and had to strike a second one.

A pool of flickering light spread round the room and she looked into the corner where she had been convinced she heard a noise: nothing but bare wood. She stood up, back to the wall, peering round and listening hard. She was covered in a film of sweat, her hand still shaking, so the lamplight shifted and swung.

Suddenly, out of the corner of her eye, she saw something coming towards her. She screamed and almost dropped the lamp in panic before realising it was a large white moth, drawn to the light. Its wings flapped and it smacked against the glass of the lamp. Instantly Kitty realised that was the sound she had heard earlier in the darkness; it must have flown into a window.

'You idiot!' she whispered, still feeling shaken. She walked across the floor and opened the cabin door, placing the lamp on the porch so the moth would follow it out. The night air was cool and she padded barefoot down to the water's edge, feeling the sweat evaporating on her skin. There was just a sliver of moon among hosts of faraway stars in an ink-black sky, and the water and trees were utterly still. An owl hooted, breaking the silence.

Suddenly there was a loud, distinctive rustling in the trees to one side of the cabin, and the terror returned. Kitty rushed to the end of the jetty, ready to dive into the lake if a wild animal ran out. What creatures might there be? Most likely it was a deer, she told herself. They wouldn't have bears or wolves by the lake – or would they?

She crouched on the end of the jetty, scanning the forest, alert for any further rustling sounds. The distance to her cabin door seemed huge. Something might pounce on her as she crossed the space. Her heart was racing. What if she were mauled to death by a wild animal out there miles from anywhere? It would be days before her body was found. She would die alone, in pain and terror. She hoped at least it would be quick, unlike the gruesome deaths of the Romanovs.

A morbid mood descended as she crouched beneath the vast twinkling sky. What difference would her death make? Tom would miss her. So would a few friends. But she had left no mark on the world. The Romanovs had their place in history, Dmitri left behind his novels and his descendants, but she had produced no children, hadn't achieved anything of note. She had never felt so insignificant as she did at that moment.

Why had she not written a book yet? This summer by the lake would have been an ideal time but she hadn't produced a single word. Writing was hard work and while she could force herself to do it when there was money on offer and a deadline to meet, she couldn't imagine how authors slaved for hundreds of hours without pay, on the off-chance they might one day get published. Perhaps she simply wasn't good enough. Maybe those with a genuine gift felt they had no choice but to write.

But if she wasn't a writer, what was she? What talents did she have? She thought of her mother's wish that she should study law and shuddered. That would never have worked. She had chosen journalism because English was her best subject at school, not because of any burning desire to communicate the truth or any of those worthy reasons real journalists have. Perhaps she was simply lazy, as her mum had always said. Good for nothing. Useless.

I suppose this is what they call a 'long dark night of the soul', she mused once her heart had stopped racing. There had been no further rustlings in the trees so she hoped whatever creature had been there had moved on. She decided to make a run for the cabin, slam the door and crawl back into bed.

As she stood up, the wood of the jetty was smooth and even beneath her feet.

Chapter Thirty-Five

Urals, Russia, September–December 1918

Every night as he lay in his bedding roll on the hard earth, Dmitri tortured himself with thoughts of the terror Tatiana must have felt when the cottage door was hacked down, the shouting, the rough handling she might have endured. He was still in shock about her disappearance.

Malevich was convinced the family were being held in Bolshevik territory to the west of the mountains, and Dmitri prayed he was right and that Tatiana was with them, but he felt sick to his stomach imagining alternative scenarios.

During the day, the discipline of military life kept him occupied: they rose at a set hour, tended their horses, ate breakfast then broke camp, before continuing across the Ural Mountains in pursuit of the Red Army. The terrain was steep and rough and already there was a hint of winter in the air. If they did not get to the other side of the vast range before the first snowfall, they could be stranded for months with no food or shelter to speak of, so they rode from dawn until well beyond dusk. He did his duty in a daze – riding reconnaissance, poring over maps, giving orders to his men – but all the time the shocking disappearance of Tatiana hammered on his consciousness.

One evening a newcomer rode into camp, and Dmitri was astonished to see a familiar face from Tobolsk: 'Vasily Yakovlev! What on earth are you doing here?'

Yakovlev leapt from his horse and came over to greet Dmitri. 'I couldn't bear to watch what the Bolsheviks were doing to our people. The Red Army is a hornets' nest of suspicion and back-stabbing. If I'd stayed, I would probably have been executed by now. So I switched to the side whose cause I believe in and am fighting for the Whites.'

Dmitri regarded him with suspicion. Their camp was no stranger to spies and all had been warned to be wary about what information they passed on. Still, this man had once been a friend of sorts – and perhaps he had news of the Romanovs. Dmitri poured him a coffee and invited him to sit, introducing him to Malevich.

'Last time we met, you were trying to save the royal family by diverting their train to Omsk. Whatever went wrong?' he asked.

Yakovlev shook his head sadly. 'I did my best but the railway workers took orders directly from Moscow and the matter was out of my hands. I bitterly regret that I failed, especially since the rumour is that all have now been killed.'

Dmitri's face blanched and he sat very still. 'What did you say?'

'That I hear it wasn't just Nicholas who was shot in the Ipatiev House . . .' Yakovlev seemed surprised at Dmitri's shocked reaction. 'I'm only repeating what I've heard, mind. I wasn't actually there.'

Malevich joined in. 'I have heard the same rumour but cannot believe it. This government would lose the sympathy of all its supporters and would be condemned the world over. Perhaps Nicholas is dead – even that is in doubt given that they have not produced the body – but I'm confident we will discover the rest of the family as we march on Moscow.'

Dmitri stood and excused himself from the group, stumbling into the woods at the edge of the camp. Once out of sight he bent over and threw up violently, the bitter taste of bile scorching his throat. *They can't be dead. They simply can't.* If they were, he had failed utterly. He was directly responsible for the fate of the farm girl Yelena. He had bungled all his attempts to rescue the family. It was possible their deaths were his fault because the guards panicked when they realised that Tatiana had been freed.

Malevich appeared behind him and flung an arm around his shoulders. 'Don't listen to him. Stay strong.'

Dmitri looked up in despair: 'If I discover Tatiana is dead, I cannot go on living.'

Malevich spoke sternly. 'First of all, I simply don't believe the Bolsheviks would be so stupid as to kill them all. And even if they did kill those in the Ipatiev House, you have no proof Tatiana was there. I firmly believe she is out here somewhere, and she's waiting for you to find her. You owe it to her to carry on looking.'

Dmitri turned and smashed his forehead against a tree. 'I miss her so badly. I can't bear this agony.' He drew his head back to smash it again and Malevich caught him by the shoulders.

'You can and you will,' he said firmly. 'Imagine she is watching you, and do as she would want you to do.'

Dmitri felt the sense of his words and they gave him the strength to pull himself together. One day, if he found Tatiana, she would ask what he was doing in this period, and he hoped to be able to say he behaved with courage. He vowed he would never give up searching until he found her, wherever she might be.

At first, momentum in battle was with the White Army. With the help of arms supplied by the British government, and with a ragtag band of recruits from various different factions who were disenchanted with the Bolsheviks, Admiral Kolchak's men marched steadily towards Moscow. As they went they liberated villages from Bolshevik control, freed prisoners and overturned socialist reforms that had been imposed. White Army morale suffered a blow in November when the British withdrew their support after signing an armistice with Germany, but the advance continued and soon Kolchak's troops reached the River Volga, only a hundred miles east of Moscow.

By now the snow lay deep and temperatures were dropping daily. All the men stopped washing because to expose bare skin in such cold would be a sure way of catching frostbite. They requisitioned food for men and horses from farms they passed. Dmitri felt ashamed to be depriving the occupants of their winter stores, but there was no alternative if they were to free the country from the lunatics who had taken charge.

In December Dmitri's division was dispatched further south to the strategically important town of Tsaritsyn, which the Red Army refused to abandon, and straight away there were fierce clashes. The Soviet 10th Army they faced had twice as many men, dozens of machineguns and artillery placements, but still it seemed the White Army was creeping into the suburbs, winning over the town street by street. Dmitri took a few men with him on daily reconnaissance missions to check where the big guns were placed before each assault. They needed their wits about them in the hostile terrain, but his superlative training took over. He knew he was more capable than these Bolshevik opponents, who could spout socialist rhetoric but knew nothing of military tactics. It would not be long before they drove them back.

On the 1st of January 1919, the White Army launched a major assault on Tsaritsyn. Within two weeks they had advanced to form a semicircle around the city and looked set for victory. One afternoon Dmitri's men were in a tall office building near the town centre, planning their next move, when suddenly shells began to rain down. He sprinted up to the roof and, peering through his binoculars, realised they were surrounded and vastly outnumbered by Red Army troops that had materialised seemingly out of nowhere. No other White Army groups were in sight. He ordered a small band of men to break free of the building and ride for help, but as he watched they were shot down in the street like wild boar on a country shoot.

While the officers were debating what to do, a shell smashed through a corner of the room, showering them in debris. As the dust settled, Dmitri saw that Malevich was trapped beneath the rubble. He was unconscious, his face white with plaster dust. Dmitri crouched to listen for sounds of breathing but couldn't detect any.

Working frantically he heaved aside the debris, urging, 'Malevich, wake up. Open your eyes. Breathe, man.' After lifting one massive block he was confronted by a hideous sight: Malevich had been cut in half by the force of the blast, his upper body separated from his lower. His guts spilled out of the torso, while his mangled legs were facing the other way. Dmitri screamed in high pitch, and couldn't stop screaming. His entire body shook in revulsion. He turned away, unable to look at the slippery coils of intestine, the blank expression on his dearest friend's face. *No, God. Please. How can you do this? Why?*

He should try to drag him clear and arrange a Christian burial but the room was empty now. There was no one left to help. The sounds of shelling were further away but the smell of blood and smoke still filled the air. Dmitri's ears rang and he was shivering with shock as he paced up and down, up and down. Eventually he decided the only thing he could do was to cover Malevich where he lay. He did that, murmuring a prayer for God to have mercy on his soul since he had allowed his body to be so hideously butchered.

When Dmitri finally went to look for his men, he realised the fighting had moved several blocks away. He ducked into doorways, making his way back towards the muster point where they had started that morning. No one was there. He headed towards the camp in the woods where they had slept the night before. Much of it was intact, the horses still tethered and bedding rolls abandoned on the ground, but there were no men in sight. He picked up his pack, which contained his most treasured possessions: Tatiana's diary and the waistcoat she had knitted for him.

Dmitri found his horse, filled a canteen with water then rode out to try and locate his troops, but wherever he went he found piles of the dead. It had been a mass slaughter. He tried for several hours but couldn't find anyone to report to, or any group of survivors numbering more than two or three. His unit seemed to have vanished into thin air.

Somehow he found himself on the outskirts of town, riding through snowy conifer woods towards open country. *I should turn back*, he thought. *This is desertion.* But he did not. He galloped till nightfall, sustained only by sips of water from his canteen. When tiredness overwhelmed him, he took a room in a cheap inn, where he was tormented by bedbugs and traumatised by vivid dreams of his best friend's body ripped in two.

Next morning, over breakfast, he saw the landlady reading a newspaper with a headline about the Romanovs, so he begged to be allowed to borrow it. The story read that Admiral Kolchak had commissioned a man named Sokolov, a local prosecutor in Ekaterinburg, to head an enquiry into the fate of the royal family, and it seemed he had found some burnt remains by a mineshaft outside Ekaterinburg: fragments of clothing, a pair of old spectacles, and some jewels that had belonged to the family. Among the more grisly remains there was a severed finger and the body of a small dog. Dmitri felt sick. The family would never have left one of their dogs behind if they could help it. Had it been poor Ortipo? And whose was the finger?

The story continued with a fresh insistence from the Bolshevik government that although Nicholas had been executed, the family were safe. It said they were being accommodated in the town of Perm. Dmitri's heart leapt. He did not trust this government one iota, but why would they specify Perm if there was no truth in it? Tatiana's Aunt Ella had lived in Perm, so perhaps they were staying with her. Oh God, he hoped so.

It was at least a thousand miles to the north, too far to ride, but if he changed into peasant clothes he could maybe take a train without raising suspicion. His mind made up, he went to enquire about train times.

Chapter Thirty-Six

Perm, Russia, spring 1919

Travel was treacherous in a country in the midst of civil war, especially when you had recently deserted from your army. Dmitri kept himself to himself on the train and did not get drawn into any of the heated discussions amongst his fellow passengers, both for and against Bolshevism.

Perm was in the hands of the White Army. It was unlikely anyone in this northern group would recognise him, but Dmitri kept a low profile all the same. He took lodgings under an assumed name, bought a horse, and began riding through the town, street by street, just as he had done in Verkhoturye. There were heavily guarded munitions factories but he could find no private houses with guards outside. He began making discreet enquiries, asking if anyone had seen the Romanovs arrive but was disheartened by the casual response: 'They're all dead, my friend.' No one seemed to care. From one café owner he heard that Tatiana's Aunt Ella and her Uncle Michael, along with several other family members, had been executed by the Bolsheviks, but still he refused to believe they could have killed the young grand duke and the duchesses. They were children! He kept busy during the day, and at night he drank himself unconscious to drown out the appalling dreams of

Tatiana being dragged away by men with axes, and Malevich cut in half.

By spring 1919, the tide in the civil war had swung firmly against the White Army: Admiral Kolchak surrendered to the Bolsheviks in May 1919 and was promptly executed. The territories they had fought so hard for were recaptured. International help dried up and the Red Army were once again advancing towards the Urals.

When he had exhausted his search of Perm, Dmitri caught a train south just before the Red Army arrived in town. A young man travelling alone would arouse suspicion and he did not want to find himself detained by a local soviet, answering questions about where he hailed from. He intended at long last to visit his mother and sisters in Lozovatka, which was in Ukrainian hands, but on the way there he heard from a fellow passenger that Tatiana's grandmother, Maria Feodorovna, and several other relatives were staying at the Livadia Palace in Crimea so he decided to go there first. If Tatiana had managed to escape her captors, that's where she would head. She had always loved Livadia.

It was mid-summer and the heat was fierce when he arrived at the Romanovs' luxurious white-granite Livadia palace to find it deserted, apart from a handful of servants.

'Where is the Dowager Empress?' he asked a housemaid who answered the door.

'They were rescued a few weeks ago by a ship sent by King George V of England. All were very relieved.'

'Were any of Tsar Nicholas's children with them?' He held his breath.

'No, we've heard nothing of them. There are rumours that they've been killed but Maria Feodorovna refuses to believe it. She said no one could be so heartless . . . You look faint, sir. Would you like to sit down awhile?'

It was another bitter disappointment for Dmitri. Somewhere in the vastness of the great Russian hinterland was his wife, the woman he loved above all others on earth, but he no longer had any idea where to look for her or even if she was alive. She could be waiting for him, despairing of him finding her, and he felt useless and impotent that he had no idea where to look.

Dmitri sent a telegram to his mother saying that he would visit within the month, then he spent another week wandering around the Livadia estate, hoping against hope that Tatiana might arrive. The staff accepted him when he explained he had been a member of the royal escort, and produced meals and refreshments as if he were an honoured guest. He tried to imagine Tatiana strolling by the fountains in the Arabian courtyard; playing croquet on the manicured lawn with a view out to sea; swimming in the clear blue waters; dining on the open-air terrace; bathing in the white marble bathrooms. It made him feel a connection with her. This was a place she had loved and he could see why, but it also made him contrast the rarefied lifestyle she had led with the realities of life for the country's peasants, something he had seen at first hand over the previous year. In Livadia, luxury was taken for granted: the paintings in lavish gilt frames, the heavy hallmarked silver cutlery, the ornate carved furniture – everything smelled expensive. The average peasant eked out the barest existence on a diet of root vegetables and rough bread, with few possessions beyond the clothes they wore on their backs. It was an inequality that should be righted, but he loathed the methods of the Bolsheviks.

Towards the end of the week, just as he was planning to leave, he received a telegram from a neighbour of his mother's: REGRET YOUR MOTHER DIED IN APRIL STOP SHE HEARD YOU WERE KILLED AT TSARITSYN STOP YOUR SISTERS HAVE SAILED FOR CONSTANTINOPLE STOP. There followed an address in Turkey.

A howl burst from Dmitri's lungs: 'No!' He ran through the park to the edge of the sea, howling all the way. The sound seemed to echo around the bay and two gulls took off from a ledge in the cliff. Dmitri fell to his knees, his forehead to the ground, and tore at his hair.

If only he had contacted his mother as soon as he left Tsaritsyn. He should have gone to visit straight after his father died. He had let her down, just as he had let Tatiana down. It was as if God had turned on him and everything he touched turned to dust. He was a failure as a husband and a failure as a son. He did not deserve to live any more.

The waves lapped against the shore with a steady rhythm, giving him an idea. He would swim out to sea and keep swimming further and further until his strength left him and he slipped beneath the waves. That way at last he would bring his torment to an end.

He stripped off his shirt, boots and trousers and stepped into the water. His body would never be found in the vastness of the Black Sea. His sisters would continue to think he had died at Tsaritsyn, and that's what Tatiana would hear if she tried to search for him.

That thought stopped him. What if his body washed up on the shore? He could not bear to have Tatiana think of him as a coward.

He sat down on the shingle, sobbing hard. No. His punishment was that he must live with the shame of his actions. He would be tortured by guilt for the rest of his life, but at least he could try to make it up to his sisters – and possibly, one day, to Tatiana.

Dmitri stayed in Crimea to fight in the White Army's last futile battles against the Bolsheviks, under the command of General Wrangel. In early 1920 he got on board one of the last ships taking refugees south to Constantinople, and made his way to his sisters' house. They were astounded to see him, and there were long days in which they told each other all that had happened in the years since last they saw each other. He wept as he told them of Tatiana; he cried more when Valerina told him of their father's death in Bolshevik custody. They suspected but could not prove he had been executed.

'Mother never fully recovered,' Valerina explained. 'Her heart grew weaker and she could not exert herself without risking collapse. When we got the news that you were killed in battle, it was almost as if she gave up on life.'

'I blame myself . . .' Dmitri began.

'Don't ever say that,' Valerina interrupted, taking his hand and squeezing it tightly. 'From what you have told me, everything you did has been for love. I don't believe God will frown on that.'

He shook his head. 'How can I live with the wrong I have done?'

Valerina had the answer: 'You will get out of bed every morning and keep going, hour by hour, day by day, and gradually it will get easier. Vera's husband will give you work in his carpet business and you can live with us. You should write to all of Tatiana's relatives, wherever they may be found, and if she escapes from the Bolsheviks she will know where to find you. But in the meantime you must grit your teeth and carry on living because to do otherwise would be hideously cruel to your sisters, who love you and have only just found you again.'

He lifted her hand to his lips and kissed it tenderly. 'I'll try,' he whispered, the words catching in his throat.

Chapter Thirty-Seven

Lake Akanabee, New York State, end of September 2016

A few days after her terrifying nocturnal experience, Kitty was planting some flowers in a patch alongside the cabin when she heard a car crawling down the track. As it got close she recognised Jeff from the vacation park along with an older man.

'Morning, Kitty,' Jeff called. 'How ya doing?'

'I'm hot!' she called back, embarrassed by the dark patches of sweat on her t-shirt.

As the men got out of the car, she saw that Jeff was carrying a Fedex parcel the size of a pillow. 'This is my granddad,' he said of the older man, who tipped his straw hat in greeting. 'I'm giving him a ride home and thought I'd stop by with this . . .' He handed the parcel over.

Kitty clutched it, surprised. 'Goodness, what is it?' The address on the label said it came from Marion, her cleaner in London. The bag was open at the top and she glanced in to see her long, chunky olive-green cardigan, a useful cold-weather cover-up. 'Thanks for bringing it over.'

'My granddad wanted to see what you've done with the cabin. Hope you don't mind.'

'No, of course not. Feel free to have a wander.'

The old man was looking round the yard. 'What are you planting?' he asked.

'Purple cone flowers, hydrangeas and some black-eyed Susan,' she told him. She'd asked advice at the Indian Lake Garden Centre about what plants were likely to survive the winter. He nodded in approval.

'Last time I was out here must have been when we found your great-granddaddy's body,' the old man commented.

Kitty was startled. 'He died here?'

'Yeah. I came out to look for him after the storekeeper told me she hadn't seen him for a couple of weeks. Found him lying frozen solid on the ground and his dog guarding the body. Half-starved that dog was. A lovely creature. I took him in myself.' He smiled. 'Kids loved him.'

'So you knew Dmitri? What was he like?'

'Well, we never got much beyond saying howdy and commenting on the weather. After he died we tried our damnedest to find some relatives but without success, so the wife and I went to his funeral to pay our respects.'

'He had a daughter, Marta, who was my grandmother, and a son, Nicholas, as well. I wonder why you couldn't find them?' Had they been estranged? The more Kitty found out about Dmitri, the more she realised how little she knew.

'I guess they lost touch along the way. Course, that was in the days before the Internet. You can pretty much find anyone now . . .'

After Jeff and his granddad left, Kitty went into the cabin to open the package. As well as the long cardigan, there was her fleecy dressing gown, the one she wore to cuddle up in front of the tele on winter nights, a bundle of post that had come through for her, a new novel by one of her favourite authors, and a family bar of Galaxy chocolate. Had Marion packed all this for her?

She opened the chocolate and munched a square as she flicked through the mail: a postcard from a friend in Costa Rica, a bank statement for her personal account, a couple of invoices, some

221

complimentary play tickets – and a letter with a note from Marion on the outside: 'Hi Kitty, I couldn't lie when Tom asked if I knew where your cabin was. I refused to give him the address but promised to send this package and let you know he's missing you terribly. We had a long chat the other day and I feel sorry for him. He's a decent man.'

Kitty was irritated. People always thought Tom was decent. That meant if there was any interruption to the normal harmony, it was automatically assumed to be her fault.

'Anyway, I'm sorry to stick my nose in where it's not wanted but I couldn't see the harm in you having this lot and the enclosed letter from Tom. Hope you are OK out there. Marion.'

The envelope wasn't sealed. Kitty glanced inside and recognised Tom's handwriting. Nerves twisted in her stomach at the thought of reading it and she decided she would wait till later, when she'd had a glass of wine for Dutch courage.

She went back out to the garden to continue her planting, wondering exactly where Dmitri was found dead. It felt kind of creepy that he had died there.

Later that evening, with a bottle of Chardonnay by her side, Kitty sat on the jetty with Tom's letter in one hand. The sunset was magnificent, all salmon-pink and mauve, and for a while she just watched. As the light faded, it felt as though she was looking through a sepia filter that was darkening minute by minute. She fetched her gas lamp, poured a second glass, then began to read.

Hey Kitty,

The weather has turned to autumn here, with rainy days and chilly evenings, and I worried you might get cold out there in the Adirondacks. It's hard to tell from your ward-robe but it looks as though you've only taken summer clothes. If you want me to ship out anything else just ask.

l. you've been reading my emails (and I hope you have), you'll know that I've been seeing a counsellor for six weeks now.

Kitty's eyes widened with surprise. Tom had never struck her as the therapy type. Wonders would never cease. She took a big gulp of wine before reading on.

I never thought I'd do something like this but it's a fascinating process that is helping me to understand why I did such a stupid, destructive thing as to have sex with Karren Bayliss. It only happened four times and it was over long before you found the messages but that's obviously four times too many. There are no excuses, of course, but I was feeling pretty low when I didn't get that promotion at work and I got the feeling, rightly or wrongly, that you were disappointed in me.

Kitty frowned. She couldn't remember which promotion he meant.

I know you're not interested in my job and think I have basically sold out to the establishment, but moving departments would have meant a more creative role. I'd like to be involved in something to do with music, even if I'm never going to be Bruce Springsteen. Anyway, I've registered with an agency to try and find another job and have a few interviews coming up.

So, my dented ego was one reason for the stupid infidelity. It's embarrassing how neatly I fit the midlife crisis criteria: approaching forty, a few pounds overweight, frustrated at work, and feeling lonely because you and I stopped communicating at some point and I miss being close to you. I won't bore you with the therapeutic term for this kind of phenomenon. I'm just disgusted with myself for

223

being a cliché, and most of all for hurting you, the person who means most to me in the world.

Kitty shivered, although it was a balmy evening, and refilled her glass. Tom was obviously taking the whole counselling thing very seriously, studying it as if for one of his accountancy exams.

My counsellor thinks I subconsciously left my phone where you would find it that day. She would like to have a session with us together but I explained that you are on the other side of the Atlantic and not replying to emails. Frankly I would rather you slapped me, yelled at me and smashed up my laptop than disappeared for weeks on end without any communication. It's excruciating to be on the receiving end of the deep-freeze treatment and not know when I might see you again.

It seems a long time since we talked, properly talked, about anything. I've been trying to work out how long and I think it started after your parents died. We'd only been married a year and I expected you to be sobbing yourself to sleep every night, breaking down during the day, drinking too much and eating too little. Instead, what did you do? You bought that big run-down house in Tottenham and spent every waking hour doing it up: rebuilding, redecorating, fitting a new kitchen, tiling the bathrooms, more or less singlehanded. Your energy was scary but you never once mentioned your mum and dad, and if I spoke about them you left the room. Since then it has felt to me as if I'm not allowed to bring up sensitive subjects, and after a while I stopped trying – and now we find ourselves estranged.

Kitty remembered that period. The house she was doing up had dry rot everywhere, wiring that was centuries out of date and dodgy plumbing, but she had welcomed the distraction. She freely admitted that she dealt with her parents' death by keeping busy. She thought back to the policewoman coming to the door with the news of the pileup on a Spanish motorway. She'd felt numb during the flight out to Malaga. Tom had to identify the bodies because she simply couldn't do it. It was as if she was anaesthetised for the first few weeks and could hardly feel anything, but when she did start to feel, the pain was intolerable. It could have destroyed her. And so she had bought that house in Tottenham, with so many problems that really it would have been easier to demolish it and rebuild from scratch.

What was wrong with distracting yourself from grief? She'd got through it: that was the main thing.

Suddenly Kitty's elbow caught the bottle of wine and it toppled and fell into the lake. She swigged the dregs from her glass then got up to fetch another bottle from the cabin before reading the rest of the letter.

Don't think I am trying to put any of the blame for the infidelity onto you. I am a messed-up piece of shit and I hate myself for what I've done. Please know that I will do anything it takes to make it up to you and turn our marriage back into the beautiful, loving, fun partnership it used to be. Tell me what you want and I'll do it. I simply can't be happy without you, Kitty.

I hope you are having a lovely summer out there. Contact me when you are ready to talk and I'll either fly out to you or we can meet in a place of your choice and see where we stand. Just don't ever doubt how much I love you and how much I regret what I have done.

Your Tom xxx

It was pitch dark now and there were bats gliding overhead, while frogs croaked a night-time symphony. Kitty drank another glass of wine and suddenly she began to cry. *What am I crying for?* she wondered, and had no answer, but the compulsion had taken hold. She grasped the letter and hugged it tightly to her chest as she wept like a child, with complete abandon. There was a painful spot deep inside and she hoped the crying jag might shift it but when she clambered up to the cabin and pulled herself into bed fully clothed, it was still there.

Chapter Thirty-Eight

Istanbul, 1922

Dmitri dragged himself through the next two years, morose and self-hating, often seeking release from the thoughts and images that tortured him in the bottom of an arak bottle. His time with Tatiana seemed a distant dream, a fairy tale from a past life in which he could distantly recall he had once been happy. He found it hard to be around his sister Vera, with her two adorable children and attentive husband, because it reminded him of what might have been. Instead he spent his evenings with Valerina, a clever, creative woman, who had never found a husband but who occupied her time painting charming pictures of the Turkish landscape.

One morning in March 1922 Valerina came rushing to his office to show him a story, just a few paragraphs long, on the inside of the front page of her newspaper.

'A woman in a Berlin asylum is claiming to be Grand Duchess Anastasia,' she cried.

Dmitri grabbed the paper. There was no photograph, and no details about where she had been since 1918, but he was elated. 'If it is Anastasia, then she might know where the others are – where Tatiana is. And surely if Tatiana is alive and reads the same story, she will travel to Berlin to be reunited with her sister?'

It said in the newspaper that the woman in question had lost her memory but Dmitri was sure he could prompt her to regain it. He had spoken to Anastasia several times in St Petersburg and she would certainly know him. For the first time in years, there was positive news and he allowed himself to become excited – although it was tinged with anxiety because there was always a chance that Anastasia could be the bearer of bad tidings.

He resigned from the carpet business, apologising to Vera's husband, packed a small brown leather suitcase and bought a ticket on the Orient Express to Munich, then another ticket to travel onwards to Berlin. On board he willed the train to go faster. He couldn't wait to see Anastasia, couldn't wait to hear what she might have to say.

It felt odd arriving in a country whose soldiers he had been attempting to kill just six years earlier. He spoke only a few words of German and had difficulty making himself understood when he asked directions to the Dalldorf Asylum, mentioned in the news story.

It was a wide, three-storey sandstone building with ivy climbing up the front, set in neat, extensive gardens. He walked up to the front door, knocked and addressed the matronly woman who answered in English: 'Might I see Grand Duchess Anastasia? I am an old friend of the family, from Russia.'

The woman replied in German and he could only catch the word 'Anastasia' but from her gestures she appeared to be asking him to leave. He tried speaking to her in French but got the same reaction.

'I *must* see Anastasia,' he repeated, looking up the stone staircase beyond, wondering where she might be. He could easily rush past this woman, but wouldn't know where to go next.

A doctor came by who spoke some French and he explained to Dmitri: 'Our former patient, who is known as Anna Tschaikovsky, has moved out of the asylum and is living with a Russian émigré by the name of Baron von Kleist.'

Dmitri asked if he had the address, but the doctor said it would be unprofessional of him to give it, although he added, 'I suggest you ask around.'

'But where would I ask?'

The doctor wrinkled his forehead: 'Try the cafés of Charlottenburg, where there are more Russians than Germans. Good luck, my friend.'

Everything was a struggle in this foreign land. Trams trundled past on electrified lines but none of them had the name Charlottenburg on the front, and when Dmitri asked for directions he found few who understood him. Eventually one woman directed him onto a bright yellow tram and told him to ask for Prager Platz.

Night was beginning to fall when the conductor called out that they had reached Prager Platz and Dmitri descended into a bustling square with a grassy area in the centre. All around brightly coloured electric signs were being illuminated outside cafés and restaurants. Everyone seemed to be in a hurry.

He chose the busiest café, called the Prager Diele, and immediately heard a group of men conversing in loud Russian.

'Excuse me . . .' he interrupted, 'but do any of you know where Baron von Kleist lives?'

'Another one looking for Anastasia.' A man in a purple cravat rolled his eyes at his companions then turned to Dmitri. 'They won't let you see her. The Baron is fiercely protective. But I have a friend who spoke with her while she was in the asylum and he swears it is not her. She doesn't even speak Russian, for God's sake.'

Dmitri's spirits plummeted. 'She doesn't?' He had pinned too much hope on this meeting, full of optimism that he might soon find his wife. What a fool he was.

'Come, have a glass with us. My name is Boris.' The man poured a generous measure of ruby wine into a glass and handed it to Dmitri. 'You've just arrived in Berlin, I suppose.'

Dmitri nodded his head and accepted the wine, feeling devastated. The men scraped their chairs closer together to make room for him. 'All the same,' he continued, 'I'd like to see her for myself. I knew Anastasia in St Petersburg when I . . .'

Boris held up a hand to stop him. 'The first rule here is that you must be careful not to identify yourself as a monarchist. Keep your counsel. There are many Bolshevik spies in town and you can never tell who you are speaking to, especially after a few glasses of good Burgundy.'

'Thank you. I appreciate your advice.' Dmitri introduced himself and learned the names of the other four at the table, all of them Russian. He could tell from their accents that two were from the St Petersburg area, one from Moscow, two from Siberia, but he did not ask their backgrounds. They refilled his glass and when the bottle was empty Dmitri bought the next one.

At around midnight, when Dmitri's words were slurred and his head spinning, Boris took him to a nearby apartment block and introduced him to the landlady, who fortunately had a small apartment available. Before he left, Boris pushed a piece of paper into his hand. 'The address you wanted,' he whispered. 'But don't get your hopes up.'

Next morning, after Dmitri had held his head under a cold tap to clear a thumping headache, then eaten a filling breakfast of sausage and sauerkraut in a café, he set off to find Baron von Kleist's apartment. Boris's note said it was on the fourth floor at number 9 Nettelbeckstrasse, which he found with the help of a street map borrowed from his landlady.

He rang the bell and when it was answered by a black-suited butler he asked, 'I wonder if I might see Anna Tschaikovsky? Tell her it is Cornet Malama.' His stomach was twisting with nerves. Was he about to learn the truth about what happened to Tatiana?

'I'm sorry, sir. She is unwell and not seeing anyone.'

'If I write a note, will you give it to her?' he asked, and the butler agreed with a slight shrug.

Dmitri scribbled a message then and there, saying he was delighted to hear Anastasia was alive, and wondering if she had any news of the others. He said he would be happy to perform any services she might require of him and signed it 'Malama'. 'I'll wait in the park across the road in case she changes her mind about seeing me,' he explained.

He paced up and down, checking his pocket watch, looking up at the windows of the Baron's apartment. Would she glance out to see if it was him?

An hour later, when there had been no word, he rang the bell at number 9 once more. 'Did she read my note?' he asked.

'As I said, I'm afraid she will not see anybody,' the butler repeated, expressionless.

Dmitri felt shattered. He had come so far and invested so much hope in this encounter that it was unbearable to have hit an impasse. There was nothing more he could do so he stopped in a café down the street to ease his disappointment with a tumbler of vodka.

Chapter Thirty-Nine

Berlin, 1922

Dmitri spent long hours in the café near Baron von Kleist's residence, watching the door in case the woman who claimed to be Anastasia might emerge, but there was no sign of her. One morning as he waited he found a copy of a Russian newspaper called *Rul* – 'Rudder' – lying abandoned on a table and flicked through it. Produced in Berlin, it reported on matters of interest to the city's Russian community. From just a cursory read, Dmitri realised there were many factions: there were the pro-monarchists, the Bolsheviks, and the Constitutional Democrats, who thought Russia should enter into the modern age with free elections. The Whites accused the Bolsheviks of being Jews seeking global domination, and argued about the best way to wrest Russia from their control, while spies from the Cheka, the secret police, infiltrated their number and assassinations were not uncommon. He could see why Boris had recommended that he keep his counsel.

Dmitri had saved some money while working in Constantinople but he would need to earn more to keep himself, and the newspaper gave him an idea. He bought a notebook and wrote an article about the last stand of General Wrangel in Crimea, and his evacuation of the last remnants of the White Army from Sevastopol on the 14th of November 1920. The Bolsheviks had executed those they captured by tying their hands and feet and dropping them overboard into the Black Sea. Dmitri had seen many trussed-up corpses in the water, eyes bulging grotesquely, as he sailed to Constantinople. When he had finished, he walked to the offices of *Rul* and sat across a desk while the editor, a man named Burtsev, read his piece.

'You write well,' Burtsev told him, 'and I have not seen a more compelling account of the final evacuation. I'll pay you 5,000 marks for this story.'

That sounded good. 'Can I write more for you?' Dmitri asked.

'Sure. If I like your articles, I will pay you. But get yourself a typewriter first.'

Dmitri bought a second-hand typewriter and taught himself to type with two fingers. He studied each issue of *Rul*, as well as its rival paper, *Golos Rossii* – 'The Voice of Russia' – which was edited by a man who had been Minister of Agriculture in the government of March to October 1917. Burtsev liked Dmitri's work, and began to give him commissions, which Dmitri asked him to publish under the family name Yakovlevich so that he would not be identified; back home everyone had known him as Malama.

He was sent to interview musicians and choreographers, writers and artists, men who had been prominent back in Russia but who struggled to find work in this modern city. Many were living in poverty, having spent any money they managed to bring with them on the journey. Some were working in menial jobs simply to feed their families: counts served as waiters, princesses as secretaries. Dmitri wrote about the sights of Berlin through the eyes of an émigré, describing the men who dressed as women to work in cabaret shows, the skinny prostitutes with sunken cheeks and haunted eyes, the street sellers with goods that looked too good to be true and broke at first use.

Gradually he began to trust Burtsev and asked him if he might write a story about Anna Tschaikovsky. He explained that he had known Anastasia in St Petersburg. Could the editor perhaps arrange an interview?

Burtsev eyed him thoughtfully. 'All my requests for an interview with Miss Tschaikovsky have been refused but I hear that Princess Irene of Hesse, the sister of Tsarina Alexandra, is arriving in town to visit the girl. Did you ever come across her?'

Dmitri had to say no, he hadn't.

'But can I say you are a family friend?'

Dmitri nodded. 'Certainly.'

'I will ask if you can talk to her after she has met the girl. There is bound to be a story in that.'

Somewhat to Dmitri's surprise, Princess Irene of Hesse agreed to be interviewed by him, asking that he come to her suite at the Adlon, the town's most luxurious hotel. He dressed with care, polishing his shoes and getting a close shave and a haircut in a barbershop.

On arrival, Dmitri was kept waiting for over an hour in the sumptuous hotel lobby, with square marble columns and a fountain of water gushing from the trunk of a stone elephant.

At last, he was shown up to Princess Irene's suite and found her sitting by a window sipping tea. She was a stout woman in her fifties, her brown hair streaked with grey, and her Germanic features bore a strong resemblance to those of Alexandra. Dmitri was overcome for a moment: this was Tatiana's aunt! He had written to her two years earlier asking her to let him know if there was news of the family but had received no reply.

'Please sit.' She waved him to an armchair, and began to speak. 'I assume you wish to hear of my meeting with Miss Tschaikovsky, and I must tell you I am afraid to say she is not Anastasia. There is no resemblance with my niece. The position of the eyes, the bone structure, both are quite wrong.'

'When did you last see the Grand Duchesses?' Dmitri asked, scribbling in his notebook in an attempt to hide his disappointment.

'I admit it's been nine years, but Alexandra used to send me photographs right up until they were taken into *captivity*' – she spoke the word with distaste – 'and I am quite certain. This girl is rude and thoughtless, in a way my nieces would never have been, and what's more she spoke no Russian. Not a word.'

'How did she explain that?' Dmitri asked.

'Baron von Kleist told me that she suffered some kind of trauma that caused her to lose her memory, and along with it her mother tongue.'

'What kind of trauma?' Dmitri reddened and his pulse quickened.

'I presume he means the murder of the rest of the family.' She took a sip of tea.

'You believe they are dead?' Dmitri held his breath.

'I have it from very credible sources that they all died in the Ipatiev House at the hands of the Red Guards.'

Dmitri opened his mouth to speak but instead a sob burst from his throat. Princess Irene regarded him with surprise as he struggled to regain control.

'Did you know them personally?' she asked.

He nodded, unable to speak at first, then managed to say, 'I was a good friend of Grand Duchess Tatiana.'

The Princess peered at him through narrowed eyes. 'Are you Malama?' He nodded. 'Alexandra thought very highly of you.' Dmitri covered his face with his hands. 'Come, come. Pull yourself together, man.'

She rang a bell and asked for a cognac, which was quickly supplied by a uniformed servant. Dmitri took a gulp and felt it burn its way down.

'Have you entirely given up hope?' he asked in a strangled voice.

'I'm afraid so. If my sister were alive, she would have found a way to get word to me over the last four years. She could have asked someone to send a note. None of the family has heard: Nicholas's mother and sister in Denmark, the English family – no

235

one knows any more than I do. We're all furious with Bertie, of course. He could easily have brought them to London back in 1917 but he got cold feet. He's such a coward. He worried about who would support them, how the order of precedence would work – Lord knows what went through his selfish brain, but the upshot is my sister is dead.'

'You just assume the worst because there has been no word; you haven't heard this from people in Ekaterinburg, have you?' Dmitri asked, clutching at straws.

'I had a letter from the British Consul Sir Thomas Preston. He has spoken to many local people, including Mr Sokolov, who has escaped overseas and is still preparing the report that he was commissioned to produce by the leader of the White Army. I believe it will be published within a year or so.' She offered Dmitri another cognac but he shook his head.

'Will you please let me know if you should hear any more news of Tatiana, or the family?' he begged.

'Well, of course.' Her expression was sympathetic. 'But you mustn't live in the past. Get on with your future. It's a terrible tragedy, but you are still young and you will recover. I, on the other hand, will mourn them till the day I die.'

Dmitri left the hotel clutching his notebook, headed into the nearest bar and ordered a vodka. Despite what Princess Irene had said, he vowed that unless someone presented him with absolute proof that Tatiana was dead, he would never give up hope. Never.

Chapter Forty

Dmitri filed his article about Princess Irene's meeting with Anna Tschaikovsky and it was published in *Rul*. A week later they received a letter from Tsar Nicholas's sister Olga in Denmark saying that she disagreed with Irene and thought Anna genuinely was her niece Anastasia. The controversy made Dmitri even more determined to meet the girl, but no matter which avenues he tried, he could not find a way through the heavy oak doors of Baron von Kleist's apartment.

Dmitri spent his days writing articles, and his evenings in the cafés of Charlottenburg, drinking with crowds of Russian émigrés. They moaned to each other about Berlin, calling it a materialistic city where everything was for sale, with gaudy advertising all around and prostitutes openly hustling passersby on every street corner. Usually one or other of his drinking companions would end up in tears of homesickness for Mother Russia once they were a few bottles down.

One evening, Dmitri was with a group who became rowdy and started smashing glasses on the floor, whereupon the doormen escorted them off the premises. Dmitri's comrades headed straight into a neighbouring bar but he sat on the grass in the middle of Prager Platz to let the cold night air clear his head. A girl who had been working in the café came running across to him.

'You left your notebook,' she said in Russian. It had all his notes from an interview that day and he was relieved not to have lost it.

'Thank you. You've saved my life,' he said melodramatically.

'I've seen you here before, haven't I? My name is Rosa.' She held out her hand.

As he shook hands with her, he noticed she had a very full bosom for someone so petite, and that she had pretty eyes and short dark hair. 'You've got a boy's haircut,' he remarked. He hadn't noticed her when she brought their drinks to the table, but close up she was definitely attractive.

She laughed. 'I have it cut in a barber's shop. It's cheaper than a women's hairdresser. Are you a writer?' Her Russian was fluent but she had a German accent, which made it sound unfamiliar.

'I write articles for *Rul*,' he said, then added, 'I'm also working on a novel.' He had no idea why he said this except that every White Russian in Berlin seemed to be writing a novel and it sounded romantic.

'What's your novel about?' she asked, sitting on the grass beside him.

'It's about love, of course. A great love affair that spans decades and continents but is ultimately doomed to unhappiness.' He was in a maudlin state, thinking of Tatiana.

'But why can it not have a happy ending?'

'Because all love affairs end unhappily,' he said, 'like all wars.' He wasn't drunk enough because depression was creeping up on him. 'Could you fetch another bottle of wine from your bar? I've got the money.'

'No,' she said firmly, 'but my shift has finished so I will get my coat and take you home. Where do you live?'

Dmitri considered. Suddenly it seemed a compelling idea to take comfort in a woman's arms, to nestle his head against that full bosom and breathe in a female scent. He had not made love to another woman since meeting Tatiana back in 1914, and he felt guilty even thinking about it . . . but all the same it was tempting.

238

He let Rosa help him to his feet and lead him the short distance to his apartment, with her arm linked through his. She helped when he fumbled with his keys, then steadied him on the way up the stairs.

Will I be capable of sex? Dmitri wondered, shortly before he passed out.

When Dmitri woke the next morning, he turned his head to see if Rosa was beside him. She wasn't, but the bed had been neatly made, with the sheets tucked in, and he was lying beneath the covers in his underwear. Normally he did not make the bed from one day to the next, simply slipping into the hollow his body had formed the night before. And the other odd thing was that he could not remember getting undressed. Had Rosa taken his clothes off? He glanced round the room and saw them neatly folded over the back of a chair.

On the bedside table there was a glass of water and a bottle of Bayer aspirin powder. The sight irritated him but he took a sip of water all the same, his mouth dry as cardboard and his breath rancid.

He heaved himself out of bed, pulled on a dressing gown and went through to the tiny kitchen alcove. He had left the sink overflowing with dirty dishes but now they were washed and stacked away and the surfaces sparkled. His irritation grew. In the sitting room, everything was neat and tidy but there was no sign of the girl. How dare she come into his home and clean it without permission!

He put on a pot of coffee then went to the bathroom to wash and shave. She hadn't cleaned there. The bath had a greasy grey tideline, while the sink was grimy with bristles. He was still annoyed, and as he performed his ablutions he considered charging round to the café to remonstrate with Rosa for cleaning up. It was only when he planned the words he would use that he realised how foolish it would sound and began to chuckle.

His notebook was sitting on the table next to the typewriter – thank goodness it hadn't got lost – and he sat down with a cup of coffee to read through his notes from the previous day. Suddenly he remembered telling Rosa that he was writing a novel. Why not? He had recently started reading novels again, borrowing them from Rodina's bookshop, which stocked Russian-language books. Many works by émigrés were self-indulgent laments, with little plot or characterisation; he was sure he could do better.

He went out to the local bakery to buy some warm pastries, then came back to eat them with another cup of coffee, and he began to jot down ideas for his novel: a boy and a girl meet in their teens and fall in love but are torn apart by civil war when their families are sent to opposite ends of Russia; then he would write of the boy's long search to find her again. Tatiana was in his head every moment and he decided to try and define the effects of love on body and soul. He found the first scene was clear in his mind: the boy, whom he would call Mikhail, watches the girl – Valerina, after his beloved sister – falling off her bike and trying desperately not to cry at the pain of grazed hands and knees. At that moment Mikhail feels the beginnings of the empathy, basically an insight into another person's emotions, the first step that will lead to love. He began to write, and the words flowed from his pen, bringing a sense of tranquillity.

Two nights later he went back to the café where Rosa worked and asked if she would like to have dinner with him on her night off.

'Well, of *course* I would,' she replied, rolling her eyes as if she couldn't understand what had taken him so long.

Chapter Forty-One

Dmitri had only seen Rosa in her tight black-and-white waitress's uniform so he was somewhat taken aback when she met him for their dinner date wearing her own rather eccentric clothes. Her frock of a yellow and purple pattern was a couple of sizes too large, as if she had borrowed it from her grandmother's wardrobe then belted it round the hips so it didn't fall down. She wore strings of multi-coloured beads round her neck and multiple bracelets that clattered as she moved her arm, while on her head there was a cloche hat with a knitted purple flower attached. When he looked closely, he saw there was a knitted bee inside the flower. It was like a parody of the flapper style worn in the more expensive clubs of Charlottenburg, but somehow it worked. While they talked, her dress slipped down to reveal the creamy flesh of her shoulder and she ignored it for a while before pulling it up with a wink.

They ate in a medium-priced restaurant, and he ordered steak for them both, followed by a rather good *apfeltorte*. Rosa asked about his life in Russia but he didn't feel like talking about that, so instead he questioned her about her own background. Born in the countryside, she said she had always longed to swap the sound of cows outside her bedroom window for the traffic and bustle of the city. She moved to Berlin when she was eighteen and shared a tiny apartment with three other girls, one of whom was her cousin, a dancer. She was now twenty-one and she loved dancing, eating good food, and meeting new people. Especially people.

'So you enjoy waitressing?' Dmitri asked.

She wrinkled her nose. 'For now. The tips are good, but some customers are rude. They look down on me for the job I do without knowing anything about me. I could be a ballerina or a scientist, an artist or a pearl diver, but they don't see past the uniform to my magnificent brain and sparkling personality.' She flung her arms out dramatically like a compére at a cabaret announcing the star guest.

Dmitri laughed. 'Tell me then, what are you?'

She cocked her head to one side and thought before answering. 'I don't entirely know yet, but I like looking after people. I want to have dozens of babies one day; *hundreds* of them.'

'I sincerely hope you achieve your ambition.'

'Well, at least I can have fun trying,' she twinkled.

Dmitri marvelled at the freedom of this woman's life, so unlike those of women in Russia. She could do what she wanted, say what she felt without fear of repression. It was refreshing.

After dinner they strolled through Charlottenberg, which she told him Germans were now calling Charlottengrad because of the high percentage of Russian immigrants.

'How did you learn to speak such fluent Russian?' Dmitri asked, because that was the language they conversed in, although she sometimes switched to English mid-sentence if she didn't know a word.

'I picked it up as I went along. You'll find I'm very chatty. Some cruel folk say it's hard to shut me up.'

'Would you like to come back to my apartment?' he asked.

'That sounds mar-r-vellous,' she replied in English, rolling her 'r' with a broad smile.

Soon after climbing the stairs, they were undressing each other and jumping into Dmitri's bed. Rosa made love enthusiastically and expertly, rolling him over onto his back so she could sit on top. It was clear she was not a virgin and afterwards, he rather ungallantly asked about her previous lovers.

'There was just one before you,' she said. 'He was also Russian. I liked him but he disappeared one day and several weeks later I got a postcard from Paris. He said he thought Bolshevik spies were following him and had to flee. I don't know if it was true or not.'

'You didn't want to join him in Paris?'

'He didn't ask,' she said in a small voice, and Dmitri felt compassion for her.

'I apologise on behalf of my countryman,' he said. 'He was a fool to lose you.'

She turned and kissed him on the mouth, an urgent kiss that moved him deep down inside.

The next day, while he worked on his novel, Rosa went to the market and bought a cheap cut of meat and some vegetables from which she produced a delicious pot of stew. They ate bowls of it for lunch, along with big chunks of bread, and before leaving to start her shift in the café she even cleaned his bathroom. She hummed as she worked so Dmitri didn't feel the need to stop her; or at least when the thought passed through his mind he was able to overrule it.

'Will I see you later?' she asked as she pulled on her coat.

A little warning bell rang in Dmitri's head. He didn't want to feel an obligation towards her. But at the same time, she was a cheerful soul and it was pleasant having her around. Besides, he could hardly say no after all she had done for him.

'I'll pick you up after your shift,' he said, kissing her goodbye. As soon as the door shut, he went back to his novel.

Before long Dmitri and Rosa slipped into a pattern of sleeping together three or four evenings a week. On her night off, she liked to drag him along to the Eldorado nightclub, which had opened in Charlottenburg earlier that year. Her cousin worked there so they could usually secure a good table from which to watch the transvestite dancers, the striptease artists and the comedy burlesque acts. Rosa often got up to dance on the tiny dance floor and Dmitri laughed to watch her in her oversized frocks, like a little girl playing at being grown-up. She mimicked movie stars with flirtatious flicks of her hemline, her mouth rounded in pretend shock at her own audacity.

Berlin couldn't have been less like the high society of St Petersburg with its unbreakable rules and strict formality. Dmitri didn't think he had ever seen a homosexual man in Russia – perhaps they did not exist; perhaps it was not in the national character – but here they were everywhere. He felt a little uncomfortable around them, not sure how to talk to them so that they would know he wasn't available. He'd often slip his arm around Rosa's waist to be doubly sure they got the message.

Sometimes, after making love with Rosa, Dmitri lay awake feeling guilty about his affair. He was a married man; he should not be in bed with another woman. How could he be happy when his wife was missing? But there was no question that if Tatiana appeared one day he would quietly explain the situation to Rosa and beg her forgiveness for leading her on. He would have no hesitation in choosing between them.

Dmitri often asked Burtsev, his editor, if there was any further news of Anna Tschaikovsky. It seemed she had left Baron von Kleist's apartment some time in the autumn and returned to hospital with a range of ailments that required medical treatment. She was not staying at the Dalldorf Asylum this time but at the Westend Hospital in Charlottenburg, not far from his apartment.

One evening, he asked Rosa if she ever heard any customers in the café talking about her, and straight away she replied: 'No, but my friend Klara is a nurse at Westend. She tells me Anna Tschaikovsky is very timid and barely talks to anyone. She has a badly infected arm.'

Dmitri stared at her, eyes wide with excitement. 'Do you think your friend would be able to get me into the hospital to see her? Can you ask?'

Rosa seemed surprised at the intensity with which he spoke. 'Yes, of course, I'll call on her tomorrow if it means so much to you.'

'Thank you.' He squeezed her hand tighter than he had meant to and she flinched.

Chapter Forty-Two

Berlin, January 1923

It transpired that Rosa's friend Klara was unwilling to help Dmitri sneak into the hospital to spy on their famous patient.

'It could cost her her job,' Rosa explained.

'I'll make sure it doesn't. Please – you have to convince her.' Dmitri was determined. 'Won't you try again?'

When Klara once more refused to help, Dmitri grew angry and threw his notebook to the floor. 'She's not much of a friend, is she? Why won't she do as you ask?'

Rosa looked at him closely. 'This isn't just about writing a story for *Rul*, is it? Did you know Grand Duchess Anastasia in Russia?'

Dmitri couldn't talk about that part of his life. 'Slightly,' he said, turning away. 'Only slightly.'

After that Rosa somehow succeeded in persuading Klara. Dmitri didn't ask how. It was arranged that they would meet her one lunchtime at a side door of the huge, sprawling hospital with its red-tiled roofs and towering spires. She would give him the over-alls of an orderly, along with a broom and dustpan, and direct him to the ward. Once there he could go in and sweep round the bed in Anna Tschaikovsky's private room, but if she panicked and started to scream, as she sometimes did at the sight of strangers, he must pretend he let himself in and must not mention Klara's name.

As they walked to the hospital, Rosa chatted about everyday matters – her boss's secret girlfriend, a new recipe for meatloaf – and for once her conversation annoyed him, interrupting the flow of his thoughts. It was almost five years since he had seen Anastasia but he was positive he would know her straight away, even if those chubby girlish cheeks had thinned out and the long curly locks had been trimmed. People have an essence, something in the eyes that makes them recognisable.

What if it was her? He would feel compelled to ask what had happened to the rest of the family, to Tatiana. As if reading his mind, Rosa remarked, 'Seemingly she speaks no Russian and very little English. Do you think you can converse with her in German? You've improved a lot.'

'I thought Klara didn't want me to speak to her?'

'But if it's her, I'm sure you will.'

Rosa seemed sad but he didn't have time to wonder why before they reached the hospital building and followed Klara's directions down a side alley to the workers' entrance.

She appeared at the appointed time carrying an overall and broom. Dmitri thanked her.

'I'll wait here,' Rosa promised as he hurried inside.

He felt strangely calm once he was in the hospital, about to meet the woman for whom he had left Constantinople and travelled to Berlin. Klara pointed down a corridor and told him to take the first staircase on the left, climb to the second floor, then go into the fourth room on the right. He thanked her and walked off, broom and dustpan in hand.

He hesitated outside the door of the private room, gathering his nerve, then pushed it open and saw a young female patient lying back on the pillows, eyes closed. He did not look at her directly at first, but when he did his heart leapt. It *could* be her. It might be. His face burned.

He swept the other side of the room first, around the window with its view across the rooftops of the city. When he turned to sweep near the bed, Anna Tschaikovsky opened her eyes suddenly. Her hair was short and brown, her eyes blue, and she had a wide mouth and a long nose. The similarity was definitely there. His heart beat faster.

'May I sweep under your bed, ma'am,' he asked in German and she nodded her consent.

'Do I know you?' she wondered, watching him work.

'Perhaps,' he replied. 'Do you think you do?'

She sighed. 'Oh, I can't tell. I see so many people from the past and have no memory of them. You are Russian, are you not? You look Russian.'

'Yes, I am. There are many of us in Berlin.'

'Did you know my family? The Romanovs, I mean?' Her voice was deeper than Anastasia's but that could have happened with age.

'I did, and was horrified to read speculation that they were killed. But perhaps if you have escaped, then some of the others might too?' This was the moment. This was when he would know. He held his breath.

'I don't think so,' she said. 'They were all butchered. Brutally butchered. Apart from me.'

'So you remember a little bit now? I heard you had forgotten . . .'

'I remember flashes of scenes, people's faces, but nothing links up. It's all a muddle.' She swept a hand across her forehead. Her other arm was heavily bandaged.

'And Tatiana? Was she killed?'

'Yes, I watched Tatiana die.'

Dmitri flinched and stopped sweeping, for a moment unable to breathe. 'When did she return to the Ipatiev House?' he asked. 'The night before she was killed?'

There was a moment's hesitation before Anna answered, puzzled, 'But she never left. None of us were able to leave after we arrived there in the spring. We couldn't even go to church.'

Blood rushed to Dmitri's brain, making him giddy. This was not Anastasia, but an impostor. Just to be sure, he asked: 'What happened to Yelena, the cleaning girl?'

'I don't know who you're talking about. Who are you anyway? Why are you here?' She grew alarmed.

'I'm a cleaner. Don't worry. I have finished my work. I'll leave you now.'

He hurried to the door and out into the corridor, where he leaned against a wall to breathe deeply. Were she genuinely Anastasia, she would remember that one of the cleaning girls took her sister's place for the second to last night they were in the Ipatiev House. He felt angry with Anna Tschaikovsky for pretending, but his anger didn't last long. She was a poor creature, very nervous and hesitant, and clearly mentally ill.

Most of all he felt a huge sense of deflation. Had it been Anastasia, he might have learned what happened during the family's last twenty-four hours, might even have learned what became of Tatiana. But now he was back at the start, with no leads at all. He had come to Berlin for nothing . . . Although he supposed that wasn't entirely true. The journey had been valuable in that it made him start writing, and he found a sense of peace when engrossed in his novel that had been lacking from his life in Constantinople.

Once he recovered his composure, he retraced his steps downstairs to the side entrance, slipped off the overalls and left them in a corner with the broom. He pushed open the door to step outside, and somehow the sight of faithful Rosa waiting for him in her red wool coat and man's grey trilby hat brought tears to his eyes. If only he could love her the way she deserved to be loved.

'Was it her?' Rosa asked, rubbing her hands and stamping her feet against the penetrating cold.

He shook his head and wiped his eyes with the back of his hand.

'Now will you tell me what this is all about?' she asked. 'I think you owe me, don't you?'

*

Dmitri and Rosa went to the nearest café and sat at a corner table. They ordered hot chocolates and a slice of Black Forest cake with whipped cream to share. Outside it was starting to snow, light flurries drifting past the window making passersby turn up their collars and pull down the brims of their hats. Rosa was uncharacteristically silent, blowing on her hot chocolate to cool it while waiting for him to talk.

'I used to be in the imperial guard in St Petersburg,' he told her, 'and I fell in love with Tatiana, the second-eldest of the Tsar's daughters. She also fell in love with me and in 1916 we were secretly married.'

Rosa gasped and her eyes widened with shock.

'You understand why I haven't told you this before . . . it could have made me a target for Bolshevik spies. On paper, the marriage puts me in line for the Russian throne, so they would be keen to eliminate me if they knew.'

'Do you *want* the Russian throne?' she asked, clearly flabbergasted.

'No, of course not. But I desperately want to find out what has happened to Tatiana, and that's why I was so keen to meet Anna Tschaikovsky.'

'But your wife must be dead,' Rosa said. 'How could she possibly have lived? Where could she be? I understand it is hard to give up hope, but surely there can be none?'

Dmitri felt cross with her. 'Actually, I have reason to hope. She was not in the Ipatiev House the night before the family disappeared.' He explained what had happened and Rosa listened carefully.

'But if she were alive, she would have contacted her family by now. Princess Irene, Grand Duchess Olga . . . She would have tried to find you.'

Dmitri spoke tetchily. 'Anything could have happened. You don't understand how dangerous the Bolsheviks are, even overseas. Just two weeks ago a distant cousin of the Romanovs was shot dead in his Paris apartment.'

Rosa sighed. The cake lay untouched between them. 'So you are telling me that you will wait until you find out what happened to Tatiana before you marry again? Did you not think I had a right to know this, since we have been lovers for four months, nearly five.'

'Is it that long?' Dmitri asked, then instantly realised from her hurt expression that it had been the wrong thing to say. 'I only meant that it feels so fresh and new. I like being with you, Rosa. We have fun.'

'But you are married. Thank you for letting me know at last.'

On the way home, he could tell she was trying to shake off her bad mood, telling him some anecdote about the brother of a girl at the café, but he wasn't listening. He was bitterly disappointed that Anna Tschaikovsky was not Anastasia. It meant he had hit another dead end.

That night, after they made love, Rosa whispered, 'I love you.' Dmitri froze, unable to say it back, even casually. Instead he tilted her face to his and kissed her tenderly, hoping that would do.

Afterwards, he lay awake, thinking of Tatiana: her voice, her smile, the way she moved. She still filled his heart so completely there was no room to love anyone else. He didn't want to lose Rosa, who brought joy and laughter and womanly comfort, but it would be a lie to tell her he loved her.

Chapter Forty-Three

Lake Akanabee, New York State, end of September 2016

In the days after reading Tom's letter, Kitty tipped into a depression. She could feel it happening and didn't try to resist because it felt as though it had been brewing for a while. Besides, it matched the climate. Although the days were still warm, she could sense the end of summer, with a sharp breeze in the evening and random leaves turning golden-brown and floating down from the trees. It made her realise that her days there were running out, with just over two weeks left before her flight home.

The contents of Tom's letter swirled around her head as she worked in the garden she had created. Would it have helped if she had let him comfort her after her parents died? She had chosen the only route that felt manageable: keeping busy. The enormity of the loss had simply been too much to bear. Now her parents filled her thoughts as she dug the soil.

Her dad had been a quiet, undemonstrative man, with a character that was steady and true. She loved the fact that he had treated her the way he would have treated a son: sending her up ladders to help with the guttering, teaching her carpentry skills, assuming she could change a plug from an early age. She could tell when he was proud of her by a secret smile and a faraway look in his eyes.

Although they seldom talked about emotions, she always felt he was her ally. A memory came to her of a night before a school exam when she had a classic full-scale panic attack that made her tremble and retch convulsively. Her dad had taken her by the hand and led her out to the back garden, where he set out two deckchairs. They sat side by side in the darkness while he identified the constellations above them – Ursa Major and Minor, Andromeda and Pegasus – until she was calm enough to go to sleep.

Her relationship with her mum had been far more volatile. All the pressure she put on Kitty to succeed had meant they were not close during the difficult teenage years. Her mum fussed too much over Kitty's health, her finances, and her fashion choices, as well as her exam results. After she left home, there were times when Kitty let the answer machine pick up any calls because she couldn't face her mother's critical onslaught. Even now, looking back, she felt cross about the pressure she had been under, although she recognised it had been motivated by love.

'You needed pushing,' she heard her mother saying. 'You *and* your dad. If you had it your way, you'd both sit around all day whittling pieces of wood.'

She'd been critical of Kitty's teenage boyfriends but took to Tom straight away, even though he was a struggling musician, which wasn't her idea of a respectable career. She let him tease her about her exacting standards in a way that no one else got away with. 'Now, Elizabeth,' he'd smile, 'are you sure that flower arrangement is perfectly symmetrical? Shouldn't the salt cellar be a few millimetres to the left?' Tom was the only person able to make her laugh at herself; Kitty remembered the pretty sound of her laugh.

What would you advise me to do, Mum? she asked in her head, and knew straight away that her mother would tell her to go back to Tom and work things out. 'I won't have a divorcee in my family,' she would have said. 'The shame of it!'

They'd only been in their fifties when they died, after a coach careered through the central reservation of a Spanish motorway. A postcard had arrived a week later, full of holiday joie de vivre; her dad writing about his guilt when picking a lobster from the tank in a restaurant, and her mum commenting that its colour when cooked matched her dad's sunburn. By that time, Tom was helping her to organise their funeral. All those awful decisions to be made: *What clothes do you want to wear to be cremated, Mum?* Tom, bless him, had taken care of the legalities of the estate, of clearing and selling the family home where Kitty had grown up, while she – what exactly had she done? She couldn't remember now, except that as soon as the money came through she bought the Tottenham house and launched herself into a year of keeping busy.

She found herself chatting to her parents in her head while she worked on the cabin. Sometimes she even spoke out loud. *Why did no one tell me about Dmitri, Mum? Did you ever meet your grandfather? Did Marta tell you about him? What was he like?* There was no one to answer that now. Death was too final; she'd missed her chance.

Kitty had run out of plants so she made a trip to the garden centre for more, and on the way back she stopped at the vacation park coffeehouse. Tom knew she had received his parcel and would be waiting for a reply but she wasn't sure what to say. Perhaps the words would come to her.

She charged her laptop but instead of going straight to her email folder, she found herself looking up Karren Bayliss on Facebook. The only reason she hadn't done so before was because she hadn't known the surname, and now she did, she was astounded. The image on Tom's phone hadn't been very clear but she realised Karren looked for all the world like an inflatable sex doll: her profile picture showed huge breasts on display in a low-cut top like plump cuts on a butcher's slab; brown hair with blonde tiger stripes painted through it; inches-long black eyelashes; swollen lips and a fake tan the colour of butterscotch. It was impossible to think of a physical type less like her. What had he been thinking of?

Kitty almost felt like sending him a sarcastic email about his lack of taste, but that wasn't the way forward. She glanced through her inbox and replied to a few friends. There was a message from Random House in New York apologising for the delay in answering her query due to staff holidays. Kitty remembered that Dmitri's Berlin publisher was a company called Slowo; the name appeared on the copyright page of his books. She googled Slowo and found they had been started in Berlin in 1920 by a man named Joseph Gessen, and that they also published Pushkin, Tolstoy and Nabokov, as well as producing a Russian-language newspaper for émigrés known as *Rul*. There had recently been an exhibition about immigrant publishers in Berlin and she was able to find Dmitri's name in a list of authors, along with a short biography saying that he was a journalist for *Rul*. How strange that both she and her great-grandfather had the same profession; perhaps it was in their genes.

It took some searching but Kitty eventually found an article by Dmitri in the *Rul* archives. It was in Russian but she used Google translate and was able to make out from the stilted text that Dmitri had interviewed Princess Irene of Hesse shortly after she went to visit a girl called Anna Tschaikovsky, who was claiming to be Grand Duchess Anastasia. This puzzled Kitty: the article was written in 1923, and the Romanovs had been murdered in 1918. How could an imposter hope to deceive family members only five years later? She googled Anna Tschaikovsky next and found several long articles about her. It seemed the remaining Romanov family had been split into two camps, with some believing the claimant while others were adamant she was not Anastasia. In photos she looked plausibly similar.

Of course, Kitty remembered, in 1923 the world didn't yet know about the fate of the Romanovs. It was the following year when White Army investigator Nicholas Sokolov published his report concluding that the family had all been killed in the Ipatiev House. He had found witnesses who told of the blood-soaked basement scarred by bullet holes and frenzied knife thrusts, and had taken photographs of personal possessions found in a burnt-out mine-shaft. Even after that, rumours persisted that one or more of the children had escaped. Anna Tschaikovsky maintained her story and it led to lawsuits that were only settled after her death when a DNA sample found she had been a Polish factory worker called Franziska Schanzkowska. Why did so many people believe in her? Kitty imagined it was because the truth – that all the royal children were slaughtered – was too horrific to contemplate.

In his article, Dmitri seemed sure that Anna Tschaikovsky was not Anastasia, and he speculated on the reasons why the poor woman lingering in a Berlin hospital bed might keep up such a bizarre pretence. He suggested that maybe something terrible had happened in her previous life, and she was sublimating the memory by assuming a new identity. The psyche was so deep and mysterious that he guessed she had come to believe the story herself. 'People can persuade themselves of virtually anything,' he wrote, 'as we have learned through the writings of Messrs Freud and Jung.'

Kitty's thoughts turned to Tom again. Would she have been more upset if he had chosen a mistress who resembled her? Wouldn't that mean he was trying to replace her? What was he doing choosing someone who clearly offered sex on a plate?

The word 'obvious' came into her head. The counsellor had told Tom he wanted to be found out when he left his phone in the hall. He chose someone who looked like an obvious sex object. He was trying to get Kitty's attention, to make her sit up and take notice. *Well,* she thought, *he had certainly done that.* If she emailed him now, sarcasm would almost certainly slip into her tone.

What did other couples do in their position? Have a huge fight to clear the air? Arguing and confrontation had never been her style. Perhaps it was something to do with being an only child. She hated to feel out of control, but at the same time she realised that bottling things up could make them worse. It was her avoidance of emotional issues Tom was talking about in his letter. Maybe if she was able to tell him how she felt about Karren Bayliss, they could start an honest conversation – but she couldn't think how to begin.

'Dear Tom, How *could* you?' That wasn't her style. She'd leave it for another day, when she had decided on the words.

That evening she looked through Dmitri's novels. The first one, published in 1924, had no dedication, but *Exile* was 'For Nicholas', and *The Boot that Kicked* was 'For Marta', her grandmother. The last two novels, published in America in the 40s, were 'For Rosa' but in the acknowledgements pages he thanked Alfred A. Knopf for having faith in him, he thanked his family for their support and he thanked Irena Markova, his English translator, for her talent. She flicked back to his first novel and thought what a shame that Irena Markova had not translated that one, because it was such a clunky read. Even in a poor translation the description of first love was overpowering. Dmitri described the sense of completion that comes from having another brain to bounce ideas off, the secret joy of watching another person across a crowded room and knowing exactly what they are thinking at that precise moment, the miracle of a partner who knows you better than you know yourself.

One phrase stuck in her mind: Mikhail talks of his great fondness for Valerina's 'intimate imperfections' – a tiny mole behind her ear, the way she nibbled the corners of her nails when nervous. An image sprang into Kitty's head of Tom trying to hide the bulge at his waistline by pulling his shirt out an inch or two in a blouson style; he'd suck in his belly while examining the effect in the mirror, unaware she was watching. That made her smile. And then she thought of him singing along to 90s pop songs in an off-key falsetto. Her face broke into a grin. There was no doubt she still loved him.

Could they save their marriage? With all her heart she hoped so.

Chapter Forty-Four

Berlin, 1924

When Dmitri first moved to Berlin it had been a cheap city in which to live, but in 1923 prices began to rise stratospherically as hyperinflation was triggered by the government's decision to print more money. A loaf of bread that had cost 163 marks in 1922 was selling for 200 million marks by November 1923, and wages could not keep pace. Dmitri was forced to ask his family in Constantinople to wire money, which he found humiliating. He would have left Germany entirely, but for the fact that a Berlin publishing company had offered to publish his novel.

Burtsev, the editor of *Rul*, had passed his manuscript to the Slowo publishing house, which was part of the same company. Much to Dmitri's astonishment, it was accepted and in spring 1924 *Interminable Love* was published to moderate acclaim. Dmitri was invited to give a reading at Rodina's bookshop, and many Russian émigré papers ran favourable reviews. A friend of the owner of Rodina's asked for permission to translate it into German, and another woman wrote asking if she might do the English translation. Dmitri was reluctant, because he felt it was a quintessentially Russian novel that would be impossible to translate, but he needed the money and so he agreed.

Throughout, he felt ambivalent about the publishing process. He found it embarrassing to have the intimate feelings of his characters – which were in essence his own – exposed to the public. He would have preferred to remain anonymous but Rosa was overjoyed by his success. She recommended his novel to all the customers in her café, and often wandered into bookshops to move it to a more prominent position.

When the German edition of *Interminable Love* was published, he gave her a copy but if she read it she never told him. Putting himself in her position, it would be hard to read about his love for another woman. She must guess it was about Tatiana. Perhaps she decided not to read it after all, but still she helped promote it and most people who knew them assumed it was about Rosa.

They began to be invited to literary salons and Rosa was intellectually out of her depth in the conversations about art and literature but everyone liked her for her open, friendly nature and admired her off-beat dress sense. She bought her clothes in flea markets and deliberately chose mismatching colours such as lime green and purple, hot pink and orange, when throwing outfits together: Dmitri described her look as like 'an explosion in a garment factory'. There was no artifice about her and that was refreshing in a town where so many people were hiding their true natures, especially amongst the Russian community.

Soon Rosa had many more friends in Berlin's literary set than Dmitri did, and she invited them back to their apartment to drink schnapps and listen to poetry being read aloud. He watched her sometimes and marvelled at her ability to remember the names of friends' children and the fine details of their lives. She complimented people on their writing and laughed at their witticisms, making them feel good about themselves. Perhaps that was the key to her social success.

At a salon one evening in summer 1924 Burtsev told Dmitri that the Ekaterinburg prosecutor Nicholas Sokolov had finally published his report into the fate of the Romanovs.

'It seems Sokolov escaped the Red Army by fleeing through Siberia with a box of the items he found in the Ekaterinburg mineshaft,' the editor explained. 'During the intervening years, he has interviewed émigrés and Romanov family members, making copious notes, until he felt ready to present his findings to the world.'

Dmitri's hands were shaking. He put his glass on a nearby piano. 'And his conclusion, no doubt, is that they all perished.'

'That's his opinion.'

'And yet, I do not believe he has found the bodies, has he?'

'He makes the rather grisly claim that they were hacked to pieces, dissolved in sulphuric acid and then thrown onto a fire.' Burtsev screwed up his face in disgust, and Dmitri felt sick to the pit of his stomach. He leaned on the piano so as not to collapse.

'Do you have a copy of the report?'

'I will bring it to your apartment tomorrow.'

The report contained photographs of the items Sokolov had brought out of Russia in his infamous box. Dmitri knew about some of them from the 1919 press reports, but he pored over the images looking for a clue as to whether Tatiana's remains were in the mineshaft. There was the Tsar's belt buckle; a pearl earring of the type that Tsarina Alexandra always wore; some shoe buckles from the grand duchesses' shoes – but not the type Tatiana had been wearing when last he saw her, Dmitri was sure of that; the eyeglasses and false teeth of the family's doctor, who had died with them; some icons; a jewelled badge; and that grotesque severed human finger. The body of a dog had been found at the bottom of the well, and Dmitri shuddered to think it could be Ortipo's.

Rosa arrived while Dmitri and Burtsev were talking about the report, and began preparing a meal. Dmitri could tell she was straining to hear what was being said but he did not include her in the conversation. It was nothing to do with her.

Burtsev asked if Dmitri would write an article about the Sokolov report, and he agreed. He already knew what he would write: that without any bodies, there could be no definitive proof the

Romanovs were dead; that it was still possible the adults had been killed and the children imprisoned somewhere. News was beginning to filter out of Russia about the prison camps established by the Bolsheviks: horrific places, where inmates were routinely beaten, starved and tortured. He hoped Tatiana and her siblings were not being held in such a place, but that they were together, under house arrest in decent accommodation. When the government was overthrown and the exiles returned to their homeland, the Romanov children would be found and liberated.

His article was published a few months later, and Rosa read it but made no comment.

One evening in November 1924, Dmitri and Rosa went to Eldorado nightclub with some Russian friends. While Rosa danced in her inimitable style, Dmitri chatted to his comrades about the Russian writers who were returning to the Union of Soviet Socialist Republics, as it was now known, tempted back by overtures from the Communist government. Alexei Tolstoy had just announced his departure for Moscow, Andrei Bely had already returned and Boris Pasternak, a supporter of the regime, had never left.

'I don't trust them,' Dmitri said. 'I love my homeland as much as any Russian but I will not return until the Bolsheviks have been overthrown. The farcical trials and the inhuman prison camps demonstrate the true nature of their rule and I think it is wrong for writers implicitly to condone these.'

His friend agreed. 'Did you hear about the prison on the Solovki Islands? A favourite punishment there is mosquito torture whereby they tie a man naked to a stake in the midst of a swarm. It is barbarian.'

They were interrupted by a commotion on the dance floor and when Dmitri stood to look, he saw Rosa lying on the ground. He rushed over.

'What happened?' he asked, kneeling beside her. Her eyes were closed but he could hear her murmuring.

'She collapsed with no warning,' someone said.

The manager approached with two of the doormen. 'Let's take her to a backroom where she can recover,' he suggested. One of them lifted Rosa and carried her through a curtain to a room with a stained red velvet sofa and little else. She opened her eyes as she was laid on the sofa.

'Dmitri? Where am I?'

'In the club. You fainted,' he told her, squeezing her hand. 'How are you feeling?'

'I'm all right. Just a little dizzy.'

'Please call a doctor,' Dmitri instructed the manager. 'I can pay.'

While they waited for the doctor to arrive, Rosa rested with her eyes closed and Dmitri looked around the room. He guessed this was where the female staff brought favoured customers for 'special treatment', in return for generous tips. There was a nicotine-stained mirror on one wall, and a reproduction painting of naked shepherdesses on another.

When the doctor arrived, he took Rosa's pulse, listened to her heart through his stethoscope, then asked her a string of questions in rapid German, which Dmitri could not follow. He prodded gently around her stomach and nodded to himself.

'What do you think it is?' Dmitri asked.

The doctor finished his examination before he replied. 'Your wife is pregnant, sir. Congratulations.'

Rosa gasped and covered her mouth with her hand. Dmitri looked at her. 'Are you sure?'

'Yes, I can feel the top of the uterus. In my opinion the pregnancy is more than twelve weeks along.'

Rosa still had a hand over her mouth but Dmitri could see from her eyes that she was delighted, and he smiled reassurance at her, although he felt shell-shocked. His first reaction was panic: he couldn't have a child with Rosa; he would be tied to her then. Tatiana would be devastated if she found him and discovered he had a child with another woman. She might divorce him. But what could he do? He had no choice in the matter.

Dmitri followed the doctor outside to pay him. As he counted the notes, the doctor said: 'Your wife should rest and eat well. No more nightclubs.'

'She's not my wife. I'm already married so it is rather a delicate situation . . .'

The doctor gave him a sharp, unfriendly look. 'You've got yourself into rather a mess, sir. I hope you will behave with decency.'

Shamefaced, Dmitri called a taxi to take Rosa home.

'Isn't it strange?' she exclaimed as they sat in the back seat, Dmitri's arm around her. 'I had no idea. I thought I had put on a little weight, that's all. Do you think it might be a girl or a boy?'

Dmitri shrugged. 'No idea.'

'I would prefer a boy so he could grow up just like you.' She seemed nervous. She always talked too much when she was nervous. 'If the doctor is right about it being twelve weeks, then he will arrive in May next year. That would be lovely – just in time for the summer. You don't mind about this, do you, darling?'

'It's still a bit of a shock,' he admitted.

'Yes, for me too. I didn't think we had taken any risks.' Dmitri usually withdrew when Rosa was in the fertile part of her monthly cycle. 'And I hadn't noticed that I had missed my monthlies. But now it has happened . . . it will take some getting used to but do you think you will be happy?'

'Give me a little time to get used to the idea,' Dmitri said, but he gave her shoulders a reassuring squeeze.

'We'll need a bigger apartment,' she continued. 'Not straight away but our son will need a bedroom of his own . . .'

Dmitri laughed. 'You are convinced he is a boy, even though you knew nothing of his existence until a couple of hours ago!'

'Yes,' she agreed. 'It's strange, but I am.'

Back in the apartment he helped her into bed then climbed in beside her and switched off the light.

In the darkness, Rosa asked timidly: 'Dmitri, could we please get married before the baby comes? It would mean so much . . . And my family will ask . . .'

'I can't,' he told her gently. 'I'm already married.'

'Yes, to a ghost,' she said sadly. 'How can I ever compete with that?'

Chapter Forty-Five

Berlin, 1925

The baby was a healthy boy, with sandy blonde hair, blue eyes and Russian bone structure. He looked remarkably similar to Dmitri's father.

'What would you like to call him?' Rosa asked, unable to take her eyes off him as he sucked greedily at her breast. She was blooming, her cheeks pink and her short hair lustrous. Dmitri had been worried that neither of them would know what to do with a baby, but straight away Rosa seemed to have an instinct for motherhood. She was so calm that the child stopped crying the instant he was snuggled in her arms.

'I like the name Nicholas,' he said. 'How about you?'

'Nicholas is lovely!' she cried. 'Do you mean after your tsar?'

'No, our tsar was a fool. I just like the way the syllables fall from the tongue. Nich-o-las.'

Rosa had found a crib for the boy and arranged his things in the corner of their bedroom. She sang as she rocked him to sleep, or changed his nappy, or played with him on the rug; it was obvious she was happy. She had given up asking Dmitri to marry her but only insisted that he buy her a ring so that people thought them married, and to that he consented.

After the birth, he had planned to take his typewriter to a café on the corner to work without interruption, but found that he liked being at home, with the babble of their voices in the next room and the smell of his lunch bubbling on the stove. Rosa was careful not to disturb him while he was working: as well as continuing to write articles for *Rul* he had started a new novel.

Like his first novel, *Exile* had elements of autobiography: the main character was haunted by a terrible act he had committed in his past, before being banished from his homeland, and living a shadowy half-life, unable to forget. Dmitri analysed the experience of being a stranger in a foreign land, with a culture quite different from his own, and concluded that in many ways it was liberating. In Berlin he could reinvent himself outside the strict rules of Russian society. Had his father been alive, he would never have been able to become a writer; he would have been expected to pursue a military career all the way to the top, amassing medals as he went. And yet, he still felt a sense of dislocation, as though he was leading someone else's life. Not being fluent in German annoyed him; somehow he couldn't get to grips with the staccato rhythms of the language. And his relationship with Rosa still felt temporary; she was someone to keep him company until Tatiana returned. Even with the baby he couldn't shake that feeling, although he knew it was unfair to Rosa.

He had no complaints about her. In many ways she was the perfect wife: cheerful, affectionate and forgiving. She asked little of him: a roof over their heads, money for food, and not much else. When her mother and sister visited, he was polite and welcoming, although their disapproval of him was visceral.

'Why do you love me?' he asked Rosa once. He genuinely couldn't understand it.

'Because you need me,' she replied. 'Because I want to try and make you happy.'

'It won't work,' he told her. 'Melancholy is the condition of the Russian soul.'

And yet, Rosa could make him laugh, almost against his will. When she returned from the daily shopping trip, she usually had a vignette of some tiny incident with which to entertain him: a housewife scrubbing her front steps with vigour then a bird defecating on them with a huge splat just as she turned to go indoors; a bad-tempered tram conductor who was unaware someone had stuck a notice on his back saying 'I've not had a bath since 1917'.

They no longer went out in the evenings, because they could not afford a *Kinderhüter* never mind the cost of alcohol in the cafés and nightclubs, but Dmitri would pour himself a vodka at home. Sometimes they invited friends for supper, but mostly they read books or listened to the radio. He was not unhappy. At night, they often made love. Rosa had a remarkable enthusiasm for sex and a talent for arousing him even when he felt exhausted. Cool fingers, the touch of her lips, her luscious breasts pressed against him, all had a miraculous effect on his libido. She had assured him that it would be impossible for her to get pregnant again while she was breastfeeding little Nicholas, so they were both astonished to find, when the baby was just seven months old, that she was wrong about that. Their doctor confirmed another was due the following year.

'Wouldn't it be lovely if we had a bigger apartment, where the children could have their own room,' Rosa sighed. She didn't nag – never nagged – but he knew it was a reasonable request. He asked his publisher for an advance against the next novel and managed to pay the deposit on a two-bedroom apartment not far away, where they moved just before a little girl was born in the summer of 1926.

'Can I call her Marta?' Rosa pleaded. 'I always wanted a daughter called Marta.'

'Of course,' Dmitri replied, his voice a little husky. 'Marta is a pretty name.'

The strength of his feelings when he looked at his baby daughter amazed him: a combination of protectiveness and sheer awe at her innate femininity. Even as a newborn she held her hands daintily, like a ballerina, and gazed up at him with innocent adoration. How could they have created someone quite so beautiful? Sometimes he almost fancied she looked like Tatiana – although that was, of course, impossible.

'Hello, little girl,' he whispered, and she clutched his finger in a surprisingly strong fist. Nicholas had begun to crawl and annoyed him by grabbing at his papers, knocking over cups, falling down and wailing even though he could not possibly be hurt. Secretly Dmitri admitted to himself that he loved his daughter more. Nicholas was clumsy and needful of attention, reminding Dmitri of himself as a child, while Marta seemed graceful and sure of herself, completely unlike him. When he said anything of the sort to Rosa, she laughed and chided him: 'They're babies! You can't possibly judge their characters yet.'

In summer 1927, *Exile* was published, and it proved rather more controversial than *Interminable Love*, with much debate over Dmitri's views of life in exile. The discussion was taken up by the German press when it was published in translation, resulting in many more sales. The book was reprinted and for once they had a little money to spare. Dmitri gave Rosa cash to buy new clothes for herself and the children, and one summer's day they took a day trip to the countryside with a picnic that Rosa had carefully packed in a wicker basket.

Watching the children playing on the grass, completely caught up in the moment, and watching Rosa hum as she cut big hunks of bread and cheese to serve with beer and sausage, Dmitri felt the closest he ever came to happiness. He examined the sensation, suspicious of it, feeling he did not deserve it. What about Tatiana? What about the way he had let her down?

Rosa handed him his food, then leapt to her feet, tucked one child under each arm and began to spin them round and round. Nicholas and Marta shrieked and chortled from deep in their bellies and suddenly Dmitri found himself laughing too. It was still an unfamiliar sensation for him but it got easier every time.

On the way back on the train, as the children slept on their laps, Rosa asked him a question that had obviously been on her mind: 'Would you go back to Russia if the Communists were overthrown?'

He frowned. 'It's not going to happen in my lifetime. They are too firmly entrenched.' He realised from her disappointed expression this wasn't the answer she wanted.

'But if they were to fall? What would happen to me and your children?'

'Rosa, I will always look after you. I promise. You have nothing to fear.'

She was playing with the ring on her wedding finger, about to say more, but instead she turned with an almost imperceptible sigh to look out of the window. Suddenly Dmitri saw the situation from her point of view and realised he was treating her appallingly. She loved him, she had borne him two children, and still he was not committing himself to her. It wasn't fair.

'Wherever I go, you three will come with me. You are my family,' he said, and meant it.

Rosa grinned and leaned over to kiss him, carefully, without waking the babes. Deep down Dmitri felt uneasy. What if Tatiana came back? But then a voice said, 'What if she doesn't?' He had made a life, albeit by default rather than choice, and now he must stick with it.

Chapter Forty-Six

Lake Akanabee, New York State, 1st October 2016

The 30th of September was warm and sunny but a cold front swept in overnight and Kitty woke to a chilly, overcast morning on the 1st of October, almost as if the weather was following the calendar. She thought she had been pretty thorough with her repairs, but draughts mysteriously found their way in, making it hard to warm up when she came out of the cold shower. How had Dmitri survived here in winter? He must have been very hardy.

Did Rosa stay with him? Did the children visit? She had found out a few things about his life in Berlin but virtually nothing about what they did in America, apart from the date of their arrival: June 1934.

Kitty had to go to Indian Lake for food and on the way she stopped at the vacation park coffeehouse.

'Only two weeks until we close for winter,' Jeff told her. 'You're my first customer today and I don't expect there will be many more.'

'I'm only here till the fourteenth,' Kitty told him. 'But I'll be back next year. When do you open again?'

'Easter. It can still be snowing, but we get some hardy souls who venture out.'

Kitty plugged in her laptop and sipped her coffee. She had hit a brick wall researching Dmitri so she decided to see what she could find about Rosa Liebermann through her genealogy site. Straight away she found that she had lived in the Albany area after her arrival in the US, that she served on the Parent-Teacher Association at the high school and volunteered at the hospital. Her mother and sister had come over from Germany in 1936 and lived nearby. She supposed that Dmitri and Rosa must have discovered Lake Akanabee while living in Albany. Were they outdoorsy types?

She remembered Bob saying that he had never seen anyone with Dmitri: no woman, no children. And there was the mystery about why no one had been able to contact the children when he died. Had they divorced and the children took their mother's side? Kitty searched but could find no record of a divorce.

It was easier to find information about her great-uncle Nicholas, who had moved to California at the age of thirty and got work at a winery in Sonoma Valley. He'd married a Californian girl but they didn't have any children and she was shocked to read that he died in 1970, before Kitty was born. He'd only been forty-five years old. Kitty vaguely remembered Grandma Marta saying how close they had been as children and how much she missed him when he was gone. They used to have little chats when Marta came to stay over to let Kitty's mum and dad go out for the evening. Kitty would crawl into her grandmother's bed in the morning, smelling the familiar old-lady smell of talcum powder and gawping at her teeth in the glass by the bed.

Marta had moved to Britain in the late 50s and Kitty assumed she had come for love, because she married a Sheffield businessman. Kitty's mum, Elizabeth, had been born in 1960, an only child, and had Kitty in 1981. So the family was geographically spread out, but she couldn't understand why the police had been unable to find any of them when Dmitri died in 1986. Didn't he have an address book, for goodness' sake?

Kitty asked Jeff for another coffee and opened her email folder. The usual rush of messages popped up one after another. Tom, Tom, friends, spam, Tom, Amber, Tom . . . Random House New York. Kitty clicked to open the Random House message.

Dear Ms Fisher,
I am afraid there are no editors remaining here who knew your great-grandfather Dmitri Yakovlevich but I can see from the historical accounts that he was a much-valued, very successful Knopf author from the 1930s through to the 1970s. My intern found some of his old manuscripts in our archives and, if you would like to have them, we'd be happy to send them on.

I haven't read any of his works yet but plan to have a look at *In the Pale Light of Dawn* and *Toward the Sunset* as soon as I can find the time. I warn you that there is not much demand for reprints of 1940s novels unless there are special circumstances but I will approach them with an open mind.

Many thanks for getting in touch.

All best wishes, Rebecca Wicks

It was nice to feel that Dmitri's work was appreciated, even though his contemporaries had moved on. She would like to see those manuscripts but couldn't decide where to have them sent. She could give the address in London's Crouch End but what if she never lived there again? A tight band of panic encircled her chest as she thought about renting a flat, getting a job and starting her adult life from scratch. That wasn't what she wanted.

Suddenly she began to type an email to Tom, the words flowing, fingers dashing across the keyboard:

Dear Tom,

I have read and considered your letter but have to tell you that the last thing in the world I want to do is to sit in a dingy consulting room with some smarmy counsellor telling us what's wrong with our relationship! You knew when you married me that I tend to avoid emotional confrontation; it's part of who I am and I am not about to change.

Anyway, how did this come to be about my shortcomings? You are the one who committed the marital faux-pas of dipping your pen in another woman's inkwell. I'd like to throw this discussion right back at you and ask first of all whether you want an open marriage? If you don't, how can you convince me that you would never do this again, either with Ms Karren Bayliss or some other woman? What if you miss out on a promotion at another job? What if you even get sacked? I don't know how this works but perhaps you have concocted some plan in your therapy sessions. (Please spare me the counsellor-speak in your reply.)

I will be back in London in a couple of weeks and I suppose we should meet to talk. I don't feel quite ready to see you yet but . . .

She stopped. This email was all wrong. She didn't feel angry with Tom any more. It felt as though there had to be some kind of reprimand in her first communication, but not like this. When she thought about seeing him, she knew she would want to run straight into his arms. She was dying to sit down and chat to him, properly chat like they used to do in the old days. There was so much to tell him. But where should she start? She saved the email into her drafts folder and decided to return to it later, perhaps on the way back from the shops.

At the supermarket she picked up another crate of Chardonnay. The check-out girl didn't comment any more, just scanned it through with tight lips. On the drive home, the white wine was calling out to Kitty: she needed a dose of liquid anaesthetic, so she drove straight to the cabin, took her shopping indoors and opened the bottle. She felt better already when she heard the glug-glug sound of the golden liquid swirling around her favourite glass. Over the lake, the sunset seemed more vivid than ever, like some kind of exaggerated hyper-reality. She sat on the jetty to watch, listening to the birds and frogs winding down like clockwork toys with the fading of the light. She felt entirely present in the moment, but somehow it was as though she was a visitor in someone else's life – Dmitri's maybe – rather than a protagonist in her own.

Chapter Forty-Seven

Berlin, 1930

One day Rosa brought home a women's magazine called *Das Blatt der Hausfrau* with an article about the many people scattered around Europe who claimed to be missing Romanovs. There were dozens of them now, but the magazine profiled the main contenders, with photographs of several. Dmitri had heard that there were such folk but none of their stories had sounded convincing enough for him to pursue. Now that Rosa opened the magazine in front of him, with a quizzical look, he stopped to look, pausing over the German text.

- Michelle Anches, who claimed to be Tatiana, was said to have escaped Russia via Siberia in 1925 and arrived in Paris, where she took a small apartment. After she wrote to Tsar Nicholas's mother in Denmark, saying that she was preparing to come and visit, she was shot dead in her apartment, friends blaming the Bolshevik secret police. Dmitri did not doubt that the Cheka had killed her, but looking at the photograph she was plainly not Tatiana: the face was broader, the chin more pointed, the eyes not so intelligent.

- Marga Boodts claimed that Kaiser Wilhelm II of Germany himself had recognised her as Olga when she arrived in that country after a long journey through eastern Russia and China. She gave interviews to many journalists about the brave Red Guardsman who rescued her from the Ipatiev House, but the story was laughable since she did not even slightly resemble Olga.
- Nadezhda Vasilyeva had been arrested in 1920 trying to escape from Siberia into China and was now being held in an insane asylum in the USSR, from which she wrote regular letters to monarchs around Europe proclaiming herself to be Anastasia. She had an angular face and looked much older than Anastasia would have been, so Dmitri moved on.
- Eugene Nikolaievich Ivanoff, who lived with a parish priest in Poland, claimed to be Alexei and explained that an old Cossack had helped him escape from Russia. Dmitri paused over this story because the photograph did look similar to Alexei and it seemed he suffered from haemophilia, unlike most other Alexei claimants. Could it be? Should he travel to Poland to meet him? He couldn't help thinking it would be a wasted journey. Somehow the story didn't quite add up.

The article made Dmitri wonder what Tatiana could do to make herself known if she ever managed to find her way out of Russia. She would most likely go to one of her relatives but what if they failed to recognise her, or weren't sure? She wouldn't know where to look for him but he was certain that twelve years on he would recognise her in an instant. She would be thirty-three years old now; she might have wrinkles at the corners of her eyes and perhaps her hair would have streaks of grey. Would her slender figure have thickened? No matter; he would know her anywhere.

Thinking about her brought on a weight of sadness and he turned to stare out the window. Rosa brought a cup of coffee and sat beside him, her hand on his arm.

'Why do people pretend to be Romanovs?' she asked. 'Does it make them feel important? Do they hope one day to sit on the throne of Russia?'

Dmitri shrugged. 'There is talk that Tsar Nicholas kept vast amounts of money in overseas banks and a successful claimant could access those funds. There are many reasons to try, but in truth they all seem poor creatures who struggle with their sanity.'

Rosa squeezed his leg. 'It must be hard for you . . . But I brought the magazine because I thought you might like to see . . . Did I do the right thing?'

'It's fine.' He shook his head as if to dispel the memory.

Nicholas and Marta were sitting on the floor playing at being shopkeepers. Nicholas put a single potato into Marta's basket and said, 'That will be twenty marks and I'm not giving you any more because you don't even like potatoes.'

Marta handed back the potato saying, 'It is too expensive. I think I will shop elsewhere today.'

Dmitri and Rosa laughed, but it was a sensitive point. The German economy was once again in trouble; the Great Depression that hit America the previous year had caused mass unemployment and business failures around the globe. Every street corner in Berlin had a woman in rags begging for a pfennig or two to feed her children. Men got up at dawn to queue for poorly paid labouring jobs. Dmitri still earned just enough from his articles for *Rul* plus royalties on his books to pay for their food and cover the rent but there was no surplus and he knew Rosa haggled with the best of them when she shopped for food. All the same, it was bittersweet to hear their four-year-old daughter doing the same.

For someone who worked as a journalist, Dmitri mused, he had twice failed to spot emerging political apocalypse until it became unmissable. In Russia, he had been aware of the grumblings against the monarchy and knew that revolution was in the air, but the November coup led by Lenin and Trotsky had seemed to him to emerge from nowhere. Similarly in Berlin, he was aware that men in brown shirts, known as the *Sturmabteilung*, were stirring up street brawls, and that they attacked anyone who did not support a minor fringe party known as the National Socialists, but he was astonished when that same minority party won eighteen per cent of the vote in the 1930 elections.

Burtsev asked him to write an article for *Rul* about the National Socialists' claim that Communism was part of an international Jewish conspiracy, and Dmitri had no trouble at all in rubbishing that notion. In Russia the grass roots Bolshevik movement had gained strength from the disgruntled poor of all religions. Trotsky might have been Jewish but Lenin and the new leader, Stalin, were not. Who was supposed to be organising this Jewish conspiracy? None of it made sense, and he was scathing in his critique.

Rosa was worried when she read his article. 'Perhaps it would be better not to draw attention to ourselves. It leaves you open to accusations of bias since I am Jewish.'

Dmitri had never given a thought to Rosa's religion because she did not practise, and their children were not being raised in any particular faith. He had long since decided that organised religion was an absurdity and she agreed with him.

'I can't temper my journalistic opinions because of our personal circumstances,' he replied. 'Someone needs to stand up and point out the dangers of this new creed.'

Rosa was worried though. 'Adolf Hitler is rapidly gaining supporters because he is restoring German pride. He needs scape-goats to blame for the economic ills and Jews and Communists are easy targets.'

'That's ridiculous! He looks Jewish himself! There might be a few unscrupulous Jewish moneylenders, but he can't blame an entire race.'

Dmitri soon realised how short-sighted he was being as the political landscape mutated rapidly and street fights turned some districts of Berlin into battle zones. Brown-shirted *Sturmabteilung* and the so-called Hitler Youth, young boys in *leiderhosen* spouting the party message on purity of race, were suddenly everywhere. The neighbours' sons, who had previously seemed nice young men, mutated into snarling bullies full of hatred.

Dmitri did not realise that Rosa had become a target of this vitriol until their son Nicholas asked him over dinner one evening: 'Papa, what is a *hure*?'

Rosa tutted and tried to hush him, her face flushing.

'Where did you hear that word?' Dmitri demanded.

'Mama said it to Mrs Brandt.'

Rosa shook her head, and motioned to Dmitri that she would tell him about it later, before saying, 'Mama was wrong to use that word and you must forget about it and never repeat it.'

Later she told Dmitri that Mrs Brandt had spat in her face and called her a 'filthy Jew' as she walked home from the butcher's holding the children by the hands. 'I lost my temper,' she said, 'and yelled "At least my mother wasn't a *hure*." And then I remembered the children and their big ears.'

'How does she know you are Jewish?' Dmitri asked. Rosa used his surname, Yakovlevich, and her dark looks were more Southern European than Jewish.

She shrugged. 'I don't know. People talk. My sister has lost her job and she is sure it's because she is Jewish, although her employer didn't say as much.'

'You must tell me if it happens again,' Dmitri insisted. 'I will not stand for this.' The thought of Rosa being subjected to such treatment was painful to him. She was a good person who never harmed a soul; on the contrary, she went out of her way to help others. She collected shopping for an elderly neighbour who could no longer walk, and she often looked after a friend's children so she could work, going to her apartment so as not to disturb Dmitri.

But one Sunday afternoon when Dmitri took the family to the zoo, he became intensely aware of whispering and pointing in their direction. Rosa ignored it, and the children were only interested in seeing Sammy, the giant sea elephant, at feeding time. As the day went on Dmitri's temper became increasingly frayed so when a man approached and said to Rosa, 'Your sort shouldn't be allowed in here', Dmitri pulled back his fist and punched him hard in the face. There was a cracking sound and blood spurted. The children began to cry, and he knew he should not have done it, but at the same time he was glad to take action, proud that at the age of almost forty he could still produce a punch like that.

Rosa bustled them away before there were any repercussions. 'It doesn't help,' she whispered. 'I've found it's best to ignore them.'

But Dmitri couldn't ignore this new movement that had turned his peace-loving girlfriend into a social pariah. It made him sick to his stomach and he decided to take a writer's revenge, by writing a novel about it. Ostensibly it would be about the rise of Bolshevism within one particular village in Russia, and the way it affected ordinary villagers who had previously lived together in harmony – but actually it was about what was happening on the German national stage. As he wrote, the ideas flowed and he could feel in his fingertips that this was going to be the most important book he would ever write. He wanted it to have a mythical quality but at the same time show readers the lunacies of a system that favours one racial group above another.

His novel was published in February 1933, just two weeks after Hitler was appointed Chancellor, with the title *The Boot that Kicked*, an obvious allusion to the jackboots worn by the *Sturmabteilung*. Several newspapers interviewed Dmitri and publicly he always maintained that it was about the rise of Bolshevism in Russia rather than Nazism in Germany, but he added that if people wished to draw parallels, that was their prerogative.

Almost overnight, the level of harassment Rosa experienced in their street increased until she was afraid to go out of doors. She sent Dmitri to buy food and if she took the children out for some fresh air in the park, Dmitri had to accompany them. He wasn't a particularly tall man but he had learned how to handle himself during his imperial guard training. In response to taunts, he squared up and stared the perpetrator directly in the eye in a way that left no doubt he was ready for a fight, and they invariably backed down.

'We can't live like this. Perhaps we should go to stay near my mother in the country,' Rosa suggested.

'It will happen in the countryside as well,' Dmitri argued gloomily. '*Mein Führer* is encouraging anti-Semitism and everyone wants to curry favour.'

One evening, they returned from a day out to find the front door of their apartment smashed in. They looked inside to see a chaos of destruction. Pages had been ripped from Dmitri's books and scattered like dead leaves on the floor. Clothes were strewn around and a bag of flour had been emptied over them. Limbs had been torn from Nicholas's toy animals and Marta's dolls. Dmitri's typewriter had been smashed to pieces and his reporter's notebook stolen. Cups and plates were broken, furniture overturned. Dmitri rushed to the bedroom and was relieved to find that they had not opened the brown leather suitcase in which he kept Tatiana's diary. He couldn't bear anything to happen to that.

When he returned to the front room, the children were in tears and Rosa had sunk to her knees to comfort them.

'Who did this?' Marta lisped through her tears, and Rosa hugged her before replying, 'Bad people.' Nicholas's lip trembled. Dmitri looked at the three of them huddled together in the midst of the carnage and felt a wave of primal emotion. He couldn't bear for his family to be upset, couldn't stand them being hurt. And he realised that, although he still clung to the memory of the exquisite love he had experienced with Tatiana, this feeling was just as true a kind of love. He would lay down his life to protect these three souls.

The atmosphere in Berlin, of whispering and bullying, mistrust and betrayal, reminded him powerfully of St Petersburg in 1917. Back then he had been too slow to react. If he had arranged to have the Romanovs rescued when they were under house arrest in St Petersburg, just a few hundred miles from the safety of Denmark, they would be alive today. Instead he had hesitated, with tragic consequences. This time he was determined he wouldn't delay.

Later, when the children were asleep, he said to Rosa, 'We have to leave Germany until this madness is over.'

She looked sad: 'But where would we go? This is our home.'

'We both speak good English, so it makes sense to go to an English-speaking country. I won't go to Britain because I can't forgive them for abandoning the Romanovs. How about America?'

Rosa was astounded. 'It's so far! When would I see my family? My mother and sister?'

Frankly, Dmitri didn't much care if he never saw her mother and sister again but he offered, 'They could come too, if you like.'

'Would America accept us? How do you go about applying?'

'I'll ask at the consulate tomorrow. I can't have my family subjected to this.' He took her face in his hands. 'There's something I've never said to you before, Rosa. I want you to know that I do love you. You and the children mean the world to me.'

She gasped, and the joy that shone from her eyes made him feel guilty that he had never said it before. They had been lovers for eleven years, had created two children together, and he had made her wait all this time to hear the words she yearned for. He didn't deserve a woman as patient and good as her – but he was determined somehow to become worthy of her love.

Chapter Forty-Eight

Lake Akanabee, New York State, 4th October 2016

With only ten days to go before she had to leave the States, Kitty drove to Gloversville to collect Tatiana's notebook from Vera and to return the books about the Romanovs she had borrowed. Over a cup of coffee she shared the information she had gleaned about Dmitri's life after he left Russia.

'I assume he went to Berlin because it was a meeting point for White Russians after the civil war. He met his wife Rosa and they had two children, but perhaps they left in 1934 to escape the Nazis, because Rosa was Jewish. Dmitri would have been forty-eight when the Second World War began, so wouldn't have been called up to fight, but I have no idea how he earned a living or why he only wrote two more novels after coming to America.' She took a bite of the home-baked cookie Vera had put on a plate beside her. It was gooey with peanut butter.

Vera couldn't help. 'You assume in this day and age that you can find anything you want to know on the Internet but it's simply not true.'

'Are you working on anything interesting now?' Kitty's mouth was gummed up with peanut butter, making her words sound indistinct.

'I'm translating a novel from Russian. It's very gloomy, although with undoubted literary merit. The characters endlessly analyse their motivations till you want to shout "Get on with it, buddy!"'

Kitty smiled in recognition: 'Yes, the same is true of Dmitri's novels. His characters are incapacitated by guilt – except in his anti-fascist novel *The Boot that Kicked*, where they are energised by fury. I rather like the introspection. I wish more men were introspective.' Of course, that's what Tom was doing with his counsellor: trying to understand what made him tick. Kitty admired him for the effort. It couldn't be easy.

On the way back to the cabin, she stopped at the hardware store in Indian Lake to ask the owner's advice on winter-proofing her cabin. Now she had spent so much time and effort on repairs, she didn't want to arrive next spring to find it had fallen apart again.

'You've applied the weatherproof varnish,' he said, frowning in concentration, 'and it's not leaking anywhere?'

'Nope.'

'You could fit some shutters or board over the windows,' he suggested. 'Do the eaves have enough overhang so that water from the roof runs off clear of the walls?'

Kitty nodded. 'A good six inches.'

'And what's drainage like around the cabin? You want to avoid water pooling round the foundations.'

She frowned. 'Actually, there is an area to the side where a puddle forms after heavy rain. What should I do about it?'

'Easy. Dig a trench to let it run off.'

That made sense. Kitty thanked him and headed back to the cabin to start digging. With the edge of her spade, she marked out a channel that led from the hollow of the puddle down towards the lakeshore some fifteen feet away. The ground was mushy from the rain of a few days earlier and her spade cut cleanly through, only snagging on tree roots and mossy undergrowth.

She would miss Lake Akanabee. *Maybe I'll bring Tom here in the spring*, she thought then added mentally, *all being well*. She'd likc to show him this magical place. Perhaps they could hire a boat and explore the coves. Did that mean she had forgiven him? She never thought about Karren Bayliss now, so she supposed she had.

All of a sudden her spade hit something hard. She assumed it was a rock and tried to dig around it but a foot along the hard object was still there, about three feet below the surface. She cleared some of the earth above it and realised her spade was hitting a wooden crate that was about two feet wide. Had Dmitri buried it? Perhaps it was a treasure chest containing family heirlooms. Kitty was excited, wondering if she was about to solve the mystery of her great-grandfather's later life.

She kept digging along the line of the box, which was longer than she had expected. It lay on a slope so she had to remove more soil at the upper part than the lower. When she had worked about six feet along there was a cracking sound as her spade pierced an area of rotten wood. She used the blade as a lever to prise open a corner of the box and bent to peer in. There was something yellowy-white, round. Suddenly a scream burst from her lungs as she realised there was a human skull staring up at her. She'd uncovered a coffin.

Kitty ran indoors, irrationally terrified, as if the skeleton might be pursuing her. Her voice was trembling as she dialled the number of the police station and told them of her grisly discovery.

'Someone will be there within the hour,' she was told. 'Don't touch anything in the meantime.'

Kitty couldn't face waiting on her own for an hour with a dead body outside. She rang Bob's cellphone, told him what she had found and asked if he could please come over to wait with her.

'Be right there,' he said. 'Pour yourself a stiff drink.'

She took his advice and poured a glass of Chardonnay, then stayed indoors, her heart pounding, until she heard Bob's outboard approaching the jetty ten minutes later.

'It's over there,' she gestured from the porch, and as soon as he tied up the boat, he went to have a look.

'Well, I'll be damned,' he called. 'Course it could have been there for decades. Maybe it dates from before Dmitri's time.'

'I hope so. I hope we're not about to find out my great-granddad was a murderer.' Kitty tried to speak lightly, but she felt choked with worry. Had someone from Dmitri's past caught up with him? Had there been a fight that went too far and he was forced to hide the evidence?

When the police arrived they tied plastic ribbon around the area and erected a tent over the coffin. She and Bob sat on the jetty drinking wine and watching as a forensics team arrived and pulled protective suits over their clothes.

'You're probably not going to be able to stay here while they investigate,' Bob said. 'You're welcome to our guest room.' He gestured to his house on the other side of the water.

'Thanks, but I'll probably stay at the vacation park. I expect they'll give me a deal this late in the season.' It would feel spooky to sleep in the cabin, even after the coffin had been taken away. That skull would haunt her dreams.

An officer came to take her statement and get her cell phone number. 'You can move back in a few days,' he told her. 'It looks as though the body's been there a while. Don't worry – you're not under arrest.' He laughed.

Kitty and Bob glanced at each other. It felt disrespectful to joke. She packed some clothes, food and her laptop into a holdall then drove to the vacation park. The cabin they directed her to had heating and hot water and she ran herself a hot bath that evening, the first she'd had in months. She was very shaken by the discovery and couldn't stop wondering who might be buried at Dmitri's cabin. Any explanation she could think of involved criminality.

Did Dmitri have enemies? Is that why he lived in such a remote spot? Had he killed one of them in self-defence? Did his children know about the murder? Is that why they were estranged? Her phone lay on the table and she wished she could just dial home and discuss it with Tom. She couldn't predict what he would say but knew his opinion would be worth listening to. She missed him terribly.

One thing was for sure: whoever buried a body at the cabin had not wanted the death to be discovered, and Kitty couldn't think of an innocent reason for that.

Chapter Forty-Nine

Brooklyn, June 1934

When Dmitri wrote to tell his sisters that he was emigrating to America, Vera's husband Alex replied, asking if he would care to represent their carpet company in New York. They had just begun to export Ottoman rugs to America but felt they were being exploited by the agent they used, and Alex would be delighted if Dmitri were to take over the role. He knew enough about the business from the two years he had spent working for them in Constantinople.

Dmitri was not remotely interested in being a carpet import merchant but he would need money to establish his family so it seemed a useful temporary solution. He could not expect to make a living from journalism commissions on this new continent. His spoken English was more or less fluent now but when he tried to write in English, the words would not flow. He could write business letters but could not think imaginatively in any language but Russian.

He and Rosa found an apartment in Brooklyn, and enrolled the children, now aged eight and nine, in school, while Dmitri set up an office for the carpet import business. His editor at Slowo had given him a letter of introduction to a New York publisher called Alfred A. Knopf, who was said to favour Russian and European literature, but he felt nervous about making an approach and kept putting it off.

'Dmitri, I did not fall in love with a carpet salesman. I fell in love with a brilliant writer. You must be true to yourself,' Rosa coaxed. 'Besides, I'm sure you will find that this Mr Knopf has already heard of you and will be happy to meet.'

Dmitri wasn't convinced. 'What will he say when I tell him I don't write in English?'

She shrugged. 'I don't know how publishing works but if I were in his place, I would introduce you to a good translator.'

Dmitri agonised over his letter to Alfred Knopf, then watched the mailbox for days until an envelope arrived with a Knopf logo on it.

'Look!' he showed Rosa, unable to contain his excitement. 'They have a Russian wolfhound in their logo. It's like a sign. It's meant to be.'

'Open the letter, you dunderhead,' she laughed. 'I want to hear what it says.'

'Mr Knopf would be delighted to meet you at 3pm on the fourth of October in his office in the Hecksher Building at the corner of 57th St and Fifth Avenue,' Dmitri read out loud, before grabbing Rosa for a hug and twirling her around.

The Hecksher Building was a modern skyscraper, almost like a cathedral with its pointed steeple on top, and the vast lobby decorated in Art Deco style. Dmitri gave his name to a receptionist and sat down feeling ridiculously nervous: what if he was told he would never be published in America, that his books were not good enough for their sophisticated readers, that he had been fooling himself to think he had any talent?

He hardly had to wait five minutes before he was taken up in an elevator and shown into Mr Knopf's office. A short dark-haired man with a thick moustache and an extremely elegant suit came bounding across the room and enveloped him in a bear hug.

'I'm Alfred,' he grinned. 'I'm honoured to meet you, sir. *The Boot that Kicked* is one of the bravest pieces of work I've ever read. Come, sit down. Can I offer you a drink? I have Russian vodka.'

Two hours later they were still talking about literature, history, politics and the quirks of human nature, and although Dmitri was viewing the world through a vodka haze, he knew he had found a kindred spirit. They both liked Tolstoy and Gorky, Kuprin and Bunin; they both feared political extremes, whether to the right or the left; they both loved dogs.

'Whatever you decide to write next, I want to publish,' Alfred said before Dmitri left. 'Let me know when you are ready to deliver and I will find you the best translator in New York. And if you want an advance, you need only ask.'

When Dmitri walked back into the evening sunlight, he felt a sensation he had not felt for a long time. Even though he was in a foreign country, it was like coming home.

Dmitri marvelled at Rosa's ability to become part of a social group in no time at all. He'd arrive back from the office to find the kitchen of their Brooklyn apartment full of women chatting while their children played in the communal yard outside.

'Where did you meet them all?' he asked, after they had dispersed to their own apartments.

'Oh, in the grocery store, outside the school gates, you know . . .' She waved her hand airily.

There were invitations to pot luck suppers, Thanksgiving dinners, Fourth of July celebrations, and summer cook-outs, with the children always included. They weren't people Dmitri would normally have picked as friends but they had enough in common to pass a pleasant evening. He often watched Rosa as she mingled at a social event and wondered at her ability to thrive in this new society yet still retain her sense of self. As she aged, she had never toned down her quirky style; if anything her clothes had become more colourful in this new country and she still had boyish short hair. Dmitri bought her a Singer sewing machine for her fortieth birthday and she was able to run up new frocks with lightning speed, often making garments for friends as well.

He knew she missed her family and that it had been a big wrench for her to cross the ocean to this new continent, but she never once complained. Nicholas and Marta were learning English faster than expected, and already spoke with American accents. They liked Superman and Flash Gordon comics and each had their favourite baseball teams. All would have been well, Dmitri thought, except that he couldn't seem to get started on a new novel. The strong feelings that had inspired his earlier works just weren't there. Perhaps it was because he was content. Did he have to be miserable to write?

In 1936, they moved to Albany, 130 miles north of New York City, where Dmitri was able to afford a three-bedroom house with its own spacious garden, and within months Rosa had made a brand new circle of friends. Her mother and sister arrived later that year, their immigration sponsored by Dmitri, and they moved into a house a few blocks down the same street. Nicholas and Marta were delighted and often ran to visit their grandmother, for reasons Dmitri could never understand. He found her cold and unfriendly but the children seemed to adore her.

Sometimes Dmitri sat back and watched his children and wondered who they were. When they were little it had been easy to see what motivated them because the emotions were on the surface: 'I want that toy and Nicholas is playing with it'; 'I'm exhausted and really need to sleep but I'm fighting it in the hope of getting another story'. But now, as they entered their teens, they had become independent people who had learned to tell fibs, to have secrets, and to rebel against his authority.

'Count yourself lucky: my father would have horse-whipped you for that,' he told Nicholas, who was sobbing after receiving a clip round the ear for using coarse language.

291

'Your father sounds like an asshole!' Nicholas shouted through his tears, and Dmitri couldn't help but admire his courage as he dealt out a punishment with the flat of his hand on bare legs.

Rosa never hit them but Dmitri knew he had to protect them from their own impulsiveness so they didn't get into trouble when they were older. He would never beat them with a whip, as his father had beaten him, but every child needed chastisement to keep them in line, for their own sakes.

Hitler's invasion of neighbouring countries and the outbreak of a new war only twenty-one years after the last tipped Dmitri suddenly and emphatically into depression. He couldn't believe that no lessons had been learned from the mass slaughter of the trenches. He couldn't understand why no assassin slipped through the cordons that surrounded the Führer to end the world's misery. He was anxious that he would no longer be able to support his family if naval blockades prevented the import of rugs. Suddenly, he could see no happiness in the life that had previously seemed so sunny; it was as if a shutter had come down that made everything dark and hopeless. Men were intrinsically evil the world over, from the Red Guards who had slaughtered the Romanovs to the brown-shirted *Sturmabteilung* who were shipping Jews and Communists off to live in segregated ghettos.

Rosa did her best to buoy him, remaining her cheerful self and asking nothing of him except his presence. He felt guilty that he had been such a poor choice of partner for her: he had spent their first ten years hankering after another woman, and now he was nothing but a dead weight, who found it hard to get out of bed in the morning. His adolescent children irritated and exhausted him: Marta was too interested in boys for a girl of her young age and when he confined her to her room, she would climb out the window; Nicholas never missed an opportunity to argue with him. Everything he said or did was wrong, as far as his kids were concerned.

Once America entered the war in both Europe and the Pacific, Dmitri sank to new depths of depression and stopped going to work. There seemed little point, since they had only occasional shipments to process. Alex continued to wire money, and that made Dmitri feel useless – a grown man who could not support his own family – but he could not afford to refuse it. He spent his days poring over the newspaper or listening to reports of the war on the radio and often did not bother to change out of his pyjamas. He was too old to fight, and of no further use to the world.

Sometimes he took Tatiana's diary from the old brown suitcase where he still kept it, the one he had brought with him from Istanbul in 1922. When he read her descriptions of those last days in the Ipatiev House, it reminded him once again of his failure to save her and made him feel more useless than ever. In the evenings he drank until he passed out or made himself sick, then suffered the following morning. After a night out drinking in Berlin in the old days, he'd felt no more than a little stuffy-headed but now hangovers wiped him out. A symptom of age.

Up till then, Dmitri had caught the train to New York once or twice a year to have luncheon with Alfred Knopf. They were always convivial occasions at the city's great restaurants – the Waldorf, Barbetta, the exclusive 21 Club – and the meal would last from twelve-thirty through to four or five in the afternoon, by which time copious quantities of alcohol would have been consumed and Dmitri would have to stagger back to Grand Central to catch the train home. Alfred's secretary would telephone three weeks in advance to arrange these luncheons, but when she rang in March 1942 to set a date Dmitri told her he would not be able to make it.

'Mr Knopf will be disappointed. What reason shall I give?'

'Just say that I can't condone the expenditure at a time when the world has gone mad. I'm sure he will understand.'

An hour later, when Alfred rang personally, Dmitri refused to take the call. Rosa closed the kitchen door but he could hear her explaining that he was depressed about the war because it brought back too many memories from the past. She promised she would persuade him to telephone and set a new date for luncheon once he felt up to it.

The following week a van pulled up outside their house and a deliveryman knocked on their door.

'I have a gift from Mr Alfred Knopf,' Dmitri heard him say to Rosa. He got up to look out the window and saw a Borzoi, a Russian wolfhound, just like the one on the Knopf logo. It was black with a white undercoat, and had the bounciness of a puppy. He felt like crying that the American publisher should care enough to send such a thoughtful gift.

Rosa called for him and he walked out to the porch and crouched to look at the pup. It was a beautiful animal, with intelligent eyes set in a small head, the exquisite curve of the haunches giving that famous silhouette, a coat that felt like silk. It was a boy, he noted. The pup licked his face and he felt just a fraction of the ice within him begin to thaw.

'Malevich,' he said. 'I'll call him Malevich.'

Dmitri was not the kind of man who had many friends: Malevich had been his closest friend during the last war, and Alfred was his closest during this. He wrote to express his undying gratitude and promised he would be well enough for that luncheon soon.

It was a turning point in more ways than one: Dmitri now had to go out twice a day to take Malevich for walks, and during those walks he began to analyse his depression and attempt to understand it. Was it some kind of affliction, like measles, that clogged up brain function? Why did everything bad come to the forefront, so that activities he had previously enjoyed no longer held any pleasure? What was the weight that caused his feet to drag, that made it too much effort to brush his teeth or comb his hair? It was lack of hope, he realised. Somehow any hope for the future had been extinguished, but Malevich's uncomplicated enjoyment of life had brought back a flicker of light.

He began to write a novel about a man going through a period of melancholy that tips over into full-blown depression and leads him to attempt suicide. Instead of a puppy, Dmitri's character was rescued by his secretary, a young woman of eccentric appearance and cheerful disposition whose random thoughts on the universe were pivotal in adjusting the faulty wiring in his brain so that he could hope once more. He called the secretary in his novel Gloria but in essence she was a tribute to Rosa.

Chapter Fifty

Lake Akanabee, New York State, 7th October 2016

Three days after the discovery of the body, a detective came to visit Kitty at the vacation park. He was a tall man with friendly eyes. She invited him to sit on the floral sofa while she took a chair by the pine dining table.

'I need to ask some questions about your great-grandfather,' he began, taking out a notebook and rooting around in his briefcase for a pen.

'Have you identified the body yet?' Kitty interrupted.

He tapped his pen on the arm of the sofa before answering. 'She was a woman, in her seventies when she died, and forensics can't find any signs of broken bones or bullet wounds. They think she could have been buried forty-odd years ago, although it's not an exact science.' He paused to let that sink in. 'Now, your great-grandfather purchased the cabin in 1956 so it seems likely that he owned it at the time the body was buried.'

'Oh God!' So Dmitri could have been responsible. It was her worst fear.

'We checked to see if it might be his partner, Rosa – your great-grandmother – but it seems she died in 1955 and is buried in a cemetery in Albany.'

'So he bought the cabin a year later. Perhaps he wanted to be alone.' She imagined him there, grief-stricken, introspective, living a quiet life, but the detective's next words shattered that vision.

'Have you ever heard of a woman called Irena Markova?'

Kitty nodded. 'She was the translator of Dmitri's later novels. He thanks her in the acknowledgements.'

'We've checked Dmitri's bank records and it seems he made monthly payments to Irena Markova from 1948 through to 1975. Quite substantial amounts. You never heard anything about her, perhaps from your mother or grandmother?'

Kitty shook her head, baffled. 'Maybe she did other translation work for him. Or perhaps she acted as his secretary.'

'We thought of that. We checked the records of the carpet import business where Dmitri Yakovlevich worked on his arrival in the United States, but there was no employee of that name.'

Kitty was amazed. 'He worked in a carpet import business? I never knew that.'

'He retired from carpets in 1951, on his sixtieth birthday. By that time he was relatively wealthy because the movie adaptation of his novel *In the Pale Light of Dawn* had come out, and he owned a share of the box office. The receipts from that and the follow-up, *Toward the Sunset,* kept him comfortably for the rest of his life.'

Kitty was gobsmacked. Call herself a journalist? She'd been trying to find out about Dmitri all summer and hadn't even turned up the fact that two of his novels had been filmed. It made her all the more astonished that no one had told her about him when she was growing up. She'd often sat down to watch old movies on Saturday evenings with her mum, dad and Grandma Marta. Why had none of them mentioned the family connection to movies?

'I see this comes as a surprise,' the detective continued, 'so you probably won't be able to help us fill in any more of Irena Markova's life story. We know she came to the US from Czechoslovakia in 1948 and set up home in Albany, but we have no record of her death in this country. We got in touch with her stepdaughter, Hana

Markova, in a place called Brno,' – he pronounced it 'Burr-know'. 'We tracked her down using the address on Irena's immigration papers but she says they didn't hear from her after 1948.'

'Do you think it might be Irena Markova who was buried at my cabin?' It was horrible to think of the body as a person with a name, an identity, someone with living relatives who would be upset to hear of her death.

'It's only a possibility,' the detective said. 'We may be able to make an identification from dental records, or if we find a blood relative who can give a DNA match. But it might be someone else entirely. Perhaps it's a stranger buried there without your great-grandfather's knowledge and we may never identify her.'

Kitty shook her head in astonishment. 'I'm sorry I can't be of more help, but it seems you know more about my family than I do. Dmitri had lost touch with his daughter Marta when he died and I have no idea why.'

'I can't help you there.' He consulted his notes. 'Dmitri's son Nicholas died at the age of forty-five of cirrhosis of the liver. Marta moved to England in 1958 and we don't know what she did after that.'

'Cirrhosis!' Kitty was alarmed. 'So he was an alcoholic?'

'Not necessarily – but I believe that's the most common cause.'

Oh Christ, that means I have a gene for alcoholism, Kitty realised. She knew she had been drinking far too much that summer. She'd have to rein it in.

'Anyway, you are free to move back into your cabin now,' the detective said. He stood up and handed her a card. 'Get in touch if you think of anything that might be pertinent.'

'Before you go . . . would it be possible to put me in touch with Hana Markova? I'd really like to speak to her.'

He gave her a sharp look. 'I don't think that would be right, in the circumstances, do you?'

It was only then she realised they were seriously investigating her great-grandfather for murder. Could it be true? Had she misjudged him all along? Maybe he had been involved in the murder of the Romanovs and this woman, Irena Markova, was blackmailing him, threatening to expose the truth. Perhaps in the end he killed her to silence her.

It would be horrible to learn she had the genes of a murderer, but one way or another, Kitty was determined to find the truth.

Chapter Fifty-One

Albany, New York State, 1947

Dmitri was bemused by the success of his fourth novel, *In the Pale Light of Dawn*, and even more baffled when the film rights were snapped up. It was not his favourite of his novels, with its dark core about depression contrasting with the comedy of the quirky, eccentric Gloria, but readers seemed to identify with it. He received hundreds of letters from people telling him of their own struggles with depression. The children had both left for college so Rosa had time to reply to them as his unofficial secretary. Dmitri was invited to Hollywood to visit the film studio but he refused. He didn't feel protective of his work in this new medium; let the producers do as they wished. When the movie came out, he recognised little as his, but the substantial cheque in his bank account was welcome.

In the Pale Light of Dawn was not just successful in America but was translated into several European languages, and his overseas publishers were quick to snap up the sequel, *Toward the Sunset*. In autumn 1947, his publicist asked if he would be willing to do a three-week, six-stop tour of Europe to promote his books. They would like him to visit London, Paris, Geneva, Milan, Vienna and Prague, giving a speech in each location and signing copies.

300

Dmitri was reluctant. 'Who has money for books after the war?'

'You'd be surprised how many do,' his publicist told him. 'Especially yours, because of the anti-Nazi stance you took in the early 1930s.'

He hated fuss and was embarrassed by the arrogance of standing on a stage and talking about writing as if he was some kind of expert.

'But you *are* an expert!' his publicist exclaimed. 'Readers want to know how you get your ideas, they want to know about your writing process.'

Alfred Knopf was amused by his hesitation. 'You don't have to do it, of course, but why not? All you have to do is spend an hour or so in each city being fawned over by a crowd of your most ardent fans.'

Dmitri finally consented when he realised it would be simple to tack on a trip to Istanbul to see his sisters. He had visited a couple of times in the Berlin years but he hadn't seen them since he moved to America.

'Come with me,' he urged Rosa. 'We deserve a holiday.'

She shook her head and gave a little shudder, and he knew what that meant. A number of her relatives and old friends had perished in Hitler's concentration camps and although his tour would not take in Germany, she couldn't bear to return to European shores. For her, the entire continent had been tainted by anti-Semitism.

'I'd better stay here in case the children need me,' she apologised. 'They're not as independent as they think they are.'

She bought Dmitri some smart new suits and shirts, shiny black shoes and a pale grey raincoat and fedora hat, and helped him to pack. He felt a pang as the taxi arrived to take him to the station. He would miss Rosa. Life was better when she was around.

Chapter Fifty-Two

Lake Akanabee, New York State, October 2016

Immediately after the detective left, Kitty grabbed her laptop and went to the coffeehouse to use their wi-fi. Once again she was the only customer, and they were no longer serving food as they had cleared the stores ready to close for winter.

She opened her laptop and googled 'In the Pale Light of Dawn' and immediately a listing for the movie came up. It had starred William Holden and Ann Blyth, and premiered in 1948. A still showed him sitting on a rock by the seaside looking serious and moody while she posed in a flouncy tropical-print skirt, a coconut-shell bra and a huge floppy sunhat.

The movie of *Toward the Sunset* had come out in 1950 starring the same pair, this time pictured in camping gear, although Ann Blyth would have struggled to clamber into a tent wearing that skin-tight plaid skirt and sweater, all in clashing shades of shocking pink, lime green and purple. She must try to find copies of the films and watch them, although she suspected they would not stand the test of time.

Next she opened her email account and winced at the volume of emails that flooded in from Tom. She should write and suggest a meeting on her return. She'd punished him enough.

First, she wrote to the editor at Random House, asking if they had any records concerning Irena Markova, her great-grandfather's translator. Could they shed light on those monthly payments? Next she went into the genealogy website she used and asked how she would track down someone in Brno in the Czech Republic, giving all the details she had. In her experience people on genealogy forums went to great lengths to help each other.

She sat back to sip her coffee, wondering if there was anything else she could do to find out about Irena Markova. She noticed that her Random House email wasn't getting through but was sitting in the out-folder while the rainbow circle span round and round, implying the connection wasn't working. She pressed the 'Send and Receive All' button and instantly something shifted. The Random House one went through, and then another, the one from her drafts folder, the angry one to Tom.

'No!' she cried, trying too late to click to stop it as it disappeared into the ether. A second later it popped up in her 'Sent' folder. *Oh Christ, what have I done?* Kitty thought. Now she would have to write to apologise for her sarcasm.

Her flight left on the 14th of October, the following Wednesday, and arrived in London at dawn on the 15th so she supposed she could meet Tom that evening. She would be jetlagged though. Maybe she should stay with a friend and wait till the weekend.

As she hesitated an email arrived. It was from Tom and the header read 'If you don't love me any more, please just tell me . . .'

There was no text inside. Her eyes filled with tears. It wasn't fair to punish him like this. She typed a brief reply: 'I'm arriving back next Thursday. Meet me at 6 p.m, in the bandstand.'

It was a spot in their local park where they used to meet back in the days before they lived together. She would rush there, stomach fluttery with excitement, desperate to see him again even if they had only parted that morning. Suddenly, thinking about the forthcoming meeting, she felt that same buzz of anticipation.

Chapter Fifty-Three

Europe, autumn 1947

Dmitri was ashamed on arrival in London to realise how much Americans had been cushioned from the impact of the war. Back home they had suffered no physical hardships but here there were gaping holes between buildings where rockets had destroyed people's homes, leaving whole streets looking like mouths with missing teeth. The central London hotel in which he was accommodated was shabby and faded, with unreliable electricity and strictly limited hot water. The food was terrible: greasy stews with meat of indeterminate origin that got stuck between his teeth, served with watery boiled potatoes. The smell of cabbage permeated the hallways. He was glad he had brought his own coffee, although it did not taste the same with the milk powder he was offered in lieu of fresh.

In Paris people were starving. Women offered themselves on street corners, while ragged children clung to their legs. When they called out their fees Dmitri realised he could have hired a prostitute for the equivalent of less than a dollar had he been so inclined. Instead he handed out cash to those he passed, and they mumbled their thanks without meeting his eyes. Who was he to think he could write about depression? These people knew far more than him.

In each city he gave a short speech to a crowd, usually around fifty souls, then answered their questions. What did he think of the movie of *In the Pale Light of Dawn*? 'No comment,' he said to general laughter. Had *The Boot That Kicked* really been an anti-fascist book, as was thought at the time? 'That was absolutely my intention,' he said, 'but I hope it can be read as a diatribe against any form of oppressive state control.' 'How did he feel when reviewers compared him to his compatriot Vladimir Nabokov?' 'I wasn't aware they did, but would be immensely flattered if that were the case.'

A few copies of his books were sold, then he was usually taken to dinner by his local publisher plus wife. Dmitri had never been comfortable talking to strangers, despite all the lessons he had learned from Rosa over the years. He struggled with these foreign publishers, all of them speaking a language that was not their native tongue, talking about books he had not read, and he wished Rosa was there because she would have made the conversation flow smoothly.

His favourite part of the tour was the long train rides between cities when he could gaze out the windows at farm workers bringing in the harvest, at small villages with bustling marketplaces and churches that had lost their steeples in the war, at vast forests on the lower slopes of mountain ranges that already had snow-crusted peaks although it was just early October. It was a time for contemplation.

He had no desire to live in Europe any more. America had welcomed him with open arms and he hoped their constitution and ethnic mix would prevent any extreme political parties taking power as they had in Russia and Germany. He'd noticed some anti-Russian sentiments in the press – mostly comments on the territory they had grabbed in the post-war scramble and fears that Communist sentiment might spread across the Atlantic – but it did not worry Dmitri as he agreed with them. His hatred of Communism was stronger than ever.

He was concerned about the last stop of the tour, in Prague, because the previous year the Communist Party had won thirty-eight per cent of the vote. *What were the Czech people thinking?* he wondered. Had they not heard of the Soviet show trials and mass executions, of the Siberian prison camps with forced labour, of the secret police who arrested you for nothing but a sideways glance at the wrong moment? Why had they invited him, a known critic of the Soviet regime, to speak there? Could it be a trap?

His Czech publisher met him at the train station and seemed nervous as they took a taxi to the hotel.

'There will be spies from the Interior Ministry at your speech this evening so I suggest you steer clear of politics. We don't want to have a famous American author arrested while in our care.' He gave a little laugh, as though trying to make light of it, but Dmitri saw the nervous dart of his eyes and recognised it from Russia in 1917, when you could never be sure of the allegiance of anyone you spoke to.

'I don't plan to discuss politics but my audiences have invariably asked my views at previous stops on this tour,' Dmitri said.

The publisher nodded. 'I think you'll find they won't here.'

The talk that evening was in the Café Slavia, an Art Deco establishment on the banks of the Charles River with a view towards the castle. It was famous as a meeting place of Prague intellectuals, such as Franz Kafka and Karel Capek, but Dmitri's audience seemed composed of a mixture of down-at-heel students and elderly ladies, one of whom had a miniature dog on her lap. Dmitri hoped it would not interrupt him by yapping. To the side of the hall stood two men in long dark coats. He could tell from the hostile way they regarded him that they were secret police. Unwanted memories came flooding back and he hurried to the lectern to begin his speech. He was booked on a train to Istanbul the following morning and suddenly couldn't wait to get on board.

He talked about the Russian literature that had shaped his literary tastes, about the way his own life experiences fed into his writing, and about the influence of America with its movies and fast food and ubiquitous advertisements leading to consumer culture and a generation who were no longer satisfied with the lives their parents had led.

When he finished, the questions flooded in. How many drafts of each novel did he write? There were gasps when he replied 'Around twenty.' Had he started a new book to follow *Toward the Sunset*? 'Not yet,' he replied, explaining that he could not write on demand but had to wait for inspiration. The men in the dark coats stood expressionless.

When the last questioner had taken her turn, Dmitri announced that he would sign books at a table in the corner. A waiter brought him a glass of sweet wine and a cream cake, and he signed twenty-one books – rather more than he had sold at any of his other European events. The Czechs liked their literature, he mused.

The last book had been signed, and Dmitri was sipping the wine, waiting to say goodbye to the publisher, when a shadow fell over the table.

'Hello, Malama,' a soft voice said.

Chapter Fifty-Four

Prague, October 1947

Goosebumps broke out all over Dmitri's skin and the hair stood up on the back of his neck. He looked up and it was her. Tatiana. Utterly herself after all these decades.

He couldn't speak, but tears welled up. He pressed his knuckles to his eyes in an attempt to stop them.

'We had best get out of here,' she said in Russian. 'Come with me.'

When Dmitri stood, his knees almost gave way beneath him. Tatiana took his arm and led him down a side street into the Old Town. Neither of them spoke, but Dmitri breathed the cold night air deep into his lungs in an attempt to compose himself, surreptitiously wiping his eyes. She turned down a short flight of steps that led to the wooden door of a cellar bar. It was dark and quiet inside, with only three other customers. They took a corner table and asked the waitress to bring two glasses of red wine.

'Is it really you?' Dmitri breathed, gazing at her face. She looked almost exactly the same, apart from a deep furrow between her brows and little grooves, like symmetrical scars, on either side of her mouth. Her long hair was pinned into an old-fashioned bun at the back of her head.

'I brought something so you would be sure it is me,' she said, and fumbled in her pocket before producing the jewelled dog tag she'd commissioned Fabergé to make for Ortipo.

'How could you think . . .?' he began, a fist squeezing his heart.

'I heard there have been many people pretending to be my sisters or brother and couldn't bear it if you hadn't believed me.' Her voice was the same as ever, soft and low.

He shook his head in amazement. 'I would have known you anywhere. You haven't changed a bit.'

'Oh, I have.' She raised an eyebrow. 'Of course I have. So have you.' She looked at his crumpled face, his receding hairline, with a fond smile. 'I think you are more handsome than ever.'

He felt the tears welling again and blinked rapidly. The wine arrived and they raised their glasses to each other in a silent toast then drank, and he was glad of the warmth in his throat.

'I've read all your books,' she said. 'They're wonderful. I would have known they were yours no matter what name you put on the cover.' They had been published under the name Dmitri Yakovlevich.

'Why did you not contact me before?' he asked. 'You could have written to my publishers. They would have forwarded a letter.'

'I only discovered you were a writer just before the war. I saw a newspaper article, with a grainy photograph alongside, and couldn't believe my eyes. I had been told you were killed at Tsaritsyn in 1919 so my shock then was similar to yours tonight. I rushed out to buy your books straight away and when I read *Interminable Love* . . .' She sighed deeply. 'It was as if your soul spoke to me through the pages.'

'It was a love letter to you,' he said. 'I prayed you would read it one day.'

Her face lit up. 'Really?'

'Of course. Oh, I wish you had got in touch then.'

Her face clouded over. 'The years under Occupation were diffi-cult. The Germans would have considered it suspicious if I tried to write to the author of *The Boot that Kicked* at an address in New York. People were executed for less.'

A spasm of pain twisted her mouth and suddenly Dmitri couldn't bear any more casual chat. He grabbed her hand and looked into her eyes. 'Are you all right, Tatiana? Is everything all right?'

She gave a little laugh. 'No, not really.' She was struggling to contain her emotion but her face gave her away, the way it always used to when she was younger. 'But seeing you, I am more than all right.'

A blast of love for her knocked Dmitri sideways as though he had been struck by a giant wave in the ocean, as though someone had kicked the chair from beneath him. His face felt hot and he could hardly breathe. The love he felt was every bit as vast and overwhelming as it had been on the night they married in St Petersburg, on the night she disappeared from his cottage in Ekaterinburg. How could that be, when it was more than thirty years since they last saw each other? His ears were buzzing. He even wondered if he might be having a heart attack. He picked up his wine and took a gulp, then another, yearning for intoxication to still his rampaging emotions.

Tatiana put a hand over his and asked, with a smile, 'Would you like to lean your forehead against mine so we know what each other is thinking?'

He put his arm around her and leaned forwards till their heads touched. She smelled different now. Not jasmine, but a muskier, more womanly scent. Lust swept over him, causing a stiffening in his groin. It was extraordinarily erotic, sitting in that darkened bar with their foreheads pressed together.

It seemed Tatiana felt the same way because she asked quietly, 'Shall we go to your hotel room?'

He nodded and they rose immediately, leaving the rest of the wine.

*

Dmitri was nervous as he made love to Tatiana for the first time. He felt shy as he undressed, scared that he would disappoint her. He reached out tentatively, watching her face for signs that it was all right to do so. She was still slender, with long limbs and cool skin, like a china doll's, although her hands were rough and red, her nails short. He explored her, kissing tiny scars on her arms, noting the softness of her breasts, which were fuller than they used to be. Her tummy was rumpled and he guessed she had had a child. He felt a stab of jealousy. Whose child? Between her legs was warm, with a few grey hairs nestling amongst the brown. He laid his head on her belly and explored with his fingers, while she stroked his back, breathing deeply, pulling gently on his hair.

When at last he parted her legs and pushed inside her it was so excitingly different that he couldn't last long. With a cry from the back of his throat he came then clung to her in embarrassment. He began to apologise but she pulled his face to hers for a long, tender kiss.

'My wife,' he breathed as he pulled away.

'But you have another wife,' she said, not accusing but factual. 'I read about her in an article.'

'No. Rosa and I never married,' he told her. 'I would never have married while there was a chance you were alive.'

'Poor Rosa,' she mused.

'What about you?'

'I got married,' she told him. 'I had to. Besides, I thought you were dead.'

'Where is your husband now?'

Tatiana put a finger to his lips. 'Can we please not ask these questions? Not yet. Perhaps never. Some things are too painful to revisit. Can we just pretend that we met for the first time tonight, at Café Slavia?'

That floored him. He was desperate to know where she had been all those years, what had happened the night she disappeared

– and yet, perhaps she was right. Certainly it would be better left for another time.

She rose to wash at the basin in the corner of the room and he saw that she was more than slender; her ribs and hipbones protruded as if food had been scarce. He instinctively sucked in his own midlife paunch.

'Have you had dinner?' he asked. 'We could go for a late dinner.'

She shook her head. 'Breakfast tomorrow will be fine.'

'I'm supposed to catch a train to Istanbul in the morning to stay with my sister Valerina. She and Vera live there. But I'll telephone and say I've been delayed.'

'I'd like to spend some time with you, if possible. It's been so long . . .'

She unfastened her hair from its pins and he saw it was almost waist length. It suited her. She came back to lie in his arms, her face on his chest, and he marvelled at how well they fitted together, like a familiar pair of gloves.

A question came to his lips and he blurted it out before he could stop himself. 'Did any of the others survive? Do you know?'

'I don't think so. I don't see how they could have. I only survived because of you – and for a long time I wished I hadn't.' Her voice was flat.

Dmitri felt the weight of his old familiar guilt. 'I looked everywhere for you – all over Russia. When Anna Tschaikovsky appeared in Berlin, claiming to be Anastasia, I went straight there to see her.'

'And?' she asked, without hope.

'Definitely not.'

'You didn't go to see any of the people who claimed to be me?' There was a spark of irony in her voice.

'I saw photographs. There was little resemblance.'

'Huh! Such a strange thing to do.' She tilted her face to kiss his lips, savouring the luxury, then asked, 'Tell me about your children. You have two, don't you? What are they like?'

She laid her head on his chest to listen as he described them. 'They're in their early twenties, and both at college, where they live in residence. Marta is very popular and has dozens of boyfriends, who call on the telephone or arrive on the doorstep at all hours when she's at home. Nicholas is more of a loner, like me. I worry about him more . . .'

He couldn't think what else to say. The children never confided in him, the way they did in Rosa. He'd catch them sitting in the kitchen chatting about their friends, their classes, but they'd change the subject when he entered. He did not have Rosa's facility for making them open up.

'I have a Borzoi as well,' he added. 'A beautiful animal called Malevich.'

'After your army friend,' she remembered.

He shivered, a vision of what happened to Malevich flashing to mind. 'He's a sensitive creature, very smart and affectionate. There's something about his nature that reminds me of Ortipo. He's no longer a puppy but he still runs after birds, even though he knows they will take off at the last minute. It's a game he plays with them. He's a happy creature.'

'I loved Ortipo so much,' she said with passion. 'You'd be surprised how often I think of her, even now.'

'How did you come to have her tag with you?' Dmitri asked, stroking her hair.

She cuddled closer, burying her face so he could hardly hear her words. 'Those last weeks, we sewed jewels into the seams of our clothes. The tag was in the boning of one of my undergarments. I escaped with a few more gemstones but had to sell them over the years to get by.'

'Why didn't you . . .' he began, but Tatiana hushed him by kissing him. It was a long, hungry kiss that touched him deep inside and soon they were making love again, this time for much, much longer.

Chapter Fifty-Five

Lake Akanabee, New York State, 10th October 2016

Rebecca Wicks, the editor at Random House, emailed Kitty a couple of days later with a response to her question about Dmitri's translator:

> Our accounts department has two letters on file from your great-grandfather regarding Irena Markova. In the first, dated July 1958, he asks that in the event of his death a monthly payment of $300 should be paid to her from his royalty account, and gives an address in Albany. In the second, dated May 1975, he tells us that Irena has recently passed away, and that his royalties should be held in an interest-bearing account until one of his descendants gets in touch to claim them.

That's me! Kitty thought, with a start. It felt as if Dmitri expected her to find out about him one day, as if he was reaching out a hand to her from the past.

The second shock came when she calculated that Irena Markova had died forty-one years earlier so that meant she really could be the body at the cabin. The dates fitted. But why would Dmitri have buried her there? *Did* he murder her? There was still so much she didn't know about him . . .

Why had he been so concerned to keep paying Irena in the event of him dying first? The blackmail scenario didn't fit. She wondered if they had maybe fallen in love after Rosa's death. Perhaps that was the case, and Nicholas and Marta couldn't forgive him for it. That might explain the rift between them.

But it seemed implausible that the grandmother she remembered as generous and fun-loving could have been so cold-hearted as to cut off her own father. She must have had a stronger reason. Kitty remembered her mum saying that Marta and Stanley were short of money after Stanley's business failed. Why did she not ask Dmitri for help? And then it occurred to her that maybe Dmitri had been the one to break off contact. Could it have anything to do with the body found in his cabin? He didn't want to risk them finding out . . . Kitty felt as though she was going round in circles.

She logged in to her genealogy forum to find there were some replies to her question, and scrolled down the list. Several mentioned websites in the Czech Republic but these would only be useful if she could post in Czech. She'd need to find a translator. One came up with a link to the immigration papers of Irena Markova, which gave an old address in Brno. But then, near the end of the list, she found a post in English, from a woman called Hana Markova, which said, 'I think I am the person you are looking for. I am the stepdaughter of Irena Markova and this week I had a call about her from the New York state police. I work as an interpreter at a conference centre in Brno' – she gave the telephone number – 'and it is best to catch me between 12.30 and 2 p.m.'

Kitty was amazed. The Internet had come up trumps after all! She googled and learned that New York was six hours behind the Czech Republic, so that meant calling between 6.30 and 8 a.m. in the morning. While packing her bags to move back to the cabin for her last few nights at Lake Akanabee, Kitty made sure her mobile phone was fully charged. This might be a long call.

Chapter Fifty-Six

Prague, October 1947

The following morning, Dmitri opened his eyes and turned to look at Tatiana breathing quietly beside him, her soft auburn hair fanned across the pillow. It was the most precious moment of his life. He raised himself on an elbow to examine the curl of her lashes, the curve of her ear, the slender neck, and he was choked with the enormity of his love for her.

As if she could feel his gaze she opened her eyes and smiled up at him. In that instant there was no past, no future, nothing but the two of them. Without words they kissed then began to make love and it was glorious, the fulfilment of all Dmitri's yearnings since 1914 when, at the age of twenty-three, he first set eyes on Tatiana in a hospital ward.

They bathed and dressed slowly, with many kisses and caresses. By the time they got downstairs the hotel had stopped serving breakfast so they went out to a café in Wenceslas Square and ordered dark bread, cold meats and cheeses. They sat close, their knees pressed together, as they ate.

'Where is your home?' Dmitri asked, smoothing a loose strand of hair from her brow and tucking it behind her ear. 'Am I allowed to ask?'

He still couldn't quite believe it was her, and kept touching her, gazing at her, making sure.

She finished chewing a mouthful. 'I don't have a home any more. This is something I need to discuss with you. I have a proposal.'

'Anything you want. You only have to ask.'

'I need money to rent a place . . . but I don't want to take a gift from you – although I know you would offer without hesitation.'

He was automatically reaching for his chequebook but stopped.

She continued: 'I don't know if you're aware that the English translation of your first three novels is dreadful: clumsy and wordy and not an accurate reflection of the delicacy and precision of your Russian prose. I was going to ask if you might consider hiring me to retranslate them. I know I could do much better.'

'Oh God, of course! I'd love you to do that.' He was excited at the thought.

She continued. 'Once I have a track record as a translator, I hope I can find enough work to earn a living. I have been doing farming work till now' – she held out her roughened hands to show him – 'but I have trouble with my back and can't work long hours any more.'

He couldn't bear to think of her farming, of her back aching. She was a Romanov, a grand duchess. 'Tatiana, I have plenty of money. You don't need to work ever again. Please let me give you a regular sum, whatever you need. You're my wife, after all.'

She leaned across to kiss him then pulled her chair round so that she was close enough to wrap her arms around him and hold him so close he could feel the beating of a pulse in her neck.

They spent the day walking around the town: across the famous Charles Bridge lined with lifelike statues of saints, up to St Nicholas Church and the atmospheric old Castle, back to the Jewish cemetery with its thousands of tombstones all toppling over each other, and around the majesty of Wencelas Square. Tatiana spoke fluent Czech so Dmitri imagined this must be where she had been living.

Perhaps she had been rescued from Ekaterinburg by the Czechs in the White Army. Bless them, whoever they were. He'd be forever in their debt.

Towards evening they collected her belongings from the left luggage office at the railway station – a battered holdall containing a few items of clothing and her copies of his books.

'Do you want to stay in Prague?' he asked later, over dinner. 'I'm worried about the growth of the Communist Party here. It feels like St Petersburg in 1917, with people checking who is listening before opening their mouths to speak.'

'I know. I'm worried too, but I don't have anywhere else to go.'

'Do you have children?' he asked, tentatively.

'No,' she said quickly, not meeting his eye.

He hesitated, sure she was lying, but she didn't continue. 'You don't want to get in touch with your family? I met your Aunt Irene in Berlin, and I know there are still Romanovs in Denmark.'

She winced. 'I couldn't bear to become a newspaper story, to have all these strangers queuing up to decide whether or not they recognise me. The only person I ever wanted to find was you.'

Dmitri spoke without thinking. 'Come to America then. I'll help you.'

Her face lit up, then a cloud passed over it. 'I will not be responsible for taking you away from the mother of your children, Malama.'

A vision of Rosa came into Dmitri's head and he felt stricken. For the last twenty-four hours, since meeting Tatiana, he hadn't given her a thought. Now her sunny smile, her generous body, her optimistic nature came to him as if in a vision. He could never hurt Rosa. He loved her too much. How could he have betrayed her so thoughtlessly? What could he do?

'I'll tell you what will happen,' Tatiana told him, while he hesitated. 'I will come to America with you and I will translate your books into good English but I will live alone. I have become a solitary person over the years and I think that would suit me best.'

Dmitri frowned: 'But you are my wife. I want us to be lovers.'

She took his chin between her fingers, looked him in the eye, and said. 'Yes, I rather think that is inevitable.'

Chapter Fifty-Seven

Lake Akanabee, New York State, 11th October 2016

In the few days since she was last there, it felt as if the temperature on the lake had dropped ten degrees. Kitty slept huddled in her fleecy dressing gown with her thick green cardigan piled on top of the bedding roll but still she woke several times shivering. The alarm on her phone was set for 6.30 a.m. and for the first time she caught the sunrise over the lake. If anything, it was more spectacular than the sunsets, with streaks of flamingo-pink and tangerine heralding a shimmery white sun. A black bird with red wings was crying 'Coralee, coralee' as if searching for a lost love. She made herself a cup of instant coffee and took her phone to the end of the jetty, where the signal appeared to be strongest.

There were clicks and buzzes before a phone began to ring thousands of miles down the ether. A voice answered in Czech, so Kitty said slowly and clearly, in English, 'Could I speak to Hana Markova, please.'

'Yes, of course,' the voice answered, with traces of an American accent.

While she waited to be connected, Kitty wondered briefly about the cost of the call then decided that this is what Dmitri would want her to do with his money. He would want her to clear his name.

A voice came on the line: '*Ahoj!*'

'This is Kitty Fisher. Is that Hana Markova?'

The voice switched to flawless English. 'Well, hello. Kitty! My goodness, am I really speaking to Dmitri's great-granddaughter?'

Kitty paused, puzzled. 'Yes, did you know him?'

'Not personally, but my father said Irena often spoke of him. And when she left in 1948, he was pretty sure she had gone to find Dmitri.'

'How did *she* know him?' Kitty felt as though she was being particularly slow, as though Hana was several steps ahead of her.

There was a pause, and she couldn't tell if it was a delay on the line or Hana's hesitation. 'They met in Russia, during the war. The First World War.'

'But then she married your father?'

'Yes, that's right.'

'And she was your stepmother?'

'No, I was born after Irena left. My mother was Dad's second wife.'

Kitty paused, but there was no point to this call unless she was straight. 'Did the police tell you that a body I found buried near Dmitri's cabin might be hers?'

'Yes. They asked if I knew anyone who could provide DNA or dental records but I'm afraid I can't help with that.'

Kitty chose her words carefully. 'They seem to think Dmitri might have had something to do with her death. But from what I know of him, I can't believe it. That's why I wanted to call you, to see if you can tell me any more about them.'

There was a muffled sound that could have been a laugh, or an indignant snort. 'That's ridiculous. He would never have harmed a hair on her head.'

'Were they lovers?'

Hana sighed. 'It's a big story, and not one that should be told on the telephone. But as Dmitri's great-granddaughter you have the right to know . . .'

321

Kitty spoke impulsively. 'Why don't I come to see you? I could fly out next week.'

Hana was surprised. 'You would come all the way from America to Brno?'

'I've got to be in London on Thursday but I could come to you on Friday.'

'And you have no idea what this is all about?' Hana sounded incredulous.

'Perhaps I have an inkling,' Kitty said. 'I have a Russian diary dating from 1918. I'll bring it with me.'

Chapter Fifty-Eight

Istanbul, September 1948

Two days after they found each other again, Dmitri and Tatiana caught a train to Istanbul, then sailed in a caïque across the Bosphorus to his sister Valerina's house. It was in a walled court-yard surrounded by dark green forest on all sides and looked out over the sparkling water from a high vantage point. Dmitri hadn't told his sister he was bringing another guest and when he walked in with Tatiana, Valerina recognised her immediately. Her eyes widened in shock and she caught her breath before she bent her knees in a curtsey.

'Please don't,' Tatiana begged. 'I am no longer royalty. For many years I have been a farmer's wife.'

'Come, sit down,' Valerina fussed, pointing to a comfortable armchair by a window. 'You must be tired from your journey. I will have a room prepared.'

Dmitri looked at Tatiana then back at his sister before he spoke: 'We would like to share a room – if it is acceptable to you.'

'Well, of course . . .' Valerina was momentarily flustered but soon regained her composure. 'Of course you would. I'll make arrangements. Are you well, Your . . .?' She paused, unsure how to address her guest.

'Please call me Tatiana. These last decades I have been known by the name Irena Markova but I miss the name of my birth.'

'So you were brought out of Russia by men from the Czech Legion?' Valerina asked.

'One man. Yes.'

Dmitri was consumed by jealousy. Who was this man? Was he the one she had married?

'I can't even begin to imagine what you have been through,' Valerina said softly. 'You are welcome in my house for as long as you like. Both of you.'

Dmitri hugged her. 'Thank you. I knew you would say that. I am going to apply for a passport and visa so Tatiana can come to America with me and I don't know how long it will take, so if we could stay here in the meantime . . .'

'Of course.'

Dmitri was astonished by how quickly the women became friends. Tatiana may have told him she did not want to talk about what had happened in the years since they last saw each other, but Valerina had soon coaxed most of the story from her, after serving them glasses of sweet amber-coloured sherry.

'The man who brought me to Czechoslovakia is called Vaclav Markov,' Tatiana said. 'He is a good man, a Czech soldier, as you guessed, and he smuggled me out of Russia and all the way to the village of his birth, outside Brno. I was in the depths of despair after hearing the fate of my family. Although I hoped desperately that it was not true, I had a feeling right from the start that it must be. We all knew death was close those last weeks. I think we accepted that we were unlikely to survive once we arrived at that wretched house in Ekaterinburg – even little Alexei.'

She shook herself as if to expunge the memory.

'I wrote to your mother' – Tatiana looked at Dmitri – 'and received a reply saying that you had died at the battle of Tsaritsyn. And that's when I gave up all hope . . .'

Dmitri was furious with himself. *If only he had written to his mother so she knew he was alive . . . Everything would have been different.* 'Malevich died at Tsaritsyn,' he explained. 'I couldn't bear to stay in the army after that. I left to continue searching for you.'

Tatiana gave him a look of compassion. 'It's all so long ago. We've both had to live with the decisions we made. I married Vaclav because it was the only way to stay in that village without attracting attention. We always worried that the Bolsheviks would find me so we lived unobtrusively on a farm. That's where I've been all these years.'

'Did you have children?' Valerina asked. It was the question Dmitri had felt unable to press her on after she told him she didn't, but from his sister it felt natural.

Tears welled in Tatiana's eyes. Up to that point she had been composed, but now she could not speak. Valerina rose, knelt at her feet and took her hands. 'I'm so sorry,' she said quietly.

The tears began to flow as Tatiana spoke. 'My only son, Jaroslav, was executed by the Nazis. It happened five years ago but feels like yesterday.'

Dmitri came to put her arms around her shoulders and she leaned her face into his waist and wept. He felt useless, lumpen, that he was unable to take away her pain.

'It was too cruel,' she sobbed. 'After everything else. Then that.'

Valerina and Dmitri caught eyes. There was nothing to say, so they remained there, holding Tatiana, until her crying passed. Dmitri felt the scale of her loss keenly – her homeland, her family, her son. It was unthinkable.

'But now I have you.' She looked up at him through wet lashes and he knew that whatever happened he must keep her close for the rest of his life.

The passport and visa came through, in the name of Irena Markova, since that was what she was called in her Czech documents. Dmitri and Tatiana bade farewell to Valerina and flew to New York together in early December 1948. It was a long, gruelling flight with six stop-overs between Istanbul and New York, but much faster than a ship's crossing. Rosa had been expecting Dmitri weeks earlier – he had been absent for three months rather than one – and despite several expensive international calls from Valerina's house, he knew she was anxious.

He and Tatiana caught a train from Grand Central station and she gazed out the window at this country that would be her new home. Light snow was falling and the grass sparkled with frost, while stark trees waved against a white sky, almost like their Russian homeland. As the train neared Albany, Dmitri walked along to alight from another compartment, as he knew Rosa would be waiting on the platform. He had given Tatiana an envelope full of money, instructions on where to find the taxi rank and the address of a good hotel – and thus his double life began.

When Dmitri saw Rosa on the platform, wearing a coat the colour of raspberries with three oversized black buttons down the front, and a pillbox hat with two black feathers sticking up jauntily, he felt a gush of warmth for her. She ran along the platform and threw herself into his arms, and Dmitri couldn't help glancing over his shoulder to check if Tatiana was watching. He couldn't see her, so he hugged Rosa and kissed her on the cheek. This was going to be hard. Already he felt torn: on the one hand he worried that Tatiana might not find her hotel safely, that she might feel lonely on her own in a strange land, and on the other he was nervous that Rosa might sense his infidelity, might smell it on his clothes or detect it in his manner. She had always been good at reading his moods and he was not practised in deception.

Back home, he was greeted by Malevich, now a rather elderly dog with grey whiskers and arthritic joints, but still retaining a puppyish enthusiasm. He could no longer jump up but licked Dmitri's hand and wouldn't stop following him all evening. It was midweek and the children were at college, but Rosa had made a feast of his favourite Russian dishes: Borscht soup, *pirogi* dumplings filled with meat and cheese, and a salmon *coulibiac*, with fish, rice, spinach and hard-boiled eggs wrapped in pastry. As he ate, Rosa told him the latest news: the children's examination results, a neighbour who had been admitted to hospital, her worries for her mother, who was getting increasingly frail. Dmitri half-listened, making appropriate murmuring noises, and trying to calm her with his still presence, because she seemed agitated.

'So these problems with the company, you are sure they are sorted?' This was the excuse Dmitri had used for his delayed return. He nodded vaguely. 'I wish you would leave the job now that we don't need the money any more.'

'They're family,' he soothed. 'I can't leave them in the lurch. But I've told Alex I'm resigning soon and he accepted it. I just have to find someone to take over.'

Rosa was pleased. 'Do you have an idea what you will write next? Did Europe provide any inspiration for a new novel?'

'Perhaps. I haven't decided yet. As you know, I can only write in the peace and quiet of my own home.'

After dinner they went up to the bedroom where he opened his suitcase and gave her the presents he had brought from Europe: a bottle of the coveted Chanel No. 5 perfume from Coco Chanel's rue Cambon shop in Paris; a recipe book from Vienna, written in German; and a length of fine silk from Milan, the iridescent turquoise of a kingfisher's wings. He'd also brought gifts for the children, and for her mother and sister, and she admired them and complimented his taste.

And then came the moment he dreaded as Rosa leaned in to kiss him and reached her hand between his legs.

'It's been such a long time,' she murmured.

He froze and began formulating the words to tell her that he was tired from the journey and needed to bathe, but his penis betrayed him by responding to her touch. Rosa knew his body intimately; his cells held a memory of all the sensual delights of their past decades, and it proved impossible to resist her. He liked the familiar way she used her muscles to grip him, the places she touched him, the little cry she gave as she came. That's how Dmitri found himself making love to Rosa just twenty-four hours after he last made love to Tatiana.

Afterwards, as she lay in his arms, Dmitri experienced new depths of guilt. Of all the bad things he had done in his life this was the most despicable. He listed them in his head: he hadn't visited his parents before they died because he was too busy trying – and failing – to rescue the Romanovs; he had almost certainly caused the death of the farm girl Yelena through his blinkered selfishness; he had done his best to save Tatiana but in doing so he might have sealed her family's fate; he had let Rosa fall in love with him even though he loved another. But now, this huge infidelity – this was inexcusable.

During their stay with Valerina his sister had warned him he would never be able to manage an affair, that it would tear him apart. But how could he hurt either of these women? He couldn't bear it. He loved them both in different ways, wanted them both to be happy and to be part of his life.

Rosa seemed to have no idea of his turmoil. She curled her body around his with a sigh of contentment and fell asleep in his arms.

The following day, Dmitri left home at the time he would normally go to the office, despite Rosa pleading with him to rest and recover from his jetlag. He drove straight to the town-centre hotel where Tatiana was installed and hurried up to her room, where he found her reading by the window, quite content to wait for him.

'Is Rosa all right?' she asked, smiling as if it were the most natural thing in the world for her to ask.

'Yes, fine.' He was uncomfortable talking about Rosa. 'And you? Is the hotel to your liking?'

'It is utterly luxurious. I had a delicious dinner last night then spent an hour in the bath so I feel quite pampered.' She smiled and stretched, cat-like.

He sat down on the bed. 'Tatiana, I don't think I can do this. The dishonesty feels fundamentally wrong. I think I should tell Rosa that I've found you and that we have to be together. She will be devastated but at least I won't be lying to her.'

Tatiana shook her head decisively. 'What you're saying is that you would rather make Rosa suffer than live with your guilty conscience.' She held his gaze. 'If you hadn't met me, would you be leaving Rosa now?'

'Of course not.'

'Well, our relationship need not change anything between you two. In her position, I would rather keep the man I love, with whom I had raised two children, than be left on my own.'

Dmitri sighed and pursed his lips.

'You will get used to it. All will be well.' Tatiana rose to put her arms round his neck, pulled his head to her breast. 'First, we need to find somewhere for me to live.'

Dmitri resigned himself to the situation for now. 'We can visit a real-estate agent this morning and pick out somewhere.'

She shook her head. 'It's best that we are not seen together around the town. Why don't you choose? Pick an area where Rosa seldom goes but not too distant that you can't visit easily. Whatever you like is fine with me, so long as it has a little outdoor space where I can grow a few plants. I will wait here for your return.'

She seemed to have thought it all through, Dmitri mused. Perhaps women understood these matters better. He found the whole idea of the deception abhorrent. It certainly didn't come naturally to him.

He followed Tatiana's instructions and found her a two-bedroom cottage in Buckingham Lake, just walking distance from his rug import office but on the opposite side of town from their home and the area where most of Rosa's friends and her mother and sister lived. He opened a bank account for her and put in plenty of money so she could furnish the cottage and buy all that she needed in the way of clothes and household goods.

Back at the hotel they had lunch together and talked about the translation of *Interminable Love*, which she was keen to start. To anyone watching from the outside, they could have been two old friends. But after lunch they went up to her hotel room and made love, still discovering each other, still overwhelmed by the force of their feelings for each other after thirty years apart. While in her arms, Dmitri didn't think of Rosa once.

He pulled up in his driveway at six o'clock, the time he would have got home from a day at the office, and Malevich came limping out to greet him.

'Are you OK?' Rosa asked as he kissed her in greeting. 'I called the office and they said you hadn't been in.'

Dmitri picked up the mail from the kitchen table, knowing he would be unable to look her in the eye while telling an outright lie. 'I had a long meeting with a wholesaler. He took me for lunch.' He tore open an envelope but stared without focus at the letter inside, while he waited to see if Rosa had any more questions.

'It's chicken supreme for dinner,' she said. 'Nicholas called to say he'll come home on Friday evening and he'll stay till Sunday. I hope Marta can come too but you know what her social calendar is like! We'll be lucky if she can squeeze us in for a lunch.' She laughed, proud of her gregarious daughter.

'Good. Well, that will be nice.' Dmitri seemed to have got away with it this time but he was useless at dissembling. This is where the arrangement would fail: he had never been good at telling lies. Rosa had believed his excuse today but what about next time? And the time after that? Would Tatiana become impatient if she didn't see enough of him? He realised Rosa was talking and he wasn't listening because his head was full of the problem of loving two women and not wanting to hurt either of them.

It was relatively simple on a practical level for Dmitri to see Tatiana on weekdays. He could slip out of the office, ostensibly for a

330

meeting, or use the time when Rosa had engagements: she volunteered at the local hospital, attended a weekly flower-arranging class, and often went for coffee with friends. At weekends, he could use the excuse of taking the dog for a long walk, but more than once his plans were thwarted when Nicholas or Rosa decided to accompany him.

Dmitri usually drove to Tatiana's cottage in his Lincoln Continental Cabriolet. Physically, he could be there in ten minutes, but it was harder to make the mental adjustment from one woman to another because he was a different man with each. With Tatiana he discussed literature, politics and history, while with Rosa he talked of their children and mutual acquaintances and they laughed at lot. He was utterly besotted by Tatiana, just as he had been in the old days – she was the creature of his fantasies, his great love – but sometimes when he was with her he found himself thinking of Rosa's indomitable cheerfulness. When he was at home with Rosa and his thoughts turned to Tatiana he flushed to the roots of his hair at the strength of his feelings. Rosa had been a wonderful mother and companion but she would never be his soulmate; she would never totally understand him because she did not share his Russian heritage.

Tatiana was different from her teenage self. She seemed strong and self-reliant now, quite content with her own company. She never asked that he visit her more frequently but was always pleased to see him when he arrived. There was no sign of her making friends in the neighbourhood; she seemed to live a solitary life when he was not around, working on the translation of his novel or cultivating her garden. She had furnished the cottage in a simple, functional style, devoting all her creative energy into growing vegetables, herbs and flowers in the little twenty-foot by twenty-foot yard out back. He was surprised to find that she could cook now.

'Do you remember when you were learning to make bread?' he asked. 'I was shocked that a grand duchess should have to do such a thing.'

'That was in Tobolsk . . .' Her voice trailed off and a haunted look came into her eyes. Dmitri knew she was thinking of her family.

'I have your diary,' he said. 'The one you left in my cottage. Would you like to see it?'

'Never.' She shuddered. 'No.'

'And I still have the waistcoat you knitted for me that Christmas,' he told her, 'but it is a little snug around my middle.'

'I have done a lot of knitting since then,' she said, 'and made my own wool too. We kept sheep.'

She let slip odd facts from time to time and he stored them up, putting the pieces together. Still there was much she wouldn't talk about – the night she disappeared from the cottage, how she got back to Czechoslovakia, her dead son Jaroslev – but he would never push her. Frankly, he wasn't sure he wanted to know, at least not for a while. He was still trying to find his balance in this strange seesaw life he had created.

Chapter Fifty-Nine

London, 15th October 2016

London was drizzly and overcast when Kitty arrived at Heathrow. She shivered and wrapped her green cardigan tightly around herself. There wasn't a chink of sunlight, just solid grey cloud cover, like a lid closed over the city. She missed the colours of Lake Akanabee. Even in wild weather it had been like an artist's palette of pinks, purples, greens, reds, gold, and every shade of blue.

She caught a train into the centre of town then took a taxi to Crouch End, fumbling in the bottom of her case for door keys. There was a moment of panic: Tom wouldn't have changed the locks, would he? What if he hadn't gone to work yet but was sitting at the kitchen table – or upstairs, still in bed?

The door opened and the first thing she saw was a neat pile of post addressed to her on the hall table. It felt as though she was an intruder. Everything was clean and orderly, and the air smelled of furniture polish. It was as if the house had been uninhabited since she left.

She went to the kitchen and made a cup of tea, glancing into the fridge as she took out the milk. There wasn't much fresh food, but the freezer was full of ready meals and that made her sad. Poor Tom.

She dozed on the sofa for a couple of hours then began to unpack the clothes she'd taken to America and lay out the ones she would take to Brno. As six o'clock approached she had butterflies at the thought of meeting Tom, and smiled at herself. Would they make love that night?

She arrived at the park early and stood beneath the shelter of an oak tree, wanting to watch Tom as he approached the bandstand. Even from a distance she could tell he had lost weight. His jacket hung loose and he'd forgotten to bring a raincoat or umbrella so was getting soaked in the drizzle, but he was valiantly carrying two takeaway coffees as well as his briefcase. She felt a pang of love for him.

When she stepped out to say hello, she saw his eyes were rimmed by shadows. There was a moment when they both held back then she leaned in to give him a kiss on the cheek before taking one of the coffees.

'You look tired,' she said. 'Are you OK?' She had done this to him; it was her fault he was so thin and grey. And then she remembered what he had done to her by sleeping with Karren. Suddenly it seemed like ancient history, something that had happened in another lifetime.

'It's good to see you looking all tanned and beautiful, Kitty-kat. Your summer on the lake obviously suited you.'

'The cabin is gorgeous. You'll have to . . .' She stopped. They weren't there yet.

They sat on the wrought-iron bench inside the bandstand, where Hula-Hoop packets and Irn-Bru cans littered the ground, and she took a sip of her coffee: a soya latte. He knew what she liked.

'You were right,' she began. 'There was a lot of work to do. It was covered in creepers and had a tree growing through the steps when I arrived, but it's all fixed up now.' She showed him some photos she'd taken on her phone. 'I had to rebuild the porch and the jetty from scratch. I made that swing seat as well.'

'What a beautiful spot.' He scrolled through the pictures. 'So is that what you've been doing all summer? Working on the cabin?'

'I've also been finding out about the great-grandfather who left it to me. There are lots of gaps in his story but I'm flying to the Czech Republic tomorrow to meet someone who can tell me more.' Tom looked alarmed so she added quickly: 'Just for the weekend.'

'Will you come back to our house tonight?' She had never heard him sound so unsure of himself.

'I took my bags there this morning. Was that all right?'

'Of *course*.'

They were like strangers. Kitty decided to cut through the formality. 'I'm sorry I haven't been in touch. I needed space to think. Not just about us; I needed to try and work out what I'm doing with my life.' She gave a little laugh. 'I suppose I want to find a sense of purpose. Other people have children and that gives them a focus but we decided against them. Now I want to find a way for my life to mean something. Does that make sense?'

He was listening closely. 'If you want to put the children issue back on the table we can discuss it.'

'No, not really.' She looked into his eyes, trying to read his expression. 'Unless you do?'

'I thought about it this summer, but mainly because if we'd had kids you wouldn't have been able to leave me for three months without any communication. It's been horrible, Kitty. I felt as if I was emailing into a black hole but I couldn't stop because it was the only slender hope I had of getting through to you. Were you reading my mails?'

She gave a guilty shake of the head. 'I read your letter. It made sense.' Suddenly she badly wanted to kiss him. It felt too soon, though. 'Are you still looking for a new job?'

'I had an interview last week with a company that raises funding for the arts and I just heard two days ago that I've got the job.' He looked boyish in his excitement. 'They're based in Shoreditch in a converted factory. I love the atmosphere and the people there.'

'That sounds brilliant! Congratulations!' She grinned at him. 'What will you have to do?'

He described the role, and Kitty thought how perfect it sounded for him to become an enabler for artists, someone who would help them achieve their dreams.

'Did you do any writing over the summer?' he asked.

She sighed. 'Not a word. I'm beginning to realise I'm not cut out to be a writer. Sure, I can string a sentence together but I don't have anything I passionately want to say. That's why I keep abandoning everything I start. My great-grandfather, on the other hand . . . he was a famous novelist in his day. His books are powerful insights into human emotion.'

He was regarding her affectionately. 'You never mentioned having a writer in the family.'

'No one ever told me. I can't think why Mum never said.'

'It seems odd, but I remember her saying she never met any of her grandparents: all four died before she was born . . .'

'Did she?' Kitty screwed up her forehead trying to remember. 'But that's not true. Dmitri only died in 1986. It seems there was some big falling out between them. That's why Dmitri's inheritance eventually came to me; they couldn't find any family members when he died.'

'Is this why you are flying to the Czech Republic? So you can solve the mystery?' He smiled indulgently.

'I'll tell you more about it over dinner. Can we go and eat now? I'm starving.'

They walked to their favourite restaurant, a tiny French bistro two streets from home, and first she told him what she had learned about Dmitri Yakovlevich. They ordered their usual – French onion soup, pepper steaks and a bottle of Burgundy – and never stopped talking throughout the meal. There was so much to say.

'If you have decided that you don't want to be a writer any more, then what?' Tom asked.

'I don't know. I didn't get that far.'

'If you want to develop another property, we could easily raise money against the house.'

Kitty wrinkled her nose. 'I don't know. It's stressful, and there are tedious problems. Besides, I'm not sure the market is going in the right direction. There could be a crash on the way.'

Tom was watching her, eyes narrowed. 'Show me those photos of your cabin again.'

She handed him her phone and he flicked through them once more. She'd taken long shots from the end of the jetty, and also some close-ups of the stairs and banister leading up to the porch.

'I know what you should be,' he said, handing the phone back to her. 'A carpenter.'

She opened her mouth to object then stopped. She loved working with wood. 'But how would I earn a living at it?'

'That's up to you. You could set up a website and distribute leaflets offering to make bookshelves and fitted cupboards . . . or you could design your own bespoke furniture. Why not?'

She frowned. 'I'd need to upgrade my tools. I've already got contacts in that wood yard in Kentish Town. Perhaps I could build a shed at the end of our garden as a workshop.' Tom let her think out loud, nodding encouragement. She had the strangest sensation as all the pieces slotted into place. It was as if it was predestined. This was one of the extraordinary things about a close relationship: it was possible for your partner to know you better than you knew yourself.

'Mum wouldn't have approved,' she said. 'She wanted me to be a lawyer.'

'Maybe, but most of all she wanted you to be happy.'

Kitty knew that was true, and loved that Tom knew it as well. He provided continuity in her life now that he had become her sole family member. She had drunk two glasses of wine and was about to pour another when she stopped, remembering her great-uncle Nicholas and his cirrhosis. Tom didn't want any more either, so they put a cork in the bottle and carried it home.

Once they were in the hall, she grabbed the collar of his jacket and pulled him in for the kiss she'd been wanting to give him for the last few hours. 'I'm sorry,' she whispered, and she meant she was sorry for leaving him alone all summer. He didn't reply, too busy lifting her sweater over her head. She unfastened his trousers, lifted her skirt and pushed her knickers aside then stood on tiptoe and hooked one leg around his waist so he could enter her. Now, she thought, now at last I am home.

Chapter Sixty

Albany, New York State, 1955

Dmitri's double life continued for seven years and neither of the women he loved challenged him. Tatiana never seemed to resent the fact that he spent most weekends and holidays with his family and sometimes couldn't see her for days on end; Rosa never questioned his whereabouts, just accepting whatever excuse he made to explain a few hours' absence. On the drive home from Tatiana's he often stopped for a beer to clear his head. Guilt had become a familiar companion but he still believed there had been no choice: he couldn't have left Rosa, the woman who had entwined her fortune with his and brought him so much happiness, but at the same time he couldn't resist the potent magnetism of his decades-old bond with Tatiana.

During those seven years, both of his children got married. Nicholas had never brought home any girlfriends and by his late twenties they were beginning to worry about him until one weekend he presented a long-legged, sun-kissed Californian girl called Pattie and announced they were engaged. The whole family flew out to Santa Barbara for a wedding in Pattie's home church, followed by a party at her parents' glamorous beach club. At first Dmitri and Rosa were dazzled by the champagne cocktails, the palm trees set around a turquoise swimming pool, and the glitzy people wearing ostentatious jewellery, but Rosa was soon circulating and befriending their new in-laws. She was wearing a rose-pink lace off-the-shoulder dress with a mauve satin sash, and a tiny hat decorated with pink and mauve fresh flowers and in Dmitri's opinion was by far the best-dressed woman at the gathering.

Marta had brought one of her many boyfriends as her 'plus one': a staid, prematurely balding Englishman called Stanley who owned a company that manufactured silver cutlery. He had a strange accent from somewhere in the north of England, and Dmitri found it hard to make out what he was saying. After a while it became awkward asking him to repeat himself, so he nodded and smiled vaguely whenever they were forced to make conversation. Marta obviously had no such difficulty because a few weeks after the Santa Barbara wedding, Stanley came to ask Dmitri's permission to marry her.

Dmitri hesitated. 'Of course, it is my daughter's decision, but I hope you do not plan to take her back to England with you. My wife and I would miss her terribly.'

'Naw, I'm going to be here awhile,' Stanley promised. 'America's the fastest-growing market in't cutlery trade and we'll most likely set up home near Albany.'

'And you think you can keep my daughter and any children you might have in comfort with your earnings from this business?'

Stanley launched into a speech about profit margins and the potential growth of the company, and Dmitri stopped concentrating. He wasn't sure what Marta saw in this man, who was no more than average-looking, but perhaps she liked the foreignness of him. When he discussed it with Rosa later, she said he treated Marta like a princess but Dmitri couldn't see how. At any rate, the marriage went ahead, in a church in Albany, followed by a reception for eighty guests in a swish restaurant. After the meal, a swing band played and everyone crowded onto the tiny dance floor.

Dmitri and Rosa held each other and swayed to the unfamiliar beat.

'We've done our duty as parents.' She smiled. 'Now I look forward to being a grandma.'

The thought hadn't even occurred to Dmitri and when he considered it he felt sad that he and Tatiana had not been able to have a child together. His direct bloodline would continue into the future but Nicholas and Alexandra's would not.

Just after Marta's wedding, Dmitri's dog, Malevich, fell ill. His belly swelled up and he was in obvious pain, pressing his head against the wall and whimpering. A vet was called, who told them the liver had failed and there was nothing he could do. Dmitri held Malevich's head in his hands, looking into those trusting brown eyes, as the vet administered a fatal injection. Once the dog stopped breathing he put his arms around him and sobbed into his coat. His head filled with images of all the friends he had lost, of his parents, of Tatiana's family. He thought of the concentration camps where many German friends had died; of the hard-labour camps in Siberia. Why was life so relentlessly brutal, just one challenge after another? Why did evil so frequently triumph?

For a while it seemed as though losing Malevich, the dog who had alleviated his depression at the onset of war, would tip Dmitri into another full-scale episode. The old symptoms returned: a feeling of uselessness, believing that there was no point in getting out of bed, or dressing or shaving. Senator Joe McCarthy's Subcommittee hearings to root out Communism had begun to take on the repressive nature of the very ideology they opposed and Dmitri feared he might be forced to leave America, the land that had become home. He went to Tatiana's house two or three times a week but was taciturn and moody with her. When she tried to make him talk about it, he growled at her to leave him alone and she shrank back, unprepared for this new side of him.

341

But Rosa knew what to do. About a month after Malevich's death, Dmitri came home to find a Borzoi puppy scrabbling round the kitchen floor on unsteady legs. It leapt up at him, licking his outstretched hand, eager to make friends. The puppy's coat was white with brown patches and it was only a few weeks old. He looked questioningly at Rosa.

'It's a girl.' She smiled. 'But she's not house-trained yet so we're going to have our work cut out!'

He crouched and let her lick his face as he ran his hands over the silky coat. 'Let's call her Trina,' he said. 'She looks like a Trina.' In his mind, he was thinking of the ladies' maid who used to take messages between Tatiana and him when she was under house arrest.

Tatiana was charmed when she met Trina, and pleased at the name Dmitri had chosen.

'I wonder what became of Trina?' she mused. 'I hope she found a good husband.'

Dmitri didn't like to tell her it was unlikely. Most of the Romanovs' staff had been imprisoned and several were executed by the Bolshevik regime.

One sunny September day, when Rosa had told him she would be out until dinnertime, he and Tatiana drove up to the lakes to take Trina for a long walk. Dmitri stopped at a remote spot on the shore of Lake Akanabee and Trina ran into the water, taking to it instinctively. She never tired of swimming for the sticks they threw, bringing them back and soaking the two of them as she shook the water from her coat. They laughed to remember their failed efforts to train Ortipo back in St Petersburg; this Trina seemed either more intelligent or just more obedient than Ortipo had ever been.

The sun had already set when Dmitri dropped Tatiana back at her cottage and drove home, his forehead pink from the sun. He was late for dinner and hoped Rosa wouldn't mind.

'Sorry, darling,' he called as he came in the kitchen door. 'I was walking Trina and lost count of the time.'

Rosa was sitting at the table, her head in her hands, and he could tell she had been crying.

'What is it?' he asked, alarmed. Rosa never cried.

She took a deep breath. 'I found a lump in my breast a few weeks ago. I didn't like to worry you because I was sure it was nothing but I saw the doctor today and he says I have breast cancer. I have to start treatment straight away.'

Dmitri sat down hard on a chair, the breath knocked out of him. 'You should have told me.'

'You were depressed. I didn't want to add to it. But I'm going to need you to be strong now, Dmitri. Is that OK?'

He got up to put his arms around her, careful not to touch her breasts. He wondered which one the cancer was in, but didn't like to ask.

'Of course it is. How could you ever doubt it?'

She rested her head on his arm, eyes closed, and didn't reply.

Two days later, Dmitri accompanied Rosa to her appointment with the doctor who was treating her, Dr Eisenberg. He was a bald man with freckles all over his shiny head, and he wore heavy black-rimmed glasses and a dark suit and tie. His manner was businesslike.

'I am recommending a radical mastectomy of the left breast, as is standard procedure. We'll remove all the breast tissue, the lymph nodes and part of the muscle of the chest wall. That should excise all the cancer cells but as a precaution we'll follow it up with a course of radiation therapy, which we'll start as soon as the wound has healed sufficiently.' His tone sounded as though he was reading from a textbook. He looked up. 'Any questions?'

'Yes,' Dmitri said. 'When will you operate? How long will Rosa be in hospital?'

'I have her booked in for next Monday, and I would expect her to stay with us at least a week.'

343

'And the radiation? How long will that last?'

'Twelve weeks is standard.'

Dmitri counted in his head. 'So she could be cured by Christmas?'

The doctor sighed, almost imperceptibly. 'We don't talk about a cure, Mr . . .' – he consulted his notes – 'Yakovlevich. We talk about being in remission. And I'm afraid Christmas is a little optimistic.'

He talked on and Dmitri listened hard, latching on to anything that sounded optimistic and memorising the phrases so he could reassure Rosa with them later, reassure himself: 'state-of-the-art technology', 'gold-standard therapy', 'I'd recommend the same for my own mother'.

That evening they telephoned Nicholas and Marta to tell them the news, one after the other, and both insisted they were coming home to help look after their mother.

Rosa protested a little but gave in with a smile. She wanted her children by her side. Dmitri's first thought was that it would be difficult for him to slip out to see Tatiana with them there, but immediately he felt ashamed of himself. That was hardly the most important thing.

The operation lasted six hours and Dmitri was shocked to see how ill Rosa looked when she came round afterwards, her chest bandaged like an Egyptian mummy and tubes draining fluid from her sides. It took all her energy to speak, and he ushered the children away after half an hour, realising that she needed to rest. As they walked down the antiseptic-smelling hospital corridor, Dmitri looked at the dusty overhead pipes, the bright lights, the peeling paint on the walls, and knew they were going to become very familiar over the next few months.

That evening they were all invited for dinner with Rosa's mother and sister but Dmitri cried off, saying he had a headache, and drove to Tatiana's instead. She took him in her arms and ran her cool fingers through his hair, massaging his scalp.

'I got a book from the library about cancer,' she told him. 'It is important that she eats lots of good food to stay strong. The X-ray treatment is very successful but it will take a lot out of her.'

Somehow it seemed natural that Tatiana should be comforting him during Rosa's illness, helping him to present a strong front at home. She had never shown any jealousy of Rosa; instead she was curious about her, wanted to see photographs of her, asked about her likes and dislikes, her hobbies and volunteer work. Once she said that if circumstances had been different she would have liked to be Rosa's friend. That was an odd thought, but Dmitri could imagine they would have got on. Rosa got on with everyone.

Over the weeks and months of her treatment, Dmitri remained positive in front of Rosa and the children, but he was able to express his fears when he went to Tatiana's. Sometimes he cried when he described to her the agonising burns the radiation caused on Rosa's already raw flesh. Often he talked through his worries about the side effects: the fatigue, the inability to taste food any more, Rosa's tortured breathing when she finally managed to get to sleep, and his own sense of helplessness that there was little he could do. She had become so thin that clothes were falling off her so he bought new ones in loose, soft fabrics, garments that could be slipped on and off without aggravating her wounds. He couldn't bear to watch while she changed or bathed; couldn't bear to see the jagged line where her left breast had been. He used to love her pert, shapely breasts.

'It will pass,' Tatiana told him. 'Life will go on.'

As the new year of 1955 dawned, it seemed Rosa was in hospital more than she was at home. Things kept going wrong. She grew so tired she could barely get out of bed; her blood counts were poor; she collapsed with a blood clot in her lungs. One day, when Dmitri visited, she clutched his hand suddenly.

'There is something I must say and I want you to listen.' She couldn't raise her head from the pillow but she sought his eyes, forcing them to meet hers before she continued. 'When I am gone, I don't want you to feel guilty about anything. I know you torture yourself with guilt for all kinds of things that were never your fault but don't ever feel guilty about us. Please believe me when I say that I have loved our life together. You have been a good husband – although we never married.' She gave a little smile.

Tears began to gather in Dmitri's eyes. 'Rosa, please don't talk that way. I want you to fight this thing and get well. You mustn't give up. We need you.'

She reached for his hand. 'I don't think I'm going to beat this, my love. I'm too tired and running out of fight. But I can't bear to think of you being miserable when I am gone.' She took a deep breath that made a rattling sound in her throat, then said, 'Dmitri, I know you found her. I know you found Tatiana. And when I am gone I want you to be together, and I want you both to be happy. Do you promise me you will?'

A sob burst from his throat and the tears flowed. He wanted to say 'sorry' but couldn't even form the word.

'Promise me,' Rosa insisted fiercely, her fingernails digging into his palm, and he gave a little nod.

Chapter Sixty-One

Albany, New York State, 1955

Around ten o'clock one February evening, a nurse rang to tell Dmitri that Rosa was very weak and unlikely to make it through the night. Nicholas and Marta piled into the car and they collected Rosa's mother and sister then drove to the hospital. Rosa was no longer conscious but lay with her mouth open, gasping for every breath like a fish lying on a riverbank. They all spoke to her, told her they were there and that they loved her, but there was no reaction. She was too far along the journey to the next place. Chairs were brought, cups of coffee offered, and they sat with her as the breaths became fainter and further apart.

Dmitri perched close to Rosa's head, whispering to her, wetting her cracked lips with a damp sponge, as he had learned to do after her bouts of vomiting. He felt panic welling inside him at the thought of life without her, but at the same time he couldn't bear her to suffer any more. He must be strong tonight for the sake of his children. Marta was crying and Nicholas was white-faced. Somehow they would get through this.

'You should take the wedding ring off her finger now,' a nurse advised. 'It's harder to do once she's gone.'

Rosa's mother and sister glared at him as he slid off the gold band and slipped it in his pocket. They both knew, although the children did not, that there had never been a wedding.

When the end came, none of them recognised it at first because the breaths were already so far apart. They listened, scarcely moving a muscle, watching her throat for a tiny flicker, but after several minutes with no movement Rosa's mother sobbed, 'She's gone.' A nurse came to confirm it and recorded the time of death as 3.20 a.m.

Dmitri wanted to be on his own with her, to whisper his last private messages of love, but he couldn't; she belonged to all of them, not just him. He was dry-eyed, shocked, and extraordinarily tired. He failed to smother a yawn, and Rosa's sister shook her head and tutted.

Before long, the nurse came to tell them that the body must be moved: that's what Rosa was now – a body. They trailed out to the car and Dmitri dropped off Rosa's mother and sister then took Nicholas and Marta back to the house. They were exhausted and went up to their rooms to sleep, but Dmitri sat at the kitchen table, head in his hands, feeling utterly bereft. He couldn't bear the emptiness, the terrifying hole Rosa had left in the universe. He wanted to cry but at the same time was scared of crying because it might make him fall apart completely.

On a sudden impulse he got up and slipped out the back door, closing it quietly behind him. He climbed into his car, pulled out of the drive and headed across town to Tatiana's, knocking on her door at five o'clock in the morning. She answered, wearing a long satin dressing gown, wiping the sleep from her eyes.

'She's gone,' he said, a frog in his throat. 'I had to see you.'

She pulled him inside and held him close for several minutes. 'I'll get some vodka,' she said. 'Sit down.'

He took off his jacket, loosened his tie, which suddenly felt as though it was choking him, and kicked off his shoes.

'To Rosa,' Tatiana toasted, handing him a shot of vodka.

As Dmitri drank he heard a banging on the door. 'Who can that be?' he asked. 'I hope I didn't wake your neighbours.'

Tatiana shrugged that she didn't know and went to see. He heard a voice in the hall – 'Where the hell is he?' – then Marta burst into the room, her face scarlet from crying.

'You bastard, how could you? Mum's not even cold!' She picked up a glass of vodka from the table and threw it over Dmitri.

What could he say? He took a handkerchief from his pocket to wipe his cheek.

Tatiana gathered her wits. 'You must be Marta,' she said. 'I am an old friend of your father's, from Russia. Please sit down.'

'Forget it! I'm not accepting hospitality from a whore!' Marta cried.

'Marta!' Dmitri rebuked. He was too exhausted, too drained to deal with this.

Marta was hysterical, spitting out her words. 'Nicholas and I followed you in my car because I suspected you might come to your other woman. Oh yes, I've known for ages: all those long walks with the dog, and mysterious errands, and fictitious meetings. I warned Mum there was someone else, but she would never hear a word against you. All the time she was struggling with cancer you were coming here . . . I just thought you might have the decency not to come tonight. Have you no respect at all?'

'Have a drink,' Tatiana urged. 'You are overwrought. You don't know the facts but we will explain if you sit down. I'll go and invite your brother inside . . .'

'You must be joking,' Marta screamed. 'Sit down for a chat? In your house? Frankly, I never want to see either of you again.'

She turned to leave. 'Marta, wait!' Dmitri called, and stood to go after her, feeling utterly useless.

Tatiana put a hand on his arm. 'Leave her. You can explain tomorrow when she has had some sleep and calmed down a little. Talk to both of them. I don't mind what explanation you give. It's up to you.'

*

A few hours later, Dmitri drove home. He expected to find his children sitting in the kitchen over breakfast, but neither of them was there. Trina whined and nudged his leg, desperate to be let out to empty her bladder, and equally keen for her breakfast. There was a short note on the table telling him that both Marta and Nicholas had gone to stay at their grandmother's house. He sighed, imagining the character assassination that would be going on over that breakfast table. It would all come out now. How could he talk to his son or daughter with the disapproving in-laws present?

He made the necessary phone calls to tell friends of Rosa's death and spoke to an undertaker about organising a funeral then called his mother-in-law's house to consult them on the date. Neither Nicholas or Marta would come to the telephone and Dmitri didn't know what to do, short of driving round and forcing his way over the threshold. Tatiana suggested that he write to them, and he did: 'We need to stick together to get through this terrible loss,' he wrote. 'After we have buried your mother, I will tell you anything you want to know about my long friendship with Tatiana. Be assured it is not what you imagine.'

Worrying about the rift with his children stopped him grieving for Rosa. He went through the motions of ordering flowers, choosing a coffin, and picking hymns for the service, with only brief phone calls to his mother-in-law's house to ask their wishes. On the day of the funeral they made their way separately to the church and when Dmitri walked in, he saw that his children, their partners, and Rosa's family had occupied the front row, forcing him to sit one behind. After the service, they huddled together at the graveside leaving no room for him, just glancing across red-eyed and accusing when the minister called Rosa a 'beloved wife and mother'. From their sneering expressions, he suspected Nicholas and Marta had been told he never married their mother: one more sin that would have to be explained.

In his head Dmitri asked Rosa, 'What should I do?' She would have known how to fix this, just as she had smoothed over every family argument through the years, but there was no reply because she was in the cold earth.

He telephoned that night and Nicholas answered the call.

'Won't you meet me, son?' he begged. 'We need to talk. Please let me explain . . .'

'I don't care about your private life, Dad,' he said wearily. 'Nothing will bring Mom back. I can't come out tonight because Pattie and I are flying to California in the morning and I'd like to spend the evening with my grandma.'

'What about your sister? Is she there?'

'Marta and Stanley have gone back to their place. I'd leave her to calm down a while if I were you. She's taken it hard.'

Dmitri couldn't stop trying though. The day after the funeral he drove to Marta's house with Rosa's jewellery box. Stanley opened the door but refused to let him in.

'Please,' Dmitri begged. 'She's my daughter.'

Stanley was immoveable. 'She's been telling me some horror stories about her childhood, about how you used to beat them both, and to be honest I'm surprised she didn't disown you long before now. She kept her feelings to herself because she didn't want to hurt her mother, but now she says she just wants you to leave her alone.'

Dmitri was surprised by the accusation. Didn't everyone smack their children? 'I'm the first to admit I wasn't a great father, but surely I deserve a chance to explain myself? Tell Marta that her mother knew about my relationship with Tatiana – she had always known.'

'I don't reckon that's going to help, somehow.' Stanley folded his arms. 'It don't make it right that you went to see her before Rosa's body was cold, when your own children needed you.'

'I thought they were asleep!'

There was no sense in arguing with this pig-headed man, who seemed to have positioned himself as Marta's new protector. Dmitri begged to be allowed to see her, but Stanley would not budge.

Eventually he handed over the jewellery box. 'Will you at least give this to my daughter? She should take what she wants and send the rest to Nicholas's wife.'

Stanley tucked it under his arm. 'I know there are more things she wants from the house. Perhaps you could make yourself scarce while she collects them? Tomorrow afternoon, maybe?'

'Whatever she wants, she can have,' Dmitri agreed, and he kept to his word, going to spend the day with Tatiana. On his return, he looked around, trying to see what was missing: a few ornaments here and there, a painting, some kitchen items. He didn't notice till much later that Marta had taken the old brown leather suitcase in which he kept Tatiana's diary. Rosa had begun to store the family photos in there, not realising the significance of the diary at the bottom, not realising that suitcase dated from a time before he met her when he was still searching for Tatiana. Asking for its return would only inflame the situation, so he let it be.

He hoped that Nicholas might be able to intercede with his sister and placed a call to California one evening, but Pattie came on the line and said he was too drunk to come to the phone. She was worried about his drinking but supposed it was just his way of dealing with grief. Pattie promised she would have a word with Marta when she spoke to her next, but did not sound particularly optimistic.

Dmitri and Tatiana often discussed the estrangement but they could find no solution. When his children's birthdays rolled around, he sent thousand-dollar cheques, which he was pleased to see both of them cashed. He wrote telling them he planned to sell the house, which was too big for him, and asking if they wanted any furniture, but there was no reply. In truth, he couldn't bear to live there any more without Rosa's warmth. In the old days, they used to gravitate to whichever room she was in, whether she was cooking, ironing, or sewing by a sunny window. She had been the centre of the home, but now it was just a series of rooms without any focus.

He moved into Tatiana's cottage, but her garden was not big enough for Trina, a lively dog who needed a lot of exercise. One day while they were walking by Lake Akanabee they spotted a cabin for sale and straight away Dmitri wanted it. The location was stunning, at the remotest end of the lake, not overlooked by any other properties. He went to the real-estate agent and paid cash for it that afternoon. It was just four walls and a roof but he hired a carpenter to build a covered porch and a dock sticking out into the lake; he got it plumbed into a well further up the slope and had a septic tank and bathroom fittings installed. Tatiana chose a bed, a table, a sofa and armchair, a thick rug and curtains, pictures for the walls. A pot-bellied stove gave off enough heat to cook, to warm water, and keep the interior cosy. And Dmitri bought a fishing rod, planning to fish from the end of the dock.

'Is this the equivalent of a hairshirt?' Tatiana asked as she bathed in lukewarm water on a frosty autumn morning. 'I hope you are not trying to do penance for your sins by coming here.'

'No.' He shook his head. 'I want my life to be simpler. I'm sixty-four years old and I've had enough of other human beings – apart from you, of course.'

'I'm not sure I can stay here all year round,' Tatiana laughed. 'It's beautiful, but I shall keep my cottage for the months when bugs fill the air and torment me with their bites, and for the winter when it is impossible to get warm.'

Dmitri had written to his children giving them his new address and when Christmas came around, Pattie sent a Christmas card. He telephoned from Tatiana's house to thank her and to ask if there was any news.

'Marta is pregnant,' she told him. 'Her baby is due next April.'

Dmitri was moved. 'Perhaps, with the arrival of the little one, it might be a good time for me to try and make the peace.'

Pattie hesitated. 'I've tried, but she simply refuses to talk about you. She has a very one-track approach: her mother was a saint and you were a sinner. I don't think Stanley helps, to be honest.'

Dmitri sighed. 'And you?' he asked. 'Are you and Nicholas happy?'

'He's still suffering from the loss of Rosa. I don't know how to snap him out of it,' Pattie confided, 'but I'll keep trying.'

'Tell him that he still has a father and that I'm here if ever he wants me.' Dmitri had no advice to give her because he realised he hardly knew his adult son, could see few similarities between him and the little boy they had raised. It didn't occur to him to pass on the advice that was helping him through his own grief: solitude, long walks, and the beauty of the outdoors.

In February 1956, on the first anniversary of Rosa's death, Dmitri wrote heartfelt letters to both his children. He described his own strict upbringing back in Russia and apologised that he had been an emotionally distant father. He had tried to be different but somehow the childhood influences were too deeply ingrained and he found himself acting in ways that reminded him of his father, for which he was sorry with all his heart. He told them about the losses he had suffered during the Russian Civil War, including the disappearance of his wife, Tatiana, and the bouts of depression he had battled ever since. He tried to explain his sorrow at having to leave his homeland. It didn't look as though he could ever return now that the Communist regime was so firmly rooted. It was even possible that Russia and America might try to blow each other to smithereens with their deadly atom bombs.

He told them that he and Rosa had loved each other dearly and been good partners to each other for over thirty years. And he explained that she had known from the early days he was already married to Tatiana, and had accepted the situation, had even wished them happiness after she had gone. Finally, in his letter to Marta, he wrote: 'I know I have been a failure as a parent to you, but I did the best I could. I hope with all my heart that I will be allowed to meet the grandchild you are carrying. Please know that I love you deeply and will always be here if you want anything from me.'

From Nicholas there was no acknowledgement. Marta's letter was torn into tiny pieces and sent back to him in the original envelope marked, in Stanley's handwriting, 'Return to sender'.

Chapter Sixty-Two

Brno, Czech Republic, 16th October 2016

As she sat in Stansted Airport waiting for her flight to Brno, Kitty listened to all the voicemails that had filled her phone. Most were pleading messages from Tom, left early in the summer, and there was a long, heartfelt one from her friend Amber.

> Kitty, I'm *so sorry* you found out about Tom's fall from grace the way you did and I wish to God I had told you straight away. It was complete fluke that I saw them together in a bar in Kings Cross station when I was collecting my mum from the train. It was obvious they were more than friends so I charged up to Tom and yelled at him. To give him credit, he was mortally ashamed, said he had made a huge mistake and begged me not to tell you. He promised it was over – in fact, he told the woman in front of me that he wouldn't be able to see her again. She shrugged and didn't seem bothered, so it's not as if it was some big romance. I told Tom I would be watching him like a hawk, that he needed to sort himself out, and if he put a foot wrong again I'd be on the phone to you faster than he could pull up his zipper. But in retrospect I should

have told you anyway. We girls should stick together. I'm sorry for getting it wrong. I just didn't want you to be hurt. Please call me, Kitty.

Her flight began to board just at that moment so she quickly texted Amber: 'I'm an idiot and don't deserve a friend like you. Going to Brno for a few days. You'll have to Google it to find the correct pronunciation, as I had to. Will call and tell all on my return.'

She took her seat on the plane and was about to switch off her phone for take-off when a message came back: 'I love you. Always have, always will. Text me your return flight time and I'll collect you from the airport.'

It was late afternoon when Kitty arrived in Brno and caught a bus to the town centre, then a taxi to the address Hana Markova had given. It drew up outside an old-fashioned brick-built house that opened directly onto the street. When Kitty knocked it was flung open by a big-boned woman wearing an apron, who looked to be in her fifties or possibly sixties. She had a ruddy complexion with sparkling blue eyes and short brown hair streaked with grey.

'Come in, come in,' she cried, stepping back to let Kitty pass. She gestured for her to go through to an oak-panelled kitchen with windows looking out over a children's play park. Kitty sat down at an oak table scarred by the scorch marks of generations.

'I feel as though we are family,' Hana said, 'but I can't quite work out the relationship. Welcome to my home!'

She put the kettle on to boil and produced a plate of apple cake, although Kitty could smell something aromatic cooking in the oven, presumably dinner.

'It's very good of you to invite me,' she said. 'The mysteries of Dmitri's life have got right under my skin and I'm desperate to find the truth. It all started when I found this at the cabin.' She held out the oval pendant she wore round her neck. 'A jeweller told me it's Fabergé.'

'Let me have a closer look.'

Kitty removed the chain and Hana held it by the window to examine the markings on the back in the best light.

'Do you know what this says?' she asked.

'I'm told it is the maker's mark.'

'No, above that. It says "Ortipo".'

Kitty was none the wiser. 'What does that mean?'

'Ortipo was the French Bulldog that your great-grandfather gave to Grand Duchess Tatiana back in 1914, soon after they met. She was nursing him in a military hospital in St Petersburg. The piece you are wearing is a ludicrously expensive dog tag.' She handed it back with a smile. 'Beautiful, isn't it?'

'Wow! Was Dmitri her lover?' Kitty's eyes widened.

Hana smiled. 'They were in love, yes. But they were not lovers in the physical sense as you and I understand it today.'

'That's why he had Tatiana's diary, then.' Kitty opened her handbag, pulled the diary out of the padded envelope in which she had been protecting it, and passed it to Hana. 'I've had this translated into English, if you want to see the translation?'

'No, it's fine. I speak Russian.' Hana scanned the pages, then checked the date on the last page: 14th July 1918. 'I have the diary she wrote immediately after this one. The handwriting, the style of placing the dates above the entries is the same.'

Kitty was puzzled: 'But she died two days after this was written. Did she write another diary in her final days?'

Hana offered her a slice of cake, but Kitty shook her head, totally captivated by the story. 'Here is the truth that you have flown all the way over to hear: Tatiana did not die in the Ipatiev House. Dmitri helped her to escape.'

It crossed Kitty's mind to wonder whether she was visiting a crazy person. There had been many conspiracy theories about the Romanovs, with dozens of impostors popping up through the decades, but scientists had proved categorically that they all died. 'Surely that's not possible? I read that forensic scientists have proved the exact number of people who were in the graves, and their heights and ages all fit. They cross-matched bone samples with people who have Romanov DNA, including our Prince Philip. How could the weight of so much scientific evidence be wrong?'

Hana was nodding. She knew all this. 'If you've read about the investigation, you'll know how badly the samples were contaminated over the years. What the scientists won't admit is that they kept finding DNA they couldn't match and they brushed it under the carpet, deciding it must belong to someone working in one of the labs that handled the material. But it didn't. There was another girl in there, the same height as Tatiana, just a local farm girl whose disappearance didn't warrant a police investigation during the upheaval of the times. She had taken Tatiana's place on the 15th of July, and it was her who died in the brutal slaughter of the night of the 16th. Tatiana lived.'

Kitty couldn't take it in. 'So if Dmitri rescued her . . . where did she go?'

'Let me read you the story from Tatiana's diary. My father found it in a drawer long after she had gone. It is distressing but you are Dmitri's direct descendant and you deserve to know.'

She walked across to a sideboard and pulled a tattered notebook from one of the drawers. It was flimsy, unlike the solid leather-bound one Kitty had found in the box of family photographs, but the handwriting inside was exactly the same.

Hana began. Although she was translating from Russian to English, she spoke without hesitation. It was clearly something she had read many times before.

359

Chapter Sixty-Three

A Tent East of Ekaterinburg, July 1918

I asked Vaclav to find me a pencil and notebook because in the past writing a diary used to help me order my thoughts. Somehow I need to pass the hours until I leave this world and perhaps I should make a record so that historians of the future will know what became of the last and most wretched of the Romanov grand duchesses.

It seems incredible that just five days ago Mama, Papa, OTMA and Alexei were all together for that emotional service led by Father Storozhev, where he said the prayer for the dead. If only we had taken poison that night and died in each other's arms, it would have been a better end. I don't think any of us had hope any more: the guards were too disrespectful, their behaviour towards us too callous for us to believe we would be allowed a dignified and peaceful exile. But then came that note from Malama on Sunday afternoon and for a short while hope was renewed.

15th July, Monday
Papa was concerned about me leaving the house while the cleaner took my place but he trusted Malama. We all did. She was a sweet girl, by the name of Yelena, and she was terribly nervous as she

slid off her blouse, skirt and headscarf and swapped them for my gown, while Olga and Maria kept watch by the door. I thanked her for her loyalty and promised that I would see her in the morning. As I walked out with the other girl, Yelena's friend, I saw Anton, the vilest of the guards, watching us and kept my head down, fiddling with my sleeves, waiting to feel a hand on my shoulder at any moment. Suddenly we were on the street and it seemed so bright and open, I was dazzled by the light. I didn't know where to go but the girl led me to a street corner and there was my beloved Malama and he was smiling. Oh, the joy of that moment, when all my fears were momentarily banished! We rode back to a cottage he had rented and we embraced and talked and talked and embraced, and it was beautiful. I loved him more than ever that afternoon. Such sacrifices as he has made for me could never be repaid.

I didn't want him to leave the cottage that evening – perhaps I had a premonition of what was to come – but he was confident of his plan to rescue us all. So I bolted the door and while I waited, I looked round at Malama's few possessions. His spare clothes, the meagre bread and cheese in the kitchen, his tooth powder and brush, and I loved them for being his. Oh, I would give anything to leap back to those moments, the last moments of innocence.

I heard horses approach and the door being rattled and I ran to hide in the wardrobe. Why there? It was the first thought that came to mind. There was nowhere else. With terror, I listened to the sound of the door being hacked down then there were men's voices in the cottage. The wardrobe was pulled open and when I saw the ugly pockmarked face of Anton the guard, I knew I was doomed. He grabbed me by the hair to pull me from the wardrobe and spat in my face, calling me *prostitutka* and all kinds of awful words. I ordered him to let me go and he slapped me then threw me to the ground. He didn't care if I was hurt, had no concern about what my father might say. 'We followed you here, you and your boyfriend,' he said. 'Did you really believe you could get away? You royals think you are above the law.'

He tied a dirty rag over my mouth so I could not scream for help, and secured my wrists behind my back. When he hauled me onto his horse's back, I assumed we were returning to the Ipatiev House. At that stage I was not afraid for myself but for what they would do to Malama if they caught him. The two men riding alongside did not look at me. They seemed to take orders from Anton. I suspect it is because he is a bully and they are scared of him.

When the horses stopped, it was not at the familiar house but outside some dirty hovel. Anton pulled me from his horse and shoved me hard in the back to force me inside. There was no one in the street, nowhere to run. It was dimly lit but I could see there were two rooms with straw mattresses on the floor and little else. Anton pushed me into one of the rooms and shut the door and I stood there shivering, deeply shocked. Malama would be back at the cottage soon. What would he do when he found me gone? How would he ever discover my whereabouts? If only there had been time to write him a note, give him a clue – but it all happened so suddenly.

I could hear the men drinking next door, their voices becoming increasingly raucous, and I wondered when Yurovsky, the commander of the guards, would arrive. I would appeal to him to return me to my family immediately. When Anton opened the door he laughed a truly evil laugh, and I could feel how much he despised me. All those times I spoke haughtily and reprimanded him had sown a deep hatred and now he wanted his vengeance. He hit me hard across the face, knocking me backwards onto the bed, then he fell on top of me, ripped at my clothes, and violated me. The pain was indescribable, his rancid smell utterly repulsive, but worst of all was the thought of Malama, my husband, and what it would do to him if he ever found out that his precious wife was no longer pure. I can't bear for him ever to know.

362

16th July, Tuesday

While Anton slept I crept up and tried the door, but it was locked and there were no windows. I could feel blood between my legs where he had ripped me open and a dull ache in my belly as if he had damaged something deep within. I could see from a chink beneath the door that it was dawn outside and worried myself sick thinking about poor Yelena, the cleaner. If I could not get back to the house that morning, she would be stuck inside and my family would be terrified for my safety. Why had Anton not taken me there? Did Yurovsky know of my escape? For all that he was unsympathetic to our plight, I could not believe he had condoned this brutal attack. Anton must have planned this on his own and persuaded his two cronies to help.

I decided that when he woke, I would be nice, pretend to like him, and try to persuade him that I would tell no one if he would just take me back to the house. I had worked the rag off my mouth by now although my hands were still tied and as soon as he woke I spoke kindly, using terms of endearment. My attempts did not persuade him for one moment, though. He violated me again then tied me securely, feet as well as hands, before leaving. The hovel fell silent. I rolled to the door and nudged it with my shoulder but it wouldn't budge. I knew Malama would be looking for me and couldn't bear to think of his distress. What would he do? Where would he turn?

I tried everything I could think of to get free during those long hours, pulling and twisting my ankles and wrists until they were bleeding. I was raked by savage thirst and when I drifted into sleep I dreamed of cool, clear mountain lakes and woke even thirstier than before. The light faded and now it was night again, with no chink of light coming from the outside. Anton and his friends returned and I realised this must be the house where they slept.

He was drunk when he barged in, swinging a lantern that made me blink. And then he said the most hateful words in the world:

'Your family are all dead and it's your fault. By trying to escape you signed their death warrants and tonight the executions were carried out. How does that make you feel?'

He tore the rag from my mouth, wanting to hear my reaction, and I screamed as hard as I could from deep down inside and only stopped screaming when Anton hit me on the head and knocked me unconscious.

17th July, Wednesday

The next morning when I awoke, Anton had brought me a glass of water but I knocked it over. I wouldn't take anything from him. 'We are going to make a little trip today,' he said. 'I thought you would like to see where your family died before you join them.' And it may sound strange but I was comforted by this. I believed him when he told me they were dead and all I wanted was to join them in the hereafter, the sooner the better. 'You must behave as I tell you when we reach the house,' he said, 'or else I shall bring you back to this place and keep you here as my slave to use as I wish. Remember that.' He wrapped me in a long cloak with a hood, which was stifling in the summer heat, then we rode through the streets until I could see the Ipatiev House. My heart was beating hard. Might Malama be somewhere nearby looking for me? Might Anton have been playing a trick and my family were still alive?

The guards were not at their usual posts but two of them were sweeping the yard, backwards and forwards in a scrubbing motion. Anton took me in through a side door and down a flight of steps that led to the basement. Twenty-three steps, I counted. 'This is where it happened,' he whispered, and straight away I could smell the salty metallic scent of blood. It turned my stomach. Anton had his arm through mine and dragged me along to a storeroom and as soon as I saw it I felt faint. Someone had tried to clean up but there was so much blood that their efforts had only served to smear it across the floor, up the walls. In places it had congealed into dark lakes. 'This is where they died,' Anton told me. 'Your mama had a chair in the middle here' – he stood on the spot – 'and little Alexei beside her.' My knees were collapsing and I leaned back on a wall as Anton demonstrated where each one had stood. I could feel their presence in the room and sense their terror, their screams. And then he told me that the girls had been slow to die so they were slashed with bayonets. And he showed me the slash marks in the floor, the bullet holes in the wall, and there was a buzzing sound in my ears. I must have collapsed because suddenly I was lying in the blood and it was all over me. The blood of my parents, the blood of my sisters, my baby brother.

Anton took out a gun. 'Brace yourself,' he said, pressing it into the back of my head, 'because now you will join them.' I prayed that he would hurry up, then I prayed that Malama would have a good life without me, then I prayed for the souls of my family, but still the shot did not come. I opened my eyes. Anton was leering down with sadistic enjoyment. 'Perhaps I will not kill you yet,' he sneered. 'No one knows you are still alive so no one will seek you. I will keep you for a few more nights, until I get bored of you.' I froze at his words. The thought of going back to that room was abhorrent.

'Please . . . if you have any mercy, please shoot me,' I begged, but that made him laugh.

'I like to hear you beg,' he said. 'Tonight I will make you beg some more.'

He yanked me up by the hair and bundled me outside. I thought of screaming for help from the two guards sweeping the yard but Anton clapped a filthy hand across my mouth. I don't think they knew who I was. I was stunned, incapable of action, and then we were back on Anton's horse and galloping across town to the hovel and I sank into a state of utter hopelessness. No one knew I was there apart from Anton and his two acolytes. Did Yurovsky think I was free? Is that why he slaughtered my family? Was he looking for me even now?

That night was worse than before as Anton violated me in different ways, forcing himself into my mouth, biting my breasts and thighs and hurting me in every manner he could think of. I could hear the other two men next door and knew they must hear my cries but neither of them intervened. I was utterly alone.

Anton fell asleep at last and began to snore. I lay awake, every part of me in pain. I could not get the smell of blood out of my nostrils; it was caked in my hair, on my skin. The blood of my loved ones. Oh God, may no one else ever have to experience that.

The door to the room opened slowly and one of the men beckoned me to come. At first I thought he planned to violate me too but he put a finger to his lips and opened the door to the street outside. I staggered to the opening, grabbing what clothes I could, my legs barely able to support my weight. 'You do not deserve this. Take a horse. Run,' he whispered.

'What is your name?' I asked him, but he wouldn't tell me. So I untied a horse and climbed on its back and I rode east towards the dawn.

Chapter Sixty-Four

Brno, Czech Republic, 16th October 2016

Kitty sat in silence while Hana was reading, feeling the horror of the words written almost a century ago. Goosebumps pricked her flesh. Hana stopped and fetched some beers from the fridge, flipped open the tops and poured them into glasses.

'My father found Tatiana the day she escaped. He said she was raving like a madwoman and trying to hang herself from a tree but the rope kept slipping. When she told him she was a Romanov grand duchess, he thought she was delusional. It was only when she showed him the jewels hidden in the seams of her undergarments that he began to believe her. He took her back to his tent and fed her some broth, then persuaded her to rest a few hours while he decided what to do.'

Kitty tried to imagine Tatiana's state of mind. She must have been in profound shock, but somehow this man had won her trust. 'Your father was clearly a good person,' she said.

'The very best. They don't often come like him.' Hana smiled proudly. 'Papa was a member of the Czech Legion fighting the Bolsheviks, but he took time away from the front line to nurse Tatiana. He told me he knew that if he left her for so much as an hour, she would have found a way to kill herself. She couldn't bear to be alive any more, knowing what had happened to her family.'

'Didn't she want to find Dmitri?'

Hana tilted her head and nodded thoughtfully. 'Sometimes she tore her hair with yearning for him then at other times she said she would die of shame if he found out what had happened to her. There were moments when she blamed him, saying if he hadn't rescued her the rest of her family might still be alive, but then she would change her mind and cry out for him. As soon as the Czech Legion reached Ekaterinburg, Papa made enquiries but was told Dmitri had left town and no one knew how to reach him.'

'So your father kept Tatiana with him?'

'Of course. The Bolsheviks would have stopped at nothing to kill her had they realised she was still alive. She maintained she wanted to die and Papa had to coax her to eat. At night she woke screaming from terrible nightmares of men slashing at her with bayonets.' Hana got up to check on the casserole bubbling in the oven and there was a blast of hot air then a fragrant meaty smell as she lifted the lid and stirred it. 'To be honest, I don't know how he managed. He says they followed along behind the front line and he kept Tatiana out of sight because once her face healed from the wounds that guard had inflicted, she would have been recognisable to any Russian civilian.'

Hana took out some gaudily patterned red and purple plates and heaped spoonfuls of casserole onto each then added slices of what looked like spongy white bread before passing one to Kitty. 'Goulash with dumplings,' she said. 'A local speciality.'

Kitty inhaled the scent of paprika and garlic and her stomach rumbled. 'How did they get back to the Czech Republic?' she asked before taking a forkful. It was delicious, the goulash rich and flavourful, the texture of the dumplings soft and gooey.

Hana started her own meal. 'The Czech Republic didn't exist back then. When a declaration was made in October 1918 that the Czechs and Slovaks could form an independent republic from the old kingdoms of Bohemia and Moravia, the Legionnaires were overjoyed. It's what they had long campaigned for. The civil war was not going well for the White Army and my father persuaded Tatiana to come back here with him, just until the Bolsheviks were defeated. Of course, everyone thought their downfall was imminent, that Communism was a passing phase people would get sick of. Who could have guessed it would last the rest of the century?'

Kitty watched her, wondering what it had been like to live under Communism in Czechoslovakia. That era had only ended in 1989 when student protests brought about democratic elections. Hana did not remotely match her mental image of an Eastern European of the Communist era. She had a matronly figure but she was smartly dressed in a grey skirt and pale pink blouse, and she wore a pearl necklace and matching pearl stud earrings. She probably had to dress smartly for her job. There was no sign of a husband or children in the house and she wore no rings on her fingers. Kitty was curious but didn't like to ask about her marital status. Instead she asked when her father had told her about Tatiana.

'He told me gradually, over the years. I always knew he had been married to someone before my mum and bit by bit the rest came out.'

'Did you never consider telling the story publicly? To the press, I mean?'

Hana shook her head emphatically. 'Why would I want to bring a media circus down on my head? What purpose would it serve?'

Kitty considered. 'Maybe the truth should be told for the sake of historical record, if nothing else. And your father's role is so heroic that I would have thought you would want it to be acknowledged.'

Hana smiled. 'No one who knew my father was in any doubt about his heroism. He needs no more accolades than those he received in his lifetime. But this is your story too, so I suppose if you want to publicise it, that is your prerogative. I would rather not be identified, but otherwise you can reveal what you like. I will let you have copies of some photographs, if that would help.'

After they'd finished eating, Hana cleared the table and brought out a worn photograph album. The first picture in the book showed a group of men in military greatcoats and hats against a snowy landscape.

'That's my father, on the left,' she said. He was taller than the others, very clean-cut and handsome.

The next pictures showed a farm and in one there was a silhouette of a woman hoeing in a field. 'That's Tatiana.' Kitty peered hard but could make out nothing except that she was willowy thin.

The following photos showed some kind of village party, with flags in the street, then Kitty turned the page and there was a woman looking down at a baby with utter adoration, in a classic Madonna and Child pose. Kitty raised her eyes in question.

'That's Tatiana with her son Jaroslav, my half-brother. He was born in 1922, three years after they arrived in the Czech Republic. By then, she had married my father and taken the name Irena to protect her identity.'

Of course! Irena Markova, the translator of Dmitri's books, and Grand Duchess Tatiana were one and the same person. Kitty had realised there was a connection but hadn't made that final step. So she had come to Albany to be with him.

Even wearing the clothes of a farmer's wife's, with a scarf tied round her hair, Tatiana was recognisable as the second daughter of Tsar Nicholas. The fine bone structure, the intelligent eyes, the distant, self-contained air – of course it was her.

'What happened to Jaroslav? Is he still around?' If he was, he would be the direct heir to the Romanov dynasty.

'No, he died in 1943. It was awful. I don't think either Tatiana or my father ever recovered.' Kitty flicked through pages of photographs of the boy at different stages of his life: a toddler, a schoolboy, a handsome teenager, while Hana told his story. 'Jaroslav was always a headstrong boy. He'd been brought up to hate repression so when the Nazis marched into our country in 1939, he joined a partisan guerrilla group that sabotaged supply chains and helped to smuggle Jews out of the country. For four years he dodged capture but all the time his parents lived with their hearts in their mouths. And then in 1943, his luck ran out. He was arrested, probably tortured, and executed.' Hana sounded emotional recalling the death of the half-brother she never knew. 'I can't begin to imagine how Tatiana survived that period. It's unthinkable for one person to lose so much.'

Kitty paused over a photograph of a simple grave with a tiny vase of flowers beside it, and a headstone carved with the boy's name and dates. 'I know she came to America with Dmitri in 1948. How did he find her?'

'*She* found *him*. Just before the war she came across an article about him and she was astonished because she had been told he died in 1919. She showed it to my father and he says he knew from that moment that she would leave him one day.' Hana rose to clear their plates. 'They had been good companions for each other and she was grateful to him for protecting her but she never loved him the all-consuming way she loved Dmitri. Of course, the war intervened, and then she was in deep mourning for Jaroslav's death, but one day in 1948, after they'd brought in the harvest, she told my father that it was time for her to leave. She thanked him for all he had done for her and wished him the very best. It broke his heart but he didn't try to stop her. He knew she was going to Dmitri.'

Kitty felt sorry for Vaclav. It seemed a shame after all he had done for Tatiana. 'Did she not keep in touch?'

'I think there were occasional letters. I don't have copies of them. My father met my mother a few months later and I was born in 1949, so he didn't hang around for long!'

'Did he divorce Tatiana?'

'I believe he had the marriage dissolved, because he married my mother when I was three. I got to be a bridesmaid at their wedding. As you can imagine, this was considered shocking back in the 1950s!' She laughed and rolled her eyes.

'I'm glad he had another family. He deserved to be happy.'

'We were. The three of us had a good life. I hope Tatiana found happiness too.'

Kitty wondered about that. She knew little about Dmitri's life in America, never mind his time with Irena. 'I hope so too. But I wonder about the body found near his cabin. If it is her, and he was not responsible for the death – which sounds unlikely given how much they loved each other – then why would he not report it to the authorities in the normal way?' She guessed the answer as she spoke but it was Hana who said it out loud.

'Do you remember the furore over the bones of Romanov imposters? Anna Tschaikovsky's remains were exhumed for further DNA tests several years after she died. I imagine he didn't want that for Tatiana. It's a shame it is happening now . . .'

Kitty was quiet. Hana had said the decision about whether to expose the truth was in her hands. Did she want them testing these bones? Or should she ask that they be buried in her great-grandfather's grave and let the two of them rest in peace? It was a tricky decision.

The next morning a friend of Hana's, a woman called Erika who looked roughly the same age, came to take them out in her car. When she arrived, she kissed Hana on the lips and Kitty realised they were lovers, although they did not announce it.

Erika drove them out to the karst lands and they caught a cable car over lush forested slopes down into a spectacular gorge with a river splashing through. They toured a collapsed cavern known as the Macocha Abyss, then some caves with elaborate stalactites and stalagmites, like spooky pointing fingers. There was a sense of ancient history that went back millions of years, long before the existence of man, and Kitty loved the otherworldly atmosphere.

As they walked around the footpaths of the gorge they talked a little more about Tatiana and Dmitri and Kitty realised Erika knew the story.

'I admire the fact that she was able to adapt to being a farmer's wife after an upbringing of such wealth and grandeur,' Erika said. 'Hana tells me she did the heaviest farm work without complaint.'

'Did she never consider trying to reclaim any of the Romanov fortune?' Kitty asked.

'Oh, no,' Hana replied. 'Once, when they had financial difficulties, Vaclav travelled to Prague to sell some jewels she had smuggled out of Russia and so many questions were asked that he ran away. In the end he sold them to a black marketeer who did not question their provenance, but he probably got far less than they were worth.'

'She said she never wanted to be a royal,' Erika added. 'She liked a simple life.'

'And your father: didn't he want to be rich?' Kitty asked Hana.

'Never! Money had no importance for him.' Hana laughed. 'He was a wise man.'

'Do you think the story would be worth a lot of money now?' Erika asked Kitty.

'Probably,' she agreed, 'but Hana and I have been discussing it and I'm not sure either of us wants to be in the media spotlight.'

'But you are a journalist, are you not?' Erika asked.

Kitty liked these honest, down-to-earth women and in answer to their questions she told them about her decision to change career and work as a carpenter. 'There are plenty of journalists in the world, talented writers with drive and ambition, and I'm just not one of them. But I'm proud of the work I did on Dmitri's cabin this summer,' she finished. 'If you ever want to borrow it for a holiday, you'd be more than welcome.'

'What a lovely idea.' Hana put her arm round Erika and gave her a squeeze.

Chapter Sixty-Five

Lake Akanabee, New York State, December 1968

Dmitri and Tatiana chuckled when they read in December 1968 of the marriage of Anna Tschaikovsky, the woman who claimed to be Grand Duchess Anastasia, to an American genealogist called Jack Manahan, who was twenty years her junior. She had made an entire career of her claims and had many influential supporters, although she had never been accepted by the living Romanov family members. Now Jack Manahan announced himself as the new 'Grand Duke in waiting' from their home in Virginia, a claim met with scorn by the Romanovs.

'Don't you want to go and visit your *sister* now that she is in America?' Dmitri teased.

'Goodness! Whatever for? She looks nothing like Anastasia, and she sounds rather a disturbed creature.'

'No one would believe us if we announced that you are Grand Duchess Tatiana. It would be very hard to prove, although to me you look the same as the first day I set eyes on you.'

Tatiana had celebrated her seventieth birthday the previous year. She was still slender, with glorious cheekbones and the same intelligent grey eyes ringed with violet she'd had as a girl. She was careful to wear a straw hat to keep the sun off her pale skin and was not nearly as lined as Dmitri. At the age of seventy-seven, his cheeks hung in folds and his forehead was scored by deep furrows.

Tatiana leaned over to trace his wrinkles and frown lines with a finger. 'I think I have been the cause of most of these,' she smiled. 'We didn't choose the easiest paths in life.'

'Do you ever think about leaving a record of the truth for future historians to find long after we are gone?' Dmitri asked. 'I would like my children to understand why I was unfaithful to their mother, even if they don't forgive me.'

'You can write it if you like. I don't care what is said when I am gone.'

'Why don't we write it together?' Dmitri suggested. 'Starting from 1914 when you floated like an angel into the hospital ward where I lay with my wounded leg and we talked about dogs and then books.'

'There are so many horrendous memories that would have to be included alongside the beautiful ones, I fear it might upset us to revisit them.'

'It's all such a long time ago,' Dmitri said. 'I think I can cope if you can.'

And so they began reconstructing their joint story. Dmitri wrote the first draft in Russian – he still couldn't express himself as poetically as he wished in English – then Tatiana translated it, adding in her own perspectives. He knew most of her story already – she had even confided in him about the horrors she had endured at the hands of Anton – but now they looked back they could see how quirks of fate had played with them.

If only one of the many attempts to rescue the Romanovs had been successful, he and she could have led a life together in exile. They could have had children together. If Alexei hadn't been ill in April 1918 and Vasily Yakovlev had managed to get them to Omsk; or if Armistead had arrived on the 13th of July 1918 and spirited them away . . . These things didn't bear thinking about. There was no purpose in regret.

They realised they had missed each other by days after the murder of her family. When the Czechs entered Ekaterinburg in late July and Vaclav tried to find Dmitri, he was away in Verkhoturye, hunting for the Romanovs. If only Vaclav had gone to see Sir Thomas Preston, the British ambassador, he would have told him. 'I should have suggested that,' Tatiana sighed. 'I wasn't thinking clearly.'

When she received the letter from Dmitri's mother saying he had died at Tsaritsyn in 1919, she should have stayed in touch, or asked to be put in contact with his sisters, then they could have been reunited the following year when he arrived in Constantinople.

'All that time we wasted . . .' Dmitri mused. 'And yet we have each other now, and somehow this is enough happiness for one lifetime.'

'Let's not pretend that you weren't happy with Rosa too,' Tatiana smiled. 'I regret I never met her. She was a remarkable woman.'

'And Vaclav was a hero. I'm still amazed that he took such good care of you and asked nothing in return.'

'It's true. He was a gentleman who never tried to come into my bed until I invited him. We were both lucky in the people who rescued us – although I'm not sure they were quite so lucky.'

Both Rosa and Vaclav featured in the book they wrote together. Chapter by chapter they drafted, translated and polished, reading and commenting on each other's work. It got to the stage that when Dmitri reread it and found a phrase he admired, he could no longer remember whether it was his or Tatiana's, so intertwined were their words.

They spent all summer at the cabin and came at weekends in winter too, but they repaired to Tatiana's Albany house during the height of bug season in May and June and during the coldest weather, when the lake was frozen and the damp ate into Dmitri's elderly bones, making his leg injuries ache more than fifty years after they were inflicted. They transported their typewriter and the growing stack of pages to and fro in Dmitri's new Pontiac motorcar, which had room in the back for Trina, the Borzoi.

'Where should we end our story?' Tatiana asked one day. 'I think it should stop with me finding you at the Café Slavia in Prague.'

'But then it will not answer my children's questions . . .' Dmitri mused. 'I want them to understand that there was never any question of me leaving their mother, and that you agreed. I want them to know how sorry I am about the way they found out about you, and how much I miss being part of their lives.'

'Marta might not like you writing for publication that she is no longer communicating with you,' Tatiana said. 'It paints her in a bad light.'

Dmitri pondered that. 'Why don't I send both her and Nicholas a copy of the manuscript, saying that I will be happy to cut anything they don't want published? I hope they will be tempted to read it knowing it concerns their lives.'

They agreed on this plan and had two Xerox copies made. One was posted to Nicholas in California and Dmitri drove to Marta's house in Albany to deliver the other, only to have the door answered by a stranger.

'They moved to England years ago now,' the woman said. 'I had a forwarding address but I think they've moved on.'

Dmitri called Nicholas's house in California and spoke to Pattie, who told him that Marta and Stanley lived in a suburb of London, where he sold insurance since the cutlery company had gone bankrupt. She gave him the new address.

'How old is my grandchild now?' he asked.

'Elizabeth is nine. Marta absolutely dotes on her.'

'I thought she'd be older. Didn't Marta get pregnant soon after Rosa died in 1955?'

'She did but she lost that baby, and several more, before Elizabeth was born. It's not been easy for her.'

'I'm so sad to hear that,' Dmitri sighed. If only she had turned to him; but he was the last person she would have wanted to talk to. 'How is Nicholas?' he asked. 'Has he read my book?'

There was a long pause. 'I'm afraid that Nicholas and I are separated. I had to kick him out when his alcoholism got out of control. He lives in an apartment near the beach so I took your parcel to him but I doubt he's read it.'

'I'm so sorry . . .' Dmitri was stricken. 'I wish I had known. Is there anything I can do? I could pay for him to go to a clinic.'

'I tried that, but he won't go. He's not interested in stopping. I know he loves me and I love him too. I've told him he can come home if he gives up drinking but he simply can't do it. He manages one day, two at most, then the least little thing sends him back to the bourbon. I'm sorry, Dmitri, but I think he's beyond hope.'

'I'm coming out. I'll fly there next week.'

Pattie gave a big sigh. 'I doubt it will make a difference, but you can stay here if you want to try.'

Dmitri flew to Santa Barbara in March 1970 and was met at the airport by his daughter-in-law. She drove him to Nicholas's apartment in a rundown block with some rusty old motorcycles out front. He knocked on the door but when Nicholas opened it and saw his father he slammed it shut again. All Dmitri noticed was that he had long straggly hair and an unkempt beard.

It was difficult with his arthritic joints but Dmitri slid down to sit on the floor in the corridor outside and called through the door.

'I used to drink too much, Nicholas. Way too much. It was your mother who saved me – first of all by motivating me to write novels, and then by giving me children and forcing me to look to the future. Pattie is a good woman. Please let her help you, the way your mum helped me.'

He waited but there was no sound from within. He wasn't sure if Nicholas was listening.

'I miss your mother every day. I'm sure you do too. But imagine what she would say if she could see you now, son. Try to pull yourself together for her sake.'

No reply. He sat there for hours, calling through the door. He'd come all this way and there was no point in giving up, although he supposed he would have to go back to Pattie's at nightfall. He was too old to spend the night outside. Suddenly the door opened and Nicholas glared at him. 'Will you not leave me in peace?' he asked, bleary-eyed and exhausted-looking. 'I don't care about your book, or Tatiana, or any of it. Publish what you want. You don't need my approval.'

He was shoeless, his shirt hanging open, and he smelled rank, as if he hadn't bathed for a long time. Worse than that was his nose: it was bulbous and red, etched with purple spider veins, a true drinker's nose. Dmitri remembered such noses on the men back in Russia who drank vast quantities of home-made vodka and usually died young after passing out in the snow or choking on their own vomit.

'Son, you're ill. Please let me take you to a doctor.'

'It's too late, Dad. You can't wave your money around and make this go away. Unfortunately I inherited the melancholy gene from you rather than the happy gene from Mum and I don't want to go through life like this. The drink is merely a means to an end.'

Dmitri protested: 'You're only forty-four years old. Your whole life is in front of you. You can do anything you want. Anything!'

'Good. Because what I want is to drink myself to death.' He tried to close the door but Dmitri stuck his arm in the way.

'Come for a drink with me then. Let me buy you a beer at your local bar.'

Nicholas shrugged and agreed to that. He slid his feet into some battered beach shoes but didn't bother to fasten his shirt or comb his hair. Dmitri's joints were aching from sitting on the ground and he limped heavily as they walked down the road to a dingy bar with a Budweiser sign out front. Dmitri ordered two beers and let Nicholas have a bourbon chaser then they sat in a booth and talked man to man for the first time in their lives.

'I never felt you were really there, Dad,' Nicholas told him. 'Your head was always somewhere else. I certainly never got the feeling that you loved Marta and me. We were an irritation to you, a duty. I suppose when I found out you'd had another woman all that time, it finally made sense: *Oh, that's why he was like that. It wasn't because of me.* In a way it was comforting. I know Marta was furious for what you did to Mom but I don't have any anger. I just feel like you're a stranger.'

While he spoke, tears rolled down Dmitri's cheek. He took out a handkerchief and dabbed at them. 'I know I failed as a father. I always hoped you'd turn out fine because you had such a wonderful mother but maybe you needed me too.'

'I don't know what caused this thing I have: alcoholism, depression, call it what you will. I'm not sure it would have been any different if you'd been the perfect parent. There's no use you blaming yourself. I've screwed up all by myself.'

'What can be done to make you want to live?' Dmitri asked.

'Nothing,' Nicholas said firmly. 'Some things are unfixable.'

'Will you not try? If I find the name of the top expert in California and pay for a consultation, will you at least see him? Maybe there's a pill you can take, or electric shock therapy, or surgery. I climbed out of the kind of morass you are in, so I know it's possible. Please try, son.'

At last Nicholas agreed. With Pattie's help, Dmitri found an expert and paid for a course of detoxification treatment. He left feeling optimistic, but when he telephoned on his return to Albany, Pattie told him that Nicholas had not even attended the first appointment.

There was more bad news. Two weeks after his return, a lawyer's letter arrived from England saying that Marta would sue him for defamation if he published the book.

'That's that, then,' he told Tatiana. 'We'll have to forget it.'

'Why don't you talk to Alfred?' she suggested. 'When are you next seeing him?'

Dmitri still had occasional lunches with Alfred A. Knopf in New York City. His company had merged with Random House and he had semi-retired but he still dabbled in editorial matters and kept in touch with his favourite authors. When Dmitri met him that spring, at Barbetta, their usual Italian restaurant, he mused that his publisher had barely changed from the day they first met. The moustache and hair were white rather than jet black, and his waist was a little thicker, but the lively eyes and the gregarious character were unchanged.

Dmitri handed over the manuscript. 'Prepare to be surprised when you read it,' he said. 'I don't want an advance but my only stipulation is that it mustn't be published in my children's lifetimes. Marta might live another fifty years, so perhaps it could be pencilled for publication in 2020. Is it possible to arrange that?'

'It's out of the ordinary but I don't see why not. I could leave it in the archives flagged with a note for someone to revisit it in 2020.'

A week later he telephoned, having read the manuscript.

'Are you kidding me? We've been friends for thirty-five years and you never told me you're married to one of the goddamn Romanov royal family? Well, I'll be damned. Is there no chance I can persuade you to publish now? I'm sure our lawyers could see off your daughter's objections.'

'No, I don't want to upset her any more than I have already. But thanks, Alfred.'

He wrote to Nicholas and Marta telling them both he had decided not to publish, and was pleased to receive a postcard from Nicholas. It had a picture on the front of some kids playing volleyball on a beach and it read 'Thanks for coming over to see me, Dad.' That was all, but it was nice.

Six months later, Nicholas died of cirrhosis of the liver. Pattie wrote to tell Dmitri since there was no phone at the cabin and she'd been unable to reach him at the house in Albany. At last his boy was at peace, after a tortured life. Dmitri flew to California for the funeral hoping that Marta might be there and that he'd have a chance to talk with her. Perhaps there could still be a rapprochement at this sad time. His hopes were dashed when she didn't show up.

'Since Rosa died Marta has never been able to deal with anything emotionally challenging,' Pattie told him. 'She pulls down the shutters and pretends nothing is wrong. I'm sorry to say it but I don't think she'll ever change.'

'Is she happy?' Dmitri asked.

Pattie shrugged. 'I don't think her marriage is perfect. She once told me that Stanley has a wandering eye. I guess that makes it even harder for her to forgive you. But she adores her daughter. Elizabeth is the centre of her life.'

When he got back to Albany, Dmitri rewrote his will, leaving enough for Tatiana, should she outlive him, and the remainder of his estate to whichever of his descendants came forward to claim it. Perhaps his little granddaughter would come to find him one day. He surely hoped so.

Chapter Sixty-Six

Lake Akanabee, New York State, February 1975

Dmitri celebrated his eightieth birthday at the cabin with Tatiana. She made his favourite Russian *Pashka*, a dessert similar to the Americans' cheesecake, and stuck a candle in the top that dripped wax down the side while he struggled to find the breath to blow it out. They lived very simply now, eating vegetables she had grown in the garden around the cabin and the occasional fish he caught from the end of the dock (although in truth he never had much patience for fishing). They still commuted between there and the Albany cottage but spent most of their time at the lake, keeping the stove stocked with firewood on the cold days and talking, always talking.

They joked that if they were to live another twenty years, they would never run out of conversation. They discussed religion and philosophy and tried to agree upon the ideal political system; they fretted over news reports of the Vietnam War, worried about whether America was right to get involved; they talked about books and music and remembered theatrical productions they had seen back in St Petersburg before the First World War; they talked about people they had known, and they speculated on what Tatiana's brother and sisters might have been like had they lived.

Each expressed whatever was on his or her mind at the moment and it flowed back and forth in a fast-moving current of companionship. If they woke at night when the wind blew hard outside and rain hammered on the cabin's tin roof, they resumed the conversation they'd been having earlier.

In his head Dmitri sometimes compared the two women he had loved. Sex had never been especially important in his relationship with Tatiana; Rosa had been much more enthusiastic in that department, and she had brought him great pleasure with her skills. There had never been the meeting of the minds he had with Tatiana, though. When you were in your eighties, that became most important. To feel that another human being truly understood the core of you and loved what they saw, while you felt the same about them – that was the best feeling of all. In some ways, he thought, it was the highest achievement of humanity. He had failed in all his other close relationships but at least he got the most important one right.

One spring day he drove to the store in Indian Lake – slowly, peering through the windshield because his glasses were not strong enough and the road appeared as a blur. He bought a few items then on the way back remembered he had forgotten tea, the one thing Tatiana had expressly asked for, so he turned round to get some.

When he drove down the track and the cabin came into view, he saw Tatiana lying on the soil and his first thought was that she must have lost an earring. Trina was sitting nearby, whining. He got out of the car and hobbled towards Tatiana.

'Angel?' he called. 'Is everything OK?'

When she didn't reply, he limped across and sank to his knees, turning her onto her back. She wasn't breathing. Gulping back a sob, he put an ear to her chest but couldn't hear a heartbeat. He had never given artificial respiration but he'd read about it in a magazine so he tried frantically pressing down on her chest and blowing into her mouth. All the time he knew, deep inside, that she had gone. He was simply delaying the moment when he must accept it. The expression on her face was calm. At least she had not felt any pain.

When he had tried to revive her for several minutes without getting any response, Dmitri gathered her in his arms and howled, the sound echoing across the lake. He howled again and again. 'Don't go, Tatiana, don't go, come back, don't do this to me.' He cried out loud, tears spilling as he rocked her back and forwards, trying to shake her out of death's grip. The pain was so appalling he thought he must be dying too and he looked up at the sky and prayed that God would take him now. 'You don't understand. I can't be without her. I can't survive.'

A light rain began to fall but still Dmitri sat there, holding her, stroking her hair, kissing her cold lips, squeezing her to see if there was one ounce of life left. 'Can you still hear me, darling? If you can, *please* try to come back. Oh, you must come back to me. I can't bear it.' Her face was changing, tightening in death. The lips were pale and thin, her cheeks alabaster.

Dmitri knew he should call the police. They would come and take her away to an undertaker's. Perhaps there would be an autopsy to establish the cause of death. What did that matter to him? She was gone and he would never find her again if he searched the world over. *I'll keep her with me a little longer*, he thought. *Just a while.*

The sun had started to lower in the skies when he decided that he did not want anyone to take her away, not ever. He would keep her with him at the cabin. No one need know. He would have to work fast because he couldn't risk someone coming by and finding them like this. He lifted her head off his lap and rose with great difficulty, his hips and knees locked in place from sitting too long. Trina followed as he staggered to the cabin for his tools and some planks of wood he had bought for repairing the porch. Along with a couple of wooden boxes they used for storage, there would be just enough for a makeshift coffin.

He wasn't a proficient carpenter but he managed to fashion a coffin of a size that would accommodate her. The edges were uneven, the angles askew, but it would do. He hobbled around looking for the perfect spot. Just to the west of the cabin there was a grassy bank between the silver birch trees, with a view out across the lake. The ground was malleable beneath his spade and the moon came out as he worked. He didn't stop to eat or drink, not once, because he was scared he might collapse and be unable to finish. His back was aching, his hips and knees screeching complaint, and he was wheezing for breath in the cold night air, but he kept going, deeper and deeper. He welcomed the work because it stopped him thinking about the infinite vastness of his loss.

Tatiana lay on her back, looking more beautiful than ever, the moonlight glowing on her skin, her eyes closed as though she was simply asleep. He hoped she would approve of what he was doing.

Dmitri kept digging until he'd made a hole that would accommodate the coffin, and he lowered it inside. Next he lined it with a rose-coloured satin quilt so the rough wood could not scratch her skin, and he put in a little pillow for her head. Clouds scudded across the moon and stars twinkled but it was utterly silent on the lake, apart from the lapping of tiny waves on the shore and Trina's snuffling. No owls hooted, no whip-poor-wills sang.

He found he did not have the strength to lift Tatiana so he slipped his hands beneath her shoulders and pulled her, legs dragging, to her resting place. As he arranged her so she was comfortable, he noticed that she was wearing Ortipo's oval dog tag on a chain around her neck, with the tiny sapphire, ruby and imperial topaz stones set within fancy swirls. On a whim, he took it off and fastened it around his own neck instead.

It was April and he had seen some wildflowers blooming in the woods. Tatiana loved flowers. She should have had magnificent roses and orchids, lilies and cherry blossom, but all he could find were some tiny pink, purple and white flowers hidden in the grass. He picked a few handfuls and sprinkled them around her.

When he was done, the sky was turning salmon-pink over the eastern part of the lake as the sun nudged the horizon. It was time. He lay down and leaned into the grave to kiss her one last time, letting his lips move all over her face, her neck, her hands, in a frenzy of kisses. He could still smell her scent and he took a deep breath as if to preserve it within him forever. Then he wrapped the quilt round her to keep her safe and warm and that's when the tears started.

As he hammered the lid on her coffin and covered it with soil, he couldn't stop crying. Something had broken inside him and he knew it would never be fixed.

Chapter Sixty-Seven

London, November 2016

When Kitty got back to London, there was an email waiting for her from the editor at Random House, New York, asking if she was able to go for a meeting with them. She replied that she was in London and unlikely to be back in the US till the spring, whereupon they asked if she could visit their London offices, which were on Vauxhall Bridge Road, just behind Tate Britain. Kitty wondered if they wanted to talk about reissuing Dmitri's novels. She hoped so.

She gave her name in the glass-fronted reception area and in no time at all a dark-haired, bespectacled girl called Annabel arrived to lead her upstairs to a pokey office, where she was introduced to a girl called Olivia. She had the grand title of Publishing Director, although Kitty thought she looked as if she was fresh out of university.

'This is an unpublished manuscript of your great-grandfather's that we found in the archives,' she said, indicating a stack of pages covered in an old-fashioned typewriter font. 'There was a memo attached from Alfred A. Knopf, the founder of Knopf Publishing, which is part of Random House.' She handed it to Kitty, who read it quickly.

'To the editorial director of non-fiction in 2020: This is dynamite! Believe me when I tell you that you have a bestseller on your hands. My good friend Dmitri Yakovlevich wanted us to publish it but not until after the death of his daughter, Marta, as she was opposed to publication for reasons that will become clear when you read it.' He gave the last known address for Marta and asked them to liaise with any descendants they could trace. 'Publish it sensitively,' he advised. 'You will not be able to prevent the sensationalist press having a field day but this man is a writer of great literary merit and I would hate for that to be lost in the furore that will undoubtedly erupt.'

'What on earth is it?' Kitty asked.

'I read it at the weekend,' Olivia told her. 'It's the story of your great-grandfather and his love affair with the Russian Grand Duchess Tatiana Romanova. It's quite astounding.'

'Who wrote it?' Kitty asked.

'They both did.'

'Wow!' Kitty grinned. 'I had no idea they'd done that, but I'm delighted!'

'This is a delicate question,' Olivia said, 'but is there any way of proving it's true? There have been so many Romanov impostors over the years.'

Kitty showed her Ortipo's dog tag, with the jewels set in a pretty golden oval. 'This dates from the very beginning of their relationship,' she said. 'But the only way of proving it categorically will be if we have DNA tests carried out on a skeleton that I found a few weeks ago at Dmitri's old cabin in New York State.'

Now that she knew Dmitri and Tatiana had wanted their story to be published one day, she would make sure it was. She would call the detective in Indian Lake to tell him of her suspicion that the body would prove to be a member of the Romanov royal family and suggest he contact the laboratory in Stanford University that had done recent tests on the Romanov remains. Once all the legal paperwork was completed, she would rebury Tatiana's body in Dmitri's grave in the Cedar River cemetery near Lake Akanabee. She and Tom could organise an appropriate service to mark the occasion.

'Might I borrow a copy of the manuscript to read?'

'Of course!' Olivia agreed. 'It's your copyright so we will need to contract you in order to publish it. If we can prove this was co-written by a Romanov grand duchess, we will be able to offer a substantial advance.'

Kitty started reading on her journey home. It began with Dmitri wakening from a laudanum stupor to see an angel in a white dress, with whom he fell in love almost immediately. The writing was elegant and spare.

When Kitty got home she made coffee and curled her feet beneath her on the sofa to read about their secret marriage in 1916, of Tatiana's eighteen months of house arrest, and then the shocking night of their separation in July 1918. She stopped to have dinner with Tom then returned to the sofa to read long into the night about Dmitri and Tatiana's reunion in Prague in 1948, followed by the difficult years when she was his secret mistress in Albany and finally the traumatic rift with his children.

That explained why Kitty had never met him. She was surprised that Marta, the sweet grandmother she remembered, could have held a grudge lasting thirty years. Perhaps she avoided confrontation, like her granddaughter, and the result was that the wound was never able to heal. She felt sad that her mother had never learned the truth; surely she would have found a way to bridge the chasm between Marta and Dmitri and he could have died knowing he was forgiven. But Marta had told Elizabeth that her grandparents died before she was born. A lie like that, once told, can never be untold. Had Marta regretted it? Dmitri was still alive when Kitty was born. Did her grandmother consider breaking her silence then or was she too stubborn?

If only Dmitri had tried harder to heal the rift with his children. Perhaps he simply did not know how. Men of that generation did not have much practice at dealing with complex emotional situations. Perhaps he felt he was doing the right thing by respecting Marta's choice. It was such a shame.

Honest communication was the only way through an emotional impasse; Kitty had learned that over the summer. Brooding never helped anyone to heal, but talking did. She had also learned that infidelity need not be the end of a relationship – some things are more important. Tragically Marta never learned that and the upshot had been a lifelong estrangement.

Dmitri and Tatiana's lives had been full of tragedy. And yet theirs had been such a strong love, lasting through the decades and transcending all obstacles, that you could also say they had been fortunate. Not many people find such life-affirming intimacy. Kitty's thoughts turned to Tom. What other man would have put up with her running away for three months? He knew her inside-out and still he was prepared to stick around, and she realised she was incredibly lucky. It must have been difficult being her partner during all those years when she clammed up and refused to talk about her parents, or anything else that was upsetting her. It had taken the thunderbolt of Tom's infidelity to shake her out of her cocoon, and now she was almost glad it had happened.

She thought of Tatiana and Dmitri living in the cabin in their seventies, supporting each other as they succumbed to the ailments and indignities of old age and continuing what they described in the book as a lifelong, never-ending conversation. Suddenly she knew she wanted to have that with Tom. She wanted to be with him when they were both in their seventies. She liked the sense of history coming around. If only there was a way of letting Dmitri know how much he had helped her; she hoped he would have been pleased.

Chapter Sixty-Eight

Lake Akanabee, New York State, 1986

One night in the winter of 1986 Dmitri woke with an acute pain in his chest and knew it was a heart attack. 'Tatiana!' he cried, then rolled out of bed, landing with a bump on the floor. Ortipo followed, licking his face. The pain came in waves and between them he scrabbled across the cabin floor to the door, managed to open it and hurl himself down the steps. The chain around his neck caught on something and the Fabergé dog tag with its sapphire, ruby and imperial topaz jewels was ripped off. Ortipo was whining and nudging him to get up.

There was no one left in his life now, no one to live for. If only Marta was nearby; if only she'd forgiven him. He thought of his daughter, so lively and popular as a teenager; somehow he had never understood her. After Tatiana died, he had written her a heartfelt letter about his grief at their estrangement and told her of his profound loneliness. Deep down he knew he could expect no sympathy; she'd rejoice to hear about the death of the woman she considered to have been his mistress. There was no reply and after that final attempt, he became a virtual recluse. He got rid of the Albany cottage and spent all his days in the cabin. Once a week he drove into Indian Lake to do some shopping, pick

392

up a newspaper that he would never get around to reading, and collect his mail from the sorting office, but he dreaded it because too often the letters told of the deaths of people he had known.

His sisters Vera and Valerina lived till their late eighties then died within a year of each other. Their funerals had already taken place by the time he picked up the letters informing him. He wrote to Vera's children, with whom he had barely kept in touch over the years, offering his belated sympathies.

His dog Trina died and he bought another Borzoi. This time he called her Ortipo, after the first dog he and Tatiana had tried and failed to train. She was a beautiful creature with a rich copper coat and white underside, a sensitive, timid dog who shrank behind him when they met other dogs in the street and hovered close by his side when he worked around the cabin. At night, Ortipo slept on the bed next to him, helping to keep him warm.

Dmitri received notification from a new editor at Random House that his books had gone out of print and he could buy the remaining stock cheaply if he wanted, but he didn't see the point. His lunches with Alfred A. Knopf petered out around 1980 when Dmitri could no longer face the long train journey into the city. Soon he had no social contacts at all, apart from the lady who worked in the grocery store and a fisherman called Bob who lived on the other side of the lake. Bob married a girl called Sue and Dmitri gave them copies of his novels as a wedding present because he couldn't think what else to give. Tatiana would have known. Rosa would certainly have known.

He knew he was becoming forgetful. Sometimes his memories of the two women joined up so that they were all sitting together in a glorious sunny field enjoying a picnic and it came as a shock when he remembered that they never actually met. There were days when he awoke and called to Tatiana, as if she were outside working in the vegetable patch, and it could be several minutes before he remembered that she was no longer able to reply. A few times he thought he saw her in the woods, and that was a nice feeling. He often spoke to her out loud, asking what he should do about the rip in his shirt, or how the heck she stopped her scrambled eggs sticking to the pan, or commenting on a dark storm cloud looming over the lake.

And now, in his final moments, his only thoughts were of Tatiana. It was just fifteen feet to the trees by the shore but Dmitri had no breath left. Who knew it would hurt so much? He clung to clumps of frozen grass, pulling himself along, until finally he was lying on top of the earth where his great love was buried. And he smiled in spite of the agony, and spread his arms wide across her grave in a final embrace.

Historical Afterword

I hope you've enjoyed reading *The Secret Wife* as much as I enjoyed writing it. The seed of the story came about in conversation with my very talented friend Richard Hughes, who gave me the greatest gift anyone can ever give to a novelist. He had just watched a BBC2 documentary about the Russian grand duchesses and was intrigued by the love affair between Tatiana and an officer called Dmitri Malama. 'Could this be your next novel?' he asked, and I instantly fell off my chair in excitement.

I'd long been fascinated by the tragic story of the Romanovs. Back in my teens I read Anthony Summers and Tom Mangold's book *The File on the Tsar* and desperately wanted to believe their theory that some of the family had survived. I read other books about the Romanovs as they were published and I knew that both Olga and Tatiana had flirtations with officers they treated in the Tsarskoe Selo hospital but I'd only come across Dmitri Malama as a footnote. Once I started reading about him, and realised how handsome and courageous he was, and how close he and Tatiana seem to have been, the plot of *The Secret Wife* fell into place.

During my research I discovered that Dmitri Yakovlevich Malama was born on the 19th of July 1891 in Lozovatka, the son of a cavalry general, and he had two sisters, Vera and Valerina.

He trained at the prestigious Imperial Corps de Page in St Petersburg, which brought him into contact with the royal court. In August 1912 he graduated and became a cornet in the Uhlan Lancer Guard Regiment, of which Grand Duchess Tatiana was honorary colonel. Two years later, during the opening week of the First World War, he was wounded in the leg while their regiment was under attack but he refused to leave the field, earning him the Golden Arms sword with an inscription that read 'for bravery'.

Dmitri was brought to hospital in Tsarskoe Selo in September 1914 and there he got to know Tatiana, who had volunteered as a nurse. There's a chance he might have encountered her before but now they became so close that he gave her a gift of a French Bulldog she called Ortipo. I slightly tinkered with historical fact at this point: in fact, he asked her permission to buy her a puppy and she excitedly said 'yes' straight away, then had to write a note apologising to her mother and asking if it would be all right. He had the puppy delivered to the palace, but as a novelist I couldn't resist altering the facts to have him surprise her with the gift.

Tatiana's 1914 diaries list what she has been doing and who she has seen *without* much commentary, but it is easy to read between the lines with entries such as these:

27th September 1914. Malama took photographs. He is awfully sweet. He is already walking by himself, but of course still limping.

23rd October 1914. Talked to Malama sweetheart in the hallway for a little then went to his ward and took photographs. Today my darling Malama is being discharged from the infirmary. I feel such horrible regret.

28th October 1914. After dinner at 9.15 Malama came over and sat till 10.15. I was terribly glad to see him, he was very sweet.

A 1914 shot of the family showing Olga and Tatiana standing behind, Maria seated left and Anastasia on the right, with Alexandra and Nicholas in the centre and little Alexei in front.

21st November 1914. Had tea at home with Mama [we] four, and Malama sweetheart was [here]. [Was] awfully glad to see him. And we said goodbye as he is going to the front soon.

If Dmitri and Tatiana corresponded while he was at the front, the letters have not survived. A year and a half later, once he had returned to Tsarskoe Selo, Alexandra wrote of him to Tsar Nicholas: 'He had matured, though still a lovely boy. I have to admit, he would make an excellent son-in-law. Why are foreign princes not like him?'

Had it not been for the Revolution, there is a good chance Malama and Tatiana could have married: Malama's family were part of Russia's old nobility and there were precedents because Nicholas's sister Olga had married an army officer in 1916. Tatiana also had an admirer called Volodya, but there is no doubt Malama was her favourite from the many times she mentions him in her diaries and from the numerous photographs she took of him. In my story I departed from known historical fact when I had them engage in a secret marriage, although there is a precedent for this in the Russian royal family: it is rumoured that Catherine the Great secretly married her lover Grigory Potemkin in 1774, and I have borrowed some details of the moonlit chapel downriver in which this might have taken place.

After the Romanovs were placed under house arrest in February 1917, it seems to me only natural that Tatiana's brave young lover would have been part of at least one of the many plots to rescue them. At first it was assumed that George V would bring the family to live in the United Kingdom but he hesitated. Who would support them? How would the order of precedence be affected at court? They were related to virtually every other European royal family – the Danish, Greek, German and British – but in wartime, the world's attention was focused elsewhere and, shockingly, no one stepped out of line to save the Romanovs.

There were several rescue attempts while they were in captivity, including the one in which Red Guard commander Vasily Yakovlev tried to redirect their train to Omsk, and another led by British merchant Henry Armistead. In the novel, I imagine Dmitri leading an attempt that goes horribly wrong just before the fateful events of the night of the 16th–17th of July 1918. In fact, according to record, he joined the White Army after the October 1917 Revolution and achieved the rank of captain, fighting as bravely against the Bolsheviks as he had previously fought the Germans. After rumours of the murder of the Romanov family leaked out, it is said that he lost heart and was killed at Tsaritsyn in June 1919.

But what if he wasn't? What if both he and Tatiana survived? Would she have been able to convince anyone of her identity in those days before DNA testing? There were dozens of people claiming to be Romanovs, of whom Anna Tschaikovsky/Anderson was the most famous. Many in the extended Romanov family took the claims seriously while others loudly refuted them and it led to protracted lawsuits. Perhaps Tatiana would have decided to keep her head down and get on with her life as a private citizen.

Lenin almost certainly gave the order for the Romanovs to be executed, although he made sure there was no paper trail connecting him to it. At first the Bolsheviks only admitted to killing the Tsar but, after the publication of the Sokolov report, in 1926 they had to agree they were all dead. The chief executioner, Yurovsky, left a written account of the murders, which he is said to have greatly regretted in later life.

The mass grave was first discovered in 1979. Skulls were removed from it and their measurements used to form tentative identifications. In 1991 the grave was dug up and bones were taken to different laboratories, in Russia, the UK, and later in America. It was only in 2007 that the remains of Alexei and Anastasia (or possibly Maria) were found about 70 metres away from the original grave. DNA comparisons were carried out with a number of distant relatives, including Prince Philip of Great Britain. There is no doubt that the remains were contaminated over the years, but most experts now agree that Tsar Nicholas, his wife and his five children were executed by Yurovsky and his team in July 1918.

But what if they weren't? I believe that if any of the Romanovs were going to escape, it would have been Tatiana, who was the most level-headed and, in my opinion, the most intelligent of them all. And although Dmitri disappears from her diaries and then from the history books, surely that fits with them having a secret romance and even a secret marriage? I like to think it could have been true: that they were reunited and lived together in seclusion, far away from the lavish life of the court that neither of them particularly relished. Perhaps a memoir by the pair of them, telling of their lives together, will surface round the centenary of the 1917 Revolution and Civil War, just as I imagined it. Wouldn't that be wonderful?

Sources

An excellent website, www.alexanderpalace.org/palace, run by Romanov expert Bob Atchison, contains detailed descriptions of their palaces and gardens, the family history, translations of diaries and letters by family members, and masses of fascinating information. It's a complete treasure trove for fans and a goldmine for historical novelists.

Anthony Summers and Tom Mangold's *The File on the Tsar*, originally published in 1976, is the book that first sparked my interest in the Romanovs with its plausibly argued hypothesis that they did not all die at Ekaterinburg. It's still worth a read.

Helen Azar has produced English translations of Olga's and Tatiana's diaries. These were extremely useful to me for accounts of the family's day-to-day life in captivity and for a glimpse into their individual personalities.

I love Helen Rappaport's writing, and devoured both *Ekaterinburg: The Last Days of the Romanovs* and *Four Sisters: The Lost Lives of the Romanov Grand Duchesses*. Both are highly recommended for their authority and insight. Andrew Cook's *The Murder of the Romanovs* was also useful, and so was Robert K. Massie's account of the investigation into the identification of the remains in *The Romanovs: The Final Chapter*.

For background on the ostentatious lifestyle of the Romanovs before the Revolution, I used Stefano Papi's *The Jewels of the Romanovs* and the Mississippi Arts Pavilion's *Palaces of St. Petersburg*, both of which are lavishly illustrated. For background on Berlin in the 1920s and 1930s, I found Andrew Pitzer's biography of Vladimir Nabokov particularly valuable, as well as Peter Kurth's book *Anastasia: The Riddle of Anna Anderson*.

Many more books and TV series are planned as the centenary approaches. Already in 2016 we have had Simon Sebag Montefiore's comprehensive history of the dynasty, *The Romanovs 1613–1918*, and Lucy Worsley's excellent BBC series *Empire of the Tsars*. There is bound to be new light shed on the family's fate, and I for one will be catching them all.

Acknowledgements

Huge thanks to Richard Hughes for the idea for this novel, and for reading an early draft and making astute observations. Karen Sullivan, the founder of new fiction publisher Orenda Books, was also a first reader and gave me pages of clever notes, proving the old adage that if you want something done always ask the busiest person you know. And the lovely Vivien Green, who has been my agent for seventeen years, gave her usual wise insights and steady support.

I switched editors just as the manuscript was being delivered and in the handover period I was lucky enough to get editorial feedback from both Eli Dryden and Natasha Harding – all of it utterly invaluable. Eloise Wood has been a star and I've really felt the backing of the whole Avon team with this one, so big hugs to Oli Jameson, Helen Huthwaite, Phoebe Morgan, Caroline Kirkpatrick, Kate Ellis, Helena Sheffield, Hannah Welsh, Camilla Davis, Jennifer Rothwell – and also to Jo Marino and the sparky PR team at Way To Blue.

The period around publication is always stressful but for me it has been made much easier by the support of a bunch of lovely book bloggers, some of whom have been following my novels since *Women and Children First* in 2012. A really warm thank you to Amanda at One More Page, Sharon and the team at Shaz's Book Blog, Julie at Boon's Bookshelf, Sarah at Reading the Past, Kate at

For Winter Nights, Laura and Helen at Novel Kicks, LindyLou at Lindy Lou Reviews, Holly and Allison at On My Bookshelf, Heidi at Cosmochicklitan, all the team at Bookbabblers, Laura at Laura's Little Book Blog, Hannah at Echoes in an Empty Room, Anne at Books with Wine and Chocolate, Ananda and Marina at This Chick Reads, Jody at A Spoonful of Happy Endings, Kate at A Bookish Blog, Sarah at Today I'm Reading, Bettina at Trip Fiction and Karen at My Reading Corner. And a special mention for the inspirational Lor Bingham.

Thanks also to the wonderful friends and family who've gone out of their way to help support my novels: Anne Nicholson, Christina Jansen, Sue Reid Sexton, Katie Bailey, Daisy Bata, Louise Kerr, Kirsty Crawford, Barbara Massey, Clémence Jacquinet, Lee Ryda, Martyn Swain, Fiona Williams, Neville Farmer, Jim Paul, Joyce McElroy, Peggy Vance, David Boyle, Julia Mackenzie, Carol Cornish, Dee McMath, Avril Broadley, Anna Sullivan, Patte Griffith, Catherine Lamb, Marnie Riches and Kerry Fisher. Love you all!

And thanks to Karel for making me laugh.

If you enjoyed *The Secret Wife*, read Gill Paul's sumptuous and enchanting novel *No Place for a Lady*

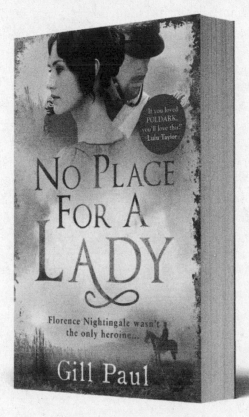

'A terrific adventure story, full of romance and atmospheric detail – a great escapist read'
Liz Trenow

If you enjoyed ... ove Gill Paul's
richly e... ...ettable

Women & Children First

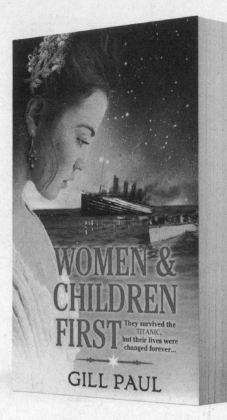

'A thrilling, moving story of lives caught up in an
extraordinary event – vivid and engrossing. I loved it'
Lulu Taylor